GREED
AND
DECEIT

A BRICE MILLER AND ANNIE YOUNGBLOOD NOVEL

BOOK III

BUCK RAMSEY

ALSO BY BUCK RAMSEY

The Last Stand of Dark Horse

The Last Days for Bad Men

Buck Ramsey Copyright © 2019

This book is a work of fiction. Names, characters, businesses, places, events and incidents are either the products of the author's imagination or used in a fictitious manner. Any resemblance to actual persons, living or dead, is purely coincidental.

With respect to historical details that are scattered throughout this book, these details were drawn from a variety of published sources and are dramatized within the context of a fictional story. They are not to be viewed or relied upon as accurate or truthful. Certain long-standing institutions, agencies, and public offices are also mentioned in this book, but the characters involved are wholly imaginary.

Some of the character names in this book are the names of friends who have given me their prior permission to use their name within a fictional context. However, the description and development of these fictional characters is completely of a fictional nature and bears no relation whatsoever to the actual individual.

All of the political opinions, character development and or moral judgments portrayed in this book reflect my views alone.

Editorial credit goes to the erudite team of Tom Burns, Jim Feiteleson, Jim Grimes, Mike Hall, Terry Kaltenbach, Fred Remington, Elroy Voet, and Bob Watts. My wife, Lynne, also helped me with the editing. As she has for the past forty years, she kept me on point and curbed my runaway imagination.

Photograph credits- "Kabul Bazaar," Wikimedia; "Hindu Kush Mountains," Flickr Creative Commons, Photographer Ninara (Donation made by author); "Ahmad Shah Massoud (part of original photo)" on Massoud's letter to the American people. Photo by U.S. Navy CPO2 David Quillen, taken at Afghan Minister of Defense talk, April 13, 2010. Author photo by David Harper.

Map credits- The U.S. CIA; the University of Texas Libraries; Wikimedia; and My Google Maps.

Floor and site plans- Joseph's Home Designs.

Book cover (front and back) and formatting- Damonza.com.

This book is dedicated to Alan Fischer, Jim Grimes, and Mike Hall, three longtime friends. They are all loving family men, generous humanitarians, veterans, and great Americans. It has been my honor to laugh with them and know them as friends.

Author's Opening Note

This book is at its heart a historical novel. When I first began to write this story, two years ago, I quickly realized that my memory and understanding of times, places, and events in Central Asia and the Middle East was not as accurate as I initially thought. Thus, I put down my pen and began reading non-fiction books and news articles that covered those regions. I began with Steve Coll's books on Afghanistan. Then, I read books by Joshua Partlow, Chris Alexander, Philip Haney and Art Moore, Kenneth R. Timmerman, Michael Hayden (former Director of the National Security Agency and the CIA), and Robert M. Gates (former Secretary of Defense). Among Gates's many achievements was his unique service to eight presidents. At last count, I'd read over thirty books and taken countless notes.

In addition to the books, I read hundreds of articles from major international news sources: *The New York Times (including their international edition), The Washington Post, The Atlantic, The Guardian, The Express Tribune (Pakistan), Al Jazeera, Israel Hayom, BBC, CNN, CBS, NBC, etc.* I also scrutinized U.S. Congressional reports and private research reports from the likes of the Brookings Institution, Stratfor, Foreign Affairs and Critical Threats. Lastly, there were a number of bloggers who I followed. A partial list includes Daniel Greenfield, Michael Hughes, Dr. Farhan Zahid, Animesh Roul, Jason Burke, and Yobie Benjamin.

As you read this book and come across a historical detail that seems hard-to-believe,check it out on "Google."

In closing, the series's main characters, Brice Miller and Annie Youngblood, are in the midst of career changes. They don't appear until the end of this novel.

I hope you enjoy this story.

BR

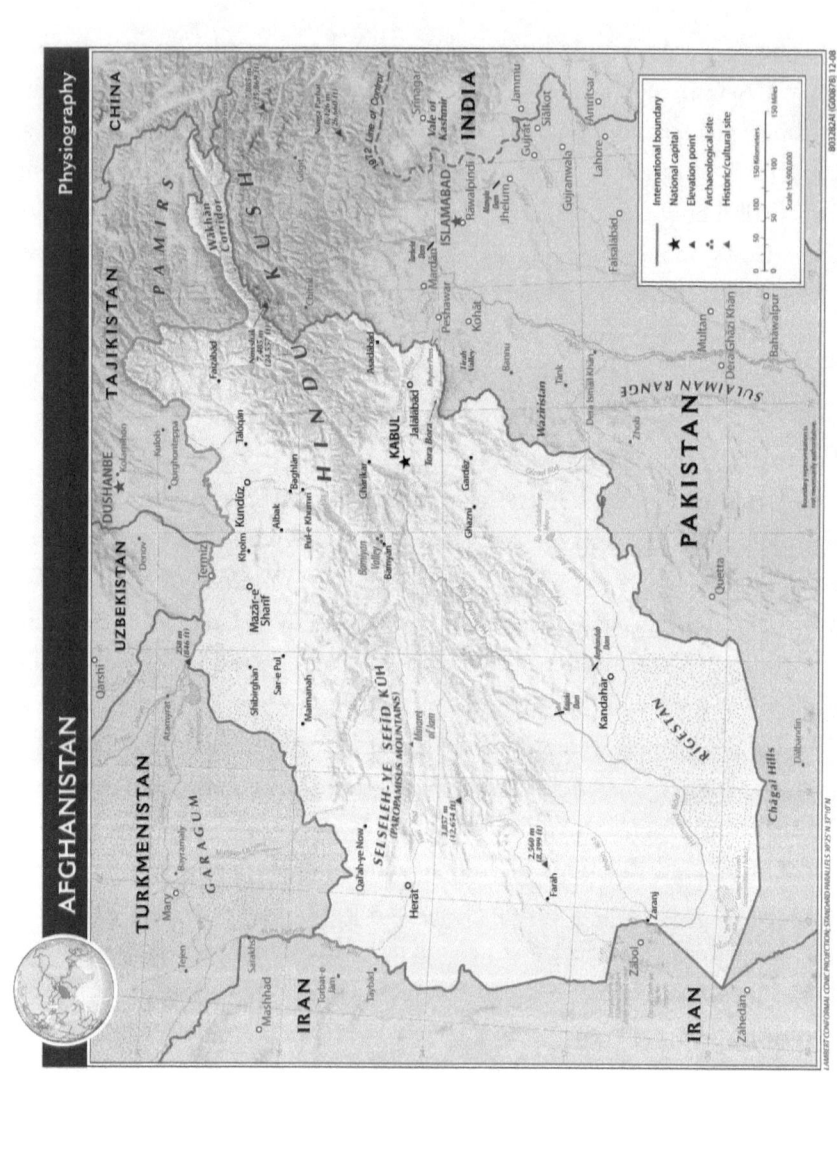

AFGHANISTAN

Physiography

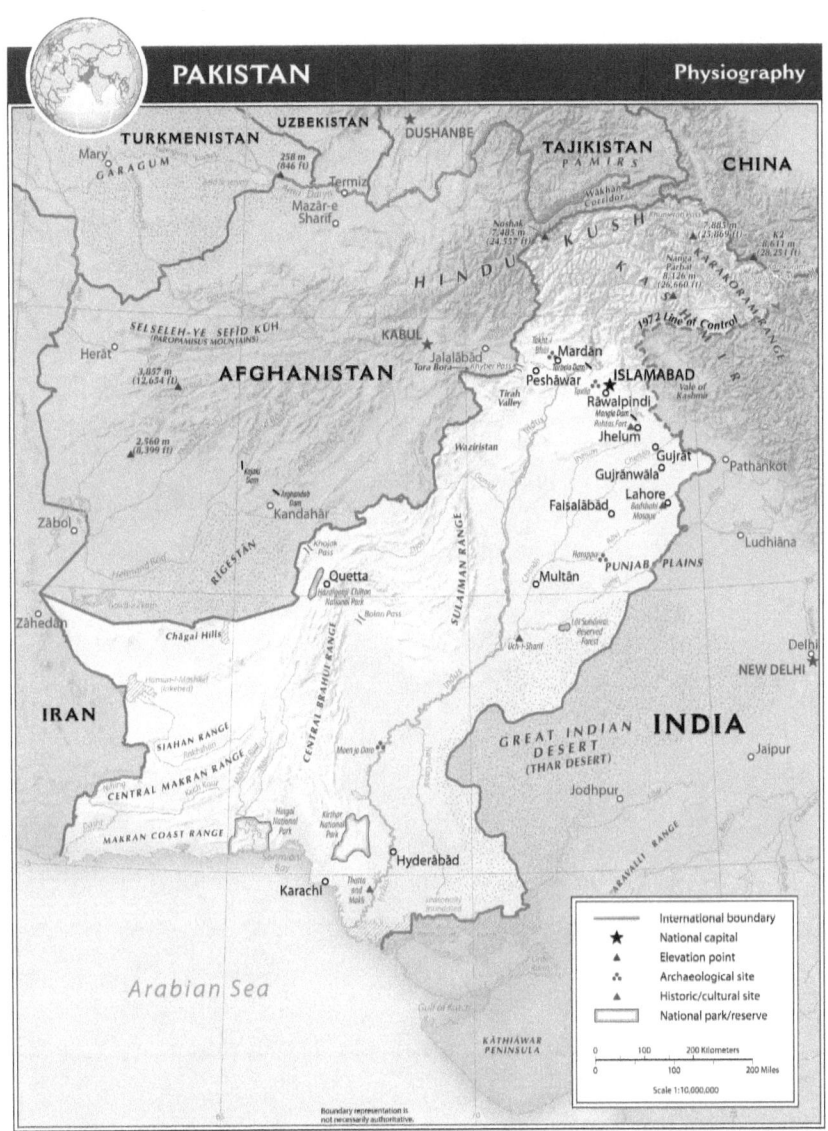

PAKISTAN

Physiography

TURKMENISTAN
UZBEKISTAN
DUSHANBE
TAJIKISTAN
CHINA
Mary
GARAGUM
258 m
(846 ft)
Termiz
Mazār-e
Sharīf
PAMIRS
Wakhān
Corridor
Noshak
7,485 m
(24,557 ft)
HINDU
KUSH
7,885 m
(23,869 ft)
K2
8,611 m
(28,251 ft)
Nanga
Parbat
8,126 m
(26,660 ft)
SELSELEH-YE SEFĪD KŪH
(PAROPAMISUS MOUNTAINS)
KABUL
Jalālābād
Tora Bora
Khyber Pass
1972 Line of Control
KASHMIR
KARAKORAM RANGE
Herāt
3,857 m
(12,654 ft)
AFGHANISTAN
Tirah
Valley
Peshāwar
Mardān
ISLAMABAD
Rawalpindi
Attock Fort
Vale of
Kashmir
2,560 m
(8,399 ft)
Khojak
Sam
Jwgwdwk
Dam
Kandahār
Waziristan
Jhelum
Gujrāt
Pathānkot
Gujrānwāla
Lahore
Bādshāhi
Mosque
Zābol
RĪGESTĀN
Khojak
Pass
Quetta
Hazarganji Chiltan
National Park
Bolan Pass
Faisalābād
Ludhiāna
Zāhedan
Chāgai Hills
SULAIMAN RANGE
Multān
PUNJAB
PLAINS
Uch-i-Sharīf
Uch Sharīf
Reserved
Forest
Delhi
NEW DELHI
IRAN
Hamun-i-Mashkel
(lakebed)
SIAHAN RANGE
CENTRAL MAKRAN RANGE
CENTRAL BRAHUI RANGE
Mehrgarh
GREAT INDIAN
DESERT
(THAR DESERT)
INDIA
Jaipur
Jodhpur
MAKRAN COAST RANGE
Hingol
National
Park
Kirthar
National
Park
Thatta
and
Malls
Hyderābād
ARAVALLI RANGE
Karachi

Arabian Sea

KĀTHIĀWAR
PENINSULA

Gulf of Kutch

Legend
— International boundary
★ National capital
▲ Elevation point
⁂ Archaeological site
▲ Historic/cultural site
▢ National park/reserve

0   100   200 Kilometers
0   100   200 Miles
Scale 1:10,000,000

Boundary representation is
not necessarily authoritative.

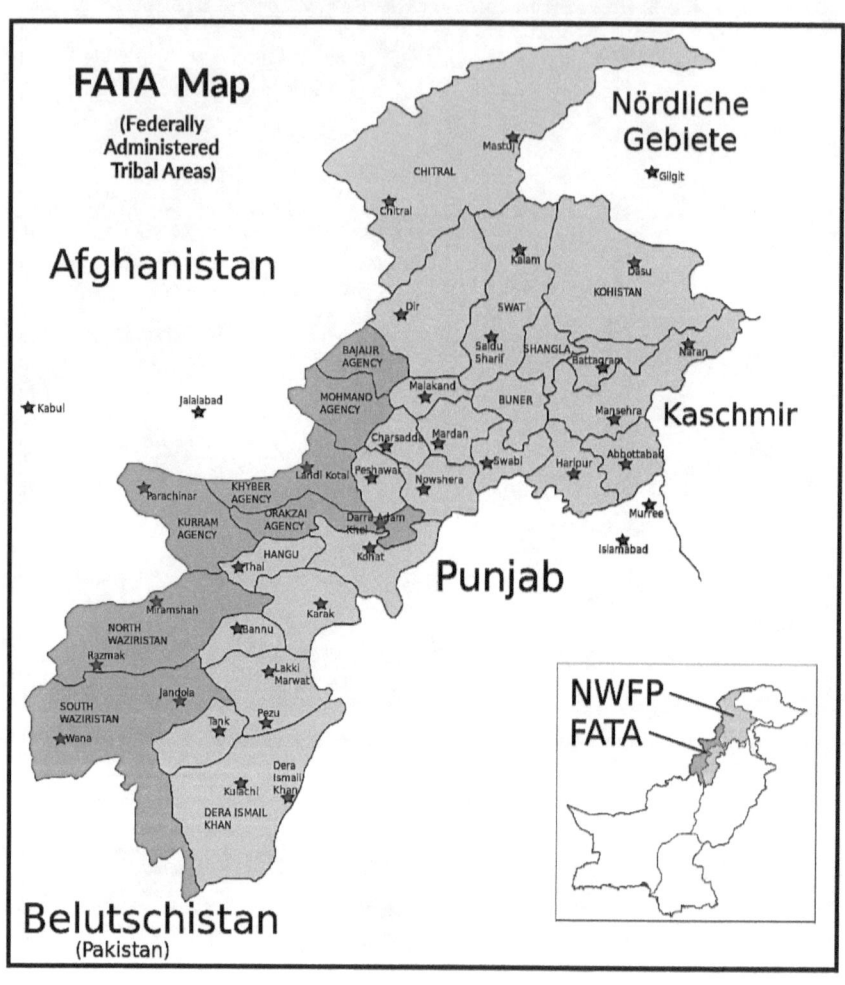

FATA Map
(Federally Administered Tribal Areas)

Afghanistan

Nördliche Gebiete

Kaschmir

Punjab

Belutschistan
(Pakistan)

CHITRAL

Mastuj

Gilgit

Chitral

Kalam

Dasu

KOHISTAN

Dir

SWAT

Saidu Sharif

SHANGLA

Battagram

Naran

BAJAUR AGENCY

Malakand

BUNER

Mansehra

MOHMAND AGENCY

Charsadda

Mardan

Jalalabad

Kabul

Peshawar

Landi Kotal

KHYBER AGENCY

Swabi

Haripur

Abbottabad

Parachinar

ORAKZAI AGENCY

Nowshera

Darra Adam Khel

Murree

KURRAM AGENCY

Islamabad

HANGU

Thal

Kohat

Miramshah

Karak

NORTH WAZIRISTAN

Bannu

Razmak

Lakki Marwat

Jandola

Pezu

SOUTH WAZIRISTAN

Tank

Wana

Dera Ismail Khan

Kulachi

DERA ISMAIL KHAN

NWFP
FATA

Kabul, Afghanistan to Islamabad, Pakistan

Key Locations- *Greed and Deceit*

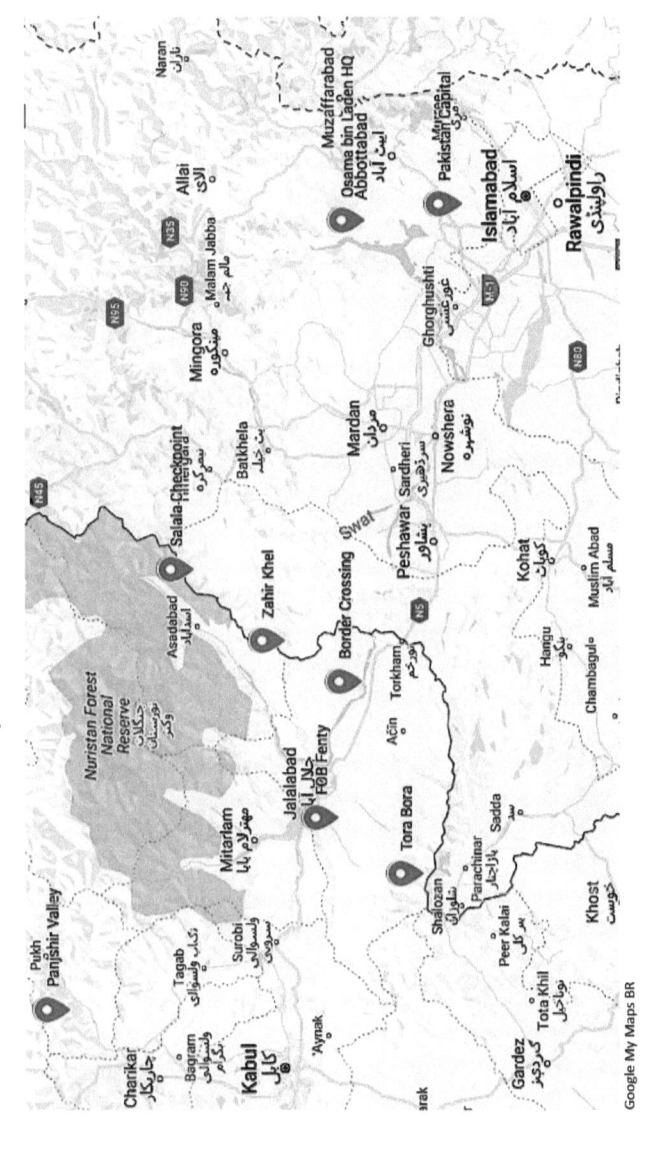

Google My Maps BR

List of Characters

(all fictional characters unless otherwise noted)

The White House

President Jed Adams
Vice President Tim McCracken

Department of Justice

Deputy Attorney General Max Smithson
Associate Attorney General Lena Jones
Deputy Assistant Attorney General, Criminal Div., Charles T. Hightower, Jr.

Federal Bureau of Investigation (FBI)

Director Thomas Milton
Deputy Director Byron Weeks
Special Agent Hook DeLuca

Department of State

Secretary of State Ted David
Acting Secretary of State Susanna Thomas

U.S. Embassy, Kabul

Director Cultural and Religious Section Dr. Mary Phillips
Interpreter-Driver Jamal Waleed
Bureau of Diplomatic Security (DS)

DS Senior Security Technical Specialist Lane Peters
DS Security Technical Specialist Joe Michaels

Department of Defense

U.S. Marine Corps

2nd Lieutenant Brice Miller

U.S. Army

Staff Sergeant Sam Smith, Medical Corps

Department of Homeland Security

Secretary of Homeland Security Jim Agnew

Central Intelligence Agency (CIA), Kabul

Station Chief Mike Hall

United Kingdom- Secret Intelligence Service (aka MI6)

Senior Intelligence Officer, Oliver

Islamic Republic of Afghanistan

President Hakim Qazi
Justice Minister Abdul Sharif
Finance Minister Jamee Nabi
Chairman, Provincial Council-Kandahar, Azim Qazi

Northern Alliance

Leader-Ahmad Shah Massoud*
Major Nazir Waleed

Police Department, Kabul

Chief of Police Safi Khan
Lieutenant Din Pirooz

New Hope Girls Schools

Director Beena Waleed

Israeli Defense Force (IDF)

Israeli Navy

Segen Mishne (rank similar to U.S. Navy Ensign) Yossi Levy

Zahir Clan

Malik (leader) Jan Zahir

Laila Zahir- Jan's wife
Elder Abdul (intelligence-spying)
Elder Mohammad (military-security)
Elder Sayd (logistics-finance)
Elder Kochi (farming-ranching)
    Farid (guard)
    Ali (guard)

---

* Ahmad Shah Massoud was the actual leader of the Northern Alliance. He is not a fictional character. Beena and Jamal Waleed, Massoud's niece and nephew in this novel, are fictional characters.

Civilians

Charles T. Hightower, Sr., President, VA Trucking
Mick Phillips, Maine lobsterman
William "Bill" Tidwell, planner, VA Trucking
Annie Youngblood, 6th grade teacher, Dennis, MT

List of Terrorist Groups

These groups are mentioned throughout this novel for background purposes. The leaders of these groups, as of the beginning of this novel, 2011, are listed in parenthesis.

Pakistan, including the FATA*

Al-Qaeda (Osama bin Laden)
The Afghanistan Taliban (Mullah Omar)
The Haqqani Network (Jalaluddin Haqqani)
Tehrik-i-Taliban (Baitullah Mehsud). Also known as the Pakistan Taliban or TTP.

Libya

Libyan Islamic Fighting Group (Abdelhakim Belhaj)

List of Ethnic Groups in Afghanistan

Their percentage of the overall population is in parenthesis.

---

* FATA is the abbreviation for Pakistan's Federally Administered Tribal Area. The FATA is a mountainous area in northwestern Pakistan—10,000 square miles in size—that adjoins the eastern border of Afghanistan. Though part of Pakistan, the seven agencies that comprise the FATA are like small, self-governing countries. They receive no financial aid from Pakistan, and as a result of that, and other factors, Pakistan has little control over their activities.

Pashtun (42%)
Tajik (27%)
Hazara (9%)
Uzbek (9%)
Others (13%) Includes Aimak, Turkmen, Baloch, and others less than 1% each.

Nobody cares how much you know, until they know how much you care.

Theodore Roosevelt

PART 1

PANJSHIR VALLEY, AFGHANISTAN

1999-2001

CHAPTER 1
THE NORTHERN ALLIANCE

September 9, 1999 | Thursday, 4:31 p.m.

AHMAD SHAH MASSOUD sat alone on the rusted and twisted tail section of a Russian helicopter, a Mi 24 gunship, which lay awkwardly on its side in the middle of a small, grassy plateau. The forty-six-year-old military commander was comfortably smoking the last of his French cigarettes while he read poetry. His dog-eared book of Persian poetry was always at the ready, often tucked into an inside pocket of his familiar safari vest. Several hundred feet below the plateau, the turquoise waters of the Panjshir River raced and tumbled through the mountainous valley toward Kabul, 100 miles to the south. The setting sun, framed in a cloudless azure sky, warmed his weathered face, and the sound of the rushing river soothed his soul.

He was dressed much as he had been for most of the last twenty years, with his multi-pocketed working vest draped over a well-worn woolen shirt. His baggy and loose-fitting faded green pants were tucked into the top of his high leather boots. Pushed back atop the right side of his head was a soft, round-topped woolen cap (a pakul cap) that revealed a thatch of his graying, black hair.

As the commander of an irregular army, the Northern Alliance, he was not a physically imposing figure. He was of medium height and build, with a friendly face and easy manner. Easy, that is, until he was involved in military tactics. Then, his greatness emerged. Greatness that was the product of fighting better equipped Russians for ten years, and battling the twisted Islamic beliefs of the Taliban for much of the last seven. A greatness that was also shaped by his high level of energy, cleverness, and compassion. He cared for the well-being of all of his men.

When he reached the end of his cigarette, he took a final puff and ground the embers out between his thumb and forefinger. He slipped his book of poetry into his pocket and gazed thoughtfully at the rugged Hindu Kush Mountains that surrounded his patch of peace and quiet. His thoughts turned to his wife, six children, a nephew, and a special niece. They were all safe, secure, and provided for by relatives and friends who lived in areas away from the fighting. *But how long can that last?* he wondered as he heard the distant rumble of friendly, outgoing artillery fire. His army was losing a war.

From Kabul, one traveled northward across the Shomali Plains to the Panjshir Valley. A narrow gorge, at the mouth of his verdant valley, greeted all visitors. The gorge's near-vertical granite walls compressed the Panjshir River's southbound waters and determined its safe passage. Travel through the gorge during periods of heavy rains or modest snowmelt runoff was dangerous and nearly impossible during higher water. Other manmade obstacles, especially for unwelcome visitors, included cliff-top artillery and hidden machine-gun emplacements, which covered every inch of the gorge's entrance.

During the Russians' ten-year occupation of Afghanistan, the gorge had stopped eight Russian attacks, save for one. The one Russian attack that the gorge didn't stop fulfilled a more deadly role. It trapped the advancing Russians in a valley from which very few escaped. This killing gorge now checked the Taliban that was little more than ten miles from his current sanctuary.

Leaning forward, Ahmad closed his eyes and held his head in his hands, visualizing his loved ones. They each gave him strength. When his thoughts settled on his fourteen-year-old niece, Beena Waleed, he smiled. Smart, fearless, and mature beyond her years. *I'm her favorite uncle. She wants to be just like me. Who in their right mind would want to follow in my footsteps? Apparently, Afghanistan's wannabee Joan of Arc, Beena! The prospective target of thousands of Taliban and al-Qaeda fighters!*

A tall, broad-shouldered man silently approached Ahmad from the rear. When he was within several yards of him, he boomed in Arabic, *"As-Salaam-Alaikum, Ahmad!"* Peace be upon you, Ahmad.

Startled out of his reverie, Ahmad jumped to his feet and instinctively reached for his AK-47 rifle, which rested beside him. When he spun toward the man, he was relieved to find that he was facing a longtime friend and supporter. Excited, he smiled broadly, bowed his head politely, and replied in Arabic, *"Wa-Alaikum-Salaam, Jan! Laqad faja'atani!"* Peace be upon you, as well, Jan! You surprised me!

After a moment, Ahmad continued in Dari. "It's a good thing we're fighting on the same side. How did you sneak up on me like that? I have guards posted in the trees."

"I bribed them with a pack of those foul-smelling French cigarettes that you like, Gauloises! Plus, they know me," said Jan Zahir. After he removed his backpack, the two hugged one another like brothers.

They were an unlikely pair of friends. Ahmad Shah Massoud was an ethnic Tajik from the northern part of Afghanistan, and Jan Zahir was a Pashtun* from the *Spīn Ghar* Mountain Range (translated "White Mountains") in the Khyber Agency of Pakistan's FATA.†

The Zahir clan owned and occupied a naturally protected, fertile valley sixty miles east of Jalalabad, Afghanistan, just inside the western border of the Khyber Agency. A principal source of revenue for his clan was Khyber Pass toll collections. In 1947, the Zahir clan signed an official treaty with Pakistan that gave them the exclusive rights to Khyber Pass tolls in exchange for road maintenance and the protection of thru-traffic.

As a teenager, Ahmad attended the *Lycée Esteqlal* in Kabul, one of the most prestigious Franco-Afghan high schools in the country, where he excelled in languages. Aside from Dari, the official language in Afghanistan, he possessed a good command of French, English, and Pashto. Ahmad and

---

* Pashtuns widely believed that they were a superior ethnic race to Tajiks, Hazaras, and Uzbeks. Tajiks are descendants from the Republic of Tajikistan, a country that adjoins Afghanistan's northern border. Tajikistan was formerly part of the Soviet Union.

† FATA is the abbreviation for Pakistan's Federally Administered Tribal Area. The FATA is a mountainous area in northwestern Pakistan—10,000 square miles in size—that adjoins the eastern border of Afghanistan. Though part of Pakistan, the seven agencies that comprise the FATA are like small, self-governing countries. They receive no financial aid from Pakistan, and as a result of that, and other factors, Pakistan has little control over their activities.

Jan first met at the *Lycée Esteqlal*. The Zahir family kept a small home in Kabul, which they used primarily for boarding their sons while they attended Kabul schools. After high school, Ahmad and Jan both attended Kabul University, where they each majored in engineering. After graduating from Kabul University, their lives and the lives of their ethnic groups diverged.

Jan, who at six feet, towered over his friend by a good six inches, held Ahmad at arms' length as he appraised him. His neatly trimmed mustache and diamond-shaped goatee framed an even mouth, which formed the region's most well-known smile. Uncharacteristic lines of fatigue, however, were evident on his friend's lean bronze face, which was punctuated with a hawk-like nose. Lethargy was not a trait he associated with his friend. At first, it worried him until his eyes fell on Ahmad's deep brown eyes.

Both men believed that one's eyes were the window to their heart. In Ahmad, Jan sensed that the fire that had always motivated him—an unwavering resolve to unite Afghanistan—was still burning brightly. A month earlier, the Taliban had driven Ahmad's Northern Alliance army—along with 500,000 civilians— from the general area of the Bagram Airfield, forty miles north of Kabul. Unfortunately, hundreds of civilians had drowned in the Panjshir River during this sixty-mile, overnight race to Ahmad's impregnable valley.

In light of his friend's recent setback, he was reminded of a French history class in high school. He and Ahmad were sitting next to one another in class when their flamboyant teacher quoted a famous observation made by General Charles de Gaulle in 1940. With a flourish, Jan said, "*La France a perdu une bataille, mais la France n'a pas perdu la guerre.*" France has lost a battle, but France has not lost the war. He then added, *"Maintenant cela s'applique à votre armée!"* Now, that applies to your army!

"*Oui!*" smiled Ahmad with a look of appreciation.

Jan released Ahmad and began rummaging through his backpack. "This is for you. Happy birthday! A carton of Gauloises Caporal cigarettes, the perfect smoke for freedom fighters like you. '*Liberté toujours!*' Freedom forever! By the way, these particular cigarettes are apparently bad for one's health. They're discontinuing them," he said with a sarcastic smirk.

Ahmad laughed and slapped his leg. "Yes, yes, very dangerous to my health, especially when I'm dodging bullets and bombs. I'll keep that in mind."

"And, this is a French bottle of medicinal grape juice, called a Cabernet Sauvignon. Your doctor friend with Médecins Sans Frontières asked me to deliver this bottle to you. He knows that you're a good Muslim and are prohibited from drinking alcohol. He informed me that he's prescribed this to you before and that you should only drink it whenever you're under extreme stress."

"I'm a moderate Muslim! I believe in medications."

"*Moi aussi!* Me too! That's one of the many reasons why we're friends."

"That and the fact that I saved your life."

Jan bobbed his head as he unconsciously turned away from his friend. He grimly studied the near-vertical rock face, thirty yards behind them. When his eyes settled on a rock outcropping, fifty yards above the plateau, he closed his eyes and shook his bowed head. He still carried the humiliation of his actions that occurred on that outcropping thirteen years earlier, in 1986. "I'd never seen a flying machine, up close before. I was mesmerized."

"That you were. And, you'd never seen the 'Hind' (the nickname of the Russian Mi 24 helicopter gunship) spit its deadly fire."

"No, I hadn't. I was a fool!" Jan said shamefully.

"Not a fool, just inexperienced. But, the two of us shot that dragon down with a U.S. Stinger missile (a shoulder-launched guided missile) that you'd brought to my men and me from Pakistan."

"Yes, it was one of many Stingers that I delivered to you. Thanks mainly to the charity and goodwill of America's CIA."

"And," interjected Ahmad, "the *insistence* of the Americans that those weapons reached their destination. The Pakistanis then, like now, would have preferred that we bled to death."

"Yes, yes. The Pakis are always playing a double game. Someday their double-dealing will come back to haunt them!"

Ahmad smiled in agreement and gave Jan a friendly pat on the back. "Let's sit on the rusted remains of our dead dragon and talk of nicer things. By the way, my birthday was last week, September 2nd. You're a week late!"

"I know. I couldn't get you the supplies that I promised any sooner. The roads north of Kabul are packed with trucks transporting Pakistani soldiers and equipment to the Taliban's frontlines, south of here. I decided it was safer to travel through the Hindu Kush Mountains on foot, via Mitarlam, rather than traveling along roads through Kabul."

"Safer, but much steeper! How did you get through the Taliban checkpoints to Mitarlam?"

"The checkpoints through Nangarhar Province and the town of Mitarlam are manned by those who know me and value a little extra cash. Don't forget, I'm a Pashtun!"

"Yes, but not Taliban!"

"Correct! And a wise Pashtun who knows that greasing the palms of zealous Islamists tends to weaken their religious resolve."

Ahmad smiled in understanding before asking, "Do the Taliban recognize you when you travel into Afghanistan?"

"Some, particularly the pro-Taliban Pashtuns in the area around Jalalabad. I often wear disguises whenever I sneak across the border, but many know me on sight. They also know what happens to them and their families if they betray me.

"In Mitarlam, I exercised a rare level of patience. Because it's a small town, I secretly staged my supplies and mules there over five days. That's why I was late getting here. I was hoping to get here by your birthday, but I didn't want my activities in Mitarlam to attract unwanted attention."

"Mules! Did you say mules?"

"Yes! Remember those Tennessee mules the CIA gave us for transporting Stingers and other supplies through the mountains in the 1980s?"

"Uh-huh! I thought all those mules had died of old age?"

"They can live for up to forty years, though the ones I came with are five to ten years old. They're mature and strong. My father liked them. He decided our clan should breed them, which we did. You mate a male donkey (a jack) with a female horse (a mare). Their intercourse isn't particularly loving, but the results are a mule that can handle high elevations, rugged mountains, carry upwards of 300 pounds of supplies, and eat less than a horse. They're better suited to our mountains than horses or donkeys. I have thirty of them in my caravan. I'm going to leave them with you."

Ahmad flashed his charismatic smile and clapped his hands. "Wonderful, just wonderful! Our horses and donkeys are almost worthless. We end up eating them half the time and use our men as packhorses. We often have to stash much of our supplies along our supply routes for delivery at a later time."

"My mules had little trouble with thirty miles of rugged 'Kush' mountains. We couldn't have gotten our supplies to you without them."

"With all that's happened recently, I thought you might come through Mitarlam. I told my men who are guarding that mountain pass to be on the lookout for you. Two weeks ago my men killed twenty Taliban who tried to sneak through there and attack me from the rear. Those invaders were from Hekmatyar's tribe. I was worried that they might be a little trigger happy."

"Yes, your men stopped me. They recognized me and I them. Half of them were the same mujahideen who served you twenty years ago when we fought the Russians. It was like a school reunion. I gave them winter clothing, food, and munitions. I delivered the rest of your supplies, several tons in total, to your headquarters an hour ago."

Ahmad smiled absently. His thoughts were focused on his men who guarded that pass. "Those men are tough warriors and fierce nationalists. I love every one of them. Thank you for giving them winter clothing. They'll be facing a cold winter," he said with a note of concern.

The two sat together on the rusted tail section and chatted easily for the next two hours. Much of there conversation covered national and world politics that affected Afghanistan. Ahmad reminisced about the failures of his and President Burhanuddin Rabbani's former government in Kabul.

"Once we ousted the Russian's puppet government from office in 1992," began Ahmad, "I had high hopes that the country would see more peaceful days. But it was not to be! More violence erupted. It was a terrible time, ethnic wars raged throughout the country, and warlords battled one another in Kabul," he said, pausing to massage his forehead. His face radiated regret and self-reproach. "Rabbani and I were both Tajiks. The Pashtuns hated us. During those years, every ethnic group committed atrocities. We made Gulbuddin Hekmatyar, a Pashtun, the prime minister with the hope that he would reduce the violence, but he only made matters worse. He killed more Afghans than the Russians did. He was and still is a brutal man!"

At the mention Hekmatyar, Jan's thoughts flashed back to a stopover visit he had with Massoud, in 1993, at the Presidential Palace. In the lobby of the building, situated beside the Afghan flag were the names of the leaders of the Islamic State of Afghanistan on a brass plaque:

Prime Minister Gulbuddin Hekmatyar[*]
President Burhanuddin Rabbani
Minister of Defense Ahmad Shah Massoud

Jan agreed with Ahmad's view of Hekmatyar and added, "There was only so much you could do. You were in the midst of a fierce civil war. Hekmatyar didn't want to share anything. You hoped that a power-sharing pact with him, the 'Butcher of Kabul,' would bring the country together. But, he was, and still is, a duplicitous bastard. He only cares about what's best for him and his not-so-secret supporters, the Pakistan ISI and Saudi Wahhabis," he paused, reflecting on the plaque in the Presidential Palace. "Did Hekmatyar ever set up an office with you and Rabbani in the palace?"

"Not that I recall. His men were shelling the building."

"In the 1980s," Jan resumed, "he abandoned your army and other mujahideen forces when it benefitted him. He hoped the Russians would kill you. I never understood why the U.S. supported him. My Zahir clan never liked or trusted him, nor his buddy, Mullah Omar.[†] Mullah Omar and Osama bin Laden think alike. They believe that there is nothing wrong with killing moderate Muslims and non-believers who haven't caused them any harm. They've reshaped Islam to suit their sick and warped goals. What crap! The ignorant jihadists who follow their warped goals are murderers and terrorists of the lowest order."

"You and your Zahir clan are a unique breed of Pashtuns. You avoid extremism in its many shapes, forms, and disguises. You also understand the importance of education and the equality of men and women. You're an enlightened clan."

"Those are kind words, my brother. But, changing a Pashtun's behavior

---

[*] Hekmatyar and Rabbani are mentioned here for historical background purposes only. Neither of them appears later in this novel. Ahmad Shah Massoud is, however, mentioned throughout this story.

[†] Mullah Omar, the founder of the Taliban, overthrew Rabbani's Afghanistan government in 1996. As this novel develops, there are occasional references to Mullah Omar and Osama bin Laden.

and thinking doesn't occur overnight. It has taken many generations of Zahirs to reform our clan's thinking. And, it requires a constant level of reminding and reinforcing."

"Yes, I understand, but you at least have a vision for the betterment of your people. You're not like the Islamic fundamentalists who are intent on returning their followers to the Age of Mohammed."

Jan appreciated the compliment and added, "But we must remain vigilant and strong. Fundamentalism is like a virus that never dies. The starving and displaced are susceptible to the false beliefs of those who offer them temporary relief. We must never forget that."

Ahmad nodded in agreement. "When Osama bin Laden arrived here in 1996, with his bags of gold from the Wahhabis in Saudi Arabia, my world …Afghanistan… changed. He has—"

Jan raised an open hand, stopping his friend. "He changed my world, as well. Nearly all of my clan's relations with neighboring Pashtun tribes have now soured or completely collapsed. My father, grandfather, and great grandfather nurtured those relationships. Onetime friends are now our enemies. Those Pashtuns, like Mullah Omar, that support and shelter Osama bin Laden say their hands are tied. They argue that *Pashtunwali* requires them to support him because he asked for their help. What nonsense! *Pashtunwali* doesn't prescribe unending or unlimited support to a guest. Mullah Omar and other Pashtun warlords protect Bin Laden because he pays them."

"Bin Laden's presence here does not bode well for Afghanistan," added Ahmad. "Moderate Saudis and the Sudanese kicked him out of their countries. Furthermore, everyone knows that he was the mastermind behind the bombings of the U.S. embassies in Kenya and Tanzania, twelve months ago, which killed hundreds of innocent civilians and injured thousands more. He's evil. I've warned the CIA about him, but those in Washington don't seem to care. They don't view him as a global threat."

"I don't understand that. If hundreds of deaths in Africa don't warrant their attention, what will? Furthermore, without Bin Laden's support and that of the Pakistani's Inter-Services Intelligence Directorate (ISI), the Taliban wouldn't even exist."

"I know," said Ahmad, with an unmistakable note of frustration.

Jan shifted their conversation to military matters. "With the Taliban's takeover of Mazir-i-Sharif last year, from your Afghan ally, Dostum, that cut your overall forces in half. The Northern Alliance is just you and your men. You're not allied with anyone else, except, of course, the Zahirs."

Ahmad suddenly stood and anxiously began to pace. "Give me a minute, my friend." He walked to the edge of the plateau, set his hands on his hips, and took deep breaths of fresh air. His friend's mention of Mazir-i-Sharif had caused his heart to race. After Mullah Omar's Taliban seized the city, his men went on what the Human Rights Watch described as a "killing frenzy." They sought out and killed every Hazara, Tajik, and Uzbek they could find. No one, including children, was spared. Human Rights Watch estimated that 2,000 civilians were slaughtered.

When he returned to Jan's side, he shakily broke open the carton of cigarettes. He opened a pack and offered a cigarette to his friend.

Jan declined with a shrug and said, "The Taliban did horrible things there. I'm sorry I mentioned Mazir-i-Sharif. It makes me sick too."

After taking a deep draw on his cigarette, Ahmad said, "That is war. Awful things happen. You and I understand that better than most." He paused and took another calming draw on his cigarette. "This valley holds what is left of the Northern Alliance. That's no secret to Mullah Omar and Osama bin Laden. Omar has offered me a post in his Taliban government in exchange for my surrender."

Jan couldn't believe what he'd just heard. His heart and mind froze.

Several long moments later, Ahmad continued, "I told him that I would rather die a thousand deaths than join forces with him. I also told him that my life's goal is to unify Afghanistan under a democratic government that represents all of our ethnic and religious sects. He didn't like that. He said that Allah would never approve of such a Western concept. I was a non-believer, and all non-believers deserved a painful death."

"You should be careful, my friend. Spies and traitors abound in these times."

"I'm well aware of that. Regarding that, I have a favor to ask of you."

"We're brothers. What do you desire?"

"My brother-in-law," began Ahmad, "Nazir Waleed, was killed by the Taliban during my retreat last month from the Bagram area. He was one of my most trusted and respected field commanders. He was also married to one of my half-sisters. They had two children, a boy and a girl. The boy, Jamal, is fourteen-years-old; and the girl, Beena, is sixteen-years-old. His family lived in Jalalabad, Afghanistan, not far from your clan in the *Spīn Ghar* Mountains. Their children often stayed with us when I was the minister of defense in Kabul," he said, pausing to reflect on the fond memory and image of all the children playing together. " My six children and the two Waleed children are like one to me. I've kept Nazir's relationship with me a secret."

"That is not an easy secret to keep these days. Should the Taliban ever learn of that relationship, they would torture and kill every member of the Waleed family."

"Yes, I know. Three years ago, just before the Taliban took control of Kabul— displacing all of our government leaders, including me—I sent the two Waleed children to Paris. They are staying with a secret relative and continuing their education. The CIA provides them with a modest allowance. The Waleeds hope that I will someday return to power and lead Afghanistan into more peaceful and prosperous times. They also hope and pray that their family will, someday, be reunited in Jalalabad."

"Say no more! Should any of them ever need a safe home, they are welcome to live amongst my clan in the *Spīn Ghar* Mountains. I will protect them. Should they desire to live in Jalalabad, I have contacts there that can look after them. If they go beyond Jalalabad, say to Kabul, my influence there is limited. But, I do have friends there. I would do what is necessary to protect them."

Ahmad stood, and the two again hugged. With tears filling the corner of his eyes, he choked, "One more thing. The girl, Beena, is exceptionally bright. One shouldn't have favorite relatives, but she was a favorite of mine. My favorite cat even took a liking to her, which, if you'd ever met my cat, was quite amazing. Nazir told me before his passing that she very much desires to be like me, her favorite uncle."

Jan smiled.

"What is so funny?"

"Just a thought," he began, before his smile turned into laughter. "I love the goal of your young niece, Beena. Our military genius, our women's rights advocate, and our next president of Afghanistan… 'The Lion of

Panjshir'…now has a teenage prodigy." With his arms outstretched and his head thrown back as if in supplication to a compassionate Allah, he loudly proclaimed, "Be it known to all Afghans and friends of Massoud that, from this day forward, we have a successor-in-training to my best friend… Ahmad Shah Massoud! Her name is Beena Waleed, and she shall be known, from this day forward, as the 'Kitty Cat of Panjshir.'"

Ahmad laughed as did his guards in the nearby trees.

"Soon to be known," added Jan, "as the 'Lioness of Panjshir.'"

"It shall be so!" added Ahmad as he slipped a hand inside one of Jan's arms and steered him to his headquarters. "We shall eat, drink, and celebrate this day. When I am with you, you lighten my burdens and brighten my heart."

"Moi aussi! Me too! It seems like years since I last laughed. I shall mark this day, September 9th, in my calendar. The day I laughed again, the day I learned of the Kitty Cat of Panjshir, and the day I arrived one week late for your birthday. We shall always speak with one another on this *special day.*"

"Birthdays are for keeping track of aging. What fun is there in that? I will look forward to our September 9ths. Our special day of friendship!"

One year later, September 9, 2000, 2:13 p.m. AFT *Satellite phone conversation between Ahmad and Jan (CIA intercepted abstract; salutations deleted).*

Jan- This is our first September 9th reunion call. I've heard that you are in good health and that your troop levels are growing. That's good news. I've also heard rumors that the Americans have again refused to support you.

Ahmad- Yes. President Clinton, on advice from his State and Defense Departments, doesn't want anything to do with us. I've continued to warn them that al-Qaeda—and its leader, Osama bin Laden—is a threat to the West, but they ignore me. I've forwarded them intelligence that he is planning a major attack in the U.S., but they ignore my information. Fortunately, their CIA listens to me. They secretly provide me with weapons and modest amounts of cash. They've been helpful.

Jan- If you're communicating with their CIA, please let them know that the Pakistan ISI is actively recruiting and training terrorists at al-Qaeda camps near me, in the White Mountains, and further south in Waziristan. These camps are full of poor, displaced Pashtuns plus newly arrived Arab and Chechen mercenaries.

The Saudis finance madrassas (Islamic religious schools) in or near these camps where they teach the children Wahhabism (fundamentalist Islamic doctrine) while the Pakistan ISI teaches their parents how to fire weapons and make bombs. The madrassas' teachings ignore science, math, and history. The Saudis, along with al-Qaeda, also clothe, feed, and provide shelter for these people. They're refugee camps with a terrorist mission.

Ahmad- I've heard of these camps. Al-Qaeda is taking advantage of those people. There is nothing compassionate or humanitarian about that. The Allah that you and I worship does not support such practices.

Jan- Yes, I agree with you. How is your niece doing?

Ahmad- Thank you for not mentioning names over the phone. The Kitty Cat of Panjshir is doing well. She is now studying medicine and has hopes of becoming a doctor.

Jan- Old men, like us, need doctors more than ever. And, by the way, happy belated birthday! Next year, I hope we can again get together…perhaps in Kabul! Last year's visit was special.

Ahmad- That it was! I look forward to our next visit.

The next year, September 9, 2001, 5:08 p.m. AFT

Jan- Is this Ahmad? It sounds like you've just smoked a pack of those French cigarettes.

Mohammed Qasim Fahim- No Jan, this is Marshal Fahim … Ahmad's former assistant commander. We've met before.

Jan- Yes, I remember you. Ahmad has told me many good things about you. Is my friend busy planning an attack against the Taliban?

Fahim- I have terrible news for you. Two al-Qaeda spies, posing as journalists, killed Ahmad today with a bomb. One of the bombers escaped the blast, but Ahmad's bodyguards quickly caught him. Before they killed him, he said Osama bin Laden had sent them. (Long silence) Jan, are you still there?

Jan- Yes, Fahim, I am. I am sick with sadness. I promised Ahmad that I would look after his family, especially a nephew and niece. If you speak with them, explain that I will always honor that promise.

Fahim- I will do so. Before I leave you to your grieving during this dark time, I have one favor to ask. Your intelligence reports and supplies have greatly helped us. Can I count on you to continue your support?

Jan- I swear, Fahim, on my father's grave to support your cause until my last breath. Ahmad was my brother. I will do whatever I can for you.

Fahim- Thank you, my friend. May the blessings of Allah be upon you.

Jan- And upon you as well, Fahim.

Two days later, September 11, 2001

Al-Qaeda attacks the United States. For additional details see the addendum, A Summary of the "9/11" Tragedy, at the end of this book.

Postscript

Ahmad Shah Massoud's Letter to the People of America

(sent in 1998 before his assassination in 2001)

I send this message to you today on behalf of the freedom and peace-loving people of Afghanistan, the Mujahedeen freedom fighters who resisted and defeated Soviet communism, the men and women who are still resisting oppression and foreign hegemony and, in the name of more than one and a half million Afghan martyrs who sacrificed their lives to uphold some of the same values and ideals shared by most Americans and Afghans alike. This is a crucial and unique moment in the history of Afghanistan and the world, a time when Afghanistan has crossed yet another threshold and is entering a new stage of struggle and resistance for its survival as a free nation and independent state.

I have spent the past 20 years, most of my youth and adult life, alongside my compatriots, at the service of the Afghan nation, fighting an uphill battle to preserve our freedom, independence, right to self-determination and dignity. Afghans fought for God and country, sometime alone, at other times with the support of the international community. Against all odds, we, meaning the free world and Afghans, halted and checkmated Soviet expansionism a decade ago. But the embattled people of my country did not savor the fruits of victory. Instead they were thrust in a whirlwind of foreign intrigue, deception, great-gamesmanship and internal strife. Our country and our noble people were brutalized, the victims of misplaced greed, hegemonic designs and ignorance. We Afghans erred too. Our shortcomings were as a result of political innocence, inexperience, vulnerability, victimization, bickering and inflated egos. But by no means does this justify what some of our so-called Cold War allies did to undermine this just victory and unleash their diabolical plans to destroy and subjugate Afghanistan.

Today, the world clearly sees and feels the results of such misguided and evil deeds. South-Central Asia is in turmoil, some countries on the brink of war. Illegal drug production, terrorist activities and planning are on the rise. Ethnic and religiously-motivated mass murders and forced displacements are taking place, and the most basic human and women's rights are shamelessly violated. The country has gradually been occupied by fanatics, extremists, terrorists, mercenaries, drug Mafias and professional murderers. One faction, the Taliban, which by no means rightly represents Islam, Afghanistan or our centuries-old cultural heritage, has with direct foreign assistance exacerbated this explosive situation. They are unyielding and unwilling to talk or reach a compromise with any other Afghan side.

Unfortunately, this dark accomplishment could not have materialized without the direct support and involvement of influential governmental and non-governmental circles in Pakistan. Aside from receiving military logistics, fuel and arms from Pakistan, our intelligence reports indicate that more than 28,000 Pakistani citizens, including paramilitary personnel and military advisers are part of the Taliban occupation forces in various parts of Afghanistan. We currently hold more than 500 Pakistani citizens including military personnel in our POW camps. Three major concerns – namely terrorism, drugs and human rights – originate from Taliban-held areas but are instigated from Pakistan, thus forming the inter-connecting angles of an evil triangle. For many Afghans, regardless of ethnicity or religion, Afghanistan, for the second time in one decade, is once again an occupied country.

Let me correct a few fallacies that are propagated by Taliban backers and their lobbies around the world. This situation over the short and long-run, even in case of total control by the Taliban, will not be to anyone's interest. It will not result in stability, peace and prosperity in the region. The people of Afghanistan will not accept such a repressive regime. Regional countries will never feel secure and safe. Resistance will not end in Afghanistan, but will take on a new national dimension, encompassing all Afghan ethnic and social strata.

The goal is clear. Afghans want to regain their right to self-determination through a democratic or traditional mechanism acceptable to our people. No one group, faction or individual has the right to dictate or impose its will by force or proxy on others. But first, the obstacles have to be overcome, the war has to end, just peace established and a transitional administration set up to move us toward a representative government.

We are willing to move toward this noble goal. We consider this as part of our duty to defend humanity against the scourge of intolerance, violence and fanaticism. But the international community and the democracies of the world should not waste any valuable time, and instead play their critical role to assist in any way possible the valiant people of Afghanistan overcome the obstacles that exist on the path to freedom, peace, stability and prosperity.

Effective pressure should be exerted on those countries who stand against the aspirations of the people of Afghanistan. I urge you to engage in constructive and substantive discussions with our representatives and all Afghans who can and want to be part of a broad consensus for peace and freedom for Afghanistan.

With all due respect and my best wishes for the government and people of the United States,

Ahmad Shah Massoud (1998)

(Source: Afghan-web.com)

PART 2

(10 years and 1 day later)
KABUL, AFGHANISTAN

2011

CHAPTER 2

THE NATIONAL MUSEUM

Executive Conference Room
Presidential Palace | Kabul, Afghanistan
September 12, 2011 | Monday 2:36 p.m.

"My friends, thank you for all the time and money you have contributed towards expanding our National Museum of Afghanistan. I know that we all look forward to the groundbreaking of our new building adjacent to the museum," President Hakim Qazi said in English and then in Dari.

With the museum's board meeting concluded, Qazi's senior advisors, ISAF* dignitaries, and several senior members of the U.S. Embassy's cultural team began to file out of the conference room. Qazi stood near the exit and nodded respectfully to each of the board members as they departed. He was dressed formally in a long white robe, white pants, a high-collar white shirt, and a short black coat. His familiar *karakul*, a triangular-shaped hat made of Persian lamb, rested comfortably on his nearly bald head.

When Dr. Mary Phillips—a senior Foreign Service officer and the head of the Cultural and Religious Section at the U.S. Embassy—was abreast of him, he discreetly stepped forward and leaned toward her. "Please stay. I'd like a private word with you."

Mary acknowledged his request with a slight nod and took a seat at

---

* ISAF- The International Security Assistance Force is a NATO-led military force that oversees the U.N. approved security mission in Afghanistan. Other non-NATO countries are also involved in this mission.

the head of the room's long mahogany conference table. She gazed idly at her surroundings as her hand absently swept across the highly polished table. Maroon silk wall coverings— imprinted with a repeating, slightly darker Afghan symbol—filled the walls. A large gold-colored replica of the Afghanistan national emblem hung prominently from the wall beside the room's double door entrance. Hanging upright, on an ornate flagpole, on the opposite wall was a large Afghanistan flag with its black, red, and green stripes. During her current and two prior tours in Kabul, which included a dozen or so visits to this room, she realized that she'd never really studied her surroundings. The conference room was impressive.

She next turned her attention to Qazi as he greeted the last of the board members. He was of medium height with a neatly trimmed gray mustache and beard, and just a trace of gray hair at the edges of his balding head. His physical appearance reminded her of the actor Ben Kingsley when he starred in the movie *Gandhi*. But she knew Qazi was no Gandhi. If anything, he was just the opposite.

His preferred surname, Qazi, meant judge in Dari. His birth name was similar to Qazi, but Mary couldn't remember it. She did recall that it did have some reference to his tribe, but she couldn't recall that either. No matter if the President of Afghanistan liked being addressed as Judge, that was all he, or anyone else in Afghanistan, needed to change a name. Name changes in Afghanistan were a regular occurrence, even within families. For example, the oldest male child in a family typically enjoyed a name, title, and or description entirely different than that of the family's youngest daughter. Unless one knew the family, it would be impossible for an outsider to identify, by their names, the children of the same mother and father.

This name changing practice had also created a security nightmare for Western military forces in the country. These forces scrupulously kept detailed records, by surname, of Taliban spies. When a local national was caught in the act of spying, he was respectfully interviewed by a Western interrogator—no touching or raising voices—and often released, especially if they believed he was a first-time offender. Days later, the spy had a new name, and he moved on to another military installation. Interrogators, especially U.S. interrogators, became so fearful of being charged with war crimes by their own country—for an aggressive interview—that their inter-action with suspects degraded into little more than an informal interview.

As the last board member approached the exit door, Qazi whispered something to his security guard. The guard followed the member out of the room, closed the door behind him, and locked it.

The loud click of the lock caused Mary to subconsciously straightened and re-cross her legs. She saw Qazi's dark eyes widen slightly as the hem of her skirt inadvertently slipped an inch above her knee.

Though in her mid-forties, Dr. Mary Phillips was still a disarmingly beautiful woman with unreadable blue eyes and blonde hair, cut in a sleek bob. Pink lips, with just a touch of lipstick, and her healthy complexion gave her the appearance of a woman who'd just finished a five-mile run. Her complexion and sturdy, five-foot-ten physique were likely influenced by her upbringing in a small Maine coastal town. She routinely helped her single-parent father set and retrieve lobster traps in all types of weather.

Qazi settled into a chair opposite Mary and asked in English, "Shall we speak in English or Dari?"

"Your English is better than my Dari," said Mary, with a modest smile. In truth, her fluency level of Dari and Pashto—the two languages spoken in Afghanistan—was on a level equal to the native Afghans. She purposefully kept that fact a closely guarded secret.

"All of my advisors have been pleased with you. You've done good work here, and your establishment of that all-girls primary school on Airport Road has not gone unnoticed."

I'm sure it hasn't, she thought cynically. The school Qazi referred to was one of two all-girls schools, known as the New Hope Girls Schools (grades 1-8), that she and her close friend in Jalalabad, Beena Waleed, had set up during her prior tour in Kabul. Both schools provided the girls with a Community-Based Education (CBE), which meant that the schools were supported by private donations, rather than from funds funneled through the government's Ministry of Education.

One of Qazi's second cousins ran the ministry, which meant that only twenty cents of every dollar slithered through the sticky fingers of his bureaucrats and reached educational programs. A sad consequence of this corruption was that half of the government-funded schooling in the country was administered in tents, with no freshwater or toilet facilities, and teachers weren't regularly paid. Students typically had to pay for teaching supplies.

"I understand that you're returning to America," continued Qazi.

"Yes, it's been a busy and challenging year. I fly out tomorrow."

Qazi's head dipped, and his eyes settled on the bandage that was wrapped around four fingers of Mary's right hand. "I heard that you were involved in an incident last week."

During *the incident*, she'd torn off the fingernails of those fingers while fighting off her attacker. She struggled to contain her anger. But when she saw the hint of a cruel smile curl the corner of Qazi's lips, she knew her emotions had betrayed her. "I fought off a rapist. How did you know about that?"

"I read the police reports," he smiled.

Mary abruptly stood, turned her back to Qazi, and purposefully strode to the coffee bar at the opposite end of the conference room. With all the fortitude she could muster, she calmly poured herself a cup of coffee. She could feel his eyes follow her. Returning to her seat, she steadily placed her coffee cup and saucer on the conference table and stared hard at him. "I didn't file a police report."

He ignored her comment while he unabashedly leered at her. "You're a beautiful woman."

She coolly sipped her coffee and spurned his ill-timed and inappropriate attempt at flattery.

After a time, he continued, "Perhaps my chief of police, Safi Khan," told me about the attack."

Her lips tightened, and her eyes hardened. "He'd have first-hand knowledge of that," she spat.

"Your country rapes my country every day. You Americans are worse than the Russians!"

"How would you know? You never fought with the mujahideen. You and your brother, Azim, fled to Pakistan when the Russians invaded Afghanistan."

Qazi's face reddened. No one, especially women, spoke to him like that. He countered, "Safi hopes you'll return. Will you?"

* Khan in Dari means chief. Thus, like Qazi (judge), Safi used a title in his name.

She didn't immediately respond. She was tempted to remain silent about her future plans. Qazi and Safi were two-of-a-kind men with a flawed moral compass. The less they knew about her plans, the better. She opted for vagary. "Possibly. But I'd return for the Afghan children. I want to help more of them, particularly girls, get an education. And, I'd like to do what I can to end your barbaric practice of *bacha bazi*. The rape of young boys by Afghan men," she said evenly.

"But boy play is part of our Afghan culture. You, of all people, should understand that."

"'Women are for children and boys are for pleasure,'" quoted Mary.

"Exactly, my good friend. You're an expert on Afghan culture. You understand these things."

"I know that you, your family, and many of your closest friends approve of boy play. Your brother, Azim, who manages the province of Kandahar in the south, is particularly tolerant of that depravity."

Qazi was silent for several long moments before he responded. "Many of our male leaders are owed that privilege, or pleasure, because they were subjected to it as young boys themselves."

"It's degenerate behavior, and just because your men have been subjected to it doesn't mean it's acceptable. If anything, I'd think they'd want to eliminate the practice, not perpetuate it." Mary paused before adding an ironic aside. "When the Taliban governed this country, in the mid to late 1990s, they nearly abolished boy play. Should they return, I doubt they will fail a second time!"

Qazi's face was flushed with anger and indecision. He didn't know what to say. This brash Western female had openly criticized his support of boy play. Boy play was a long-standing, accepted Afghan custom. He knew, however, after working with the U.S. and other NATO governments for the past ten years, that boy play was a custom that was very much abhorred by his allies.

"Look, Qazi," she continued, "my country is strong and powerful, but sometimes a little too optimistic and impatient when it comes to trying to aid third world countries. They tend to overlook the culture, ethnic divisions, and extreme religious beliefs that have become embedded in a country's character over centuries. Your country is a perfect example.

"On one hand, your country isn't really a country. It's merely a confederation of tribal warlords and druglords. And, on the other hand, it's a haven for regional and global terrorist groups who get much, if not all, of their funding from al-Qaeda and your poppy fields in the south. Because of Osama bin Laden's fundamentalist Islamic beliefs, his appeal to jihadists, and his connections in the Arab world, he had—and his al-Qaeda successors now have—access to nearly unlimited funding for regional and global terrorism.

"His donors and supporters include, as you well know, Pakistan, Saudi Wahhabis, and other anti-West Arab states. Iran is also an unusual supporter of local terrorist groups." Mary paused. She wanted Qazi to fully digest her opinion of his country's predicament before delivering her final thoughts.

"You, and those that surround you, are corrupt to the core, and none of you give a damn about the future or current well-being of your countrymen or your country's children. Your guiding goal, as president, is to steal as much money as you possibly can before you're replaced. When the leaders in my country wake-up and realize this, we'll leave this place."

She wisely elected to omit her long-held belief that the only difference between the Taliban and Qazi's regimen was how they subjugated their citizens. Qazi's choice of oppression was widespread corruption. The Taliban chose adherence to fundamentalist Sharia Law.

Qazi didn't take long to reply. "Ah, Mary, you're a smart woman, but not a visionary. Your country views the world as one big chessboard. America covets our territory. Afghanistan is the ideal location for your country to accomplish their geopolitical goals for Central Asia," said Qazi as he began to tick off his supporting reasons with the fingers of one hand:

- Interfere, disrupt and terminate the global goals of al-Qaeda and its legions of jihadists, who move through Pakistan and Afghanistan like ghosts.

- Deny regional terrorists, like the Afghan Taliban, the possibility of overthrowing this country and sustaining itself on hundreds of millions of dollars of annual drug trafficking revenue.

- Undermine and deny the indoctrination of hundreds of thousands of displaced, stateless Muslims—living in the mountains that separate us from Pakistan—with the violent, fundamentalist Islamic teachings of Saudi Wahhabis.

- Attempt to defuse the tensions between Pakistan and India. Both countries possess nuclear weapons.

- And, lastly, keep Iran, Russia, and China wary of your presence in Central Asia.

"We're your indispensable chess piece, the powerful *queen!* You'll never leave our country, and we'll never change. The flow of billions of U.S. dollars into Afghanistan will last forever. We'll soon become your Central Asian version of South Korea or Israel."

Mary agreed with Qazi's chessboard metaphor, but she didn't buy his comparison of Afghanistan to South Korea and Israel. Afghanistan was not a modern country. Their government was corrupt. Their level of poverty and illiteracy was pitiful. And, they were cursed with never-ending ethnic conflicts. The only bright spot in their economy was their poppy fields,* which accounted for the largest production of illicit opium in the world. And that, unfortunately, drew terrorists to the country like moths to a flame.

"I wouldn't count on a never-ending stream of U.S. support, Qazi," replied Mary simply. "Our ambassador feels the same way."

"Your ambassador is nothing more than a figurehead. Your real power here is your CIA. I know this because they send tens of thousands of dollars every month to my brother, Azim, in Kandahar. Those dollars sustain many of my starving Pashtun brothers who are prevented from growing poppies."

"What! Ten cents of every CIA dollar eventually ends up in the hands of your starving brothers," remarked Mary sarcastically. "Azim's selective monitoring of opium growers also seems to be influenced by those who pay your brother a large bribe, *baksheesh!*"

Qazi appeared outraged at her insinuation.

"Save the look Qazi for our Secretary of State Ted David and our

---

* Afghanistan's poppy fields are primarily located in the southern provinces of Kandahar and Helmand.

in-country generals. This is my third tour in Kabul. I know how you, your brother, and your police chief, Safi Khan, work."

With an exasperated and perplexed look on his face, Qazi changed the subject and proclaimed, "I'm going to end all of your drone attacks! The U.S. is killing thousands of innocent Afghan civilians every year. It is—"

Mary cut him off again. "Save that *diatribe* for the liberal news media. As you well know, drone attacks didn't begin here until a couple of years ago. And, sadly, we…the U.S. and the ISAF… didn't catch on immediately to the reprehensible behavior of your Pashtun buddies. Under the self-serving banner of *Pashtunwali,* they deliberately fed us false information. Their sense of revenge superseded their interest in identifying bona fide Taliban targets.

"Furthermore, you and your five-person committee now hold final 'drone approval' for every target in your country. What you're really saying is that you want more money from your protectors for your approvals. It's also no secret that you've asked the ISAF to attack the homes and villages of some of your political rivals."

He tapped his fingers on the conference table for several long moments as he thought. He'd have to speak with Safi about this arrogant and well-informed Western woman. *She knows too much about our businesses.* He again changed the subject. "Tell me about your ambassador's boss, the Secretary of State, Ted David."

"What about him?"

"He is a forward-thinking man, much like me. As you know, I've had several meetings with him. His 'New Start' speech in Cairo, Egypt, last year was quite enlightening. His father was an Iranian Shiite, yes?"

That remark covers a lot of ground, mused Mary. First, there was Qazi's comment about David's Iranian background. Was he searching to see how well she knew the Secretary of State? And, second, there was his reference to David's 'New Start' speech. Was that a probe of her political disposition?

"David's natural father was not an Iranian, nor was he a Muslim. He was a Catholic Frenchman with likely some Algerian blood, which accounts for his very dark, swarthy appearance. When David's father was a teenager, he and his parents emigrated to the U.S., from France, in the early 1950s. They obtained U.S. citizenship under President Truman's post World War II, European refugee admission policy."

Mary noticed Qazi's eyes widen with her response. *He thought he was an Iranian Muslim. That makes sense though,* she thought. David was a dazzling performer who possessed the unique ability to cloud the judgment of the world's smartest people.

Continuing, she said, "His biological father was killed in a car accident." She left out the details of the accident. He was drunk as a skunk when he drove into a bridge abutment at 100 MPH. "His mother remarried an Iranian—a sometimes pro-Western journalist and indifferent Shia believer—who was granted asylum in the U.S. in 1979, shortly after Ayatollah Khomeini swept into power. His stepfather's well-known collection of contemporary music in Tehran, specifically the Bee Gees' bestselling album, 'Children of the World,' marked him with the Revolutionary Guard him as *an enemy of the state.* David took his stepfather's Americanized surname, David. His Iranian family name was Davud."

He nodded knowingly. "An enemy of the state ...that's a death sentence!"

"Yes."

Mary knew that, initially, Shah Pahlavi's secular goals for Iran were modernization and Westernization, which included the expansion of women's rights and profit-sharing for workers. He was especially keen to help poor farmworkers in the countryside with land reform. Sadly, the unintended consequences of that experiment backfired in a huge way. Independent farmers joined together and severed their ties with the Shah. And the poor farmworkers, who anticipated better days, soon found themselves unemployed.

The ultimate winner in the Shah's failed economic experiment was Shia Islam. In 1979, days after the Shah fled Iran during the Iranian Revolution, the exiled Shia cleric, Ayatollah Ruhollah Khomeini, returned to the country and became its political and religious leader. His Shia followers and Revolutionary Guards quickly erased all vestiges of Westernization, and strict Sharia Law became the law of the land. Within the first eighteen months of his reign, according to Amnesty International, he executed over 30,000 of his countrymen. Petty Sharia Law infractions like a woman wearing a touch of lipstick or a teenager playing a song on their cassette player could result in a death sentence. Reports of gruesome tortures filled the front pages of Western newspapers for years after Khomeini's return.

Qazi continued, "My father had some dealings with Shah of Iran, Mohammad Reza Pahlavi in the 1960s. They were both involved in negotiating the water rights of our Helmand River. My father admired the Shah. He said he was a strong, pro-Western leader who cared for the working class and the merchants. I'm like that!"

"You're pro-Western and supportive of the Afghan working class!" burst Mary a bit too hastily. She regretted the tone of her comment the instant her words passed her lips. Qazi's face reddened. *Shit!* She realized she was now on *really thin ice.* "That came out the wrong way. The Shah was forced out of his country. I don't see that happening to you," she said with an affected smile and the omission of an unsaid modifier…*at least in the near future.*

After a time, he calmed and said, "Tell me your thoughts on Ted David's Cairo speech."

"First, a little background," began Mary. "U.S. President Jed Adams's American Party cabinet is a mix of moderates from both our Republican and Democratic parties. Those he appointed to cabinet positions shared his goals for the country, and they pledged to advance those goals for the next four years. David has apparently decided unilaterally that it's no longer in his best political interests to honor his pledge. Nothing unusual about that. Keeping your word these days in Washington is more the exception than the rule. Do you understand what I'm saying?"

"Perfectly! Adams is a weak, social conservative. He was tired of the finger-pointing and lack of cooperation between both of your major political parties, so he believed that a *mix,* as you say, would work," he said, sneering and wagging his head from side to side as if he were scolding a child.

"Do you find something offensive about Adams's goals?"

"Offensive! Not to me! But only a fool would surround himself with advisors who might not follow his orders. Look at my staff. They're all loyal to me! If they're not…" He then quite deliberately paused to measure Mary's interest in his view of governing.

Though Mary didn't need to hear him articulate his beliefs, she was curious to see if he would. She knew he liked to bedevil and torment his adversaries with outrageous remarks. She also knew that he suffered from a brain disorder known as manic-depressive illness. Symptoms of this disorder included odd shifts in mood, disassociation with reality, and the inclination to change one's opinion in the blink of an eye. If one of his major support-ers—like the U.S., Great Britain, Canada, Germany, or France—confronted him about an inexplicable change in policy or his unilateral recession of an agreement, he'd typically ascribe his oversight to his illness.

Mary leaned toward Qazi and pressed him for his view. "And, if they're not loyal to you?"

With a look of indifference, he replied calmly, "They leave Kabul and get replaced!"

The leave Kabul... alive or dead? she wondered as a cold chill ran down her spine. It was time to change the subject. "David's 'New Start' speech in Cairo—"

"Yes, with his special Sunni guests—all leaders of the Muslim Brother-hood— seated in the front row," he interjected ironically.

Mary paused before continuing. *What the hell was Qazi getting at now? Was he trying to point out the paradoxes of the U.S.'s international policies vis a vis the Muslim Brotherhood? Or that 90% of the Afghan population were Sunnis.*

Oppressive regimes, particularly those that resisted democratic reforms in the Middle East, were currently feeling the backlash of the Arab Spring that began in late 2010 in Tunisia. President Hosni Mubarak of Egypt, the long-standing supporter of the U.S., had been overthrown the previous January for his halfhearted enthusiasm for implementing such reforms.

She knew that the Muslim Brotherhood was behind that overthrow. When, not if, these Islamic fundamentalists took control of the country, they would immediately institute the strict observance of Sharia Law. When that occurred, the only question in her mind was how long they could hold onto power. She guessed that the Egyptians would boot them out within a year or two. She'd been previously stationed in Cairo and was certain that modern-day Egyptians wouldn't tolerate a seventh-century Islamic way of life.

Rather than getting into a protracted debate with Qazi about Sunnis, the Muslim Brotherhood, and David's well-known interest in a regime change in Egypt, she elected to make a simple observation. "I think David was attempting to extend an olive branch to the Muslim world. It was an admirable gesture, though somewhat naïve. Islam is much more than a religion. It's a way of life with a set of laws, like our Constitution, and it..." she suddenly stopped, mid-sentence.

Qazi had stood and was now standing behind her. She felt his hand slide along her shoulders and brush her hair. Her entire being bristled. After several long moments and deep breaths, she willed herself to continue. "Americans would never accept the rules of Sharia Law. Sharia Law doesn't recognize civil rights, human rights, or women's rights."

"What do you think about my respect for those rights?" whispered Qazi into her ear.

Not much! screamed Mary's mind. He was baiting her for some strange reason. Though she didn't sense that he was going to physically assail her, there was clearly something about their interaction that sexually aroused him. Whatever his reason, she'd had enough. "We're through here," she snapped. Standing, she realized that he had moved closer to her, and their bodies briefly collided. Taking a step backward, she ordered, "Unlock and open the door!"

Qazi was frozen in place. His eyes were clouded, and a lewd smirk filled his face.

Mary coolly pulled her cell phone from her purse and held it at arm's length so Qazi could read the ambassador's name and her last text to him. "He knows about the incident, and he knows that I'm with you. I texted him just before you said goodbye to your last board member. Open the door!" she repeated.

THE ROUNDABOUTS

U.S. Embassy, Kabul | Airport Road exit area

September 13, 2011 | Tuesday 1:48 p.m.

After the last piece of luggage was loaded into the white Toyota Land Cruiser, the rear armor-plated double doors were shut and locked from within. Three embassy staff members sat, facing one another on bench seats, in that rear compartment. Their luggage was stacked between them. Dr. Mary Phillips sat in the front passenger seat.

All of them were returning to the U.S. after their yearlong tour at the U.S. Embassy, Kabul. They had introduced themselves to Mary, who was the well-known head of the embassy's Cultural and Religious Section. Amy Blake was a certified public accountant (CPA), in her late twenties, and a U.S. Treasury analyst in Treasury's Financial Crimes Enforcement Network (FinCEN). Joe Michaels was also in his late twenties and formerly in the U.S. Army. What he did in the Army and where he was stationed was a mystery, a closely guarded mystery. He was a mid-level security specialist in the embassy's Diplomatic Security (DS) department who was returning to the States for additional DS training and several weeks of vacation before he returned to Kabul for his third tour. The last passenger was an Army medic, in his early thirties, named Sam Smith. He was a veteran of several combat tours in Iraq and was in the midst of earning his master's degree in medical care, which would qualify him to become a physician's assistant.

All of the passengers wore Kevlar vests over their casual attire for the one-hour, thirty-five-mile drive from the embassy's Green Zone to Bagram Airfield. Kabul's Green Zone is a high-security area—covering approximately one square mile—in central Kabul that is the home to the Afghanistan Presidential Palace, the U.S. Embassy, the ISAF headquarters, and several other major Western embassies. Their departure time from the embassy left a comfortable cushion of three-plus hours before their flight departed Bagram. Traffic, check-in procedures at Bagram, and an occasional bomb threat—or an actual bombing—could delay their arrival at the airfield.

Mary was dressed in worn jeans, a loose-fitting cotton blouse, hooded sweatshirt, and low-cut hiking boots. She looked as if she was headed for a daylong hike in her childhood state of Maine. Her well-worn Boston Red Sox baseball cap concealed her pinned up blonde hair and proudly announced that she was a fan of the club. The other passengers were similarly dressed in casual and comfortable attire.

The first leg of their journey involved a seven-hour government flight from Bagram to the Ramstein Air Base in Germany. Ramstein is the home of the U.S. Air Force in Europe and often referred to as "Little America," with 57,00 U.S. citizens living and working in the surrounding area. It is also America's hub, in Europe, for its "war on terror." The Landstuhl Regional Medical Facility— the largest American operated hospital outside of the U.S.—is located five miles from the Ramstein Air Base. It provides specialized medical care to U.S. servicemen injured in Afghanistan and Iraq.

The Toyota Land Cruiser that they were traveling in was known as a Minerva Special Purpose Vehicle 78, or simply an MSPV 78. It was an armored plated vehicle specifically constructed for protection against assault rifles, hand grenades, and low explosive IEDs. For extra safety, the vehicle also possessed blast plates on the roof and underbody, reinforced glass windows, fuel tank protection, upgraded suspension, run-flat tires, and a heavy-duty front bumper that resembled a cattle-guard.

The driver of the Land Cruiser was a young Afghan in his early twenties. He was a member of the newly trained Afghan security force that was incrementally replacing ISAF personnel in Afghanistan. An M-4 carbine sat upright in a rifle rack between the driver and Mary. The M-4 was a shorter and lighter version of the M-16 that was first introduced in Vietnam.

Mary asked the driver, in Dari, why her friend Jamal Waleed wasn't driving them to Bagram.

"Last minute change by Diplomatic Security (DS)," he replied stiffly in Dari.

"Jamal is a good friend. His older sister, Beena, and I established the all-girls primary school several miles north of here, just off of Airport Road School. I spent many hours volunteering there this past year," smiled Mary.

The driver remained silent and looked straight ahead. Mary noticed his grip on the steering wheel tighten, and an inscrutable look cross his face.

She continued, "Is this rifle loaded?"

"Locked and loaded, but don't touch. Not for women," he grunted.

Mary ignored the comment. She was all too familiar with the sexist behavior of most Afghan males.

When the first of the security gates were raised on the eastern side of the main embassy structure—a blocky, four-story tan structure that looked like a professional basketball arena—the driver carefully wound around multiple security pylons and past a machine gun emplacement. Security precautions at U.S. embassies—especially in Afghanistan and other Middle Eastern countries—in the days surrounding the anniversary of "9/11" were particularly stringent.

The driving skills of the young Afghan reminded the passengers of a sixteen-year-old anxiously attempting to pass his first driver's license exam. He drove tentatively as he approached the last security gate. This final, sliding steel gate was connected to the thirty-foot high, tan concrete wall that surrounded the entire nine-acre embassy compound. Once through this last gate, the driver turned left onto Airport Road,* northbound toward Bagram. He then nervously withdrew a cell phone from his shirt pocket and sent a prewritten text message with a single keystroke.

Hoping to calm the anxious driver, Mary asked him casually how he liked his new job. The driver didn't seem to hear a word she said. He looked petrified. She began to wonder if there was more to his nervousness than new-job jitters. His sending of a text message also stirred her curiosity. Before she could reflect further on his behavior, an unusual sight caught her attention. Lane Peters, the surly security specialist who usually accom-

* Airport Road is more formally known as Great Massoud Road.

panied her on off-site embassy business, was sprinting with pumping arms. He had just barreled around the northwest corner of Great Massoud Circle, the intersecting roundabout of Airport Road and Wazir Akbar Khan Road. Forty yards ahead of them, on the opposite side of the road, it appeared that he was racing toward the embassy exit, which they'd just departed.

She briefly locked eyes with Peters. His look conveyed a high level of anxiety, either anger or dread. She couldn't tell which. Unexpectedly, he bounded to the edge of the road, withdrew his portable radio from his belt, and looked over his shoulder to check the southbound traffic. It seemed as if he might try to flag down their vehicle, but the traffic was too heavy. He narrowly avoided a honking jingle truck whose side mirror must have missed him by an inch. He next spoke excitedly into his radio. *Was he trying to warn them or those at the embassy of some impending threat?*

Peters's unusual behavior had also drawn the attention of the driver. As Mary leaned forward in her seat to get a better look at Peters, the driver hit the gas pedal and made a sharp right-hand turn out of Great Massoud Circle. The unexpected, wrong turn slammed her hard against the M-4, which was firmly braced in the center console. They were now headed eastward on Wazir Akbar Khan Road toward Abdul Haq Square, with no way to turn around because of the road's center median.

The Abdul Haq Square roundabout was known as one of the busiest and wildest traffic roundabouts in all of Afghanistan. It reminded her of some of the snarly roundabouts in Rome and Mexico City, except that the pushcart vendors and begging children were bolder and braver. In the center of the roundabout was a giant billboard with a picture of the square's namesake, Abdul Haq. Haq was a famous mujahideen leader who battled the Soviets in the 1980s and attempted to rally the Afghans against the Taliban, days after al-Qaeda's 9/11 attacks in the U.S. The Taliban assassinated him on October 26, 2001.

Mary glared angrily at the driver as she massaged her sore left elbow that had smashed into the rifle. The driver's high-speed turn was unnecessary. Furthermore, the idiot should have understood why the damn road they'd just left was nicknamed Airport Road. She opened her mouth and was about to chastise him when Joe, the DS security specialist, distracted her.

"Do you know Peters?" he asked.

"He was usually my DS security escort whenever I left the embassy compound. He's brusque and impatient. He didn't impress me." As an afterthought, she added, "I think he heads back to States for DS training in a month or so. You may run into him at Arlington."

"He's very unimpressive if you ask me. I think he's got his finger into illegal stuff 'outside of the wire.' Kickbacks on Afghan security contracts, the unlawful sale of U.S. weapons, selling intelligence. It's one or more of those," said Joe disparagingly.

Mary turned in her seat toward and examined him. "Those are serious allegations. Do you have any proof?"

"No, just a feeling! A couple of my DS buddies served with him in the Army when they were stationed in Iraq. Peters was arrested and charged with selling military weapons to the jihadists. He was scheduled to go up before a General Court-Martial, but his attorney negotiated a deal during his pre-trial Article 32 investigation. He should have gotten ten years at Leavenworth if you ask me. Instead, he agreed to an OTH. A stink surrounds OTH guys!"

"What's an OTH?" asked Amy.

"*Other than honorable*, general discharge. It's near the bottom of the barrel," interjected Sam.

Amy continued, "In my spare time, I've been investigating the DS section for Treasury. Their accounting is terrible, almost nonexistent. Millions of dollars are missing and unaccounted for."

"I'm not surprised. Peters oversaw all of our expenditures," said Joe. A moment later, he added, "You should also look into his relationship with the embassy's contracting and transportation departments. Peters spent more time there than he did in our DS control center."

"I'm aware of that. I've heard that he, and maybe other DS personnel, enjoy an unusually close relationship with Kabul's police department. There are rumors that Police Chief Safi Khan and President Hakim Qazi receive kickbacks from the security firms that protect our military supply convoys wherever they travel. Plus, they allegedly get a cut of toll collections, be it along dirt roads or major highways. *Major highways!*" closed Amy, chuckling to herself.

Mary asked, over her shoulder, "What's so funny?"

"Major highways. That's a *misnomer*. There are no major highways here. At best, there are a handful of old four-lane roads with brick medians."

Mary nodded in agreement.

Amy continued, "So, first, we pay over-priced security firms to escort our convoys. They supposedly provide *a level of safety*. Then, our convoys have to pay tolls on *roadways* that these toll collectors allegedly maintain and control. What a joke that is!"

"How so?" probed Mary.

"These roadways pass through areas that have already been secured by ISAF forces. All these local toll collectors do is collect tolls. They don't provide any services. Filling and repairing major potholes is beneath them. Removing abandoned or wrecked vehicles on the side of the road isn't part of their job description. And, searching for or removing IED explosives planted in the roadbed is too dangerous. They're all Pashtuns, except in the north, and most are likely Taliban. They're the ones who planted the IEDs in the road. If they aren't Taliban, then they're likely associated with the Afghan security firm that's escorting convoys in their neighborhood. So, with advance knowledge of a convoy's route, all these collectors do is collect tolls. It's the Afghan version of *highway robbery*."

"That sounds like something that Peters would be involved in," sneered Joe.

News that Peters and the chief of police, Safi Khan, might share mutual, unethical interests turned Mary's stomach. She filed that tidbit of information in the back of her mind, while she posed another question. "What about toll collectors stationed on the major, cross-border passes, like the Khyber Pass?"

"The Kyber Pass is one of the few major exceptions. The Zahir clan collects tolls, maintains the road, and they provide the trucks with security when they cross through the pass. It's a tall order, under tough conditions."

"Why a *tall order*?" queried Mary, despite knowing the answer. She was testing Amy's breadth of local knowledge.

"Approximately 70% of the ISAF's fuel requirements country-wide are delivered, via tanker trucks, through that pass. Tankers are one of the Taliban's top targets."

Mary nodded in agreement. Her new acquaintance was proving that she was not only a thorough investigator but one who also possessed a grasp of daily Afghan life. She liked that. "You said earlier that you investigated the DS section *in your spare time*. What were your main duties?"

"My primary duty was investigating the Kabul Bank debacle. In six years, the bank lost $950 million, most of that was the result of bad loans. The day after I arrived here last year, the former Kabul Bank president and Afghanistan's Minister of Finance, Jamee Nabi, ordered me to a meeting at the bank's headquarters. In short, they both told me, in no uncertain terms, that all the bank's bad loans were unsecured. And that there was nothing more that could be done to recover loan deficiencies.

"I wasn't entirely surprised with their judgment. My predecessors had already warned me about the bank's reluctance…er, hostility… to any outsider examinations of their loan documents. And to expect threats if I refused to suspend my investigation."

"Threats?" questioned Mary.

"Yes, physical threats… bodily injury, death. Violence and corruption is a way of life here. On my third day in Kabul, I changed the combination on the bank's vault. That's where all the loan docs were held. That eliminated the prospect of bank management tampering with or destroying the documents. It also royally pissed off the former bank president and Minister Nabi."

Mary turned in her seat and studied Amy. She was the first to greet her when she arrived at the embassy's loading area. Her opening compliment about her New Hope Girls School—north of downtown Kabul, off of Airport Road—had made a favorable, first impression. She was a slender, five-foot four-inch, attractive woman, with intelligent gray eyes and auburn hair, swept to the right side of her head. "Were you concerned about those threats?"

"I was scared shitless! Treasury made arrangements to have an FBI special agent accompany me every time I visited the bank."

"The FBI has agents in Kabul?"

"Yes, I too was surprised about that. The FBI has specially trained hostage rescue teams that work with our military's special forces."

Mary unconsciously squinted her eyes. That was news to her. "How did your investigations turn out?"

"Most of the bad loans, 90% or so, were made to companies controlled by President Hakim Qazi, his family relations, and/or his pals. Unfortunately for the principals of these phony-baloney shell companies—and fortunately for the initial 'seed money' investors in the bank, like the U.S.—their Afghan attorneys did a piss-poor job of protecting their clients. The loan documents that the principals signed didn't protect them from personal liability.

"Though the loans the companies took out were labeled *unsecured*, that only meant that specific assets didn't secure or back the loans. Local bank management *weakly* appealed to the shell companies for loan repayment, but their managers all screamed that they were broke. None of them provided any financial records. Failing recourse there, the bank was next required to look to the personal guarantees of the shell's principals for debt repayment. Bank management and Nabi refused to do that. When I get back to the States, I'm going to look into a couple of ideas I have for recovering more money.

"Meanwhile, I was able to recover $50 million this past year, which is peanuts. The big losers were mainly the U.S. taxpayers and, to a lesser extent, the taxpayers in Great Britain and Germany whose seed money originally funded the bank. Thousands of small depositors also lost their savings," closed Amy.

Thieving bastards! What a mess! thought Mary as she wagged her head angrily and stared at oncoming traffic. Their peculiar and inexperienced driver was about to drive them into yet another roundabout.

The rumble of honking car horns, traffic cop whistles, and roaring truck engines was rising. The busy Abdul Haq Square roundabout was seconds away. If they were involved in a car accident in this roundabout, she knew, it could easily result in hours of police investigations and angry finger-pointing by injured locals. They could all miss their flight home, which was no minor inconvenience. When they each arrived in Afghanistan, 365 days earlier, they—like every soldier in Afghanistan—began counting the days to their departure date. Today was special.

A feeling, perhaps a sixth sense, prompted Mary to sneak a peek at the driver. His face was flushed, and beads of sweat were beginning to form on his forehead. *Something more than new-driver jitters was affecting this guy?*

A moment later, their Land Cruiser was swept into the chaotic thunder of car horns, police whistles, creaking pushcarts, teenage hawkers, and several highly decorated jingle trucks that were loudly jangling. Unexpectedly, a new sound replaced all others. It was the earsplitting racket of automatic gunfire that was clanging against the left side of their vehicle.

A uniform chorus of "*what the fuck*" filled the inside of the cab. An instant later, the Land Cruiser came to a sudden and jarring stop. All of them were violently flung forward against their seatbelts. Their first thought was that the nervous driver had accidentally plowed head-on into one of the many red and white striped concrete traffic barriers that protected the traffic cops in the center of the roundabout. Wrong! The driver had jammed the brake pedal to the floor and ground the automatic gearshift into park. He then leaped from the vehicle and ran.

Their first rear-end collision was modest, probably a small car, thought Mary, who was looking straight ahead. The next rear-end impact was anything but modest. It felt like a train had rammed them. Mary turned in her seat. The small car had been pancaked into the rear of the Land Cruiser by a large garbage truck. The car's front windshield was shattered, and blood was beginning to color the driver's side of the windshield.

Mary instinctively moved the M-4 to the side and slid herself into the driver's seat and closed the driver's door. Bodies were falling all around them. Their Land Cruiser wasn't the target of the attack. The target was everything and every person in the clogged roundabout. She eased the vehicle forward and tried to ignore the excruciating sound of ripping metal as she separated the Land Cruiser from the small car that was plastered against its rear end. Once free of the small car, she began to maneuver around the confusion of stationary cars and trucks. She had driven less than a hundred feet when two bloodied traffic cops, on all fours, crawled in front of her.

Mary braked and turned sideways, so those behind her could hear her above the din of clanging gunfire. "Sam, get those rear doors open. We're picking up two injured cops. There's a first aid kit attached to the backside of my seat. We need to help these guys!"

Sam replied, "That's my job. Pull up beside them. Keep them on your right, so we're sheltered from the gunfire."

"Uh-huh," grunted Mary. *Thank God, Sam is with us! I wouldn't have thought of that.* The gunfire that was raining down on them was coming from the upper floors of the buildings on their left. This was a well-planned attack.

The next minutes unfolded in slow motion. Mary pulled up beside the two injured policemen. Sam and Joe helped each of the wounded men into the rear of the Land Cruiser. While this was occurring, Amy quickly rearranged the luggage so that both men could lie down on the vehicle's floor. She also opened and prepped the extensive first aid kit for Sam. She then slipped into the front passenger seat and turned on the vehicle's radio that connected them to the embassy.

While they all listened to security reports over the radio, Mary maneuvered around the last of the vehicles in the roundabout and stepped on the gas. After a couple of high speeds turns, she pulled the Land Cruiser to a stop at the emergency entrance of a private hospital, which was only a quarter of a mile north of Abdul Haq Square.

Both cops weakly raised their heads. When they realized where she had taken them, they began to object. One of the cops groaned in broken English, "This is a private hospital…only for the wealthy. They won't take us. Go to the military hospital, Dawood Khan Hospital. It's not far!"

Sam, the Army medic, interjected, "Mary, tell them you can't take them there. Injured Afghan soldiers are starving to death in that place, and they've run out of meds. The Afghan surgeon general and his Pashtun buddies, mainly the Qazis, stole $60 million in aid that was designated for the hospital. It's the second time that's happened. I've been there. It's a hellhole!"

The ambassador had briefed Mary and the other Foreign Service officers at the embassy about those disgraceful thefts. This, however, was not the time to discuss the matter. From the security reports she heard over the vehicle's radio, they were in the midst of a well-planned and well-coordinated terrorist attack. Pre-registered mortar rounds were pounding the embassy's compound.

She turned in her seat toward the two injured cops and said, in Dari, "This is a major Taliban attack. Terrorists are firing from the upper floors of that unfinished twelve-story building in the Wazir Akbar Khan district. They're shooting at our embassy and the nearby Dawood Khan Hospital. You're going to receive medical care here. Relax! I'll be back in a minute."

Gnawing at her thoughts was the minutes-earlier sight of Lane Peters running away from that very building on Wazir Akbar Khan Road.

She gave her Boston Red Sox cap a securing tug and jumped out of the vehicle. As Mary approached the emergency entrance, she noticed that several medical personnel, inside the hospital, were busy moving desks and couches against the entrance doors. Already a group of injured civilians was milling about outside the doors, pleading for aid. She lowered her head and muscled her way through the closing doors of the hospital.

Once inside the hospital, she barked in Dari, "I have just come from Hakim Qazi's office at the Presidential Palace. I'm a close friend of his and the chief of police, Safi Khan." She then whipped off her baseball cap, unpinned her hair and shook it out for all to see. Up until then, the medical staff didn't have any idea who this crazy door crasher was. When they saw that she was a beautiful, blonde Western woman, just the type who would likely appeal to Qazi and Safi, their opinion changed.

"The Presidential Palace, the U.S. Embassy, ISAF headquarters, Massoud Circle, and Abdul Haq Square are all under attack," continued Mary. "Go to your rooftop and look for yourselves. There are Apache helicopters in the sky attacking your enemies. President Qazi has instructed me to order you to care for every one of your injured brothers and sisters who come to your door for medical aid. *Insha'Allah!*" If Allah wills it! she barked in understandable Arabic to the Muslim staff.

With that contrived, spur of the moment proclamation Mary turned on her heels and ordered several of the staff to help her move the furniture away from the hospital's entrance doors. She next stepped outside and surveyed the growing mass of injured civilians who were converging on the hospital. From atop the entrance steps, she shouted in Dari, "Make room for your injured policemen to enter this hospital. They were injured protecting your fellow Afghans. Once they are admitted, this fine hospital will care for all who have been injured. *Allahu Akbar!*" Allah is great!

Minutes later, Mary was back behind the wheel of the Land Cruiser cautiously driving, in the slow lane of Airport Road, toward Bagram Airfield. Sam had traded seats with Amy and was now riding in the front passenger seat beside her. Mary's nerves were gradually settling as she concentrated her thoughts on a more pleasant matter, her upcoming visit with her dad at her childhood home in Maine. *Summer crowds are gone, just the locals now. Seeing elementary and high school friends. Everyone knows one another. Hi Mary! How've you been? Cool mornings with just a hint of future frosts. Leaves turning from green to shades of orange, red, and yellow.* A soft smile creased her lips, and her body relaxed.

Suddenly, a huge military truck began to nose ahead of her in the half lane, on her left. The truck towed an extended flatbed trailer with a Mine-Resistant Ambush Protected (MRAP) vehicle chained to its bed. The MRAP was the size of a small house.

Thoughts of Maine disappeared as the tow truck, and its towering load began to rumble past her leaving in its wake a dark cloud of noxious diesel fumes. While she was attempting to keep her left wheels on the roadway, a small boxy white van unexpectedly appeared from a side street, on her right. The van darted in front of her, which caused her to slam on the brakes and narrowly avoid a rear-end collision.

She took a closer look at the van. "I'll be damned!" she said to herself. A homemade decal on the rear bumper that read NHGS was the tipoff. The van was from her New Hope Girls School, which was located just a few blocks ahead of them.

In seconds, the van sped ahead of the tow truck. *That is one wild and reckless driver! He shouldn't be driving my students around the city.* She made a mental note to call the school principal when she got to Bagram. Once the military truck was well clear of her, she began to ease her right side wheels back onto the roadway. In that instant, an unexpected sight caused Mary and Sam to gasp unconsciously.

"What? What is it?" implored Amy, her nervous system still on high alert.

"That!" said Mary as she pointed to the smoking trail of an RPG (a rocket-propelled grenade) that streaked across the four lanes of traffic ahead of them. The RPG narrowly missed the van but hit a nearby bus stop. Shrapnel from the explosion tore into the front end of the van, causing it to come to a smoking, lurching stop.

The RPG shooter—along with a helper—had made the shot from a kneeling position in the slow, southbound lane of traffic, on the opposite side of Airport Road. Twenty feet behind them was their parked car, which protected them from southbound traffic.

"Sam, grab your first aid pack. That van is from the girls school, just around the corner from that next side street on our right. I opened that school with a friend. See if any girls were injured." Her instruction was delivered as she mashed the Land Cruiser's gas pedal to the floor. In the meantime, the tow truck too had sped up, though it didn't bother to stop for the smoking school van.

A few long seconds later, Mary's lead foot moved from the gas pedal to the brake. As the Land Cruiser slowed beside the van, with its darkly tinted windows, she and Sam both took a moment to study the two-man RPG team on the opposite side of the divided road.

"He's got an RPG-7 portable launcher. They're thousands of those in Afghanistan," said Sam, pausing to see what would happen next. The RPG helper reached for a nearby thirty-inch cylindrical tube with a fat pear-shaped object on one end. "Those SOBs are going to reload and take another shot at the van."

"Grab your first aid pack and take care of those in the van! I'll take care of the shooters," growled Mary.

Sam nimbly hopped out of the still-moving Land Cruiser with the ease of a gymnast who had performed the move a thousand times before.

An instant later, Mary's lead foot again jammed the gas pedal to the floor. She accelerated between a slew of northbound drivers who wanted nothing to do with the deadly RPG shooters. Over her shoulder, she shouted to Joe and Amy, "Tighten your seatbelts and prepare for ramming!"

The Land Cruiser was briefly propelled airborne when it hurtled over the raised-brick median. While airborne, Mary's brain absorbed two important details. Firstly, southbound traffic had come to a full stop. None of those drivers had interest in driving between an RPG shooter and his target. She had a clear path to the terrorists. Secondly, the RPG helper was having difficulty reloading the launcher.

Mary steeled herself as she raced toward the terrorists. The helper heard the sound of the fast-approaching vehicle. A moment before his life ended, he turned toward Mary with an angry look of resignation. He shouted something to another terrorist who was located somewhere behind her. His words had barely left his lips when the Land Cruiser's cattle-guard plowed into the two-man RPG team at 40 MPH. The sickening thud of the impact caused Amy, buckled tightly into the rear passenger compartment, to double over and vomit into an empty box of medical supplies.

The Land Cruiser came to a bumpy, rumbling stop fifty feet beyond the point of impact, at the edge of what appeared to be a horse trail. Blood and gray brain matter streaked the windshield. The empty, forty-inch RPG firing tube was wedged into the cattle-guard and protruded above the hood of the Land Cruiser at a weird 45°angle.

Without a moment's hesitation, Mary flipped on the windshield washer and wipers and shifted the vehicle into reverse. While looking over her shoulder to the rear, her lead foot again mashed the gas pedal to the floor. Tires screeched and smoked. Moments later, she yanked the steering wheel to the right and completed a high speed 180° turn. She slammed the gearshift into drive and raced forward toward the third terrorist who the RPG helper had shouted to seconds earlier. This terrorist was easily identifiable because of a heavy bag he carried in each hand, no doubt filled with explosives, and the nervous scowls he flashed her as she raced toward him.

Mary was able to traverse the center median again, but only part of one northbound lane. Northbound looky-loo drivers had brought traffic to a standstill. Cars were stopped bumper-to-bumper. The terrorist, she saw, was now hustling as fast as he could toward the entrance of the her school, fifty yards ahead of him.

Braking, she shoved her gearshift into park, grabbed the M-4 rifle, and jumped out of the Land Cruiser. She hurried to the rear of the vehicle, stepped atop the rear bumper, and settled her upper body upon the bullet-dented roof. Thankfully, the protruding RPG tube didn't interfere with her field of fire.

The terrorist was now only twenty yards from the entrance of the flat-roofed, mud-brick schoolhouse. She saw him withdraw some sort of triggering device from his vest. She switched off the rifle's safety and took several deep, calming breaths while she aimed. As she exhaled her last breath, she gently squeezed the trigger of the M-4. A click, but no round was fired. Frantically, she immediately withdrew the rifle's aluminum magazine, with thoughts of reseating it. When her eyes caught sight of the dented top of the aluminum magazine, her mind froze. There was no way this magazine could feed rounds into the rifle, and there was no time to search for a replacement magazine in the Land Cruiser.

She'd failed. Over 100 students and eight teachers would die. In a day or so, the bombing would likely be noted on the second or third pages of U.S. newspapers. Most readers would probably skim the article and its deadly statistic, one more school destroyed in Afghanistan by another demented Taliban suicide bomber. It was a faraway war, which few at home cared about and even fewer understood.

Mary's world began to spin, and her vision blurred. She felt herself floating backward. An instant before she lost consciousness and hit the roadway, she heard two loud blasts.

CHAPTER 4

THE EVIL BASTARDS

The New Hope Girls School, Kabul, near Airport Road

September 13, 2011 | Tuesday 3:07 p.m.

Smelling salts roused Mary from her unconsciousness. A man was leaning over her and saying something. She couldn't understand what he was saying. Then, a familiar face arrived. It was a young woman with a white hijab wrapped around her head.

"Mary, it's me, Beena. I shot the bomber. The girls are OK. Are you hurt?"

Mary slowly raised herself to a sitting position on the road. She wriggled her body. All her body parts seemed to be working. She next placed a hand on the back of her head. There was none of the stickiness of congealed blood, but there was definitely a lump, and her head pounded. "I think...I think I fainted. The rifle jammed. I thought..." she muttered before she was overcome with emotion. With her are arms holding her knees tight against her chest, she rested her head on her on them and rocked back and forth. Between sobs, she cried, "I heard two blasts."

"Those were the gunshots from the Glock 19 that you gave me. I planted myself sideways, legs bent, arms extended, and held the gun in both hands. The fighter's stance...just like we practiced at the shooting range at Bagram. The bomber smiled at me. It was an evil, cruel look. His eyes were glazed. I think he was high on drugs. He fumbled for a moment with the triggering device. I took a deep breath and slowly squeezed the trigger, followed a moment later by a second squeeze. I thought that part would be hard, but it wasn't. He wanted to kill all the girls. The world is a better place without him."

Mary rolled to her side and shakily attempted to stand. With Sam's helping hands, she stood. He slipped a hand inside her right arm to steady her. He turned toward her and whispered, "I caught most of you before you crashed to the road, but your head did hit the pavement. You've been out of it for the last ten minutes. I'll check you out. You may have incurred a concussion."

Before he walked her to the school, he retrieved a blood pressure cuff and a small plastic bottle of sedatives from the first aid kit in the Land Cruiser.

Minutes later, Mary was seated on a stiff wooden chair that rested on the hard-packed ground, near the school's front entrance. Behind her, the aged single-story schoolhouse looked as weary and dispirited as Mary. Sam had just performed a cursory examination of her vitals. With the blood pressure cuff, he'd confirmed that her blood pressure had spiked. The good news, though, was that her eyes were only marginally dilated. There was likely no serious head injury.

She looked at her hands that tightly grasped a glass of water. Water was splashing over the sides of the glass.

Sam knelt beside her. He placed a comforting hand on one of her wrists and said softly, "Take this sedative. It'll calm you. When we're finished here, I'll drive the Land Cruiser to Bagram. You're safe."

Mary nodded as she washed down the sedative. "Thank God for Army medics," she hiccupped.

He smiled and said, "There were no kids in the school van. The van's wild driver was a little shook up, but otherwise OK. By the way, your take out of that RPG team was a sight to see."

Joe soon joined the group. "I reparked the Land Cruiser. That's one tough vehicle." With a note of dark humor, he added, "I think we'll raise a few eyebrows when we drive up to the entrance gate at the Bagram Airfield. The RPG tube in the cattle guard, blood and guts on the windshield, a hundred or so bullet dents on the vehicle, and part of the front bumper of that little car that was squished against us in Abdul Haq Square is still attached to the rear end."

"And then there is the interior of the vehicle," added Alice. "The rear compartment looks an operating room. The cops bled a lot. There are bloody bandages all over the place. Blood even got on our suitcases. It also stinks back there. I puked," sighed Alice, with a pale face and eyes still the size of silver dollars.

A dogged, but contrived smile flitted across Mary's lips. "The worst is behind us. We'll leave here in a minute or two."

Sam's eyes squinted knowingly. He recognized grit and stubbornness. Mary's recovery from the events of the last half hour would take more than *a minute or two*. He said with an even but firm voice, "It will take at least fifteen minutes for the sedative to work its wonders. We've got plenty of time to catch our flight. You need to relax and collect yourself."

Mary offered a reluctant grunt and leaned into Beena, who was seated beside her. Her twenty-eight-year-old friend and founding partner of the New Hope Girls Schools was a special woman. They first met four years earlier, in 2007, after she had given a talk about modern women at the National Museum in Kabul. Beena assertively marched to the podium after her presentation, and confidently introduced herself. Mary was immediately taken with the young woman's command of English and her apparent level of maturity. She asked Beena if she would like to join her for a coffee in the museum's staff lounge. She accepted, and Mary soon learned of the young woman's extraordinary background.

Beena and her younger brother, Jamal, were secreted out of Afghanistan to Paris in 1996 with the aid of her uncle, Ahmad Shah Massoud. At that time, Massoud was Afghanistan's Minister of Defense. One month after their departure, the Taliban toppled the country's ruling government. In Paris, a cousin of Massoud's agreed to board Beena and her brother in a spare bedroom. The CIA provided the siblings with a modest stipend to cover their living expenses and educational costs.

Both children spoke passable French as a result of their studies in French schools in Kabul and Jalalabad. In no time, they both distinguished themselves in their respective classrooms, much as they had done in Afghanistan. Beena, subsequently, received a full scholarship to the Sorbonne University.

She majored in a medical studies program that was designed for those who aspired to be doctors. Jamal, too, received a scholarship to École des Ponts ParisTech. He majored in mechanical engineering.

When they first met, Beena was on her way to complete her last two years of residency training with Médecins Sans Frontiéres at a field hospital in Kashmir.* At that time, 2007, the Kashmir Conflict was raging in the state of Jammu and Kashmir, India. Beena's linguistic skills—fluency in French, English, Dari, Pashto, and Urdu—along with her prior medical training, qualified her for her dangerous residency posting. Urdu is the primary language in both Pakistan and Kashmir.

By early 2009, Beena and Mary had become close friends and developed a type of mentor-mentee relationship. The two decided—via numerous letters and phone calls—to start two all-girls schools, one in Kabul and the other in Jalalabad. Jalalabad is located approximately 100 miles east of Kabul. These primary schools† were funded by private donations and classified as a non-profit NGO, a non-governmental organization.

In late 2009, Beena arrived in Washington, D.C., courtesy of a round-trip airline ticket and an all-expenses-paid two-week fundraising tour, funded from Mary's savings. Beena was, by now, a formally licensed French doctor, and Mary was a well-respected senior officer in the U.S. Foreign Service. Mary was also well-liked by a large circle of wealthy and quite influential women in the Washington area.

On their joint fundraising tour, Mary began each of their presentations—to mostly women and a few husbands—with a short introduction. As her eyes grew heavier, a smile floated across her stress-free face with the thought of that memory. The sedative was working its wonders.

This is my close friend Dr. Beena Waleed. She was born and raised in Jalalabad, Afghanistan. She is twenty-six years old and has recently returned from a two-year residency stint at a field hospital in Kashmir, which was

* The Kashmir Conflict is an on-going territorial dispute between Pakistan and India that began in 1947 when British rule in India ended, and the country was partitioned. The border of the state of Jammu and Kashmir, India, is sixty miles east of Islamabad, the capital of Pakistan. Médecins Sans Frontiéres is also known as Doctors Without Borders.

† Primary girls schools in Afghanistan typically included grades 1-6. Mary and Beena's schools included two additional grades, 7-8.

affiliated with France's Doctors Without Borders. Her medical degree is from the Sorbonne University in Paris, and she is, as of one month ago, a certified medical doctor in France.

Beena is the niece of the deceased Ahmad Shah Massoud, who was known throughout Afghanistan and the world as the "Lion of Panjshir." Massoud was a staunch ally of the U.S. He opposed the Taliban with every fiber of his being. When al-Qaeda terrorists assassinated him on September 9, 2001, two days before their attacks in the U.S., he commanded the only remaining military force in Afghanistan that opposed the Taliban. Beena will present her story tonight in English. If any of you prefer a subsequent talk in French, Dari, Pasto, or Urdu, she has told me that she'd be pleased to oblige those requests.

Beena, she recalled, would then gracefully rise from her front-row seat and move to her side. She'd lightly grip her elbows as she leaned into her and delivered two little kisses…the first on the right cheek, the second on the other cheek… followed by a three-word greeting, *Merci, mon ami!* Thank you, my friend!

At these donor presentations, Beena was usually dressed in professional attire, acceptable for moderate Muslim women in major European cities, like Paris. Her attire included tailored pants; a dark blazer with a color-coordinated vest; and a formal white blouse, open at the collar. As for her head-covering scarf, her lustrous brown hair was first pulled into a high bun that was accented with a tight sweep of hair across the left side of her forehead. Wrapped neatly around her high bun was a colorful scarf that she wore in her ethnic Tajik way, which revealed her neck and chin.

The trim, five-foot three-inch beauty, with flawless bronze skin and a beguiling smile, would turn to her audience— typically a group of approximately twenty-five prospective donors— and calmly take a moment to look into the eyes of each of them. She, like her uncle, believed that a person's eyes were the window to their heart.

This time also gave each prospective donor time to take the measure of their speaker. In short order, it was evident to these prospects that this relatively young speaker was obviously quite confident and poised. None of them had ever experienced an opening pitch for money begin with five minutes of silence. That was unusual, but what most impressed them were her mesmerizing, emerald green eyes that were shrouded with long lashes.

It seemed to them that her eyes were imbued with an Eastern mystic power that could read their innermost thoughts. Several of the guests shifted uncomfortably in their seats when her eyes settled upon them. Adding to her unique bearing was her face, which was perfect in its proportions and absent any hint of timidity. It was the determined face of a crusader.

Mary's smile unconsciously dissolved when she reflected on the content of her friend's opening lines. Beena wasn't one to downplay the harsh realities of Muslim women in her homeland, nor her own experiences. She'd heard her talk so many times that she could recite it.

Thank you for welcoming me into your home tonight. I am going to tell you about my past and my hopes for the future. Generally, **my story is different** *than that of most Muslim women in Central Asia. There is, however, one terrible experience that I do share with many of my female peers. I'll start my story with that experience.*

My mother, an ethnic Tajik, is the half-sister of the deceased Ahmad Shah Massoud. He, too, was an ethnic Tajik. Because the Republic of Tajikistan abuts the northern border of Afghanistan, many Tajiks live in the northern part of my country. My father, Nazir Waleed, was an ethnic Pashtun. Pashtuns generally view all Tajiks as an inferior race. Intermarriages between the two ethnicities are rare.

After the Russians' puppet government collapsed in 1992, Uncle Ahmad became Afghanistan's Minister of Defense. A role he filled until September of 1996 when the Taliban seized control of our government in Kabul. The Taliban is comprised almost exclusively of Pashtuns. Days before this overthrow, Uncle Ahmad and his military supporters—including my father—fled north into the Panjshir Valley, 100 miles north of Kabul. My father was not only a relative and friend of my uncle, he was also one of his most reliable military commanders.

Months later, Massoud's army— then known as the Northern Alliance— counterattacked the Taliban and took control of the Bagram Airfield and the surrounding area, thirty-five miles north of Kabul. It was the Taliban's first major defeat. After that defeat, the Taliban then controlled only 80% of the country! The odds, however, of total victory by the Northern Alliance—as Westerners would say—'Weren't looking good!'

That's a little background. Before Kabul fell in early 1996, Uncle Ahmad and my father thought it would be wise if their children were sent out of the country. The Taliban were rapidly expanding their rule at that time, and they both feared for the safety of their children. Our family lived in Jalalabad, a hundred miles east of Kabul. Before that plan could be executed, however, I was raped by two of my father's longtime friends. I was thirteen-years-old. Both of these men were senior officials in the Jalalabad government. The rapists were both Pashtuns, and they each held pro-Taliban beliefs. Somehow these men learned that my mother was a Tajik and a half-sister of the country's Minister of Defense, Ahmad Shah Massoud. Massoud was a well-known Tajik, who was universally despised by Pashtuns.

When my father learned of my indignity—not from me, but others—his humiliation was nearly as great as mine. These men had disrespected him and the honor of his family. He hunted down both men and killed them in separate fistfights. Their knowledge of my family's relationship with Massoud died with them. My father's revenge killing was and still is a lawful form of retaliation that is an accepted practice in my country. This code of conduct is known as Pashtunwali. *And a revenge killing is referred to as* Badal. *In my case, this meant that justice was served. Several months later, my brother and I were sent to Paris to live with relatives.*

In August of 1999, my father was killed during the Northern Alliance's second hasty retreat into the Panjshir Valley. This latter retreat commenced from the Bagram area, unlike the retreat from Kabul in 1996.

My rape when I was thirteen years old was not different then, or now, from the fates of other young Muslim girls in my country. My Islamic beliefs, as well as those of my family, are moderate. We're not Islamic fundamentalists! We do not believe in sectarian violence. We believe that the Prophet Muhammad was respectful of women and his wives. We don't believe...

Beena gave Mary a light poke in the ribs. "How are you feeling? You look dazed."

"Uh, uh! Just lost in thought. I think Sam's sedative is working."

"Good thoughts or bad thoughts?"

"Good thoughts! I was thinking of how we met and how we raised money for this school and our school in Jalalabad."

"We've accomplished a lot in the past couple of years."

"Uh-huh! I'm glad I gave you that Glock!"

"Me too!" Beena casually wrapped an arm around Mary's shoulders and moved closer to her. She whispered in Dari, "Where is Jamal? My brother told me he was driving you to Bagram today."

Mary smiled dreamily and waved a halting hand at Sam, Joe, and the school principal who were approaching. She wished for a further moment of privacy. Turning toward her friend, she replied in Dari, "Yes, I too thought Jamal was going to drive us to Bagram. I don't know what happened. There was a last-minute change of drivers at the embassy. The replacement driver was a young Afghan security force trainee. Or, at least, that's what he told us. I think he was Taliban. He drove us into the middle of a major attack in Abdul Haq Square. He fled from our vehicle when the shooting started. See what you can learn from your brother about the change in drivers and email me the details. You have my email address?"

"Yes."

"The same goes if any school funding problems arise while I'm away. Just email me!"

Beena shook her head in understanding and offered a sad smile. "The girls, the teachers... we all love you. We're going to miss you, especially me. You're like a big sister to me," she said as her voice cracked.

Mary tenderly patted Beena's arm. "Not to worry, my little ...smarter... sister. I will return."

They stood and held one another. During their embrace, Mary noticed that the suicide bomber's triggering device still lay menacingly on the school's barren, front yard. Behind it, at the corner of the school building, she saw a bucket.

As she stepped back from Beena, she asked the school principal what was in the bucket.

"Dirty water. Just before all the activity, I was washing windows. Praise be to Allah and Beena. They saved us!"

Mary nodded and strode toward the device. After gingerly picking it up, she moved to the bucket and carefully placed it in the water. She and the others listened as it sizzled harmlessly and sank to the bucket's bottom.

"Deactivated!" she said matter-of-factly.

The two military men, Sam and Joe, were visibly impressed. Alice, Beena, and the school principal were spellbound.

Minutes later—after much hugging between Mary, the school principal, and the other teachers—the senior police officer present closed his notebook and motioned Mary to his side.

"My name is Pirooz, Din Pirooz. You and Beena saved the lives of many girls today!" he said in Dari.

Mary placed her hand over her heart and replied in Dari, "Thank you for saying that. My name is Mary."

He next explained that he'd gotten all the information required for his police report and that he'd witnessed the entire episode. "My younger brother, Titi, just phoned me. He's new to our police force. The terrorists near the U.S. Embassy have put down our force's counterattack. They're armed with mortars and other heavy weapons, we only carry handguns. My deputy and I are going to pick up heavier weapons at headquarters and help our men," he said pausing.

"Those who target vans and schools, packed with students, are evil. I hate them!" interjected Mary.

The policeman cocked his head to the side with a questioning glance. It was a skeptical look that suspicious cops the world over regularly employed. "I'm not so sure that's entirely accurate. What was the purpose of the two-man RPG team?"

"They were shooting at a school van, which they thought would be full of young girls. They missed!"

"School doesn't get out until 4:00 p.m. You know that, and I know that. I've watched you come and go from here for the past year. You've done fine work here and the girls like you. From the RPG shooters' location, I think they mistook the school's van for your Land Cruiser."

Mary considered the cop's implication. *Both vehicles were white. The van driver entered her traffic lane unseen, on the far side of that huge military truck that chugged by her, with its cloud of diesel fumes. Then, the van driver sped ahead of the military truck. All of those factors could have easily confused the shooters.*

What then was the goal of the RPG shooters? This latest attack was obviously well planned. The terrorists would have known that there were no school kids in that van at that time of day. Furthermore, if their goal was to kill as many students as possible, the suicide bomber would have simply marched into the school and blown everyone up. But, if that scenario had occurred, it would have likely shut down Airport Road and caused Mary and the others to take an alternate route to the airport. Mary shook her head at the cop with contrived incomprehension.

"I think you were the primary target," continued Pirooz. "I think the school bombing was designed to cover up your killing. Your embassy would have noted your death as collateral damage. You have enemies here. Be careful and thank you for your part in saving the girls. Two of my nieces attend this school."

Mary felt a gentle tug on her arm. It was Sam. He pointed to his watch. Turning her attention back to the policemen, she placed her right hand over her heart and said, in Dari, "You are a good man, Pirooz. Thank you for watching over the girls. I'll pray for your good health and happiness. *Allahu Akbar!*" God is the greatest!

Pirooz bowed courteously and replied in Dari, "I too will pray for your good health and happiness. *Ma'a as-salamah!* Goodbye!

She then moved to Beena. With her back to the school entrance, she gave her a final hug and said, "Tell the girls and teachers that I'll pray for them every day. I love you, Little Sister."

With tears rolling down her cheeks, Beena wordlessly nodded and spun Mary around. The teachers hadn't been able to restrain the young girls any longer. They had all piled out of the school and partially surrounded her in a semi-circle. They were chanting, "Mary, Mary!"

"I'll be back next year to help all of you with your English. I love you all. My friends and I have to leave now. We have a plane to catch!"

September 14, 2011... Wednesday 1:08 a.m.

Mary and Sam walked wearily, side by side, along the long Ramstein Air Base corridor. They were headed to the shuttle bus pick-up stop that would transport them to their transient, overnight quarters. Seven short hours later, they would board another aircraft for the final leg of their trip back to the U.S., though not to their final destinations. Mary was going to travel on to Falmouth, Maine, to visit her dad, and Sam would fly on to Atlanta, Georgia, where his wife of five years would meet him.

It was a little past 1:00 a.m. (local time) when they reached the shuttle bus stop, outside of the terminal. Joe and Alice had been picked up, minutes earlier, by friends at the base. Tuesday had been a long day. Now they were into the first hours of their second day of travel. A newspaper van slowed to a stop, thirty feet away, and a young boy tossed several bound bundles of newspapers to the curb.

Mary strolled to the pile of papers. She recognized the masthead of *The Express Tribune*. During the past year, the *Tribune* had become one of her favorite daily reads for news in Pakistan and internationally. Though the newspaper was hardly a year old, it was already ranked among the *top five* newspapers in Pakistan. Its affiliation with *The International New York Times* contributed to its regional popularity.

Sam heard Mary gasp. He turned and saw her begin to stagger. Reaching her just before she fell to the sidewalk, he steered her to a nearby bench where she sat and bent forward, her head held in her hands. A moment later, she began to sob uncontrollably.

"Mary, what's wrong?" Sam's first thought was that the rough-and-tumble events of the day had finally caught up with her. Her pent-up emotions had finally broken free. "Is this related to the Airport Road attack?"

Mary shook her head feebly and pointed weakly at *The Express Tribune*. "Front page news. Read it! There was a simultaneous attack on school kids earlier today... I mean yesterday... in Pakistan. Evil bastards, evil bastards!" cried Mary.

The Express Tribune

Mattani attack: Taliban target children

September 14, 2011

Peshawar, PAKISTAN: Taliban insurgents ambushed a school van on Tuesday, killing four pupils and the driver in a barrage of bullets and rocket fire. The attack occurred in an area known as Mattani, which is outside of Peshawar. Another eighteen people, including four children—two of them seven-year-old girls— were also wounded in the attack. The children studied at an English-language school named the Khyber Model School.

The Taliban are opposed to all types of Western education and have destroyed, in the past few years, hundreds of schools in this area as well as adjoining tribal regions.

Police explained that the van was taking the children home at the end of their school day. "The gunmen waited for the van in a field near one of its first stops. When the van neared them, they fired a rocket and bullets at it."

(abstract of actual newspaper report)

Sam shook his head in disgust and disbelief. During the past year, he'd inoculated hundreds of Afghan school kids against polio in some of the small rural villages, southeast of Jalalabad, not more than a hundred miles across the mountainous Pakistani border from Mattani. They were innocent kids. Smiling, fun-loving kids! No different than the kids in Mattani. Mary was right. The Taliban were evil bastards!

September 15, 2011 ... Thursday, 10:07 a.m.

Mary rested comfortably in her favorite overstuffed chair that was perfectly placed in front of the large bay window in her dad's living room. His fifty-year-old, single-story, white clapboard house was situated on a bluff-side promontory— sandwiched between two recently built McMansions—that provided an unobstructed view of a portion of the Maine coast, known as Casco Bay. It was a beautiful day with cloudless blue skies and shimmering green-blue water.

She gazed dreamily northward toward the white Portland Head Lighthouse and the light keeper's distinctive red-roofed quarters, which was carved precipitously out of the rocky coastline. A warm, late summer breeze wafted gently through an open window and carried with it the fragrant scent of the sea. The rhythmic sound of crashing waves helped to sooth and wash away her nightmarish memories of the last few days.

In the background, she heard the occasional rumble of boxes being moved. Her dad was rummaging through the garage in search of a set of hiking poles that he'd bought her twenty-five years earlier. Thinking he might need a hand with his search, she sipped the last of her morning coffee and rose from her chair when she heard the slap of newspaper against the front door of the house. She looked at the old ship's clock that hung in the living room, 10:10 a.m. Either the *Boston Globe* newspaper truck was late with its delivery to Southern Maine, or the paperboy had slept in. No matter. She opened the front door, picked-up the rubber-banded paper, and moved into the kitchen. She set her coffee cup in the sink, opened the paper, and dropped it on the butcher-block kitchen table. On the lower right-hand corner of the front page, a headline caught her attention.

The Boston Globe

Terrorists Identified in Attacks

September 15, 2011

While standing, she quickly read the half-column front-page report and then turned to page eight to read the remainder of the article. The U.S. State Department and the CIA had both identified the Haqqani Network as the perpetrators of the September 13th terrorist attack in Kabul. According to the article,* the CIA had intercepted several cell phone conversations between Sirajuddin Haqqani, the day-to-day leader of the network, and Pakistan's Inter-Services Intelligence (ISI) agency. ISI was Pakistan's top foreign intelligence agency, similar to the U.S.'s CIA. The phone conversations provided incontrovertible evidence of the Haqqani Network's exclusive role in the attack.

The twenty-hour attack killed sixteen innocent individuals, five Afghan policemen, and eleven civilians. Six of the civilian deaths were children. Six terrorists were also killed in the partially built high-rise that overlooked the embassy's compound. Another three suicide bombers were killed elsewhere in the city. Cited prominently in the article were the heroics of a newly commissioned Afghan police officer, Titi Pirooz, who was tragically killed in the attack.

Tears began to roll down her cheeks. She grabbed a tissue from a nearby tissue box and roughly wiped them away. Titi Pirooz was the younger brother of Din Pirooz, the policeman she'd met at her girls school, two days earlier. She distractedly opened the kitchen door and trudged to the edge of the property's ocean bluff. With her hands on her hips, she looked northward— in the direction of the lighthouse— and deeply inhaled the sea's clean, salty air. The fresh air did little to ease her sadness. The steady thump of the pounding waves now sounded like the mournful beat of a funeral march.

Turning eastward, the colors of the sea and sky displayed their splendor. Their beauty and timelessness calmed her. She closed her eyes, bowed her head, and offered a silent prayer to those departed souls, further eastward.

---

* Fictional article, but factual details..

Fair winds and following seas! A sudden on-shore breeze caught her hair, caressed her face, and dried her tears.

After a time, she returned to the kitchen and continued her reading of the Kabul attack. An unnamed source at State believed that the attack was a reprisal against the West, specifically the U.S., for two CIA drone attacks that occurred last March and allegedly killed approximately *fifty innocent Pakistanis.* The article not only misrepresented the composition of the victims, but it also elected to omit the purpose of the attack.

Mary rocked back in her chair and massaged her closed eyes. One didn't need to be clairvoyant to figure out who'd scripted State's opinion. The master dissembler of facts and the truth, Secretary of State Ted David. She was intimately familiar with the chain of events that led up to those attacks. News accounts of those attacks had filled the pages of Middle Eastern and Central Asian newspapers for weeks.

Last January, a CIA contractor in Lahore, Pakistan, shot and killed two Pakistanis. The contractor, Raymond Davis—a former Army Special Forces soldier—was behind the wheel of his car when the two Pakistanis, in their early twenties, pulled up beside his stopped car on a motorcycle. In an attempt of robbery, intimidation, or who knows what the rear passenger on the motorcycle withdrew a loaded pistol and aimed at Davis. Davis coolly grabbed his 9 mm Glock that rested on the seat beside him and shot the young man five times through his windshield. He then jumped out of his car, ran down the driver of the motorcycle—who had fled the scene on foot—and shot him to death. While standing over the dead driver, he calmly took pictures of the crime scene as hundreds of Pakistanis surrounded him.

Sensing trouble, he radioed his CIA headquarters for back-up support. They arrived within minutes, but Davis was nowhere to be found. He'd driven off. The angry crowd then converged on the back-up CIA vehicle, which in its haste to leave the scene accidentally ran over and killed an innocent motorcyclist on the opposite side of the road.

In short order, news of the incident reached the highest levels of the Pakistani government and its intelligence agency, the ISI. Who was Raymond Davis? Was he a CIA agent? The camera the police recovered from Davis's car held incriminating photographs of Pakistani military and intelligence facilities. Initial news reports indicated that the two dead motorcyclists were young thugs with criminal records. That story gradually changed, as did Davis's relationship with the CIA.

After days of CIA denials, they finally admitted to ISI that Davis was one of theirs. The CIA also reluctantly admitted that they employed dozens of intelligence personnel in Lahore. Somewhere in this blurry timeline, the true identity of the two motorcyclists also emerged. They weren't thugs with criminal records, but inexperienced Pakistan ISI agents who were assigned to simply follow Davis.

CIA personnel were soon kicked out of the country, and relations between the Pakistan ISI and U.S. CIA began to slide from bad to worse. Eventually, the U.S. negotiated a "blood money" settlement of $2.3 million for the families of the two dead ISI agents. To the U.S., this payment felt like a ransom payment. The family of the only innocent victim in the incident didn't receive any compensation. On March 16, Davis was acquitted of any crimes in a Lahore court. He was then quickly shuffled out of the courthouse and flown back to the U.S. that afternoon.

In the days leading up to the Davis courtroom drama, the U.S. State Department was forced to close its embassies in Islamabad, Peshawar, and Lahore. Riots and violent anti-U.S. protests by radical Muslims brought Pakistan to a near standstill.

While all this was happening, the CIA was in the final stages of planning the assault on Osama bin Laden's suspected compound in Abbottabad, Pakistan. This secret mission was scheduled to take place sometime within the next 30-45 days. It was a mission that the CIA kept close to its vest. No one in Pakistan, especially the Pakistan ISI, was aware of their plans.

Meanwhile, another branch of the CIA, which apparently didn't communicate with its Lahore branch, was counting down the hours before they unleashed two separate drone attacks on known terrorists...not innocent Pakistanis... in the North Waziristan Agency of Pakistan's FATA. The CIA didn't need any of Qazi's expensive and capricious approvals for drone attacks outside of his country.

The target of these attacks was a gathering of known terrorist leaders in the village of Datta Khel, a well-known al-Qaeda haven. These terrorist leaders were linked together in an organization known as the Haqqani Network. ISAF, the U.S., and the Afghans regarded this tribal network as *the most formidable terrorist organization* in the entire region. This network also happened to be connected to and supported by an alleged ally of the CIA, the Pakistan ISI. ISI routinely engaged the Haqqani Network to perform deniable dirty work in Afghanistan, which they believed would advance their national agenda. That agenda being a weak Afghanistan that couldn't sustain itself without the aid of the U.S. or India.

ISI's relationship with the Haqqani Network was supposed to be a closely guarded secret, but it wasn't. The CIA knew of their relationship, and the ISI knew that they knew. ISI and the CIA also knew that the Haqqani Network's primary benefactor was al-Qaeda.

On the evening of March 16, 2011, the first of two successive CIA drone attacks killed five terrorist tribal leaders. The next morning approximately forty more leaders were killed during a *jirga.** The Haqqani Network's leadership was enraged. The CIA drone attacks had delivered a near-fatal blow to their network.

In light of Sirajuddin Haqqani's open-net cell phone calls to ISI, it was apparent to Mary—and the CIA—that they wanted the U.S. to know who was responsible for the Kabul reprisal attack of September 13, 2011. Sirajuddin Haqqani was the day-today leader of the Haqqani Network.

Mary slammed her fist against the tabletop. The growing rift between the U.S. and Pakistan was reaching a breaking point. She wanted to scream.

Just then, her dad walked into the kitchen. "Found them! Good as new," he said, raising the collapsible hiking poles from his side in triumph.

Mary looked at him with a long face.

"What?" he said easily as he moved to the coffee pot. "You want a refill?"

Smiling weakly, she said, "That sounds good and maybe an aspirin."

"Not feeling well? You've been through a lot in the past couple of days."

"Just depressed and frustrated. At times, I feel that the real enemy in Afghanistan is not the Taliban or even al-Qaeda, but Pakistan," she said while consolidating her thoughts. *Yes, the Datta Khel drone attacks were poorly timed. But they killed a significant number of known terrorist leaders, all of whom were associated with the Haqqani Network. That's a fact! A fact that the Pakistan ISI is reluctant to publicly admit! And a fact that likely prompted*

---

*A jirga is an assembly of tribal leaders, similar to a legislative body, whose purpose is to create rules and make decisions that collectively benefit their tribes.

thoughts of a reprisal attack. What sealed the deal—at least for extreme Islamic fundamentalists—was the killing of Osama bin Laden.

Until the Red Mosque Siege of 2007, in Islamabad, moderate Pakistani Muslims didn't view Osama bin Laden as an especially charismatic or rabble-rousing spiritual and political leader. His jihad against the distant West didn't particularly trouble them. All that changed, however, after "the Siege." Fence-sitters were outraged with his violent decrees and indiscriminate attacks against fellow Muslim moderates, school children, and Pakistani soldiers.

Sighing, she added, "Our CIA has, of late, aggravated our relationship with Pakistan."

He set her refilled coffee cup on the kitchen table and settled into a chair beside her. "Was the Kabul attack a couple of days ago related to something the CIA did?"

After explaining the Datta Khel attacks to her dad, she said, "Relations between the U.S., particularly our CIA, and the Pakistan ISI are at a new low!"

"Didn't the CIA just replace their station head in Kabul?"

"Yes, they did. And, it was a change for the better. They promoted Mike Hall to station head. I've met him a couple of times and heard good things about him."

"Uh-huh," he grunted while taking a sip of his coffee and crossing his legs. "I get that the timing of the drone attacks was lousy, and the killing of Osama bin Laden pissed off his cadre of terrorists. But, I sense there is something else troubling you. Let's hear it! I told my crew that I'd be taking a few days off."

She took his hand and patted it. "Mighty 'Mick' Phillips taking a day off from lobstering! What's this world coming too?" she said as she cleared her throat and smiled. "Where to start? The Pakistan psyche is difficult to explain and even harder to understand. As you know—"

He raised a hand and interrupted, "I majored in biology, not history. I also paid a fortune for your advanced college degrees, so I don't mind a little history lesson from my brainy daughter," he said, with an affectionate smile that filled his weathered and square-jawed face.

"Great Britain and their Raj ruled British India for nearly a hundred years, until 1947. In '47, the Brits left British India, and the country was divided into Pakistan and India. The two countries were generally separated along religious lines, Hindus in India and Muslims in Pakistan. The consequences of that break-up are hard to comprehend. Upwards of sixteen million people relocated to different regions, and two million people were killed in battles. Political disputes, differences between religions, and disagreements over personal property were the causes for most of the killing. Diatribes from extremist religious leaders and chest-thumping speeches from irrelevant politicos fanned the flames of frustration. Passions, which might have been calmed, were converted into cold hatred and pointless killings. It's still like that today.

"Two oddities added to the chaos. The first quirk involved Pakistan. East Pakistan was separated from its ruling body, West Pakistan, by the breadth of India. It was a distant territory on the far eastern border of India. More like a colony... a neglected colony, in my view...than a respected and supported part of the country. In 1971, East Pakistan rebelled against West Pakistan and won their independence. It was a hard-fought, bloody revolution. World powers—except for India, who supported East Pakistan—kept their distance from that revolution and didn't support either country. East Pakistan is today, Bangladesh, and West Pakistan is now simply called Pakistan."

Pausing to study her dad's interest level, she asked, after several long moments, "Am I boring you to death?"

"Not at all. You know your history. I think I got my money's worth. What's the second oddity?" he asked, smiling.

"The second oddity involved the state of Jammu and Kashmir, located in the northwestern part of India. Its borders were not clearly defined with Pakistan. In 1949, after two years of battles, a ceasefire between Pakistan and India was negotiated with the aid of the United Nations (U.N.). The U.N. then helped both countries agree upon the borders of Kashmir. One area, within these borders, was administered and governed by Pakistan and the other by India. However, as in life, nothing is as simple as it seems. Battles still rage in Kashmir.*

"One of the most hotly debated and contested topics of today is in

* References to Kashmir apply to the state of Jammu and Kashmir.

the Kashmir area that was once administered by India. The residents of that area, including many longtime Kashmiri Muslims, were given the right to determine by a vote, which country they would prefer to align themselves with. In 1951, they voted to align themselves with India, rather than Pakistan. India welcomed them and modified their constitution to accommodate the conditions of their vote. Kashmir would autonomously govern themselves, and *non-residents couldn't own property there.* Thus, thousands of Hindus from other parts of India couldn't move into the area and prospectively outnumber Kashmiri Muslims.

"The constitutional modifications also bound India to support and protect *all of its Indian citizens there,* irrespective of their religious affiliation. Today, this is the only state in all of India where Muslims outnumber Hindus. There is also a small percent of Sikhs living in Kashmir," she said, pausing to sip her coffee and organize a couple of final points.

"According to the latest government propaganda coming out of Islamabad, Pakistan... not Kashmir... Kashmiri Muslims would love to see their region break away from India and become part of Pakistan. The Pakistani military, which has virtually run Pakistan since 1947, would also like to see that happen—as would a great many *Muslim militants.* On the opposite side of the ledger is India—"

"Propaganda! Hold it!" interrupted Mick. "Haven't the Indians persecuted the Kashmiris?"

Mary smiled, impressed with his observation. "Yes, the Indian army has... at times... mistreated the Kashmiri Muslims. However, I wouldn't categorize it as premeditated or perpetual persecution. You have to ask yourself what percentage of that mistreatment occurred in response to Pakistani-borne Muslim militancy? I'd also add...in defense of India... that, the state of Kashmir has received more Indian grants and assistance for public works projects than any other state in India since 1995. They're not a neglected state!"

After further thought, she opined, "Do the Kashmiri Muslims really want to be part of Pakistan? They've, in general, ruled Kashmir for hundreds of years and have adopted Urdu as their region's primary language. Because of that alone, they hold down many of the best government jobs there. Few Hindu's can speak and/or read Urdu, native Indians aren't a threat to their jobs.

"My feeling is that they would ideally like to rule themselves, independent of both radical Muslims and Hindus. Why would they want to be part of Pakistan? It's a country that's broke, is ruled by an insular military, and is being influenced more and more by Islamic fundamentalists, who are at their heart terrorists. Terrorists who believe they should kill all non-believers!" she closed.

"Isn't it strange how completely different Osama bin Laden, the founder of al-Qaeda, was compared to Mahatma Gandhi, the Father of a Nation, India," interjected Mick as he tilted back in his kitchen chair. "One believed in violence and killing non-Islamic-believers (jihad) the other in peacefulness and harmony. 'The essence of all religions is one. Only their approaches are different!' sayeth Gandi."

"*Veery impressive, Dad!* It is strange, and it's sickening. Where or when did you pick-up that nugget?"

"I think I first heard it during a philosophy class in college. It stuck. It may be the only thing I remember from that class."

Mary smiled agreeably.

"Back to Pakistan!" continued Mick. "I think one of your points is that Pakistanis have an inferiority complex. They feel like second-class citizens. Pakistan's Muslims have been ruled, displaced, separated, and beaten in national battles. Their honor has been tarnished. Along those lines, when East Pakistan—now Bangladesh— broke away from them, didn't that prompt them to develop a nuclear weapon capability?"

"Yes and no. Hold that thought. I'll be right back!" she said as she zipped into the living room and retrieved her laptop computer. Moments later, she was searching for a pertinent quote that she remembered from one of her graduate school lectures at Columbia. "Ah, here it is! Pakistan started their nuclear program before they lost East Pakistan in 1971, but their loss encouraged them to accelerate it. Here's the quote," she said while reading. "In 1965, then Foreign Minister Zulfikar Ali Bhutto said this:

'If India builds the bomb, we will eat grass and leaves for a thousand years, even go hungry, but we will get one of our own. The

Christians have the bomb, the Jews have the bomb and now the Hindus have the bomb. Why not the Muslims too have the bomb?'

She continued, "Bhutto secretly expedited Pakistan's nuclear weapons program. When their nuclear capability became known, the U.S. and every country in Asia, the Middle East, and Europe reappraised their relations with Pakistan. Civilized countries—those who allowed girls to attend school and believed in modern medicine—didn't like that revelation. Countries, or regions, that followed strict Sharia Law celebrated the disclosure. Pakistan could bomb India and other parts of the world back to the Age of Muhammad, the 7th century A.D.

"He, Bhutto, eventually became Pakistan's first civilian president (1971-1973) and later became the country's prime minister. In 1977, General Muhammad Zia-ul-Haq* staged a bloodless coup and removed him from power while he assumed control of the country as a military dictator. He ruled Pakistan until 1988 when he was killed in a plane crash." Mick's brooding and reflective expression prompted her to pause. "Any questions or anything you'd like to add? You look like your thoughts have returned to that philosophy class."

"Not philosophy, military history. The Ruskies invaded Afghanistan in 1979!"

"That they did. And a few short years later, the U.S. sidled up to the Pakis with buckets of cash and Stinger missiles for the mujahideen, who were fighting the Ruskies!"

Mick's faced now glowed. With a broad smile, he said, "They got their just deserts for their intervention in Vietnam. The financial and human cost of their invasion of Afghanistan broke the Ruskies back. The Soviet Union went bust in 1991!"

"Correct! Any more questions?"

"Yeah! If Pakistan is broke, how can they afford to battle India? India has more people and greater defense spending by a factor of six. And their gross domestic product exceeds (GDP) Pakistan's by a factor of ten. Are they going to experience the same fate as the Ruskies?"

---

* After this chapter, there is no further mention of Zulifer Ali Bhutto and General Muhammad Zia-ul-Haq. Both of these actual individuals are mentioned here for historical background purposes.

"Dad, you really surprise me sometimes! How did you come by all that data?"

"Hey, just because I'm a lobsterman, it doesn't mean that I can't read. I've researched the regions where you've been posted!"

She affectionately patted his hand and began, "I don't see Pakistan going bust—like the Soviet Union—in the near future, but it wouldn't take much to change those dynamics. In my opinion, three factors sustain Pakistan's battles against India. Firstly, Pakistan has a stockpile of nuclear weapons, and they don't need expensive, state-of-the-art systems to deliver and detonate them in India. A couple of mules pulling a cart is sufficient for each nuke. That's a major attraction for their terrorist supporters. Secondly, they receive financial and manpower support from al-Qaeda. The financial support comes from a variety of sources, but the primary contributors are Saudi Wahhabis and Afghanistan's poppy fields. Those poppy fields account for 90% or more of the world's illicit heroin trade, which equates to an annual export value of approximately $4 billion.

"As for manpower, Pashtun tribes in the FATA—like the Afghan Taliban—supplement their army's troop levels and are often called upon to execute deniable guerilla missions in Kashmir. Lastly, they divert U.S. aid—that was designated for counterterrorism efforts against the Taliban— to support their battles against India."

"I haven't read or heard anything about *U.S. aid diversions.* Is that common knowledge in Washington? And what kind of money are you talking about?"

"A billion or so of U.S. aid per year!"[†]

Tongue-tied at first, he then blurted, "You've got to be shitting me!"

"I'm not. The Pakis hate the Indians. It guides just about every international decision they make. That's why it's hard for Westerners to understand what motivates them. On top of that, they also have a tendency to act like a cornered, *feral cat.* If a person attempts to give the cat medical aid

---

† In 2009, two Pakistani generals told the Associated Press that of the $6.6 billion in U.S. military aid provided [Pakistan] during the previous six years, for counterterrorism measures [against terrorists fighting in Afghanistan], only $500 million had been used for that purpose. The rest of the funds were used towards Pakistan's "defense against India." (Credit-Al Jazeera, June 25, 2011).

or even food, the cat is hardwired to lash out at them. They avoid contact with humans. Pakistanis are like that with Indians and increasingly so with Westerners.

"An added complication to this behavior is that nearly all of Pakistan's government and intelligence agency, ISI, leaders have risen to their posts while actively serving in their military. ISI's ranks are led by and filled with active-duty military personnel. Instead of a country maintaining a military and intelligence service, it's a military maintaining a country."

"Hmm! From my Marine Corps experiences," he began, "I can tell you...right out of the chute...that having active-duty military personnel running all aspects of a country isn't a good idea. Take Vietnam, for example, a soldier whose unit battled the North Vietnamese Army (NVA) on multiple occasions will have likely witnessed the atrocities those bastards inflicted on our captured soldiers.

"Junior officers and non-commissioned foot soldiers that are captured on a battlefield don't possess any big-picture, tactical intelligence. The same applies to pilots and airmen who are shot down while flying a mission. In both those cases, they're just following orders. Torture for the sole purpose of inflicting pain, rather than gathering intelligence, is immoral.

"When an atrocity is inflicted on one's fellow soldier, he's not going to forget the details of who did what and when. Those details will be lodged in the back of his mind forever. Should he ever run across those bastards again, you can rest assured that he'll have some form of payback at the ready. Military men, in general, aren't *forgive and forget types!*"

Stunned, she asked, "Payback! Even in peacetime...years after a war is over?"

"I arrived by helicopter to the Khe Sanh Combat Base on the afternoon of February 19, 1967. Khe Sanh was located about fifteen miles south of the border between North Vietnam and South Vietnam. I was a twenty-three-year-old, wide-eyed 2nd lieutenant in charge of a Marine Corps platoon, which was comprised of thirty-nine men. All of them, except for three, were younger than me. There was a small airstrip at Khe Sanh with lots of hills surrounding it.

"In early March, my platoon and another one were ordered to displace the NVA from two nearby hills. They were shelling our airstrip from those locations. It was fierce back and forth fighting. Those battles are referred to today as the First Battle of Khe Sanh. On the morning of March 16, 1967, I saw what the NVA had done to one of my captured Marines. He was tortured and nailed to a tree with spikes. He was an eighteen-year-old private. Later that night, my right knee was hit during a gunfight atop one of the hills. I was MEDEVACed out of the area by a helo the next morning.

"Two weeks later, while I was recovering from my injury at Balboa Hospital in San Diego, my platoon sergeant arrived in the same hospital ward. He'd lost an arm in a hill battle. He described to me how other Marines, some in my former platoon, were tortured and killed at Khe Sanh. Eyes poked out, body parts cut off, disembowelment, etc. The NVA bastards who did that were with the 18th Regiment of 325C Division. So, to answer your question, sweetheart… yes… I still remember the *particulars of those atrocities* forty-four years later."

"You've never told me anything about Vietnam. This is the first that I've heard of your experiences there."

He considered his response. A part of him was inclined to add a derogatory comment about what he thought of the country's leadership at that time, President Lyndon B. Johnson and Secretary of Defense Robert McNamara, but he elected to remain silent. Recalling the sickening memories of NVA atrocities was enough bad juju for one day. "I was eventually medically discharged from the Marines because of my knee injury. And thanks to modern medicine, my right knee replacement is as good as new. As for memory replacements, sweetheart, there is no such thing for this Marine."

She drum-rolled her fingers on the tabletop as she considered her dad's comments. "What a mess! So Pakistan's leadership is made up of angry, *unforgiving-unforgetting* military men who feel that they've been disrespected by the British, India, Bangladesh, Afghanistan, and now the U.S."

"Don't forget their *feral cat* behavior. Or, the fact that their archenemy, India, maintains better relations with the U.S. than they do," he added.

Mick Phillips was a thoughtful and introspective individual who loved his existence in a secluded, coastal area of Maine. His Vietnam experiences may have influenced some of his reclusiveness, though Mary thought it had to do with his upbringing there. Those like Mick, who lived in these coastal areas—often referred to as Downeasters—had little interest in the pace, pressures, and mega-buck allure of big city life. They were frugal, hard-working, and trustworthy individuals who were generally unaffected by popular trends. They'd rather help a neighbor repair a barn, then spend hours surfing the Internet looking for a deal on a hot, new computer.

Mary rocked forward in her chair. Simply being around her dad had a calming effect on her. His personal experiences, like his recent Vietnam disclosure, also helped her to see and think more clearly. "The Pakistani people and their leaders better grow-up and ditch their 'woe is me, we're victims' attitude before it's too late! They're wasting time, energy, and money pissing off their neighbors and neglecting their most pressing threat…the yoke of Islamic fundamentalism! Fundamentalism that is being funded by outsiders and implemented by radicals."

"Outsiders and radicals," repeated Mick sarcastically. "Neither group gives a damn about the long-term prosperity of Pakistan or the liberties of its people. They're enforcing their deluded agenda just like Joseph Stalin did. 'Death solves all problems—no man, no problem!'"

"Was that a memory from a political science class?"

A modest smirk and raised eyebrows answered her question.

"That's enough!" she smiled as she bounded to her feet. "No more talk of religion and politics. It's a beautiful day. Let's go for our hike!"

CHAPTER 5

THE JALALABAD BAZAAR

September 19, 2011 | Monday 9:58 a.m.

WHENEVER BEENA WALEED needed to buy school supplies for her New Hope Girls Schools, she engaged a local Muslim man to escort her through the Jalalabad Bazaar. Fully covered women, unaccompanied by a male, were generally limited to buying only food and women's clothes in the bazaar. On this day, she subserviently trailed behind her escort, dressed in a fully veiled blue burqa. Wrapped around her midriff, beneath her burqa, were several towels fashioned to give lecherous males the impression that she was overweight. Her escort was a one-armed security guard whom she'd met at the Jalalabad Red Crescent clinic while volunteering there as a doctor.

The two moved inconspicuously through the open-air bazaar as they casually perused the stalls and pushcarts loaded with fruits, nuts, spices, clothes, tools, auto parts, and other necessities. Umbrellas and sun tarps of all shapes, sizes, and colors filled the bazaar and protected the merchants' wares from the sun, wind, sand, and rain. Weapons and ammunition were carefully concealed in tents behind the stalls. Sixty miles to the east, in Pakistan's mountainous Federally Administered Tribal Areas (FATA), the bazaar's merchants openly displayed such items. They were typically a bazaar's best-sellers, and it wasn't uncommon for gun manufacturers to employ a majority of the local workforce in some of the mountain villages.

All of the merchants in the Jalalabad Bazaar were male and ethnic Pashtuns. Their view of women, which had been hammered into their psyche by generations of their male forebears, was well defined—they were superior to them. Except for a few Pashtun clans, like the Zahir clan, this was a sacrosanct fact of life. Pashtuns also believed that once a girl came of marrying age, fifteen or sixteen years of age, they should be paired with a husband. Once they were married, their existence was simple. They were required to accommodate their husband's every need and producing babies, preferably male babies. They were not to be educated, well-read, or ill-disposed toward any of their husband's wishes. To support these archaic beliefs, Afghan men would simply proclaim that this was the way it had always been and would always be. If any "enlightened" Afghan male disagreed with their beliefs, he was labeled as ignorant, stupid, or a non-believer. Non-believers had obviously been brainwashed by the Westerners and were, thus, their enemy. If a wife objected to these beliefs, which was rare, they were physically disciplined by their husband or referred to the local, fundamentalist Islamic cleric who would set them straight. The Koran and the Hadith were quite clear about the subordinate and subservient role of women in everyday Islamic life.

The merchants in the bazaar knew Beena's escort, and they grudgingly accepted him into their midst, because of his former service and sacrifice to the mujahideen in the late 1980s. He'd lost an arm fighting the Russians and was now head of security for what they considered the contemptible Red Crescent* clinic. The clinic provided all those who came to their door with a wide range of basic medical care, which included prenatal care, pediatric care, and maternity care. The clinic also provided outreach care for prisoners in Afghan jails. Pashtuns viewed the clinic's care for non-fundamentalist Muslims as a blasphemy.

The bazaar's enmity toward the clinic had recently increased when word circulated among the merchants that the clinic had cared for an Afghan policeman who was shot and wounded by the bazaar's headman. The shooting occurred when the policeman heard the screams of a young boy—from one of the bazaar's secretive tents—and he interceded in his rape, *bacha bazi*, by the headman.

---

* The International Committee of Red Cross (ICRC) and the International Federation of the Red Cross and Red Crescent Societies (IFRC) are partners in the Red Cross and Red Crescent Movement. Islamic fundamentalists oppose the Red Crescent's association with the Red Cross.

Before Beena left for the bazaar, she reviewed with her escort her rules for the bazaar. Firstly, her name was Benesh, not Beena. And, if anyone questioned him about her background, he would explain that she was an outcast from the Madad family in Kandahar, and her job at the clinic was washing floors. Secondly, if anyone asked him about her physical appearance or availability, he was to describe her as a strong, fat, fifty-year-old woman with bad teeth. And that he'd only brought her to the bazaar so that she could carry his purchases back to the clinic. Thirdly, he could not indicate, in any way, that their purchases were for the New Hope Girls Schools.

Lastly, she reviewed with him her hand signals. He was the buyer. She was the silent packhorse. The index finger of her left hand on a particular item meant, "buy this." Her right-hand fingers would denote the number of units to buy. Two left-hand fingers meant, "the price is too high." These were, after all, cheap office products from China. Three fingers meant, "we'll shop somewhere else."

When the two departed for the bazaar, the wind had freshened, and trash was blowing in every direction. It was difficult seeing, and she felt as if she was in the midst of a sandstorm. For once, she was thankful that she was fully veiled. By the time they reached their destination, the wind had died. The two owners of the stall neglected their recently-arrived, and only, customers while they spiritedly debated their options for disposing of the mountain of wind-born trash that had found its way into their stall. Beena and her escort briskly began to examine the stall's wares while the merchants decided, as Beena expected they would, to simply sweep the new trash out of sight. None of the merchants were inclined to sweep the new trash into garbage bags for disposal in the bazaar's dumpsters. Why would they? Firstly, they knew that the trash wasn't theirs. Secondly, they were merchants, not garbage collectors. Furthermore, disposing of trash was a woman's job.

Except for the crowds, noise, four-story buildings—half of them were fully built out, the other half were weather-worn skeletons—and a pot-holed road packed with 3-wheeled motorized cargo tricycles, the layout of the bazaar hadn't changed much in the last fifty years. After haggling over the price of a few supplies, the stall's improvised checkout counter was soon stacked with their purchases. The escort paid for everything while Beena dutifully filled two plastic bags with their purchases.

She hefted a bag over each shouldered and turned. As she turned, she accidentally collided with a tall man who had a young girl— perhaps twelve-years-old—sitting on his back in a sling, piggy-back style. Both bags fell from her hands, and she stumbled backward into her escort. The escort, who had his back to Beena, crashed into the checkout counter, which caused several boxes of pencils and notepads to fall harmlessly to the hard-packed dirt floor.

One of the merchants grabbed a nearby cane and screamed at Beena in Pashto, *"Daa tor makh de wrak sha!"* Get your ugly dark face out of here!

An instant before the merchant's cane crashed into Beena's head, one of the tall man's hands shot out and caught the merchant's wrist. The tall man stepped toward the merchant, while maintaining his viselike grip on his wrist and whispered something into his ear. Beena couldn't hear what he said, but from the expression on the merchant's face, which turned from anger to fear, she suspected it was a threat.

She knelt, grabbed her bags, and was attempting to stand when the tall man slipped a hand under her arm and helped her to her feet. Standing, she took a moment to study her protector. He was tall, easily six feet in height, with broad shoulders and copper eyes that were now smiling at her. His weathered face was highlighted with a square jaw and high cheekbones. His brown mustache and slightly graying beard were neatly trimmed. In light of her protector's handling of the merchant and his overall bearing, she guessed that he was a senior member of a Pashtun clan in the nearby *Spīn Ghar* Range (White Mountains) of the FATA."

After taking a closer look at the man's apparel, her initial opinion began to change. His *shalwar kameez and waskat* (loose-fitting white linen pants, knee-length white shirt, and tan waistcoat) were spotless. The most telling clue to his identity, however, was his headwear. He wore a very ornamental and well-preserved green-gray Afghan lungee turban. Only respected and important Pashtun men wore that kind of turban, and they were usually aligned with the Taliban. When she stepped toward him to thank him for rescuing her from a caning, she saw two men— stationed ten feet behind him—stiffen. Bodyguards! He was a clan leader.

A groan from the young girl hugging his back drew her attention. The girl's hand went to her leg, and her face tightened with pain. An angry welt had swollen her lower leg to nearly twice its normal size. There were also two small bandages on her shin, both soaked with blood.

Beena spoke softly, but authoritatively, to the tall man in Pashto, "Follow me. Your daughter requires medical care."

The man's eyebrows arched, and his head nodded imperceptibly. The veiled woman's assertive speech reminded him of his wife, Laila. Like his wife, this woman, too, was used to giving orders.

Once the group had left the stall and was about to step into the crowded street, Beena stopped and grabbed a fistful of her escort's *kameez*. She pulled him toward her until his face was inches from her veil. "You're going to lead the tall man and me to the clinic. Show me that you're strong and don't let others influence you." She was sure word was quickly spreading through the bazaar, via cell phones and motorbikes, that the tall man had humiliated one of their own in front of an ignorant woman.

Moments later, she slipped in behind the tall man and discreetly said, in Pashto, "I'm from the Red Crescent clinic. I'd like to take a look at your daughter's leg. It might be broken."

The tall man turned toward her, with a mysterious grin curling his lips, and asked in French, "*Traitez-vous des patients ou lavez-vous les sols de la clinique?*" Do you treat patients or wash the clinic's floors?

She ignored the man's odd reply. Too many hostile merchants were studying their every move. With her head bowed, she fell back to her subservient, tail-end position of the four-man column. After a couple of minutes of weaving their way through prattling merchants and overloaded pushcarts that clanked over the remnants of a paved roadway, Beena was tempted to step forward in the column and continue her conversation with the tall man. But, a tingling in her spine gave her pause. She took a quick peek over her shoulder. Her instincts were opportune. The two offended office product merchants were following them and spreading bad tidings about their group to every other busybody in the bazaar.

So much for discretion! She suddenly collapsed to her knees, started screaming, and flapping her arms like a bird. As she did this, she pointed at the two merchants and repeatedly screeched in Pashto, "*Toray khaoray de pa sar!*" Black earth on your head!

The two merchants knew a witch when they saw one. The short fat woman in the blue burqa, who was flapping arms, certainly fit the bill. Worst of all, she was sending a curse their way. Both men, as well as several other recently recruited busybodies, turned on their heels and quickly shuffled back to their stalls.

Once they passed through the clinic's security gates and entered the small lobby of the spartan, one-story clinic, Beena motioned her visitors to several plastic chairs. She disappeared into a side room. When she reappeared, the tall man smiled knowingly, while his guards gaped at her conversion. The fat lady had miraculously lost thirty pounds. She was now dressed in a trim white lab coat, with a medical clipboard pressed against her chest. And her head was covered with a clean white scarf that wrapped around her head and neck.

Her emerald eyes held the tall man's gaze. In French, she responded to his earlier question. "*Monsieur, je suis une femme médecin. Je traite les patients. Êtes-vous Malik Jan Zahir, un ami de mon oncle Ahmad Shah Massoud?*" I am a female doctor. I treat the patients. Are you the leader of the Zahir clan, Jan Zahir, and a friend of my uncle Ahmad Shah Massoud?

Zahir smiled and gave a slight nod of his head as he said, "*Êtes-vous Beena Waleed?*" Are you Beena Waleed?

"*Oui! Voulez-vous converser en Français, Dari ou Pashto?* Would you like to converse in French, Dari, or Pashto?

He rocked on his heels as he took the measure of Ahmad Shah Massoud's niece, Beena Waleed. *The Lioness of Panjshir*, he recalled fondly. Aside from her obvious intelligence and natural beauty, he was taken with her emerald eyes. Her eyes had that same captivating and magnetic force as her uncle's. "*Pashto!*" he replied simply.

"Pashto it is. I'd like only you and your daughter to follow me into the exam room."

"Granddaughter!" he corrected.

"Ah! How old?"

"Nine."

"She is a big girl for that age!"

"She comes from sturdy stock!"

"And, smart stock!" smiled Beena.

Once they were settled in an exam room and the young girl was lying on a bed with clean white sheets, Beena began to clean her leg and ask Zahir questions over her shoulder. "What's the name of your beautiful granddaughter?"

"Emma Dil."

"*Your heart's wish!* That's the perfect name for this perfect child."

"Yes, it is. Everyone in my clan loves her. We simply call her Emma."

"So, Emma, please tell me how you hurt yourself?"

"Grandpa and I visited a building with steps this morning. None of the houses in our compound have steps, just ladders. I like steps. When we were leaving the building, I told Bubbow...that's what we call grandpa... that I would race him down the steps. I won!"

"Yes, you did Emma, but flying doesn't count," said Zahir.

Emma giggled, "After the last turn of the steps, my feet never touched the steps. I was like an angel in flight until I landed on the last two steps. That's when I cut my leg...but, it doesn't hurt!" proclaimed Emma bravely.

During the next hour, Emma calmly followed and listened to Dr. Beena's every instruction. At the end of her exam, Beena sat beside Emma with ex-ray negatives in her hand. She motioned Zahir to her side.

"Emma has broken a bone in her lower leg. This bone is called the fibula," said Beena as she held out the ex-rays for both of them to see. "It's not a major break, but it needs to be properly set...realigned... so she can beat you in all future races, Bubbow."

Zahir and Emma both smiled.

"With your permission, Bubbow, I 'd like to inject a mild painkiller into Emma's leg before I straighten it and then hold it in place with a plaster cast. The injection will minimize her pain."

"I can handle pain. Isn't that right, Bubbow?"

"Absolutely, sweetie! You didn't cry or whimper when I lifted you from the bottom of the staircase and put you on my back." He gently swept his hand through her hair and kissed her softly on her forehead. "But, I think we should accept Dr. Beena's advice. A painkiller is a good idea. She is a wise and trustful person."

"Trustful! That's a special word, Bubbow. You rarely use that word."

A modest smile curled the corner of his lips as he massaged his jaw and said, "Trustful applies to Beena."

"I like Dr. Beena. She's my friend!"

"Mine too," said Zahir as his eyes settled on Beena's eyes, the window to her heart.

"My mother has told me many stories of how you helped my favorite uncle, Ahmad Shah Massoud. He was a great man. 'A man is known by the company he keeps!'"

"Ah! An expert not only in medicine but in Greek philosophy. You've studied Aesop. I see your uncle in you."

"And I see him in you!"

SAFI'S MOLE

Presidential Palace, Kabul | President Hakim Qazi's office
October 20, 2011 | Thursday 11:30 p.m.

Kabul Chief of Police Safi Khan sat patiently by the speakerphone, in President Hakim Qazi's private office. After a minute or so, his secure phone call was connected to the U.S. Bureau of Diplomatic Security (DS) headquarters in Arlington, Virginia.

"Hello? Who's calling? I don't recognize this number," said the unidentified DS security specialist.

"One guess, 'Cannon?'" croaked Safi. Cannon was the nickname Safi used for his mole at the U.S. Embassy, Kabul.

Cannon was sitting in a temporary office that DS security specialists used when they rotated back to the U.S. from a foreign country. The creation of his nickname came to be three years earlier, on a hot summer day, in Kabul's police headquarters.

Safi and his partner-in-crime were discussing the expansion of their shakedown of ISAF (NATO) supply trucks and military convoys in the country when the electricity flickered and then went out. Though there was ample natural light from the exterior office windows, the loss of air-conditioning quickly became a problem. When the temperature rose above 85° F, his partner casually removed his long-sleeved DS shirt to cool himself.

With his partner now sitting opposite him in a sleeveless undershirt, Safi became intrigued with the large tattoo on his left shoulder. The tattoo looked like two crossed cannon barrels, with what appeared to be a grape below the intersection. Curious, he asked his partner what the tattoo meant.

"They're two crossed cigars and a grape. I think the theme came from Europe. The tattoo salutes 'the good life.' A wealthy friend of my grandfather had a tattoo like this. He lived in the biggest house in my hometown, drank the finest wines, and smoked the best cigars. I decided when I was fourteen that I wanted those things when I became a man. On my eighteenth birthday, I went to a tattoo parlor and got this," he said, proudly pointing at his tattoo. "The design is similar to my grandfather's friend's tattoo. It reminds me every day that my sole goal in life is to make lots of money and live *the good life*."

Safi laughed. "They look like cannon barrels to me. From this day forward, my good friend, I shall call you Cannon. Calling you cigar doesn't sound very noble."

Consequently, the theme of a whimsical tattoo contributed to their criminal relationship. Safi and his new partner were dedicated to accumulating wealth, by whatever means necessary, so they too could enjoy the fruits of a good life and whatever else that entailed in their greedy minds.

"Shit, Safi, these calls are monitored. Call me at home later tonight."

"No can do Cannon. I'm flying to Kandahar in an hour or so. Qazi and his brother, Azim... he's the province chief of Kandahar... want me to expand my relationship with their CIA contacts there. The CIA pay as you say, 'big bucks' for intel, especially if it comes from the Qazi family. They know the Qazis hate the Taliban."

"You mean the non-dues-paying Afghan Taliban."

"Non-dues-paying?"

"Those Afghan Taliban in the Kandahar poppy fields who don't pay Azim the going rate of *baksheesh* (bribes)."

Safi laughed. "Yes, yes, you understand these things. You're like one of us, Cannon. Those who attempt to rip-off the Qazi's soon find their name and address on a list of CIA drone targets. By the way, I learned from one of Azim's CIA contacts that a senior British colonel, on the ISAF staff in Afghanistan, is in the midst of an affair with a U.S. Navy nurse who is stationed at Camp Leatherneck, in Helmand Province."

"Nothing wrong with that, Safi. It happens all the time."

"Yes, but not if they're both married. The colonel's wife holds a senior post in Prime Minister David Cameron's government in London. And the nurse is engaged to a U.S. Congressman who sits on the U.S.'s Intelligence Committee. Perhaps we can leverage this immoral behavior into some extra money."

Immoral behavior! Talk about the 'pot calling the kettle black.' Cannon nearly laughed aloud, but he wisely checked himself. Antagonizing Safi Khan, especially over minor matters, was both pointless and dangerous. He was a heartless man who marched to the beat of an executioner's drum. At five-foot-eight and weighing in at a rock-hard 230 pounds, he was an imposing physical figure who was clearly endowed with some East Slavic bloodlines. His physique reminded Cannon of a miniature version of the 1988 Olympic Heavyweight Greco-Roman Gold Medalist, Russian Alexander Karelin. Bulging shoulders, huge chest, and a hairless, bowling-ball head. Adding to his intimidating physique were his ever-present sneer— partially hidden by a shaggy mustache— and threatening, brown eyes that smoldered from tightly stretched eye slits.

One major difference between Karelin and Safi, however, was their intellect. Karelin enjoyed the arts—music, literature, and poetry. Safi didn't appreciate anything civilized, culturally relevant, or beautiful. Except, that is, for beautiful women whose only function—in his depraved view— was to sate his supercharged libido.

"Perhaps!" replied Cannon, reflecting on the possibilities of blackmailing the two lovers. There were a few techniques that he could employ, but he'd have to be careful. Except for the Navy nurse, the participants in this honey pot were heavyweights in the government or the military. He also knew that it wasn't uncommon for the CIA to plant false stories, especially those regarding the extramarital affairs of high profile individuals. A shrewdly constructed fictional affair, which was carefully leaked, might tempt an enemy agent to reveal themselves in the course of trying to compromise one of these individuals. He'd heard from various colleagues that the new CIA station chief in Kabul, Mike Hall, was quite expert in luring his adversaries into those types of unforeseen predicaments. "Why are you calling?"

"Qazi wants the September numbers on our CIC income and fuel truck operations before a big meeting he has here tomorrow. He's meeting with the leaders of his two crews, and they'll want to know what they made last month." CIC was short for their "Coast is Clear" enterprise, or scam, that shook down all manner of ISAF and U.S. truck freight for safe passage fees on secure Afghan roads.

"Uh-huh!" replied Cannon noncommittally.

"Don't worry about U.S. agents listening in on this call. There are none. President Adams personally assured Qazi that conversations on his personal line wouldn't be monitored."

Cannon weighed the risks of divulging incriminating evidence over the phone. Had his inside sources in the White House not previously apprised him of Qazi's secure private line, he wouldn't have been so forthcoming.

"First, I've got a question for you. Tell me more about that matter that you involved me in last month. I think you referred to it as just a *little dust-up*. Simply open the security gate of that half-finished, twelve-story building in the Wazir Akbar Khan district."

"Yeah! A couple of Taliban snipers harassed U.S. embassy workers from the top floor. What of it?" he replied indifferently.

Cannon again attempted to check his emotions. This time he failed. "I wouldn't fucking call that harassment fire. The assholes in that building, and other locations in the city, killed eleven civilians…*six were children*… plus five of your own men. And they tried to blow up a girls school on Airport Road. It was a well-coordinated, twenty-hour, goddamn terrorist attack that you helped orchestrate!"

Safi replied dispassionately, "My five men were in the wrong place at the wrong time."

No pity, no remorse for his own men. His partner was a cold-hearted prick.

Safi continued, "I didn't know that you made a distinction between stealing and killing."

"Assholes are one thing, but I draw the line on killing children. I partnered with you, Qazi, and his insiders to make money, not kill children. Don't involve me in something like this again."

"Is that a threat, Cannon?"

"No, it's an ironclad condition. This call is over," he said, slamming the telephone handset into its base. He wanted to question Safi further about his instruction to change the Bagram shuttle driver that day, but the moment had passed.

He knew that Jamal Waleed and his sister, Beena, were relatives of the Ahmad Shah Massoud family. Though that was a well-kept secret, there were those in Kabul and Washington who were renowned for their loose lips. A deliberate or negligent comment to the wrong person could result in a death sentence for either one or both of them. *Maybe Safi was complying with a specific Afghan Taliban request. Isolate Jamal that day and have him assassinated. Or, kidnap him and use him as bait to entrap his beautiful sister, Beena. She was a beauty that Safi no doubt desired. Or, perhaps there were darker motives behind Safi's request. Motives related to him!* He had his suspicions.

A few minutes later, Cannon's desk phone rang again. He knew who was calling. Aside from being a cold-hearted prick, Safi was also a stubborn SOB.

"What now?" answered Cannon brusquely.

"I will not involve you in killings where children could be harmed. But I would like you to take out one individual who knows too much about our businesses."

"Who's that?"

"Mary Phillips!"

"'Shit in my own backyard!' Are you fucking nuts? No way!"

"What does that expression mean?"

"It means that I'm too close to her. It means that I might be a prime suspect." Unsaid was his thought that maybe that was precisely what Safi wanted.

Safi's pitiless eyes darkened. He didn't like to be disappointed. Regarding his and Qazi's joint decision to have Phillips assassinated—on U.S. soil, not in their *backyard*—their thinking on the matter wasn't particularly agonizing. In light of her multiple tours at the U.S. Embassy, Kabul, her fluency in regional languages, her understanding of the Pashtun culture, and her ties to the local community, they both believed that she knew too damn much about their shady dealings. And what she didn't know, it wouldn't be particularly difficult for her to find out with a few phone calls.

The highfalutin generals and embassy bigwigs that rotated through

Kabul every twelve months hadn't the slightest inkling of the depth or breadth of their criminal activities. And the brief three to four-day semi-annual visits by inspectors or auditors from Washington or ISAF countries knew even less. The only real threats to their criminal empire were the U.S. ambassador, who in their view had overstayed his welcome in Kabul; Mary Phillips; and the new CIA station chief, Mike Hall.

Safi also possessed an additional motive for wanting to get rid of Phillips. The bitch had fought him so tenaciously during his attempted rape of her— a month earlier—that he required forty stitches to reattach a partially torn ear to his head and close several deep lacerations she'd clawed into his back. To his warped sense of pride, her rejection of his unwelcome sexual advance was a direct insult of his manhood. He failed to exercise his control over a woman. This insult was generally referred to as *Ghairat* in Afghanistan, and it meant, in Safi's view, that an honor killing was required.

He'd now have to call his contact in Washington, who handled the U.S.'s "No Fly List." His second choice for the Phillips assassination was a two-man team who were prominently identified on that list. The removal of a single name from the list— a practice that his U.S. colleagues nicknamed "Visas for Sale"— would likely cost him a minimum of $25,000 each.

"Qazi needs those CIC numbers!" spat Safi.

Cannon took a deep, calming breath and said, "Got a pencil?"

"I'm ready."

"September's CIC shakedown income from supply trucks and military convoys traveling on Afghan roads was $1,180,000. That was down slightly from July and August. ISAF was busier in the summer. The splits are per our standard agreement. Your team, which includes Qazi, gets 50%. Your shakedown leaders and their toll collectors get 30%. My team gets 20%," said Cannon in a straightforward manner.

"Cannon, you know I don't like your cut—" began Safi before Cannon sharply cut him off.

"Save it, Safi! We've gone over this a hundred times before. If it weren't for me, an associate in ISAF's logistics department, and several friends who manage security companies that protect military convoys, you wouldn't have a clue about the schedules of supply trucks and/or military convoys. Furthermore, from my cut, I have to grease the skids of some very high-profile individuals in Washington. Individuals who would see to it, in a New York minute, that U.S. aid to Afghanistan be drastically reduced, or entirely eliminated if they didn't receive a rather substantial monthly fee from me."

After a long moment, Safi continued. "Yeah, yeah, yeah! I've heard that before. I don't believe you!"

Cannon was inclined to graphically tell Safi what he could do with his opinion when a better idea came to him. "Do you remember that senior U.S. general who stormed into our Justice Department offices at the U.S. Embassy in Kabul, a few months ago? He demanded to see all the criminal case files that our Justice attorneys were building against corrupt Afghan officials."

"Yeah, I remember," said Safi, with a note of condescension.

"Our military leaders in Afghanistan and Washington were, and still are, fed up with the out-of-control crime in your country. Afghanistan National Army (ANA) soldiers shooting American soldiers and getting off scot-free. Or, brazen acts of pedophilia by senior ANA officers on our military bases, etc. They don't like it, and they're pissed off with the foot-dragging of our own attorneys in Kabul."

"Uh-huh! Your high and mighty general was going to singlehandedly eliminate all of that. It'll never happen here. Your military will have to learn to live with it."

"You were one of the most high-profile Afghan officials that our Justice Department was investigating."

Safi didn't respond.

After a time, Cannon continued, "Two of our key partners, here in Washington—Max Smithson and Charles Hightower, both Justice big-wigs—were oblivious of their underlings' investigations in Kabul. After I spoke with Smithson, he quashed any further attempts by our military to examine those files. Smithson even had the balls to call a press conference and publicly denounce the general's crime-busting intentions. He said if I remember correctly, 'Afghans have the right to privacy, just like Americans! Our military has no right to examine case files or interfere with our criminal investigations in the U.S. or any foreign country, including Afghanistan.'"

Safi didn't entirely buy Cannon's story, but he didn't have the time or interest in arguing the point further. He moved on to their second profit center. "What was last month's take on the tanker trucks that we stole in Afghanistan?"

These were tanker trucks that were delivering fuel, either diesel or aviation fuel, from Pakistani refineries to ISAF fuel storage facilities in Afghanistan. In late 2011, ISAF forces were consuming a total of 1,500,000 gallons of fuel per day, or 45,000,000 gallons per month. All, but 10,000,000 gallons, of that monthly consumption was delivered into the country by trucks.* ISAF commanders estimated that the level of monthly consumption would increase by 33% within the next year.

The approximately 35,000,000 gallons of monthly trucked-in fuel began its circuitous journey into ISAF gas tanks at the Port of Karachi in Pakistan. Medium-sized tankers first offloaded unrefined, crude oil at the port. From there, it was trucked to Pakistan refineries. After the crude oil was refined, a majority of the fuel was trucked—via the Khyber Pass—to fuel terminals in the northern parts of Afghanistan. Fuel destined for consumption in the southern part of the country was trucked in via a route that ran through Quetta, Pakistan. The distances between Pakistan refineries to Afghanistan fuel terminals, before its subsequent transshipping to outlying military bases, ranged between 800-1,500 miles.

"That was our big winner last month. Your Pashtun buddies in the ANA, who posed as Taliban, did a great job of acting." He was tempted to mention that he knew they really weren't acting, but he held his tongue. "They held-up and hijacked—without injury to any of the truck drivers—thirty-two, 20,000 gallon (equal to approximately 75,000 liters) tanker trucks…all loaded with diesel, no jet fuel… from four separate convoys. We netted—based on black-market fuel sales—$60,000 per truck, for a total take of $1,920,000. Plus, we sold the tanker trucks back to ISAF and their contractors for an average price of $55,000 per truck. That sale netted us a cool $1,760,000. It was our best truck resale month ever. Most of the trucks were relatively new Freightliners. Your team gets 40% of those totals. Your

---

* Pipeline fuel imports—approximately 10,000,000 gallons per month in 2011—into Afghanistan were limited to one 600-mile long 6" pipeline that supplied primarily jet fuel to the Bagram Airfield from Manas, Kyrgyzstan. Manas fuel originated from multiple sources, north of Manas, and was delivered to Manas via rail and trucks.

Pashtun ANA actors in the field get 40%, and my team gets the remaining 20%. An hour ago, I deposited everyone's funds into their Deutsch Bank accounts in Germany. They'll see the deposits in their accounts tomorrow in Deutsch's correspondent bank in Kabul."

"Cannon, I've done a little simple math here, and I think you're screwing us on black-market fuel sales. At the current street price in Kabul of, say, $1.00 per liter of diesel that would equate to a black-market sale of $75,000 per tanker truck, not $60,000. You're skimming $15,000 per truck, for a total of $480,000."

"Christ, Safi! As I explained to you last month and the month before that, the $15,000 per truck deduction goes toward several subcontractor activities. I have to compensate the building owners who allow us to hide the trucks in their buildings or covered yards while we defuel the stolen fuel trucks; refuel smaller, distribution trucks; and then sell and deliver that fuel to hundreds of small gas stations and street vendors. It's not like we're retailing that diesel directly to the public. Repeating your question every month isn't going to change my answer. I know you're not dumb, and I know I'm not dumb," closed Canon as he waited patiently for his greedy partner to respond.

"Damn it then! Steal more fuel trucks!"

"We can't. There are only so many places we can hide those trucks because of drone surveillance. Our previous monthly high, of stolen tanker trucks, was twenty-eight."

After several long moments, Safi added, "There is another matter we should discuss. Last week, the Zahir clan captured three of my toll collectors who I assigned to the Khyber Pass. They gutted two of them and hung them from long poles that hung over a section of the pass. A third pole was empty. They gave the third man a message addressed to me. The message said that if I interfered any further in their Khyber Pass toll collections that I'd hang from that third pole."

"You idiot! You lied to me," shrieked Cannon. "You told me months ago that you'd worked out an arrangement with the Zahir clan for toll collections on a stretch of the Khyber Pass."

"I couldn't come to terms with them."

"Fuck, Safi! The Zahir's have held the toll rights to the Khyber Pass

since the goddamn British-Afghan War in 1839. Then, the Pakis signed...
as you well know... an official treaty with them in 1947. The Zahir's got
exclusive toll rights, but they have to maintain the road and protect those
...mainly trucks...that travel along it. The Khyber Pass isn't some Podunk
back road where your men can act like toll collectors at certain times. What
were you thinking?" Inwardly, he answered his own question. *Quadrupling
toll fees!* "Forget toll collections in the Khyber Pass! If you screw with the
Zahir clan, you'll lose!"

Another of Safi's shortcomings—aside from greed, cruelty, and payback
for insults to his manhood—was his loathing of a reprimand. With further
darkening eyes, which was difficult to imagine, he was thinking that Cannon
had worn out his usefulness to him. *Perhaps it's time to start searching for
another insider at the U.S. Embassy or maybe a bigwig within ISAF. That
on-going affair in Helmand Province between the married British colonel and
that U.S. Navy nurse might be a possibility,* he thought. "This conversation
is over," said Safi angrily as he slammed his telephone into its base.

A second call to Washington was now required, and this call would be
much more expensive than the first. It would also likely involve an exchange
of significant IOU favors. He would be asking a partner, who was also his
most senior contact in Washington, to ensure that a couple of laser-guided
500-pound bombs (GBU-38s), fired from a Predator drone, mistakenly
wiped the Zahir clan's compound off the face of the earth.

Cannon too was thinking about this relationship. Safi Khan was a
merciless man who didn't think twice about resolving a dispute with deadly
violence. Being one of his enemies wasn't a healthy proposition.

CHAPTER 7

QAZI'S CONFIDANTS

Presidential Palace, Kabul | Presidential Office
December 14, 2011 | Wednesday 9:31 a.m.

Attendees:
    Hakim Qazi- President
    Abdul Sharif- Justice Minister*
    Jamee Nabi- Finance Minister
    Azim Qazi- Chairman, Kandahar Provincial Council
    (Hakim's brother)
    Safi Khan- Chief of Police, Kabul

PRESIDENT HAKIM QAZI smiled warmly at the four men who filed into his large private office in the Presidential Palace. They each bowed respectfully before they sat in elegant mahogany chairs, with upholstered seats, that surrounded his ornate desk. His visitors included his brother, Azim, Chief of Police Safi Khan, Minister of Finance Jamee Nabi, and Minister of Justice Abdul Sharif. This small group represented his innermost circle of confidants.

He welcomed each man with a respectful nod of his head as he said, *"Salaam Alaikum! Chetor asten?"* Peace be upon you! How are you, my friend (Arabic followed by a Dari expression)? He next queried Nabi and Sharif

---

* Newly introduced fictional characters, Sharif and Nabi, only appear in this chapter.

on the health and well-being of their families. Qazi received regular updates on the lives of their relatives from Azim. In Safi's case, he worked with him daily and was familiar with his relationships with his wives and children.

He knew Safi treated all of his family members harshly. Were it not for his financial support of their basic needs, they would have all left him long ago. As it was, every one of his children had escaped his cruel hand by the time they were fifteen. He maintained little contact with them, and they none with him.

Nabi and Sharif enjoyed the company and relations of multiple wives and multiple families. Therefore, limiting the status of their extended families to fifteen minutes or less was no minor matter. During their narrations, he took notes, as only he could during such a private and high-level meeting. His face flushed, and his writing hand trembled when he took note of the death of one of his confidants' extended family members.

Qazi's marital and family standing in the group was unique. He had one wife and one nuclear family. He did, however, have a relatively large extended family. He and Azim were the sons of a father who enjoyed the company of multiple wives. The two brothers shared the same mother and had four full siblings plus twelve half-siblings. Their father conceived children into his late sixties when he suddenly died, according to his last wife, in her arms while sowing his last seed.

Both brothers questioned this last wife's claim, but there was nothing they could do to discredit her. Paternity tests were not a religiously or culturally accepted practice in Afghanistan. As for the total number of relatives that the two shared—including half brothers and sisters, first and second cousins, and nieces and nephews—their best guess was approximately seventy-five.

Two recent deaths particularly troubled Qazi. The first death was the result of a U.S. drone attack. He despised these insidious attacks because innocent bystanders were sometimes injured. In this specific attack, he would later learn that Sharif's first cousin wasn't an innocent bystander. The drone video, provided by the U.S. Army, confirmed that his cousin and a helper were killed while planting an IED in a roadbed regularly used by ISAF forces.

His brother, Azim, who was the senior province chief in southern

Afghanistan, reported the second maddening death. Azim officially oversaw the province of Kandahar and unofficially Helmand province. These provinces were the heartland of Afghanistan's poppy fields. Azim had learned, just minutes before their meeting, that a U.S. Marine had shot and killed one of their second cousins—a Taliban drug courier—the previous night during an attack on one the many small and secret opium gum packaging facilities in Helmand.

Qazi didn't allow the military—ISAF forces, which included U.S. forces—to perform night attacks. His view of the military had inexplicably transformed from blessed saviors—removing the Taliban from his country after 9/11— to disrespectful tenants. He would later learn that the courier was killed at 4:00 p.m. in the afternoon when the Marine returned the courier's gunfire.

He raised his hand for silence, snatched his nearby phone, and punched the intercom button. A moment later, his senior assistant answered. "I want to speak with the U.S. Ambassador and the ISAF Commanding General tomorrow morning at 10:00 a.m. in my office. Tell them it's imperative that they meet with me. No damn excuses! It's about their latest atrocities," he barked as he slammed the phone back to its base. His face was red, and his head was bobbing. "These animals are worse than the Russians. I won't stand for this!"

"Brother, will you excuse me for a few minutes. I have a short call to make," said Azim.

Qazi absently nodded his approval. It was a disoriented look that they'd all seen before. He was experiencing one of his odd shifts in mood, which was associated with his manic-depressive illness. In unison, all four men quietly shuffled out of his office.

Fifteen minutes later, the meeting reconvened. Qazi looked as if he'd just awakened from a deep sleep. His face was slack, and his eyes were a little dreamy. His meds were working.

"Let's see! Where were we?" he asked lazily.

Azim interjected, "You were just beginning to cover your agenda items, Brother, when your assistant interrupted you."

"Yes, yes, of course. My apologies, brothers, for the interruption." He flashed his visitors a half-smile and continued, "Finances, Nabi. Where do matters stand with the Kabul Bank and our offshore real estate holdings?"

"Your Excellency, the Kabul Bank no longer exists. The bank operated well— as you know—for six years until 2010, when it closed its doors. There were many bad loans. Total losses were approximately $950 million. The bank's receivers were able to recover only $50 million. The Americans absorbed most of the losses."

"What about our friends and relatives? Did they lose any money when the bank closed?" asked Qazi.

Azim chuckled involuntarily and was silenced by a sharp look from his brother.

"They were responsible for most of the losses," replied Nabi. "They borrowed heavily from the bank. Many of them, like ourselves, used those borrowed funds to acquire luxury apartments in Dubai. The real estate market collapsed there, and now everyone's holdings are worthless. When the U.S. auditors arrived earlier this year, I told them that we didn't permit outsiders to examine loan documents in Afghanistan," said Nabi officiously.

Azim again chuckled.

"Do you have something to add Brother, or are you trying to anger me?" demanded Qazi.

"Nabi should explain how he discouraged the auditors from reviewing the bank's losses," crowed Azim.

Qazi turned back to Nabi with a questioning look.

Jamee Nabi was a short man, five-foot-two, whose feet just reached the floor when he was seated. Plump, balding, bespeckled, and in his early fifties, he looked very much like the quintessential bean counter. Nabi's father had relocated his family to London in the late 1970s, shortly before the Communist Party—backed by the Russians—displaced the last Afghan king, Mohammed Zahir Shah. Nabi's father also oversaw Afghanistan's finances. When the Nabi family arrived in England, they were comforted with the far-sighted subterfuge of their patriarch. He'd cleverly diverted millions of British pounds, from Afghan government funds, into multiple, well-disguised bank accounts in London.

His fastidious son took a moment to collect himself before he spoke. "Your Excellency, I explained to the U.S. receivers that reviewing another's finances is disrespectful. We don't do business like that in Afghanistan. I also told the receivers that they might meet with an untimely death if they persisted with their rude requests. They persisted. The chief examiner—Amy Blake from the U.S. Treasury—was a particular nuisance. She insisted that borrowers, like the five of us, who personally guaranteed bad real estate loans, had to personally repay those loans from other savings."

"What? Personally repay bank loans on property that is worth less than our loans. I've never heard of such a thing. Small street loans must be repaid, but not loans from big banks. That's a risk banks take when they make a loan," said Qazi.

Nabi was, for a brief instant, tempted to explain to Qazi the meaning of personal guarantees, but he wisely elected to remain silent.

Qazi continued, "What is the present value of our offshore real estate holdings? Aren't most of our properties in Dubai?"

"Before the real estate crash, the value of our collective holdings there was approximately $30 million. When the Kabul Bank foreclosed on our real estate holdings, they sold our properties for $18 million."

"You've lost $12 million! That was our money. Money that we'll need for our retirement in Dubai, London, or the U.S.," howled Qazi.

Azim realized his brother's emotions were getting the best of him. Before he experienced another spell, he elected to intervene. "Brother, only $3 million of that money came from our savings. We borrowed $24 million from the Kabul Bank and $3 million from the Dubai developers who built and sold us the condominiums.

"The Americans are responsible for this real estate crash. They wiped out the total value of our real estate holdings when their own banks collapsed. Their greedy bankers and stupid politicians allowed this to happen. They hurt every investor in the world. Unbelievable! The Dubai developers who loaned us $3 million are screaming for their money. Nabi told them that they'd have to overthrow our country before they see any of that money," said Azim authoritatively. He deliberately neglected to mention that they also stiffed the Kabul Bank for $6 million, which was the shortfall on their primary loan.

His brother raised his thick eyebrows and nodded appreciatively.

Azim continued, "The tens of millions of U.S. dollars that we crammed into hundreds of suitcases and flew out of the country... 80% of our savings... weren't invested in real estate. Nabi invested most of those funds in high quality corporate and government bonds. Our personal accounts are secure in banks in Frankfurt and London. Nabi also, very wisely, avoided heavy losses in our common stock trading accounts in New York by buying U.S. stocks on a highly leveraged basis. When the Americans destroyed that market as well, we simply walked away from stock losses totaling about $15 million. Several New York stock brokerage houses are screaming for the money they loaned us, but Nabi told them the same thing he told the Dubai developers."

Qazi flashed the briefest of smiles. "Good work, Brother Nabi! I'm pleased to hear that you didn't let those greedy New York brokers push you around."

"Nabi and I have a plan to make up our real estate losses in Dubai and the U.S. stock market many times over. We'll explain the details of our plan at the end of our meeting," closed Azim.

His brother replied with an enigmatic grunt. His understanding of finances was limited to gains and losses. He had no understanding whatsoever of secondary notes or leveraged stock trading. His next question confirmed their views.

"Have any of our public works projects suffered as a result of the cash we flew out of the country?"

Nabi carefully removed his spectacles and began to meticulously clean them as he stalled for time. He subtly tipped his head in Azim's direction, indicating that he should answer the question.

"Brother, none of our public works have suffered because of the commissions we properly earned. We deduct a modest 2-3% on all the government contracts we negotiate. Yes, some construction projects have been delayed ... roads, rail lines, sewer projects, pump stations for freshwater, new hospitals, and schools... but they'll eventually get built. Our people have to be patient! The Americans will support us for years to come," offered Azim, with a genuine look of sincerity.

Nabi breathed a sigh of relief and said a silent prayer. *Praise be to Allah for having Azim on my side.* He knew that the 2-3% commission deduction that Azim just quoted was a flat out lie. Their commissions ranged from

5-6%, and that deduction occurred before the government bureaucrats took their cut. That last bureaucratic cut, which was above and beyond conventional general and administrative expenses, depleted the funding of every government project by another 20-25%.

Corruption—bribery, embezzlement, misappropriation, and thieving—is an embedded and accepted Afghanistan custom. Every international group that ranks countries based on their level of corruption placed Afghanistan at either the top of their list or within the top three. Had these rankings been based solely on the volume of international aid stolen, Afghanistan would have been the runaway winner.

Since 2008, the U.S. had been annually contributing $8-12 billion in aid— exclusive of U.S. military and State Department costs— to Afghanistan. This direct U.S. aid funded approximately 80% of Afghanistan's annual government budget. A majority of this aid was designated for the training of Afghan personnel—Afghan police and military forces—and the construction of essential public works projects. When rumors of training fraud in Kabul began to surface in early 2011, it sorely tested the patience of all of Afghanistan's allies, especially the U.S. In August of 2011, the U.S. confirmed the fraud. Qazi's government had falsified, by a factor of 200% or more, the number of Afghan nationals who were being trained and ultimately paid a salary. The monies designated for these nonexistent persons, or *ghosts*, went into the pockets of Qazi and his friends.

As for commerce in Afghanistan, several factors limited the country's prospects for growth. Afghanistan is an isolated country with harsh mountainous terrain (75% of the country), negligible natural resources, and an old, inadequate transportation system. Paved two-lane roads are rare, and the number of major roadways (more than two lanes) that connect cities can be counted on one hand. There is a modest rail system in the north of the country, one mainline along the Uzbekistan border, and two shorter lines from Turkmenistan. Most logistical experts compared the difficulty of getting supplies into and around the country as similar to that of supporting far-flung research camps in Antarctica.

The construction of public works projects in the country presented a different set of challenges. In 2001, 90% of all Afghans couldn't read or perform simple math. Thus, there was virtually no trained workforce, of any consequence in the country, to fill both blue and white-collar jobs. By 2011, the literacy and skills of the general workforce had marginally improved. Getting accurate data from locals on the status of on-going, major public works projects was difficult and sometimes impossible. Adding to this quandary was the cost of importing 100% of all building supplies. Importation costs plus government graft doubled or tripled the estimated cost of every Afghan public work project when compared to an identical project in Iraq.

Lastly, there was the reprehensible hand of the Taliban. They routinely destroyed newly constructed freshwater wells, roadways, electricity grids, sewer systems, communication networks, and schools. In their fundamentalist view, anything that improved the Afghan standard of living, above a Dark Ages environment, was evil.

Qazi grunted again and then turned toward Abdul Sharif, his Minister of Justice. "Minister, tell me about the developments in your department."

Sharif's body straightened, and he folded his hands in his lap as he slowly swiveled toward Qazi. His deep-set brown eyes, framed by a thicket of unkempt eyebrows, settled on the president. He was tall at five-foot-ten, rail-thin, and easily recognizable with his long, black hair and beard that always made him look as if he'd just stepped out of a wind tunnel. If it weren't for his apparel, a well-tailored short black coat that he wore over his high collar white robe with white pants, one would have thought he was a mountain nomad who'd just returned to civilization.

"Your Excellency, you appointed me to my esteemed position six years ago. I am very grateful for your trust in me," began Sharif.

Qazi smiled at his friend and confidant. "You have earned my trust, Brother Sharif."

"During my first years in office, the Americans flooded my associates and me with a mountain of rules and laws that they insisted we adopt. They threatened to abandon us and let the Taliban return if we didn't cooperate."

"That's 'hardball politics.' I hate that," spat Qazi. "They ignore our culture!"

"Yes, Your Excellency, you are wise. Our culture defines us," he replied. "Because they are the strongest country in the world, I presumed that they would make intelligent decisions. I was very wrong. If you would permit me, I'd like to describe a few of my interactions with the Americans. I think my examples will help us better deal with them."

Qazi nodded for Sharif to continue.

"Firstly, they've insisted that our laws be nearly identical to theirs. This means that we've had to adopt a constitution, a bill of rights, a representative national assembly, and strict electoral laws. In their form of government, a democracy, all the citizens have the right to vote for leaders they like. Such nonsense! We've never done anything like that. We prefer to have strong leaders like you, Your Excellency," said Sharif as he bowed his head in deference to Qazi. "Only you know what's best for the country. We can't have Tajiks (27% of the population), and certainly not Hazaras or Uzbeks (a combined 18% of the population) influence how we, Pashtuns (42% of the population), govern our country. Our northern people know nothing about our cities or our lowland farmers in the south.

"Our last presidential election was a complete failure. Outsiders, as you know, attempted to steal the election from you. Many people were threatened, some killed, and thousands of false ballots were cast. The American's Justice Department is insisting that we repeat this process again in 2014. They are also forcing me, and my office, to enact stricter electoral laws. And, you won't believe who will be aiding them in this effort!" Sharif paused for dramatic effect. After several long moments, he hissed, "Dr. Mary Phillips! She will return next September."

"But she works in the U.S. State Department, not their Justice Department," complained Qazi.

"Not anymore! Because she knows all of us and speaks our language, she'll be overseeing and managing our adoption of all these crazy laws. She's transferring into their Justice Department."

The individual reactions were mixed. Safi remained unusually quiet and indifferent. His indifference was likely buoyed by his resolve to see that Mary was dead and buried by next September.

Nabi sniffed. He hated Western women, like Mary, who thought that they deserved the same respect as men just because they could speak their language.

Azim appeared uninterested. Because he spent most of his time in Kandahar, he wasn't fully aware of the personal relationships of his colleagues in Kabul.

Qazi unconsciously increased the tapping of his fingers on his desk as his eyes held Safi's. Despite his lecherous attraction to the blonde beauty, he had agreed with Safi's plan to have the woman eliminated. She knew far too much about the workings of his inner circle of confidants.

"A second matter that shows us how the Americans think involves their bad soldiers. Several years ago, a group of bad soldiers... they were called MPs (military police)... *abused* suspected terrorists being held at the Abu Ghraib prison, west of Bagdad, Iraq. These MPs did very wicked and offensive things to their Muslim captives. Some were even tortured! You may have read about these things in the newspapers, Your Excellency?" said Sharif, knowing full well that Qazi read numerous foreign newspapers every day.

"Yes, I read about the Americans' disgraceful treatment of the prisoners at Abu Ghraib. It was behavior that I wouldn't have expected of the U.S. I think everyone in the world read about it. But, Abu Ghraib doesn't have any bearing on us!" he grumbled.

"Oh, but it does, Your Excellency! You see, the Americans regard themselves as *champions of human rights.* They were greatly shamed by what their MPs did there. The benefit to us is that if any of our people are imprisoned by the Americans for any wrongdoing—shooting an American soldier, disclosing classified military plans to the Taliban, or stealing their supplies—all they have to do is allege *prisoner abuse,* and they may very well be set free. *Prisoner abuse* is like the American term, *free pass!*"

The group was silent for several long moments as they each considered Sharif's observation.

Azim broke the silence. "Brother, Sharif is correct about this. I know that many of the Pashtun interpreters in my area, Southern Afghanistan, have relatives or close friends that serve with the Taliban. These Pashtuns often inform the Taliban of U.S. or ISAF scheduled military movements and missions. If they're caught divulging these secrets and taken into custody for betraying a mission, many of them will injure themselves...break their nose, bite their lip, slam their head against a wall, etc. It's easy to draw a few drops of blood. They'll next loudly complain that their captors tortured them.

"The Americans are petrified that they might be accused of prisoner abuse again, so they routinely release all those that they've arrested." Azim paused and rubbed his lower jaw as the glow of contented treachery filled his face. He and his brother were proud Pashtuns. "But, before these humane American soldiers release their captives, they attend to their self-inflicted wounds and pay them $2,500 for any inconvenience they may have caused them. In the case of much-needed Afghan interpreters, they change a few letters in their surname and move on to another American base and repeat the process. It's a good deal for them!"

Nabi hadn't heard any of this before. He shook his head in disbelief and asked curiously, "What happens to the American soldiers who arrested these men?"

"They treat them as if they were the ones who committed the crime. They view them as war criminals! Many of them go to prison or are kicked out of the military. It is very strange behavior," replied Azim.

Qazi excitedly chimed in. "I agree, Brother. In the U.S., *popular opinion or political correctness* is more important to them than the well-being of their own people. Unless that is, it affects a politician's relative, friend, or major donor, then the opposite applies," he chuckled. "They also don't care or understand how other cultures have functioned for centuries. Our country is a good example.

"Shortly after they kicked the Taliban out of our country, they forced us to eliminate the punishment of *stoning to death* for adultery. I've instructed Sharif to make sure that punishment is reinstated into our new laws. We're a stronger and smarter country now than we were ten years ago. I know that a great majority of our people would like to see the punishment for adultery return. The U.S. can't push us around anymore!" To emphasize his point, he clumsily slammed his fist against his desktop and beamed, with a proud sense of accomplishment.

A cloak of ambivalence enveloped the office. Azim, Safi, and Nabi hadn't heard a word about the reintroduction of this punishment. The issue that gave them pause was that they knew their former adultery laws were quite one-sided. An Afghan woman could never win an adultery case against her husband, mainly because Muslim males were allowed to have up to four wives. The old laws were solely designed to persecute women.

Azim was certain that neither the ISAF nor the U.S. would agree with his brother's latest foolishness. Rather than getting into an emotional debate with him about the matter, he simply spoke for the others when he said deferentially, "That is something to consider!"

"Americans can be very foolish and childlike at times. Finish your report, Sharif," grumbled Qazi, with an additional note of shrillness.

Qazi's confidants sensed that a combination of mental fatigue or emotional stress was beginning to cloud their leader's thinking. Irrationality and irritability were the first signs of his well-known mood swings. They knew their meeting couldn't last much longer.

"I have two final points. I'll be brief," said Sharif. "The first involves our soldiers and police. Our men view work and rules differently than the Americans."

"Yes, of course. We'll never change. It's who we are. What's your point, Sharif?"

"When our men are corrected during a training exercise or during their first days on a new job—be it a minor criticism about their skills or energy level—it's a form of disrespect... or an insult," explained Sharif. "They feel that their integrity has been challenged, and they take it very personally. We all understand *Pashtunwali*. It's the bedrock of Pashtun honor. If a stranger comes to our door for aid, we help him. If another family disrespects us, we take revenge on that family and punish them for their shameful act. The men in our culture—the heads of our families— are charged with righting a wrong!"

"Yes, yes. We all know that! Your point, Sharif?" snapped Qazi.

"Our men today respond like all brave and honorable Afghan males have done in the past. I, however, would like to see our soldiers and police *temper* their responses to what they view as an insult from our Western occupiers. Minor provocations have prompted our men to attack ISAF soldiers. They've killed or injured many soldiers over minor misunderstandings. This must change or our benefactors, those who are pouring billions into our country every year, will leave our country and never return."

Safi immediately spoke up. "Sharif is absolutely right. I've repeatedly told my police force that they can't shoot a well-meaning instructor or trainer if he attempts to modify the way they direct traffic, or they catch you accepting a bribe. My men aren't used to being publicly corrected. It embarrasses them, and bribery is hardly a crime. So, I've ordered my men to come to me personally, especially if it involves bribery, and I'll protect them."

"Yes, yes, very wise, Safi. You should all do as Safi says. I'm getting daily complaints from the ISAF about these killings. I don't want to hear any more about this issue. Is that clear?" commanded Qazi.

Nabi, Safi, and Azim vigorously shook their heads in agreement.

Sharif shifted uncomfortably in his chair. He was concerned about Qazi's reaction to his final point. "Your Excellency, my final point has to do with *bacha bazi,* sex with young boys." Everyone, except Qazi, sat frozen in place. His finger tapping became louder. More impatient, more ominous. The cadence reminded Sharif of the drum cadence that accompanied a murderer's march to the gallows.

With a flushed face and just a hint of tolerance in his voice, Qazi said, "You do understand that boy play is part of our culture! What do you suggest?"

"Your Excellency, you are our leader and a visionary. I suggest that those who partake in this longstanding institution be more discreet about their activities. That is, keep it hidden or more private. Westerners don't like or accept this institution, especially if it is forced upon an unwilling child. When the child becomes a man, then it is OK."

Azim spoke in Sharif's defense. "Brother, I think I understand what Sharif is trying to say. Some of our ill-bred men are insensitive to present-day Western standards. They take pride in flaunting their practices of yesteryear. Their unnecessary flaunting has drawn the attention of not only foreigners but also our own citizens. These men, some who hold high positions, also think nothing of kidnapping young boys from Afghan families who have repeatedly refused the demands for their sons."

"I don't like kidnapping," sighed Qazi.

"Yes, Brother, it is very wrong. Just recently, I had to relieve one of my senior police chiefs in Kandahar, who repeatedly ignored my *no kidnapping orders.* When kidnapping occurs, it draws unwanted attention to an institution that we have accepted for centuries," closed Azim.

"Brother, I know your decision to relieve your police chief was difficult. It made me very sad. That police chief was a close friend of our family. He was subjected to boy play when he was a child, so I feel that he earned that privilege."

His confidants bobbed their heads in understanding.

After a time, Sharif continued, "I have one last question on this matter, Your Excellency."

With his head held in his hands and his elbows resting on his desk for support, Qazi delivered a weak nod.

"How should we deal with our Afghan military leaders who flaunt their boy play on Western military bases? Western soldiers have intervened and protected these young boys. Foreign soldiers don't understand that this is part of our culture. It's creating many problems. I seek your guidance!"

Qazi slowly straightened himself in his chair and recommenced his death-knell finger tapping. After a time, he turned to Azim and gave him an order. "Azim, I would like you to set up a committee. But, not a committee like the Americans have where there is just talk, and nothing is accomplished. I want your committee to locate and identify our leaders who are committing these acts. Explain to them my *new ruling* on this matter. All their boy play must occur in private or hidden areas. Not on foreign military bases. My brothers, I believe this ruling is fair."

Heads nodded affirmatively.

"Your Excellency, this is a perfect example of why open elections are so stupid. All that is required is for our country to have a wise leader, like yourself," closed Sharif.

"Yes, yes!" replied Qazi proudly. "I will apprise the ISAF and the U.S. of my decision to forbid boy play in Afghanistan."

All heads again nodded, even though boy play wasn't being forbidden.

"My friends, this meeting has lasted longer than I expected," he continued. "I am tired and not feeling well. This has not been a happy meeting. We will adjourn after Azim and Nabi explain to us how we can recoup our real estate and stock losses. Be quick about it, my brothers!"

Azim began, "Yes, Brother, I will be brief. It's simple. Western military forces... ISAF forces, which includes U.S. and British troops* in the south...

---

* ISAF forces are comprised of NATO countries and select others. In this novel, the U.S. and Great Britain are occasionally mentioned separately from ISAF forces, despite their attachment to that command. It is not the author's desire to slight any other country's contribution or sacrifice to Operation Enduring Freedom. These two countries—mainly because of their high troop levels in Afghanistan— were often contacted directly by the president of Afghanistan and vice versa, rather

will soon consume nearly two million gallons of fuel per day in our country. This is a combination of both jet fuel and diesel fuel. This is twice the fuel consumption that they experienced last year.

"The leaders of these forces require their troops to maintain a thirty-day reserve of fuel in-country, at all times. A sixty-day reserve is their ideal storage level, but their consumption is outpacing their storage capabilities. We know all of this because we've just been involved with the foreign aid construction contracts that will add thirty million more gallons of in-country fuel storage.

"This recent Salala Incident and Pakistan's closure of their borders has placed these leaders in an awkward position. After only eighteen days, without fuel deliveries from Pakistan, ISAF leaders are in a panic. They're running out of fuel! They'll look like fools if their army comes to a standstill!"

"Yes, yes, we all know this, Azim. How does this benefit us?" asked Qazi impatiently.

"Virtually all of these fuel deliveries involve private contractors, not ISAF or U.S. carriers who we can't tax because of our Military Technical Agreement (MTA) with them."

"According to the MTA, we can't tax their contractors either," countered Qazi.

"Not necessarily, Brother. Nabi and I have studied the MTA. We've found *loopholes* in the agreement. We believe that we have the right to assess income tax on the employees of these private contractors who earn money while working in our country. Plus, the right to assess corporate income taxes on the private contractors who make money in our country. We also feel that we have the authority to apply asset transfer taxes on all the fuel these private contractors bring into our country."

Safi was now sitting on the edge of his chair, leaning toward Azim, focused on his every word. His CIC business and tanker truck thefts were taking a beating with this damn border closure. Finding alternate sources of income was one of his foremost concerns.

Qazi, too, was suddenly alert, startled with this latest disclosure. He pressed his brother, "Do you really think we can do this?"

---

than communicating with one another through the more customary ISAF chain of command.

"I'm certain of it, Brother. We also have leverage."

"Leverage? How so?"

"If we were to levy expensive business licenses, permits, and fees on all the private contractors, ISAF's contractors would disappear overnight," said Azim, pausing momentarily to compose his closing pitch. "If we don't back charge them for prior year taxes, I think we can easily squeeze another $15-20 million out of the ISAF this year."

"And we'll take 2-3% of that as our commission?"

"No, not at all, Brother! This was our idea…20% is proper!"

"Do it, Azim! But, back charge them for personal and corporate income taxes. Go back to 2001. You and Nabi are fine leaders. I'm proud of both of you!"

… five days later. News wires burned around the world with the following report:

Earlier today, the popular provincial chief of Kandahar, Afghanistan, Azim Qazi, was shot and killed in his provincial office. His murderer was a local police chief who he had recently demoted because he'd kidnapped a young boy from a family for boy play *(bacha bazi)* purposes. The boy's kidnapping occurred despite the family's repeated refusals of the police chief's demands for their son. The police chief was shot and killed by one of Azim Qazi's provincial security guards, moments after the murder. Initial reports indicate that the police chief's motive for murder involved Afghanistan's code of honor, known as *Pashtunwali*.

… sixty days later.

The commanding general of ISAF forces in Afghanistan handed President Hakim Qazi a check for $13 million for the first of their annual fuel-related tax payment. The ISAF check covered the tax payment for only 2011. Before the general's delivery of the check, he explained to Qazi that under the provisions of their MTA, there was a 180-day window—for the signatories of the MTA—to file a non-payment or underpayment tax claim. The filing periods for the years 2001 to 2010 had expired. Therefore, no additional taxes were due, and Afghanistan's back charge claims were invalid.

Unfortunately, ISAF couldn't recover this unexpected expense, *yet,* from their private fuel contractors because existing contracts with them clearly stated that they wouldn't be responsible for any kind of Afghan taxes.

CHAPTER 8

ZAHIR TRIBAL COUNCIL MEETING

Khyber Agency | Pakistan FATA
December 14, 2011 | Wednesday 2:15 p.m.

Attendees:

> **Malik Jan Zahir-Clan leader**
> **Elder Abdul- Regional Intelligence and toll collections***
> **Elder Mohammad – Security**
> **Elder Sayd- Logistics and finance**
> **Elder Kochi- Farming and ranching**
> **Elder Hazrat- Construction and utilities**

LATER THAT SAME day—150 miles east of the Presidential Palace in Kabul—Jan Zahir's wife, Laila, served sugarless tea to the five council elders of her husband's clan. She was an attractive, wiry woman with dark penetrating eyes. The men were seated comfortably around a warming fire pit in the oversized courtyard of Jan's home. His home overlooked the clan's ten-acre compound.

Their December monthly meeting usually took place inside their home, especially when winter began to arrive. The compound was situated at an elevation of 8,000 feet above sea level in the *Spin Ghar* Mountain Range, and it had already received its first snowfall. But, with uncharacteristically

---

* Newly introduced fictional characters—Abdul, Mohammad, Sayd, Kochi, and Hazrat—only appear in this chapter.

pleasant weather, the meeting was convened outdoors. The current temperature hovered around 10°C (50°F), the sun was shining brightly, and there was no trace of the light snowfall of a week earlier.

The *Zahir Khel's** main compound was surrounded by a mix of mature trees—firs, cedars, and pine trees, all indigenous to the northern parts of the *Spin Ghar*—and was laid out in rectangular shape, approximately 800 feet by 550 feet. In the center of the compound was a three-acre, hard-packed dirt common area that contained a small prayer hall and a modest two-room schoolhouse, which also served as a medical clinic.

Seventy single-story, mud-brick homes that housed approximately 400 clan members surrounded the common area. The roofs of most of the homes were constructed of wattle and daub, vines, and small interwoven sticks that were plastered together with mud, grass, and/or straw. Timbers typically supported these roofs. Jan's home, and a few others, was upgraded with corrugated steel roofing sheets. Some of the residents built half-walls of stone in front of their home for a courtyard, similar to the Zahirs. The courtyard provided them with a little extra living space. For others, rather than a courtyard, they built a modest animal pen, constructed of solid sticks, which held a goat or a milking cow. Many of the residents also maintained a small vegetable garden.

All of the homes faced inward, toward the common area. Their rear walls formed an unbroken, mud-brick defensive wall—approximately twelve feet high—that surrounded the entire compound. Guard towers sat above these walls at the corners of the complex.

Another 700 clan members lived in smaller clusters of homes, outside of the compound, but within the boundaries of the Zahir's well-secured, mountainous valley. Another hundred clan members were scattered throughout the region. They acted as spies for the clan. Approximately seventy-five members lived secretly amidst rival tribes in the FATA, and another twenty-five lived in Afghanistan's and Pakistan's most populous cities.

Of the sixty or so major tribes, plus hundreds more clans or subtribes that occupied the seven agencies of the FATA, the Zahir clan was viewed by other tribes as odd and standoffish. They were a secretive and relatively small group of Pashtuns, who stayed to themselves and weren't welcoming to

* Villages were often named after their leader's clan.

outsiders of any stripe. Ancestry records for over 90% of their clan members could be traced back in time by three generations or more.

The location of the clan—in a remote mountain valley—added to the clan's mystique, as did hard-to-believe rumors about their fierce and cunning fighting capabilities. For those reasons, the Russians left it alone during their ten-year occupation of Afghanistan. Outsiders knew little about daily life in the valley and cared even less about looking into it.

Before Jan began the meeting, he took a moment to savor his tea and study the faces and features of his five council members. All of them were longtime friends and all relatively the same age, their late fifties to early sixties. Jan was fifty-seven years old. They had fought, side by side, together in multiple conflicts for the past thirty-two years. Two of them had lost a leg in combat and now wore a prosthetic leg. One had limited use of an arm, and another had lost an eye. All of them had been wounded multiple times.

"I leave tomorrow morning for Jalalabad," began Jan. "The day after that, Friday morning, I have a meeting with my U.S. CIA and British SIS[†] contacts at the military base there, FOB Fenty. The two guards who accompanied me last time will be with me again."

Jalalabad, Afghanistan, was the provincial capital of Nangarhar Province, located approximately sixty miles west of *Zahir Khel*. Another hundred miles west of Jalalabad was Kabul. Jan's Zahir clan, or subtribe, was an off-shoot of the larger Shinwari tribe, which occupied much of the Nangarhar Province on Afghanistan's eastern border with the Khyber Agency of the FATA. The Kabul River separated the low-lying farmlands of Nangarhar Province from the lower reaches of the Zahir's naturally protected valley.

"Let's see Malik. Your last trip into the city was in mid-October if I remember correctly," said Abdul, who was in charge of the Zahir's network of spies. He addressed Jan as Malik, which was the traditional and honorary title of a Pashtun clan's chieftain.

"Yes, it was October 20."

"You shouldn't take the same guards. They'll arouse suspicion, even if your last visit was six weeks ago. I'll pick new men for you. All of you should wear disguises and enter Jalalabad separately if that's possible. There

---

† SIS is also known as MI6.

are thousands of prying eyes in that city. Many are Taliban with black hearts who would turn in their mothers for a few extra dollars."

Jan considered Abdul's advice for a moment before responding. Like his father, who was the clan's chieftain before him, he was a shrewd and contemplative individual. If he were to be captured or killed by the Taliban in Jalalabad, it wouldn't bode well for his clan. His oldest son was neither experienced enough, nor mature enough, to lead his clan. There were consequences for his actions.

"Yes, Abdul, I agree with you. That's good advice. By the way, when I was last in the city, I met Ahmad Shah Massoud's niece, Beena Waleed. I forgot to tell you all about that meeting.

She's a—"

"Massoud!" burst Mohammad, the one-eyed commander of the *Zahir Khel's lashkar.*[*] Animated and leaning forward toward his leader, he could hardly contain his interest in the former leader of the Northern Alliance.

The *lashkar's* current activities involved collecting tolls and providing security for supply trucks that passed through the Khyber Pass; protecting the clan's compound and other outlying homes, farms, pastures, and orchards that were located in their valley; and maintaining a small but deadly combat team that could quickly respond to the needs of the clan. Though the Afghanistan entrance to the Khyber Pass, in Torkham, was only ten miles south of Zahir Khel, it would have seemed like thirty miles to a foot soldier because of the intervening mountains and rugged terrain. Mohammad's toll collectors and security personnel typically operated from makeshift stone huts and secret trails that bordered the thirty-three-mile pass. They also utilized a well-guarded dirt road that led from the outskirts of Torkham gate to Zahir Khel.

"Massoud was a tough, bold warrior... and clever as a fox," continued Mohammad. "Back in '84, he asked your father for help. He needed someone to train his mortar teams. They were having trouble figuring out accurate firing solutions. Your dad sent me to northern Afghanistan to train them. I worked with his men for a few months. If I remember correctly, you were delivering the CIA's Stinger missiles to his Northern Alliance then."

---

* A lashkar is a sub-group within a clan, which is dedicated to a specific purpose. In this case, it was the toll collection and military arm of the Zahir clan.

Jan wagged his head in agreement.

"Well, he saved…he saved…" began Mohammad, before he was overcome with emotion.

The grizzled veteran's rare display of emotion surprised his friends. For decades, they'd referred to him in Pashto as "Cold Heart."

After a moment, he composed himself and continued. "Eight Russkies got the drop on me and nine of my trainees in a supposedly secure location. They lined us up and demanded that we tell them where Massoud's headquarters were located. I was the third man in their lineup. Their commander and interrogator started with the first man. He refused to disclose the location and was immediately shot in the head. The same thing happened to the second man. Now, it was my turn. He asked me the location, and I shook my head. The *godless animal* smiled and said, 'No easy death for you!'

"Three of his men grabbed me and threw me to the ground. They held me down while the animal put his knee on my chest and withdrew his knife. He cut this eye out and repeated his question. I shook my head again just as gunfire erupted all around me. It was Massoud and two others, three against eight. They had silently walked up behind the Russkies, armed only with pistols, no automatic rifles. They killed every last one of them." With the trauma of the memory weighing on him, he stood and moved toward Laila's kitchen. "I need some more tea!"

Once they regrouped, Jan resumed his account of his surprise meeting with Massoud's niece. "Beena Waleed is a full-fledged doctor now who volunteers at the Red Crescent clinic in Jalalabad. She received her medical degree in Paris at the Sorbonne and interned with Médecins Sans Frontières in Kashmir. I was with her when she set my granddaughter's leg in a plaster cast, and I'm going to have dinner with her Friday night, after my meetings with the CIA and SIS."

"Can she be trusted?" muttered Abdul.

"I haven't disclosed to her anything yet about our clan. And I won't until I get to know her better. Her uncle, however, spoke very highly of her many years ago." Reflecting on that moment, he clasped his hands together and subconsciously bobbed his head approvingly. "She's a good, capable doctor, with better hands and knowledge than the seamstresses that sewed up our wounds. If any of our people have serious wounds or health issues,

I'd recommend they see her. She is also one of the two owners of that New Hope Girls School on the west side of Jalalabad."

"That's bad! A girls' school is a more appealing target to the Taliban than a U.S. military convoy," stated Abdul.

All the men, except for Jan, grunted in agreement.

"I know," said Jan thoughtfully as he weighed his next statement. "I made a promise to her uncle in 1999. I promised Massoud that I'd watch over her if she ever returned to Jalalabad. If she owns that school, we're obliged to protect her interests."

Ever so subtly, the facial expressions and postures of each of the council members shifted, though not in a supportive fashion. Protecting a girls' school presented a multitude of considerations. This was new ground for all of them.

Unexpectedly, a new voice and face entered the conversation. It was Jan's one and only wife, Laila. She was the mother of his five boys and two girls. Mohammad emitted a not so quiet, nor welcoming groan. He and at least one other council member viewed her as an outspoken and impetuous woman who seemingly questioned every decision their council made.

"If you, Malik Jan," she began, by referring to her husband as the chieftain of the tribe, "made a promise on behalf of the tribe, then we're all obliged to abide by that."

"He wasn't our tribal chief then, his father was. He didn't have the authority to make that kind of promise. And it sounds like he only promised to protect her, not an entire school. Plus, it's of all things, a girls school!" protested Abdul.

"If it was a boys school, Abdul, would you feel differently?" pressed Laila.

Aside from his two sons and five grandsons, Abdul had three daughters and six granddaughters. When the first of his five children was delivered, a healthy seven-pound girl, he and his wife heard the none too quiet whispers from those in his clan. *Is a Muslim man really a man if his wife doesn't bear him a boy! A family without a son is like a home without any light!* And lastly, there was the constant prodding of a regional Islamic imam who often visited and led prayers in the Zahir's prayer hall. *The Koran allows a Muslim man to take up to four wives so long as he treats each of his wives fairly or equally*. The unsaid implication behind that prompting was a husband's Islamic duty to bear at least one son by up to three additional wives, if necessary.

Also unsaid, in the case of a wife who didn't bear her husband a son, was the interpretation of *treating each wife fairly or equally*. A wife who didn't bear her husband a son wasn't quite as equal, in the eyes of the clan or the imam, as a wife who did bear him a son. In Abdul's case, he loved his wife and had no desire to marry another woman. Fortunately for him and his wife, their next two children were boys.

With respect to this boys versus girls school issue, Abdul rightly assumed that Laila had already spoken to his wife and three daughters about this matter. He was trapped. The only certainty that crossed his mind was that the women in the Zahir clan now expressed their views more freely than they did during his father's days. Unsure of how to respond, he simply snorted a harrumph.

Laila's attention moved from Abdul to the other council members. Her fiery eyes bored into them, one after another. The familiar crackling sound of burning mulberry logs in the fire pit, which had minutes earlier relaxed them, now sounded like the cracking of a British cat-o'-nine tails. She didn't bother to question her husband's feelings. His pro-women sentiments were well known in their household.

The ambivalence of the council members motivated her to plow ahead. "You are the wise elders of this clan. We all listen to your sage advice. All of you have at least one daughter and two granddaughters?"

In unison, the five shook their heads in agreement.

"Then, I ask you this. Who among you wouldn't be proud to say that their *granddaughter* is a medical doctor... or a teacher... or even a poet?"

After several very long moments, Laila noticed one barely perceptible nod, then another. Two down, three to go.

"Consider your daughters, they're all now mothers. Who among you wouldn't be proud to say that their daughters can read, write, and understand simple math? It's never too late to learn new things. My husband has taught me how to read and write, and I'm very thankful for that."

There were a multitude of subjective factors and Islamic beliefs that shaped a Muslim male's stature within his clan. Chief among them, especially for a Pashtun, was pride. Laila was well aware of that truth. She was also mindful that Abdul was the most prideful man in all of *Zahir Khel*. After what seemed like an eternity, Abdul slowly turned to Mohammad, who was seated beside him. After they exchanged a few quiet whispers, Abdul straightened and motioned Mohammad to speak.

"We're in favor of protecting Beena and her school!"

"Schools! There is another one in Kabul," said Laila evenly. Abdul theatrically raised his eyebrows and uttered an icy grunt. He again leaned into Mohammad, and their whispering continued, though it was clearly not as even-tempered as their first exchange. After a time, Mohammad delivered their second opinion. "We're in favor of our clan using its *best efforts* to protect this second school in Kabul. Best efforts because it is somewhat out of our regional sphere of influence. But," he exclaimed as he raised a skinny finger and waved it back and forth, "our clan's livelihood is not based on protecting schools." He paused authoritatively before making his closing statement. "It doesn't matter whether they're girls schools or boys schools! Two schools are our limit. Malik Jan Zahir, do you agree with our findings?"

Jan looked at his three other council members who had not participated in Abdul and Mohammad's private discussions. Their clan responsibilities covered farming-ranching, finance-logistics, and construction-utilities. All three simultaneously bowed their heads and extended their open hands toward him, which indicated that they would defer to his final say.

Jan turned to Abdul and Mohammad and smiled. "Your findings reflect your good judgment and wisdom. I agree with your findings. It shall be so!"

Laila then added, "Since we are now going to protect two girls schools, we can't continue to prevent girls from attending or our own school. Can we?"

Heads slowly nodded in agreement. The last to nod, though sourly, was Abdul. As he scratched his tangled beard, Mohammad thought he heard him mutter, "Sneaky!"

Unexpectedly, Laila sprung forward and gave Abdul a heartfelt hug. Though the agreement only benefitted several hundred young girls, it was a big step forward for the Zahir clan. Very few, if any other, Pashtun tribes allowed girls to be educated.

"You are a strong and courageous man!" she cried as she delivered a tiny kiss to his cheek.

Abdul was again caught off guard. He didn't how to respond, especially to this surprising and very un-Muslim like public display of affection. He simply grumbled, "Women!"

"One last matter!" declared Jan. He turned toward the clan's finance-logistics elder. "Sayd, please give us your thoughts on the closure of our Khyber Pass and how it may affect our clan's finances."

Sayd carefully withdrew a small, well-worn accounting ledger from an interior pocket of his *waskat* (waistcoat). He was a small man, five-foot-three, with an intelligent face and curious brown eyes, who seemed to have an extra bounce in his step whenever he had his nose in his ledger. His ledger was similar to those that street bookies kept on their gambling-addicted customers. City names, numbers, and notes filled the pages of Sayd's ledger. In the back pages of his ledger, he kept a semi-annual, coded record of ISAF military activity throughout Afghanistan.

After double-checking a few figures, he closed the ledger and returned it to his inside pocket. He bent forward in his chair and rested his right elbow on the armrest, while he extended his prosthetic left leg. Comfortably settled, he began his report in measured speech, much like an economics professor thought Jan. "After the Haqqani's *reprisal attack* on ISAF embassies in Kabul, on September 13, 2011, Malik Jan Zahir and I decided it would be wise to increase our open market purchase of fuels. We believed that it was only a matter of time before another incident occurred between ISAF forces and Pakistan.

"The Pakistan government, especially the Pakistan ISI and the Haqqani Network, are still angry about the CIA's drone attack on Datta Khel last March that killed forty-five tribal. Leaders that the CIA believed, and we knew, were al-Qaeda terrorists. If Pakistan suffered another humiliating attack like that again—"

Mohammad interjected, "Don't forget the killing of Osama bin Laden last May!"

"Yes, that too," agreed Sayd, "though that wasn't as *personal* to the Haqqanis as the Datta Khel attack."

Jan, Mohammad, and the other council members murmured in agreement.

Sayd continued, "Whether the next incident was accidental or premeditated, warranted or unwarranted, we felt that Pakistan government would have no choice but to again close down their border passes that led into Afghanistan. This would, as you all know, prevent the flow of supplies from entering Afghanistan through our Kyber Pass and the less traveled Bolan Pass, near Quetta, in southern Pakistan. Eighty percent of all non-lethal ISAF supplies arriving in Afghanistan come through those two passes, with our Khyber Pass carrying the vast majority of those supplies.

"How long the Pakistanis closed their border would depend on their sensitivity to a specific incident. If an incident resulted in the death of Pashtuns, like ourselves, the Paki leaders in Islamabad wouldn't be terribly troubled," he noted with a condescending grin. "They refer to Pashtuns who live in the FATA as *citizens* when it suits them. When they deal with us directly, they treat us like low-class Hindus … *'untouchables!'* If Islamic fundamentalists or Paki soldiers were killed or injured in an incident, that would be an entirely different matter. In this last case, we believed that they would no doubt close their borders.

"Additionally, we knew that ISAF's fuel consumption had doubled in each of the last three years. Because there was no indication that ISAF military activity would slow, we believed that their fuel consumption would continue to increase. Or, at least, remain constant. Fuel, diesel and jet fuel, is the lifeblood of Operation Enduring Freedom. In 2004 and 2005, as you all know, we bought—through a cousin of the Zahirs in Kabul— three aging Russian fuel farms. All three of these fuel farms—Bagram, Kandahar, and Jalalabad—are located near a major Afghan airfield. We've since renovated and expanded the storage capacities at all of these facilities. When ISAF fuel reserves have run low, especially jet fuel, we've sold them fuel at a profit. Those profitable sales have fully paid off our purchase costs and renovation expenses."

Jan smiled inwardly at his friend. Sayd's understanding of basic economics—how prices were determined by supply and demand—had created a nice nest egg for the clan. A major dynamic of this financial security, unseen by most all of the clan members, was Sayd's steadfast philosophy that his fuel "buying and selling" decisions had to be grounded on his personal observations. Twice a year, he toured Afghanistan—without an incriminating camera—in an innocuous jingle truck that the Zahir's kept in Jalalabad. With two of Mohammad's toll collectors as drivers and guards, he'd observe air traffic at the major ISAF airfields as well as military traffic on the main roads. The airfields were generally located in or near Afghanistan's largest cities. Other intelligence gathering occurred at Internet cafes, along the way, where he'd dutifully followed Internet news accounts of ISAF's military activities and listened to local gossip.

While Sayd was behind a computer at these cafes, his guards generously greased the palms of fuel truck drivers and gathered further intelligence. Many of those fuel truck drivers were well acquainted with his two Khyber Pass toll collectors. They often protected and accompanied them, in some form, when they drove their fuel trucks through the Khyber Pass into Afghanistan.

In mid-summer, he toured Afghanistan in a counterclockwise manner: Jalalabad, Bagram north of Kabul, Kunduz, Mazar-i-Sharif, Herat, Camps Leatherneck and Bastion in Lashkar Gah, Kandahar, Ghazni, Khost and back home through Jalalabad. In the spring, he'd reverse his tour. Having a feel for ISAF's annual fuel consumption, including seasonal ups and downs, influenced his thinking on his fuel inventory and sales prices.

On one of his first tours, Jan remembered, Sayd rented a car and drove himself around Afghanistan. In Khost, Afghanistan, he decided he'd earned the right to do a little sightseeing on his way home. His planned route— via hitched rides or horseback—would take him through the magnificent mountains and lush valleys of the FATA's Kurram Agency. The Kurram Agency abutted the Zahir's home agency, the Khyber Agency, along its southwestern border. In his wanderlust for travel, he neglected to consider the geopolitical risks of traveling through Kurram. It was one of the main strongholds of Hakimullah Mehsud, the leader of Tehrik-i-Taliban Pakistan (TTP).

One hour after he left Khost and crossed the border into Kurram, in the bed of an old, rattling Toyota pick-up truck, TTP sentries at their ten-mile checkpoint arrested him. In his second hour of travel, he was charged and convicted of spying and thrown into a windowless storage shed to await painful questioning later that night. Fortunately for him, one of Abdul's embedded spies in the TTP recognized him and rescued him before he was tortured, questioned, and killed.

"Late last September, with the approval of ISAF, we contracted with outside sources for the supplementary delivery of 1,500,000 gallons of jet fuel and 800,000 gallons of diesel fuel to our three fuel farms. All three fuel farms reached full capacity two days before the Salala Border Post incident on November 26, 2011. Our current fuel storage total is around 5,200,000 gallons, which equals three and a half days of ISAF consumption.

"The last issue that Malik Zahir and I considered was a lengthy closure of the Pakistan border. If that happened, we knew the ISAF would have very few resupply options. Red Star, Mina, and Gazprom in Manas, Kyrgyzstan, deliver fuel via fuel trucks and a 6" pipeline that terminates adjacent to the Bagram Air Field. Monthly fuel deliveries to Bagram approximate ten million gallons of jet fuel and two to three million gallons of diesel fuel. At best, that equals a little less than nine days of ISAF monthly fuel consumption," said Sayd, pausing to interject a political note into his report.

"Red Star's fuel contract with ISAF has received intense criticism in the U.S. because of its close relationship with the former president of Kyrgyzstan, President Kurmanbek Bakiyev. He was run out of office in 2010 for stealing hundreds of millions of dollars from the country and killing anyone who criticized his thefts. All very *valid reasons* for severing a business relationship with a company that has ties with a very bad man…save for one!" he said with a critical grin. "Red Star owns the only fuel pipeline into Afghanistan. Were it not for the U.S. military's frequent and emphatic reminders to their Congress that they were fighting a war in Afghanistan, Operation Enduring Freedom, that contract would have been canceled years ago."

Jan remained silent as he considered Sayd's comment. He admired and loved the U.S., but he knew they were far from perfect. If it weren't for the singular efforts of Congressman Charlie Wilson, on behalf of the mujahideen in the 1980s, they wouldn't have kicked the Russians out of Afghanistan. He and his clansmen had transported hundreds of CIA supplied shoulder–fired Stinger missiles (now referred to as MANPADS) from Pakistani airports to tribes throughout the FATA and parts of Afghanistan.

Sayd continued, "The ISAF is only eighteen days into this latest Pakistan border closure—as a result of the Salala incident—and they are already scrambling to bring in fuel and other supplies from neighboring countries. They've burned through approximately half of their forty-day fuel reserves. They've inquired about buying our fuel, but Jan and I have decided that we're not selling at this time. Because of our current financial reserves, our clan can easily weather the absence of our Khyber Pass toll revenues for three years before we have to consider any significant spending cutbacks."

Sayd's close friend, Kochi, waved his good arm with a question. He was the elder in charge of the clan's farms, orchards, and ranch. His home was located in the lowest section of the Zahir valley, near the Kabul River. In the mid-section of the clan's fertile valley, he oversaw the growing of grapes, mulberries, pomegranates, apricots, apples, and some nuts (almonds and pistachios). Nearer his home, he managed the farming of corn, wheat, and vegetables; and the care of the lemon and orange tree orchards. His staff of approximately twenty-five clan members rotated between farm and ranch chores.

"Brother Sayd, please tell me about this Salala Border Post incident? I know nothing about it," asked Kochi easily.

His frank and honest question drew smiles from his fellow council members and Laila. Kochi was a quiet, humble man who lived in a neat hut, with his wife and dog, amidst the fragrant scents of a lemon orchard and the soothing sounds of the meandering Kabul River. Other than his wife and his son's family, the only other things that seemed to matter to him were his gardens, crops, orchards, and his dog. Those who were smiling envied him and his detachment from the outside world.

The Salala Incident was a tragic occurrence that was receiving round-the-clock worldwide news coverage. Nineteen days earlier, on November 26, 2011, at 1:00 a.m., ISAF forces were patrolling an area inside Afghanistan in Humvees. The Humvees were approximately a half-mile west of the Pakistani FATA border, inside Afghanistan, when they began to receive gunfire and mortar rounds from two occasionally manned FATA border checkpoints. This ISAF force, which was made up of predominantly U.S. troops, contacted the Pakistan command center to see if any of their soldiers were in the area. Pakistan replied that none were. After carefully following

ISAF procedures, an airstrike was approved. The strike force was comprised of two Apache helicopters, one AC-130 gunship, and several F-15 fighters. A little over one hour later, twenty-four Pakistani soldiers were dead, and thirteen were wounded.

When the dust settled, later that morning, the Pakistan government found themselves in an awkward position. In all of their major cities, radicalized, anti-U.S. Muslims took to the streets, and violent protests erupted. U.S. flags were burned, and pro-Western businesses were damaged. The Pakistan government had no choice but to close their entire border with Afghanistan.

After Sayd's explanation, Kochi's response surprised his colleagues. "Stupid Paki soldiers, who were likely drunk or high on drugs at that time of night, decided that they'd show the ISAF or the U.S. what they were made of. So, they thumped their chests and fired on Humvees that were on Afghanistan soil.* They knew the Taliban didn't travel in Humvees.

"The even stupider Pakistan Army command is contacted, and they say 'no, none of our soldiers are in that area.' They were either too dumb or too lazy to even check with their Salala checkpoint. So, Paki soldiers are killed in a humiliating attack. Who's to blame? The Pakis! What should they do? Close their border and hold the ISAF hostage for a big payoff.

"Eventually, the facts of this sad incident will come to light, and it will reveal the mistakes that the Pakistani Army made. The Pakistan government will, of course, deny the truth. They also won't have any interest in cooperating with any investigation. That would be political suicide. Radical Islamists are *a goat's hair* away from taking control of their country. They have to keep them happy.

"In the end, our Zahir clan will benefit from this tragic affair. With no cross-border traffic, the ISAF and U.S. will have a difficult time learning what's happening in Pakistan. Fewer spies mean Brother Abdul's spies

---

* The location of the attack in Kunar Province, just north of Nangarhar Province, was approximately 100 miles north of the Khyber Pass entrance in Torkham, Afghanistan. That corner of the Kunar Province was a well-known stronghold for Taliban forces because of the terrain, mountains, and heavily wooded valleys. It was also the site for some of the most violent battles of Operation Enduring Freedom. Only Afghanistan's "poppy field" provinces in the southern part of the country, Kandahar and Helmand, experienced the same level of continuous, intense fighting.

will make us more money. Selling intelligence is no different than selling produce. When produce items are scarce, their prices go up," said Kochi pausing. He then added, with an infectious grin pasted on his weathered face, "Plus, my good friend, Brother Sayd, will make our clan a fortune by selling our fuel to the ISAF when their fuel reserves are nearly empty."

Laila was the first to respond. With her hands resting on her hips, she said, "My dear husband, why is this smart man— who keeps our 1,100 local clan members well-provisioned all year round—restricted to farming and ranching activities. He should be in charge of our strategic plans."

"My dear wife," began Jan, with a twinkle in his eye, "I've offered him increased responsibilities, but he's refused my many offers. I do, however, consult with him often because of his high level of common sense," he said, pausing to add emphasis to his final point. "He's also, in my opinion, the best farmer and rancher from Jalalabad to Peshawar."

When Jan's father passed away, ten years earlier, he became the leader of the Zahir clan. If he had learned anything during the past thirty-two years of Afghan battles, it was that wars created economic and social havoc. The pernicious effects of start-and-stop commerce caused job layoffs, hyperinflation, and shortages of essentials. Based on those experiences, he knew that the more his clan became self-supporting, the better the chance they had to grow and prosper. He turned to an unlikely source, in an Islamic country, for information on communal self-sufficiency. His clan's level of independence was now very much like that of a thriving Israeli kibbutz.

In the upper reaches of the Zahir's boxed-in valley, Kochi had taught his son the basics of ranching. The son, under the watchful of eye of his father, now managed the clan's open-range ranch, which skirted just below the treeline and was a safe distance from the clan's fifteen acre-feet freshwater lake-reservoir. The ranch held a couple hundred head of cattle, approximately fifty milking cows and goats, several dozen horses, and two stud donkeys, which they occasionally crossbred with the mares when they needed to increase their population of working mules. There was also a large chicken coop area, which individual families tended.

Above the treeline, Kochi selected a shaded location and oversaw the construction of a cold room for the year-round storage of his fruits and vegetables. On the north side of the valley's highest peak, in an area that held year-round snow, he had also built a freezer room, which held not only frozen meats and poultry but also contained numerous racks and trays for the air-drying of all manner of perishable foodstuffs.

The unique geography of neighboring mountains had created, over thousands of years, a fortuitous network of rivers, holding ponds, and a small lake in the Zahir's valley. The rivers and holding ponds provided ample irrigation for the valley's terraced crops in the hottest of summers. The clan also enjoyed the modest electrical benefits of a micro hydropower generator, courtesy of the CIA and SIS. The generator was located along the banks of the main river that ran through the center of the valley. An additional benefit of the snowmelt and rainfall runoff was the accumulation of rich topsoil throughout much of the lower sections of the valley. Many of the tribes who occupied the mountainous areas south of the Zahir's unique valley were not as fortunate. Those areas were generally barren and possessed little, if any, vegetation.

Less fortunate Pashtun tribes typically relied upon the shifting and unstable generosity of al-Qaeda, the Afghanistan Taliban, or the Tehrik-i-Taliban Pakistan (TTP) for their survival. In return for aid, they were expected to press starving and displaced families into terrorist service in exchange for food and shelter. The spiritual leaders of al-Qaeda, Osama bin Laden, and the Afghanistan Taliban, Mullah Omar, originally introduced and enforced this depravity in the region. They viewed their aid, and the strings attached to it, as time-honored Islamic doctrine in support of the greater glory of Allah! The Zahir clan saw this aid-for-terrorism for what it was, taking advantage of poor, desperate souls.

When the funding for these terrorist tribes began to abate or entirely dry up, they often turned on one another. Jan was well aware of that fact, as was the clan's chief spy, Abdul, and its military leader, Mohammad. Consequently, they kept a close eye on their neighbors, particularly those who had fallen on hard economic times. Were their level of self-sufficiency commonly known, it would have made them an especially attractive takeover target.

Sayd loudly cleared his throat, interrupting Jan's thoughts.

"So sorry, Brother Sayd. I was just reflecting on Brother Kochi's fine work. Please continue."

"To offset the loss of trucked fuel deliveries through Pakistan and the insufficient fuel deliveries from Kyrgyzstan," began Sayd, "the ISAF has organized a delivery system that they call the Northern Distribution Network (NDN). It's a network of ships, trucks, and trains that deliver fuel and other cargo to Afghanistan from ports as distant as Riga, Latvia, on the Baltic Sea, and Poti, Georgia, on the Black Sea."

Abdul and Mohammad stiffened as if they'd been jabbed with an electrical cattle prod. Abdul was the first to speak, "You've got be kidding! Fuel from the Baltic Sea! Riga is 3,000 miles from Kabul, and it's not what I'd call a direct connection."

Sayd bobbed his head in understanding. "My best guess is that the cost of fuel for the ISAF will at least double in the next month. I also think it will be many, many months before our Khyber Pass re-opens. This could easily become a billion-dollar problem for the ISAF. Apologies and entreaties from the ISAF and the U.S., even if they are unwarranted, won't sway the Pakistan government. What will finally convince them to reopen their borders will be their own economy. They don't realize yet how dependent their economy is on the West's war in Afghanistan war."

Kochi kneaded his beard as his head shook resignedly from side to side. "Forget about the U.S. for the moment. The Pakis also haven't considered the damage they'll do to their relations with other ISAF member countries, like France, Germany, and Great Britain. A billion-dollar problem is not easily overlooked, nor forgotten!"

...two days later. December 16, 2011, Friday, 10:14 a.m.

Jan Zahir and his two bodyguards, Ali and Farid, sat in a dented and paint-peeling, fifteen-year-old Toyota Corolla. The driver, Ali, had just skidded to a quick stop on the side of the Torkham-Jalalabad Road, a hundred yards west of the main gate of Forward Operating Base (FOB) Fenty. FOB Fenty surrounded the Jalalabad Airport (also known as the Nangarhar Airport), which was located in a flat agricultural plain. Block walls—fifteen feet high, topped with concertina wire—separated the base from the heavily traveled four-lane road that fronted the base. Concrete guard towers—manned by heavily armed ISAF soldiers—rose above the walls at the entrance and the corners of the base. Strategically located concrete traffic barriers divided the roadway, for security purposes, as two-way traffic neared the base's main entrance.

Just west of the base, and closer to the city center of Jalalabad, was a stand of hundred-foot plane trees (known in the U.S. as sycamores), which were set back from the road—forty yards or so—to permit large trucks to park perpendicularly to the curb. On the opposite side of the road was a motley parade of aging single-story buildings, more like shacks than buildings, which offered truck drivers and motorists travel services. This area was, in general, an old and dusty version of a truck stop for drivers headed to or coming from the Kyber Pass. Behind the buildings was a thriving patchwork of farms and orchards.

The heavily guarded airport was now the exclusive domain of ISAF. It was also the frequent target of Taliban suicide bombers, in vehicles and on foot.

"ISAF guards won't allow vehicles to stop beside the airport. I'll make this quick. I spoke with my CIA contact earlier this morning. He said a man from the U.S. State Department was going to be present at my meeting this morning. I objected, but he said the ambassador insisted he attend. This new person is temporarily assigned to the U.S. Embassy in Kabul, which is run by State. I don't know anything about his duties. I do know that the CIA is not governed by State. The SIS officer also complained about the attendance of this mystery man," said Jan.

"Last minute changes, with no good reasons, can mean trouble. Abdul tells us this all the time. Be careful, Malik Zahir!" said Ali.

With Ali's formal use of his clan title, Malik, Jan wagged his head appreciatively. "Abdul spoke very highly of you and Farid. I can see why now. The SIS man flies out of here at 12:15 p.m., and this mystery man has another meeting to attend near the Jalalabad Bazaar at noon. My meeting should break-up by 11:30 a.m. I want you to follow and observe the new man.

"When I leave the base and retrieve my cell phone at the main gate, I'll call you and give you the description of the vehicle that is transporting him. Hopefully, my cell phone won't be jammed by base security. If you don't hear from me by say 11:40 a.m., use your best judgment and follow whichever vehicle you think he may be in. I'll call you once I return to our building."

Farid pointed to a large armored vehicle, the size of a large garbage truck, which had just exited the main gate. FOB Fenty security was headed their way.

"Meeting over. *Allahu Akbar*," said Jan as he exited the rear seat of the Corolla and began walking slowly toward the armored security vehicle. His arms were extended from his side, with the palms of his hands open, to indicate that he wasn't holding the trigger of a bomb.

Ali did a quick U-turn and headed toward the car rental agency, a half-mile west of their current location. The Zahir clan owned the agency and the dilapidated, unfinished two-story building behind it. The roof of the two-story building provided Ali and Farid an unobstructed view of the main gate of FOB Fenty.

Fifteen minutes later, after Jan was frisked and relieved of his cell phone at the main gate, he was escorted by an Army MP to a highly secure intelligence building. Inside the building was another structure that looked like a shipping container. It was a portable SCIF (Sensitive Compartmented Information Facility) that could be flown anywhere in the world in the belly of an Air Force C-5 Galaxy. The approximate dimensions of the windowless conference room were similar to those of a large sea-going container, forty feet long and approximately ten feet wide and high. Heating, ventilation, and air conditioning equipment was connected atop the SCIF once it reached its destination.

The walls, ceiling, and floor of the SCIF were constructed of special materials that prevented sensitive devices from surveilling activities inside the SCIF. It also prevented those inside the SCIF of sending unapproved, outgoing electronic transmissions. All those who entered the SCIF, regardless of their citizenship or position, were prohibited from carrying cell phones, recorders, electronic devices, and cameras into the room.

Jan entered the room and moved toward the two intelligence officers who he'd dealt with for the past twelve years. After friendly greetings, he stepped toward his customary seat at the head of the conference table. He was the main speaker who possessed the latest intelligence on the Taliban tribes in his Khyber Agency. On his right sat the mystery man from State, who rose lazily from his chair.

Mike Hall, the CIA's newly-promoted station chief in Kabul, introduced Jan to the mystery man, known only as Bill. The two shook hands, while they each grinned warily at the other. Jan wasn't impressed with Bill's soft hands and delicate handshake. Before he quizzed the man on his background and his reason for attending the meeting, he studied him. Medium height, slightly overweight, and young. Early thirties, he guessed. A distinctive red birthmark ran along the right side of his jaw. He asked him what position he held at the U.S. Embassy in Kabul.

"Can't say. Top secret," replied Bill.

"These men," said Jan, waving a hand in the general direction of the intelligence officers, "have told me their positions. Knowing the position of new people builds trust."

"Sorry, I can't say." The self-righteous look that was pasted on Bill's face affected Jan in a way that he would later regret. The job of a spy was to unearth secrets. Amateurs who thought they could stonewall pros often learned that lesson the hard way.

"Why is your position so secret?"

"It just is. I can't tell you what I do."

"I see. Are you an attorney?"

Bill grimaced in a manner that indicated he wasn't.

"An analyst of some kind?"

Another grimace.

He asked him in French, *"Un linguiste?"*

"Huh!" said Bill dully.

Jan repeated in English. "Are you a linguist?"

"No! That's enough of the questions."

He agreed with Bill's response. He'd satisfied his curiosity. Bill was someone's lackey and not a particularly bright one.

After withdrawing a piece of paper, filled with notes, from an inside pocket of his short jacket, he discreetly flashed a mischievous grin at the seated intelligence officers.

The SCIF's wall of maps was located on the wall behind Bill. Thirty or more 3'X4' aerial maps, which were mounted individually on Styrofoam backboards, rested loosely on three-deep rails that ran nearly the length of the SCIF. Three-quarters of the aerial maps were high definition photos taken from an elevation of 5,000 feet (scale 1:5,000), the remaining photos were taken from 20,000 feet (scale 1:20,000). The higher elevation aerial photos depicted larger areas and weren't used for pinpointing drone targets. With only a couple of exceptions, the maps generally covered the area from Jalalabad, Afghanistan, to Peshawar, Pakistan. None of the maps were labeled, latitudinal and longitudinal markings filled their edges. Those who regularly used these maps were intimately familiar with the photographed locations.

After a minute or so of moving and sliding maps along the rails, Jan focused his attention on one map. "These are the targets in Nangarhar Province, Afghanistan, that the Taliban are focused on," he said as he began to point at specific locations and explain their significance. "This intelligence is current. I received my last report from my head spy, only a couple of hours ago."

"Hold it! How did you receive that report?" crowed Bill, with a note of bombast.

"Cell phone. Why do you ask?"

"That's a violation of our security protocols. That's a crime!" admonished Bill.

Hall cleared his throat and was about to speak when Jan raised his hand and stopped him. He moved closer to Bill and peered down at him. His moments-earlier copper eyes were now angry, black specks. "Bill, I'm a Pakistani. I live in the self-governing Khyber Agency of the FATA. I'm my clan's leader, which means I govern my clan. My security protocols are more cryptic and difficult to penetrate than yours. If I followed your protocols, I would have been compromised long ago and wouldn't be standing over you now. And, just so you know, I kill anyone who even thinks of compromising me!"

Bill's face reddened. He got the message. He nodded his head in understanding and wisely elected to change the subject. He asked, "What's the deal with those maps on the far end of the rails? The ones that are hidden in jackets with OBL written on them?"

Hall rubbed his forehead as he thought. He did not want to get into a protracted discussion with this unknown individual from State regarding Operation Neptune's Spear. This was the highly classified mission that the U.S. military's Joint Special Operations Command (JSOC) planned and coordinated with senior management in the CIA to capture or takedown an individual in Pakistan who they believed to be Osama bin Laden. OBL stood for Osama bin Laden.

Seven months earlier, SEAL Team 6 and other special operation forces spent a little over a week at the Jalalabad Airport, in the very SCIF facility they were seated in, reviewing their plans for the takedown. The covered aerial maps depicted the details of that mission. On the moonless night of May 1, 2011, two MH-60 Black Hawk helicopters, loaded with approximately twenty-five SEAL team operators, lifted off from the Jalalabad Airport and headed to their fateful destination, 180 miles eastward. Osama bin Laden's presumed and unusually large compound—surrounded with twelve to eighteen-foot walls, topped with concertina wire—was located in Abbottabad, Pakistan, less than a mile from the respected Pakistan Military Academy.

Four MH-47 Chinook helicopters took off after the Black Hawks to provide back-up support, if needed. Two of the Chinooks, loaded with fuel bladders and a fast reaction force of SEALs, flew to a desolate staging area northwest of Abbottabad. In the event, any of the teams required reinforcements, the other two Chinooks—carrying addition Special Forces operators—staged in an area on the Afghanistan border.

The plan for the first arriving Black Hawk was a hovering maneuver over the compound while their complement of SEALs fast-roped to the ground. This plan failed when the high walls of the compound created a vortex ring state for the helicopter, and it crashed into the courtyard. It's tail section ended up resting on a twelve-foot wall at a 45°angle. After observing this loss of lift issue affect the first Black Hawk, the pilot of the second Black Hawk wisely decided to land his aircraft outside of the compound.

After these precarious, initial moments, the mission went as planned. Osama bin Laden was present in the compound, and he was killed while resisting arrest at approximately 1:00 a.m. on May 2, 2011. His body was transported back to the Jalalabad Airport and eventually delivered to the USS Carl Vinson (CVN 70) from whence he was buried at sea, somewhere in the middle of the Pacific Ocean. Both of the Chinooks that were standing by outside of Abbottabad were required. One Chinook transported the SEALs, which arrived in the first Black Hawk, back to the Jalalabad Airport, and the other was needed for refueling purposes.

"OBL stands for 'obsolete bombing locations.' We haven't gotten around to putting them in storage. Continue, Jan," said Hall irritably, staring hard at Bill.

Several times during his twenty-minute briefing, Jan asked Bill if he had any questions. He routinely replied with blank eyes that he understood everything. The aerial map that Jan exclusively referred to was a 1:20,000 scale aerial photo of Kashmir, the disputed territory between India and Pakistan. Bill didn't have the slightest idea of what he was looking at. The aerial map could have been of London for all he knew.

"That's it, gentlemen! Any questions?" concluded Jan.

"Yes. I have two comments. First, CIA drone attacks are killing too many innocent civilians," said Bill.

Hall responded. "Do you have specific examples, or are you speaking generally?"

"Generally! Everyone knows this. That can't continue!"

Hall and his SIS colleague blandly nodded, seemingly in agreement with Bill. In fact, his latest comment simply reinforced their opinion that Bill was someone's errand boy. All the countries involved in ISAF operations knew that the Taliban propaganda machine overstated the number of collateral civilian casualties associated with drone attacks. They also routinely misrepresented the terrorist nature of drone-destroyed targets.

Unfortunately, accidents did occur, and innocent civilians were killed, especially during the early years of Operation Enduring Freedom. In those years, inexperienced U.S. and British intelligence officers often accepted the counterfeit intelligence of their Pashtun spies at face value. Nonetheless, and unlike the Taliban and al-Qaeda, innocent civilians and/or schoolchildren were never the target of an ISAF attack.

"I see. And, your second point?" asked Hall, with hooded eyes and a bland expression.

Bill opened his briefcase and withdrew a 3"X 4" notecard with latitudinal and longitudinal coordinates written on it. In his rush to conclude his primary assignment, he neglected to close his hard case briefcase. As he handed the notecard to Hall, he said, "The State Department has learned, from a very reliable source, that there is a clan of violent Islamic terrorists who are preparing for an imminent attack on our embassy in Kabul. The coordinates on this card specify the location of the Taliban compound where they are currently training."

It was evident to Hall and the others that Bill was delivering a prepared speech. They listened patiently.

"Secretary of State Ted Davis wants this compound leveled, and the terrorists killed, by a drone attack, at your earliest opportunity. He doesn't want a repeat of last September 13th's attack on the embassy that lasted for nearly twenty-four hours. He believes that poor CIA intelligence contributed to the success of that attack."

Though Hall's temper flared, he kept his cool. He had a team that was still investigating the September 13th attack. What he was certain of, at this point in time, was that someone from the embassy unlocked the entry gates of the unfinished, twelve-story building—in the Wazir Akbar Khan district—that overlooked the embassy.

"Did you personally meet Ted David?"

"Yup! He and two others."

"Who were the *others?*"

Bill shook his head from side to side.

"You can't say!" said Hall, answering his own question. "I see. We'll certainly give this our utmost priority. Was my boss, the director of the CIA, one of the others?"

"No, he wasn't. David said he had a meeting conflict. Your boss was meeting with one of David's top men from Libya. The guy from Libya was in town for just two days before he flew back to Tripoli. He couldn't reschedule the meeting."

How very convenient! thought Hall. "Did David happen to mention what this *guy* did in Libya?" He expected another 'can't say' answer. Instead, Billy boy couldn't contain himself. His stab at validation, as a State insider, proved to be quite revealing.

"Yeah. His job is buying back missiles that the bad guys stole from Gaddafi's armories. The guy has spent $40 million in the last few months, recovering nearly all of them. I think David said that he's recovered 5,000 missiles so far," said Bill pausing. "David didn't refer to them as missiles, though. He called them MUDPUDS, I think. It was a strange name that

I hadn't heard before. The guy returned to Washington to get more money to buy back 200-300 MUDPUDS that are still missing."

MUDPUDS! Hall's left hand moved over his mouth and jaw in an attempt to hide his smile and restrain his laughter. *Where do they find these guys?* he wondered. Out of the corner of his eye, he could see that his SIS colleague was trying to do the same thing. Bill was referring to MANPADS,* not MUDPUDS.

After his private chuckle, he considered the substance of Bill's comment. His numbers were way off the mark. Before the outbreak of the civil war in Libya, approximately eleven months earlier, it was generally known that Colonel Muammar Gaddafi possessed the most extensive inventory of MANPADS of any non-producing MANPADS country in the world. His inventory was estimated to number 20,000. When the Libyan rebels chased Gaddafi out of Tripoli, last August, his weapons armories fell into the hands of the Libyan rebels. If State had rounded up 5,000 MANPADS, that left 15,000 unaccounted for, not 200-300.

He next turned his attention to Bill's notecard. He silently read the coordinates, 34° 17' 44" North and 71°10'02" East. "Looks familiar," he murmured noncommittally as he handed the card to his SIS colleague, Oliver.

It only took Oliver a second to recognize the location. He looked at Jan and said in Pashto, with just the hint of a smile, "I'll be gobsmacked! We... the CIA and ourselves... have invested millions of dollars into this village's water, electrical, sewer, and communications systems. And to think that they'd turn against! How bloody dreadful!" He then handed the notecard to Jan.

As he read the coordinates, which were of his village, *Zahir Khel,* an unusual America expression popped into his mind. "'You can't teach 'an *old horse* new tricks!'" he said in Pashto.

Keeping the dialog in Pashto, Oliver corrected Jan. "Bloody hell, Jan, it's not a horse...though we do have a horse's ass among us. The expression is, 'You can't teach an *old dog* new tricks!'"

Within weeks of al-Qaeda's terrorist attacks in the U.S. on September

---

* MANPADS is the acronym for *man-portable air-defense system*. Older versions of MANPADS are referred to generally as Stinger missiles or simply Stingers.

11, 2001, the U.S. military and the CIA arrived in Afghanistan. Their goal was to hunt down the perpetrator of the 9/11 attacks, Osama bin Laden, and remove from power the terrorist organization that hosted him and protected him there, the Taliban. The Brits arrived in Afghanistan shortly after the U.S. Both countries, in those early days, engaged well-paid Pashtun spies to provide them with intelligence on al-Qaeda and Taliban activities. Little did the Yanks or Brits know, at that time, that gathering intelligence in Afghanistan was not quite the same clear-cut proposition it was in the rest of the world. For a Pashtun spy, providing accurate intelligence ranked a distant third on his list of spying priorities.

Pashtun spies, except for the Zahir clan, firstly fabricated intelligence in a manner that benefited themselves rather than their employers. They viewed spying as an opportunity to exact justice on persons or a clan who had some time in the past, including past generations, disrespected them. That was *Pashtunwali* payback.

Their second priority, which was nearly as attractive to them as *Pashtunwali,* was to eliminate other spies who they competed against for intelligence-gathering business. This self-serving goal was nothing vengeful like *Pashtunwali*. It was merely a generally accepted business practice in Afghanistan.

The net result, unfortunately, of all this deceit was that innocent parties were sometimes injured or killed. Secretary of State Ted David and Bill were not playing a new game.

Jan guessed that the motivation behind this high-level order was in some way connected to this second priority. Some group, likely familiar with toll collections, had an interest in taking over his Khyber Pass toll collection business.

"What's with the new *lingo?* I don't understand a word your saying," grumbled Bill.

Hall replied, "Jan wasn't familiar with the location of the coordinates. We had to explain a few things to him in his native language, Pashto. We'll take care of this matter."

"You better or *heads will roll!*" said Bill menacingly. With his attention focused on the intelligence officers seated opposite him, he nonchalantly raised a hand to close the hard top of his briefcase.

An instant before his hand reached his briefcase, Jan's hand shot out, and he retrieved a little black box that was secured to the inside corner of the case. On closer inspection, he and the others saw a small hole in the corner of the case. The black box was pointing at Hall and Oliver. Jan recalled that Bill had repositioned the briefcase multiple times during his presentation. At the time, he had attributed its movement to Bill's nervousness.

"What have we got here?" sang Jan as he handed the box to Hall.

Hall popped open the box with the ease and familiarity of someone who had performed the act hundreds of times before. "A micro audio and video recorder. It's the same model we use," he said as he handed it to Oliver.

"Yes, 'same same' as ours. Here's the record button. Hey, it's on! That's a 'no-no!' Just bringing this device into this SCIF is a criminal offense! My guess, Billy boy, is that your days of recording are behind you, and your days in prison are ahead of you. Yessiree, one head will surely roll after this little powwow," said Oliver as he returned the black box to Hall and gave him a ghost of a wink.

Bill's pitiful pleas for the return of his recorder fell on deaf ears. Shortly after that, Hall adjourned the meeting. He held Bill back, however, for a private word. "I, like the others in this meeting, actively spy on others. Spying is my business, and it's a deadly business. You may have thought that your filming and recording of our meeting was simply a minor invasion of our privacy, but it wasn't. Many foreign entities would pay large sums of money for the details that we just discussed and/or the photos you took of us. Those same entities might even be inclined to have us assassinated.

"Our travel plans are kept secret, and we often have heavily armed security agents by our side whenever we're moving about. I didn't personally inspect your briefcase when you entered the SCIF because I trusted you. You get a pass on your stupid and reprehensible actions, but you're not getting your recording and filming back. I'm also going to give you a warning, if you ever pull a stunt like that again on someone not as forgiving as me, it could cost you your life."

Tongue-tied, Bill hurriedly shuffled out of the building.

Moments later, Hall caught up to Jan and asked, "Can you come back at 4:00 p.m. this afternoon for a *real* briefing? Oliver can delay his flight departure."

Jan agreed with a slight bob of his head.

Smiling, Hall added, "I was impressed with your description of Kashmir."

He returned the smile and asked, "I'd like to know more about Bill?"

"I sent his picture to my office in Kabul when he first arrived. I'll fill you in on what they've learned when you return this afternoon."

Jan's head again bobbed.

"By the way, why don't you keep this little black box. You never know when it might come in handy. I've kept Bill's recording tape from the SCIF and replaced it with a fresh tape. You can record up to twelve hours on these tapes," said Hall as he handed the recorder to Jan, along with a new box of tapes.

Mike Hall was born in 1957 in Laredo, Texas, and was the only child of a Green Beret Army sergeant. In 1967, his father was killed in Vietnam. He and his mother scraped out a meager living after his father's death, she as a secretary and he as a part-time auto mechanic after school. In 1978, he graduated from Texas A&M and was concurrently commissioned as a 2nd lieutenant in the Army infantry. His major at A&M was International Studies, with a language minor in Arabic.

Unfortunately for him, his career path—he too wanted to be a Green Beret like his father—literally and figuratively blew up on October 23, 1983, at the Marine Corps barracks bombing in Beirut, Lebanon. He was stationed in Beirut, along with a small number of other soldiers, primarily because of his modest fluency in Arabic. When he was medically discharged from the Army, because of a leg injury he incurred in the bombing, he joined the CIA in April of 1984.

After a Middle East training course at Langley that ended in early 1985, he was sent to a series of Middle Eastern hotspots. First, there was Bagdad, 1985-1986, to investigate the alleged gassing of Kurds. In Iraq, he improved his fluency in Arabic and began to develop a command of Farsi. Farsi came in handy when he interacted with his Iranian contacts. His language skills added much to his value to *the Company,*[*] though it sadly influenced—in his family's view—his itinerate postings. In 1987, he was sent to Bahrain to investigate the Iraqi jet attack on the USS Stark. After that, it seemed to him

[*] "The Company" was an often-used nickname of the CIA.

as if he was a *roving CIA investigator,* which he was because of his language skills and his military background. Additional assignments included stops in Aden, Mogadishu, Riyadh, and Doha.

In 1999, his wife of fifteen years divorced him, not because she didn't love him, but because she was worrying herself to death over the dangers he was exposed to in his hellhole stations. She also couldn't stand his clubby, blueblood superiors who rarely ventured out of the safety of their cubbyholes at Langley, Virginia. She and their two daughters moved from Laredo, Texas, to a small Southern California beach community, Solana Beach, a suburb of San Diego. All three were immediately impressed with the mild climate and the year-round availability of all types of outdoor activities. It wasn't long before his two daughters were attracted to surfing and checking out surfer dudes with long, sun-bleached hair. In the girls' eyes, these surfer dudes were quite an appealing upgrade over their bronc-riding and tobacco-chewing counterparts in Laredo.

... forty-five minutes later

Jan was sitting on a cheap plastic chair on the shabby tar papered roof of his half-built office building. It was a cloudless, clear day with the temperature hovering around 60°F, and just the hint of a breeze. As he took the first sip of a freshly made cup of hot tea, he relaxed and studied his homeland, the glistening snow-covered peaks of the *Spīn Ghar* Mountain Range to the east.

Minutes later, the ring of his cell phone interrupted his reverie. It was a call from Ali. "Malik Zahir, we followed your target to an old warehouse, near the cricket stadium. Two Kabul policemen, who Farid and I know, were guarding the entrance of the building. After your target was frisked, one of the policemen entered the building and returned a moment later with a Diplomatic Security (DS) guard. This guard was stationed at the embassy up until a few months ago when he returned to the U.S.

"We've seen him before. Last April, he was added to a large security team from the U.S. That was strange. This team was protecting two visitors from the U.S., Secretary of State Ted David, and a man from their Justice Department. The team already had too many guards. These important U.S.

men were in Afghanistan for big talks with President Hakim Qazi in Kabul. I think the name of the man from Justice was Smith."

"Smithson."

"Yes, Malik, that's his name."

"You're very observant, Ali." Jan had read the news reports of Smithson and David's visit, last April with Qazi.

"Abdul is a good teacher. He has spent many days with Farid and me in Jalalabad and Kabul. Remembering faces is important!"

"It is, and it's a valuable skill for a good spy. I will speak with Abdul about increasing your responsibilities."

Ali wasn't sure how to respond to Malik Zahir's compliment. His boss, Abdul, never complimented him, nor had any of the other leaders in his clan. He simply said, "Thank you, Malik Zahir. You honor me with your kind words."

"What do you know of these two Kabul policemen?"

"They're Police Chief Safi Khan's private guards. They go with him wherever he travels. They're mean men."

"I see. That's good to know," said Jan absently as a plan began to form in his mind. "When this meeting breaks up, if my target is left behind, bring him to me. No rough stuff. If he asks what you're about, you can give him my name and explain that I'd like to offer him some refreshments and have a private chat with him."

... thirty-eight minutes later

"Malik, we have Bill," said Ali. "When we approached him and explained that you wanted a word with him, he was grateful. The others at the meeting left him alone by the side of the road. That was very disrespectful. He seems to also have an interest in speaking with you. He mentioned a 'black box.' I don't know what that means."

Jan smiled. "I'll explain that to you later. Who were the others?"

"The others... Safi Khan, his two police guards, and the DS guard... headed back to Kabul in an SUV. There was also one other man who left the building. You know him. He's that mullah from Swat, Pakistan, who broadcasts once in a while from the FM radio station in our Khyber Agency."

"Are you referring to Fazlullah?"

"Yes, Malik. It was him!"

Jan considered the implications of that observation. *Mullah Fazlullah, the Islamic militant in the Swat Valley, ordered the shooting of that fifteen-year-old girl—Malala Yousafzai—because she supported girls' rights to an education. He and Hakimullah Mehsud were now the face and voice of the Tehrik-i-Taliban Pakistan (TTP).*

Why was Safi meeting with Fazlullah? TTP was dedicated to overthrowing the Pakistani government. He was aligned with the Haqqani Network, an extension of the Pakistan ISI and the Pakistan government. Or was he? Was the greedy Safi Khan changing sides? And what relationship did these bad men have with a personal representative of Secretary of State Ted David? This was a puzzle with many pieces, he thought while he unconsciously tapped his steepled hands together.

Fifteen minutes later, Jan and Bill were seated opposite one another in the tiny backroom office of the car rental agency. Ali and Farid stood watch outside the soundproof office for security purposes. They relieved Bill of his suitcase and briefcase before he entered the office.

Jan was sitting at his desk, turned away from Bill. He'd shed his more formal attire, which he wore in their earlier meeting, and was now dressed as an unskilled laborer. Fraying tan turban, soiled knee-length white shirt, and a ragged black waistcoat. His crossed legs rested on his desk, and on his lap was the little black box. He was rotating it as if it were a toy. "Bill, thank you for agreeing to visit with me. I think our earlier meeting ended on a sour note."

"Yeah, very sour! I want my black box back. That's U.S. government property."

"That it is, with a very incriminating tape inside. The CIA case officer, Mike Hall, has already spoken to his superiors about your recording in the SCIF. Secrecy is very near and dear to spies. The CIA will contact your Justice Department, and you may be reprimanded." With the mention of the Justice Department, he saw a trace of relief flash across Bill's face.

"Justice will tell the CIA to pound sand," Bill chortled, with a note of triumph.

"*'Pound sand!'* What does that mean?"

"It means that they'll tell them to *fuck off!* Secretary of State Ted David and two of his pals at Justice instructed me to record my meeting with you. They told me that the CIA routinely ignores intelligence from State, NSA, ISAF, and other military commands when it selects its drone targets. They described the CIA *as a rogue outfit* that targets nonthreatening Pashtun tribes and screws up their ability to negotiate a peace agreement with the Taliban and al-Qaeda. This is a test case to see how the CIA responds to a direct order—from the Secretary of State, no less—to bomb a terrorist clan."

Aside from listening to another of Bill's bullshit scripts, Jan did agree with a portion of his canned speech. The CIA did seem to enjoy greater flexibility in selecting and executing drone attacks than either the ISAF or the U.S. military. Though, from the grumblings he'd heard from both Mike Hall and Oliver on the matter, he knew it was far from any type of blanket approval.

"I see. Who provided David with the intelligence on this terrorist clan?"

"I can't reveal that."

"Bill, let me give you a little background on my clan. We're a very poor clan," he began with a note of candor that seemed to initially impress his guest, even though he too was dishing out a line of bullshit. "My clan's survival relies almost entirely on spying fees from the U.S. and Great Britain." Bill was unaware of the Zahir's Khyber Pass toll collection service. "We keep them apprised of what the Taliban are up to locally and what al-Qaeda is up to regionally. If I don't provide my clients with good intelligence, they might employ other clans for their intelligence, and my people will go hungry. Some will likely starve to death. Do you understand what I'm saying?"

"Yeah! I understand. Poverty sucks! But, that's life, and it's not my problem. Give me back that black box, or I guarantee you that you'll regret it."

The tone of Bill's reply was more bombastic than his previous comments in the SCIF. *Perhaps my disguised outfit has emboldened him. He may think I'm a lowly spook for hire,* mused Jan. Realizing that this line of questioning wasn't going anywhere, he changed the subject and asked evenly, "How long have you served in Afghanistan?"

"I arrived here two days ago. In a couple of hours, I fly from here to the Bagram Airfield and then back to the states. I can't wait! This place is a shithole. Now, give me that black box and the tape, and I'll get out of your hair."

Jan leaned back in his chair and rubbed his forehead while he studied the inexperienced and overconfident messenger. After several moments of thought, he abruptly stood, stepped out of his office, and closed the office door behind him. While explaining to Ali his purpose in meeting with Bill, he quickly rifled through Bill's briefcase. One item, in particular, caught his attention. It was an official memo from Secretary of State Ted David to Deputy Attorney General Max Smithson at the Justice Department. Below the memo's instructions were the drone target coordinates and the name of his clan. Smithson had ineffectually attempted to blackout the Zahir clan, likely with a Sharpie that was nearly out of ink.

He thought about the attempted redaction and its implications. *Bill didn't bother to study the redaction. He didn't think it affected him in any way. He doesn't know that my clan is the target of David's proposed drone attack. And David doesn't know that I'm one of Hall's top spies. Plus, Smithson likely instructed Bill to simply provide Hall with the target coordinates. Other than those who wirelessly sent a drone its target parameters, Smithson couldn't imagine that a senior intelligence officer…especially one like Hall, who oversaw all the U.S. counterintelligence operations in Afghanistan… would ever have the time or interest in familiarizing himself with specific latitudinal and longitudinal coordinates. He obviously didn't know Hall very well!* thought Jan as he sniffed at the negligence and carelessness of both Smithson and Bill.

He turned his attention back to Ali. "My visitor is keeping secrets. He's not telling me anything. He leaves Jalalabad in two hours. What would you do?"

"I think he's a messenger who has no understanding of our history or our ways. I also think he overestimates his importance in someone else's plan. His superiors likely selected him for this errand because he is expendable. If you only have limited time to get information from him, I would employ the *finger option.* I think that will loosen his lips. After that, the final step is up to you, Malik Zahir," said Ali respectfully.

"My thoughts exactly! I was thinking of offering him money for his information, but I don't like him, nor do I trust him. Get the pruning shears," ordered Jan as he folded David's official memo and slipped it into a jacket pocket.

Moments later, Ali and Farid followed Jan into the office and closed the door behind them. Farid took up a position behind Bill. Ali placed the shears—plus an additional tool, a hatchet—on the desk, while he leered at Bill.

In Pashto, Ali curiously asked, "Malik, what is that red spot on his jaw?"

"I think it's a birthmark. It's not contagious. Don't worry."

Meanwhile, the muscular Farid was rolling up the sleeves of his shirt. He was familiar with this form of questioning. Once his sleeves were rolled up and his legs spread, he nodded at Malik Zahir. He looked like a football middle linebacker preparing himself for an opponent's quarterback sneak, feet from their goal line.

Ten minutes later, after modest coaxing with the shears, Bill had divulged all he knew. Though he didn't know who provided the coordinates of *Zahir Khel* to David, he did reveal the identities of the two men who had engaged him for his trip to Afghanistan. They were Deputy Attorney General Max Smithson and the head of the criminal division at Justice, Charles Hightower, Jr. The fee for his international assignment was $25,000.

With just a minor skin break, on the pinkie of one hand, Jan additionally learned that Hightower's father—the president of VA Trucking—had secretly placed trackers on all the fuel trucks he sold to the ISAF or their contractors.

When Jan questioned Bill about Mullah Fazlullah, he had little to offer except that he'd overheard the mullah speak with the DS guard, in stilted English, about taking over Khyber Pass toll collections and his need for a more secure home for his Tehrik-i-Taliban Pakistan clan (TTP). With pursed lips, he unconsciously rubbed the palms of his hands together as he considered the implications of that information. The pieces of his puzzle were gradually coming together.

Before Ali and Farid returned Bill to the Jalalabad Airport, Jan offered him some parting advice. "Your little black box! You're not getting it back. Especially since I taped your latest *tell-all confession* of a few moments ago. I now have two of your conversations on tape." In reality, he only possessed Bill's latest confession, but Bill didn't know that. Jan paused for several moments to let the significance of that comment sink in. "It would be unwise and unhealthy for you to disclose to anyone—like David, Smithson, Hightower, or Safi Khan—what you just told me or what I found in your briefcase."

"My briefcase! You went through my briefcase. That's against the law. That's personal information!"

Jan rocked back in his chair and laughed. After a time, he collected himself and said, "I left your pornographic magazines in your case. But, Bill, you should know that possessing pornographic materials in a Muslim country is a major crime. If the Taliban or al-Qaeda caught you with those magazines, they might kill you on the spot."

Bill squirmed in his chair.

Just then, Jan's cell phone vibrated. It was an email from Hall, which he quickly perused. He continued, "The only item I removed from your briefcase was this official State memo from David to Smithson. It's an interesting read," he said as he withdrew the memo from his pocket and waved it in front of Bill.

His face turned gray.

"Yes, I understand your worries. At the bottom here, it says, 'read and destroy.' You should have done that. I think that's what you call an *oversight!*" he said, returning the memo to his pocket. He correctly believed it might have some future value.

"Please don't tell anyone about that. If my bosses find out about this, they'll kill me!"

"Ah, killing! Good point! When you return home, you shouldn't presume that you're safe! I have well-paid operatives in the U.S." To add emphasis to his closing bluff and threat, he showed Bill the screen of his cell phone, which displayed Hall's recent email in Pashto. "Can you read it?" he taunted with a smile.

Bill shook his head. The parade of wiggles and waggles was indecipherable.

"I didn't think so," continued Jan. "It's written in Pashto. It says that your full name is William Tidwell and that you are a planner for VA Trucking. It also says that you're twice divorced and live on Sandpiper Court in Newport News, Virginia."

Bill's face turned from gray to nearly white. While he sat frozen in place,

Jan grabbed the hatchet and violently swung it into the desktop, burying its blade a half-inch from Bill's forearm. "If your friends plan more attacks in this area, I better hear from you first!"

After Ali escorted Bill out of the office, Jan read a second email that had just arrived on his cell phone. It was from Beena Waleed. She was confirming their dinner plans for that night at a small restaurant in Jalalabad, which was run by one of his spies. She also added a cryptic note about Qazi's minister of finance, Jamee Nabi. Nabi was investigating the New Hope Girls School savings account at CityTrust in Kabul. The current balance of the non-governmental organization's (NGO) account, she noted, was $872,000.

He quickly sent back a confirming email that instructed her to ignore the *closed for repairs* sign on the restaurant's entrance door and to knock loudly on it when she arrived. The two of them would enjoy a private dinner together, absent the possible busybody censure of Afghan males or the black-hearted curiosity of a Taliban informer. He next closed his eyes and held his head in his hands as he thought. *Were his toll collections and the New Hope Girls School savings account somehow connected? The only common thread between the two seemed to be the greed of Afghanistan's leaders. Or, was there more to this unusual puzzle?*

PART 3

(108 days later)

WASHINGTON, D.C.

2012

CHAPTER 9

THE 2012 PRESIDENTIAL CAMPAIGN

The White House | Oval Office
April 2, 2012 | Monday 9:47 a.m.

PRESIDENT JED ADAMS sat comfortably in one of the two small couches that faced one another in the Oval Office. His walker was off to the side. Sitting opposite him, on the other couch, was his best friend in Washington and the current vice president, Tim McCracken. Adams was dressed casually in gray slacks and a white dress shirt, open at the neck. McCracken was more formally dressed in a dark blue suit, white dress shirt, and silk foulard tie, with repeating U.S. flags. Physically, both men looked like they each had one foot in the grave.

Adams's sickly complexion was the result of his stage-three Parkinson's disease. His right hand held his left wrist firmly in his lap. The tremors in his left hand and the left side of his body were worsening. His doctor, the in-house physician to the president, strongly advocated more tests. He rightly assumed that other factors were affecting the president's rapidly declining health. Adams repeatedly refused his well-meaning recommendations.

In Tim McCracken's case, his pale demeanor was not related to his health, but to that of his wife's. She had complained of lower back pain since last February. She initially attributed her back pain to vigorous yoga exercises. But when she began to vomit in mid-March, Tim decided it was time she see her doctor. Two weeks later, she received her prognosis, stage four pancreatic cancer. With accelerated cancer therapies, she might survive a year. Without painful therapies, her best-case life expectancy was six months. She chose, despite her husband's urgings, the latter option. Neither Tim nor his wife had apprised anyone about her condition.

"I'd ask you how your weekend was, but I have a sense there is something more important on your mind. You look you've been on the losing end of a bronc ride. What can I do to help you?" began Adams, with his warm Texas accent.

McCracken took a deep breath and stuttered, "Jed…Jed…" before his head dropped into his hands and he began to quietly cry.

McCracken had been his vice presidential running mate when he'd been reelected to the presidency a little over three years earlier. Before that, he'd been his attorney general for four years. He was his "go-to" ally and political advisor for all manner of issues. McCracken finished third academically in his undergraduate engineering class at the University of Michigan. Upon his graduation from Michigan, in 1979, he was commissioned as a 2nd lieutenant in the Air Force. In the Air Force, he was fulfilling his life's dream of becoming a fighter pilot. His achievement, unfortunately, came to an abrupt end when the F-15 (single-seat) aircraft he was flying— during an adversarial training exercise—was involved in a mid-air collision with an F-16 (two-seater). The new, overly aggressive F-16 pilot was found to be responsible for the collision, a collision that sadly resulted in his death and that of his navigator. McCracken incurred a severe eye injury during the accident when his canopy was shattered. His impaired vision eventually resulted in his medical discharge from the Air Force.

He returned to the University of Michigan as a law student. This time around, he finished second in his class. After multiple stints, as an attorney and senior counsel with large defense firms, he eventually accepted a position in the Justice Department. Service to his country was a more appealing option to him than bigger bucks in the private sector.

As Adams's attorney general, McCracken exhibited little compassion for U.S. attorneys whose political aspirations and/or greed superseded their primary responsibilities to the U.S. government. Nor did he ignore the wayward activities of his in-house Justice Department attorneys. During his four years at Justice, he had three U.S. attorneys disbarred and sent two of his junior attorneys to prison. The U.S. attorney disbarments involved accepting bribes, tax evasion, and the non-disclosure of a business relationship with a defendant. All three pled out to lesser charges and paid large fines.

Unlike his three U.S. attorneys who were disbarred—they were each in their mid-forties and knew they had crossed-the-line and committed crimes—McCracken's two junior attorneys at Justice were of an entirely different making. They were each in their early thirties and were assigned to an administrative section of Justice. Neither of them had any litigation experience, nor did either of them manage any other Justice employees. He had, on several occasions, issued them written warnings concerning their misleading communications with scores of U.S. attorneys—regarding Justice and the government's position on sensitive legal matters—and their propensity to publicly comment on Supreme Court decisions. When the two publicly announced together that they, and a majority of their colleagues at Justice, disagreed with a recent, high profile U.S. Supreme Court ruling—a ruling that Justice fully supported and enforced—McCracken suspended them.

When he learned, in a subsequent investigation, that the two had each received $10,000 for their showboat performance on the steps of the U.S. Supreme Court building, and that they had leaked confidential and highly classified details of the case to their news media protagonist, he charged both of them with crimes.

Both attorneys felt that their legal interpretations of the U.S. Constitution were more open-minded and "in sync" with the times than those of the high court. Neither attorney felt inclined to plead to lesser charges. Why would they? Popular opinion would protect them from the laws of the land. Furthermore, they were now in the limelight, virtual rock stars! TV stations begged them for live interviews, and newspapers printed their legal opinions on the front page of their national news sections. They were the new legal darlings of non-originalist constitutional interpretation. Once they were found guilty of their crimes, they still didn't understand their predicament. Was this some form of millennial delusion? No one would ever know.

At their sentencing hearing, they both expected—at the very worse— a perfunctory slap on the wrist and an admonishment *not to do this again* spiel. But, whether one is right or wrong, arrogance and the absence of remorse doesn't play well in a serious courtroom setting. Nor did the fact that both of them weren't particularly bright attorneys who possessed very little understanding of federal laws and their sworn duties at Justice. The presiding federal judge issued them maximum sentences and sent them to jail.

With much physical effort, Adams pushed himself off his couch and shuffled around the coffee table that separated him from McCracken. He plopped down on the couch beside his friend and massaged his back as he whispered, "Let them tears run!" The man who had supported him through thick and thin didn't come unglued over minor matters.

As tears began to roll down his friend's cheeks, he reflected on the political battles that they'd fought together. One of McCracken's unique skills, which he prized above all others, combined his encyclopedic memory with his down-home, plainspoken speech. McCracken often employed this skill in the White House news briefing room, typically a day before a close congressional vote on major legislation. He'd waltz into the briefing room—unannounced, even to his colleagues—and recite a poem, a famous saying, or a nursery rhyme. It disarmed his adversaries and roused their curiosity. What was McCracken up to now?

A smile filled Adams's face as he recalled McCracken's last, spur-of-the-moment briefing room appearance. It was 9:00 a.m., and the briefing room was packed with reporters. A majority of them were in a near out-of-control frenzy. They wanted to crucify Adams and his administration for his opposition to what they believed was a very humane and reasonable spending bill for senior citizens. Those who qualified would receive free walking aids.

McCracken began his presentation with a big smile and a quote by Confucius, "He who does not economize will have to agonize!"

His quote marginally calmed the reporters. He asked, "Who knows how long this proposed spending bill is?"

"In pages or words?" asked one reporter.

"Either one is fine."

There was silence. McCracken knew damn well that 90%, or more, of the reporters who sat before him, hadn't taken the time to read the bill. Their jobs and promotions depended on *scoops*. They didn't have the time or interest in reading proposed legislation. That was a job for their interns, or at best, their research staff.

He next withdrew a $100 bill from his wallet and waved it at the reporters. He began with flattery. "I would like to challenge this very good looking and erudite group!" He knew his sweet talk wouldn't change anyone's position on the bill, but it was a far better opening gambit than criticism. "This $100 bill goes to whoever proves that they're the most familiar with this bill. Forget about the bill's length. That's a tough question. For those of you who are inclined to 'wing it,' I wouldn't recommend that. I have a few more qualifying questions. Let's see a show of hands from those 'in the know!'"

Ten hands shot up. A small smile creased his lips. *The game was on.* Eight were "shoot from the hip" grandstanders. "Excellent, ten of Washington's finest reporters! Please stand." After the shuffling of chairs and the straightening of hair and clothes, ten reporters stood. "Because you're standing, I trust that you've read the bill or at least skimmed it. If you haven't, please take a seat." After a couple of modest grumbles, two sat. All the grandstanders remained standing.

"The formal title of this bill is on its front page. What is the title?" asked McCracken.

Four reporters offered the generic name of the bill that had been bandied about in the newspapers. He had them sit. The remaining four shook their heads. They didn't have a clue. He was zeroing on his objective.

"OK. You're honest! For that, I'll let you four remain in the game." He reached under the podium and withdrew a copy of the actual bill. He dropped it on the top of the podium and answered his original question. "From the what-it's-worth department, the bill contains 82,198 words and is 308 pages in length. President Adams and I have read it.

"The final question for my four contestants is," continued McCracken smiling, "what group of individuals receives the most benefits from this spending bill? By that, I'm referring to the percentage of the overall spending. And I'll give you a hint. It reflects over 50% of the bills total spending." Two reporters sagged into their seats. The two standing sensed a ruse but didn't move.

"Your answers please!" said McCracken as he rapped his fingers on the podium in drumroll fashion.

"Medicare seniors who can't afford the monthly Part B insurance get free wheelchairs or walking aids," replied one.

The other replied, "They don't have to be seniors on Medicare. The age threshold is fifty, but they have to pass a modified adjusted gross income analysis."

With a bright smile filling his face, he said, "You're both wrong. However, the $100 bill goes to the reporter who knew that they didn't need to be seniors on Medicare. The correct age threshold is fifty-five, not fifty. Congratulations!" An instant later, the loser began to complain. Just what he expected. "Want another chance?"

The loser nodded vigorously. The other reporters were reminded of McCracken's affability. He was a nice guy.

"OK," he said, as he removed his wallet again. He withdrew ten $100 bills. He upped the ante and, in the process, was gradually lessening the reporters' level of emotion. He knew that a factual debate, a day before the big vote, didn't stand a chance against highly charged emotion. It would be viewed as little more than whining. He also knew that he was vicariously battling the vested egos of newspaper editors-in-chief and TV station heads who supported the bill. All of their reporters towed the company line, or they were fired.

"What is your best guess of the percentage of this bill that goes toward wheelchairs and/or walking aids? And, you have to be within 10% of the correct answer. The winner gets $1,000!"

"40%!" excitedly said the former loser.

"25%!" said the other reporter.

"So sorry, you both lose again. The correct answer is 12%. The other 88% is—" he began before pausing. Turning to a young lady, who'd just entered the room with a package in her hands, he said, "Let it fly!"

She tossed him a package of pork links. McCracken deftly caught the package with one hand and tore it open. "Pork!" he exclaimed as he began to grind the pork links into the document. "88% of this bill is for earmarks, and 12% is for walking aids. This bill is the epitome of *pork-barrel spending.* Both major parties should be ashamed of themselves. President Adams and I are both card-carrying members of the American Party. We've proposed alternative legislation that eliminates pork and requires that 90%, or more, of the bill's funding be specifically directed to walking aids.

"Furthermore, those medical manufacturers who so generously underwrote the lobbying efforts of this bill… under the well-established *quid pro quo* traditions of the Congress… will be prohibited from selling their equipment to the U.S. during President Adams's remaining term in office. In the fine print, he and I were able to decipher these manufacturers' pricing schemes. It was disgusting reading. An off-the-shelf lightweight wheelchair that can be bought in any drug store in the country for around $100 was priced at $300.

"He who tries to loot gets the boot!" closed McCracken, as he flashed his engaging smile and coolly marched out of the briefing room.

The next day the spending bill was defeated. A week later, Adams's proposed bill was presented for consideration. Four months later, it was passed by both houses and signed into law.

McCracken cleared his throat.

"Sorry, 'Pardner!' Just thinking about some of our prior battles. Tell me what's troubling you."

"My wife …Chloe has stage four pancreatic cancer. The docs estimate she's got two to six months left before it takes her. For the little time that she has left, I'm going to spend every minute of it with her. I'm resigning. I'm sorry, Jed," blurted McCracken.

Adams patted McCracken's back. "You have nothing to feel sorry for. I wouldn't have expected anything less from a man like you." He then sat back on the couch and said, "I've turned off all the recording devices in the office. What we discuss next is just between you and me."

"Uh-huh!"

"I don't think I have Parkinson's."

McCracken stiffened and straightened himself. "Are your symptoms improving? Are you feeling better?"

A modest smile creased Adams's weathered face, a face that would make Willie Nelson's look like a newborn babe's. In his typically deliberate and gravelly speech, the president began to make his point. "As you know, I grew up on a hot, desolate cattle ranch in southern Texas that was better suited for horned lizards than long-horn cattle. Aside from minding cattle, I took an interest in watching the other animals on our ranch. We had horses, rabbits, pigs, one mule, a couple of dogs, and usually one or two stray cats." Adams paused as he organized his thoughts. Not only were his muscles going to hell, but his brain wasn't as razor-sharp as it once was. "All animals, even two-legged ones like ourselves, have a sense of when they're dying. When the light began to dim in the eyes of those ranch animals, and they started wandering off into the sagebrush, or one of their secret hiding places, I knew they were nearing death."

McCracken interrupted Adams. "Jed, Chloe isn't kidding herself. She knows her days are numbered."

"I'm not talking about Chloe. I'm talking about myself. I'm pretty damn sure I don't have Parkinson's. I think the docs misdiagnosed me. I have ALS, Lou Gehrig's disease. That's why I've put off my physician so many times. I know I'm dying!"

"Uh...uh...Jesus H. Christ!"

"Exactly. So, with what little time, I have left...let's see if we can put together a plan that's best for the country... rather than what's best for the Democratic or the Republican parties."

McCracken nodded and said, "Realistically, I don't think our American Party idea is going to survive the next election."

"Nor do I. But, your resignation may be a positive."

Adams had already given the matter quite a bit of thought. After several long moments, he said, "Ted David's political star rose in California because the liberals loved his looks, and he made unsustainable pension promises to state workers. That's how he was elected to the U.S. Senate. It certainly wasn't based on his accomplishments in the California State Senate, which were nil. When I brought him into my bipartisan cabinet, I hoped his charismatic appeal would help me advance the virtues of our American party. I now know that he's nothing more than an unimaginative, self-centered phony. His friends and advisors tell him what to say."

"What are you thinking?"

"Ted David moves from secretary of state to your post as vice president."

"Say what! You just said he was a phony. I don't get it!"

"Yes, he is all of that. But, if I've learned one thing, after serving two terms as president, it's that a politician's looks and smile are more important than the fiction they spout. David also possesses a quality that the news media loves... loose lips! That's a winning combination."

"Uh-huh! So, how can he help us? It's no secret on the 'Hill' that he's going to return to his Democratic party and run for the presidency in the coming months. The 'Dems' feel strongly that he can win the presidential election next November," said McCracken.

"I know, but the Republicans are going to make it a close race. If we play our cards right, Pardner, we may be able to keep some of our visions for the American Party alive."

Their visions for their party were focused on the best interests of moderates, the majority of Americans. It was a political party—unattached to special interest groups—that advanced socially and fiscally conservative programs. A medical safety net for the indigent poor, far-sighted and measured immigration reform, and benefit plans for congressmen that were similar to the plans of a majority of Americans. American Party supporters recognized the passage of ever-increasing, self-serving congressional benefit plans for what they were… a *me first dividend!*

The Democratic and Republican parties each alleged that they represented a majority of Americans, but in many ways, they didn't. Both parties were anchored to the political ways of the 1960s, or earlier. Elevator operators in the Rayburn building, sexual abuse claims quietly settled by the Office of Compliance, and enforced deference to your party's senior members whether it was warranted or not. Historically, over 200 congressmen—from both houses of Congress—had logged thirty years or more of service in Washington. And over half of them had served more than forty years. In the early 2000s, when smoking was still permitted in congressional cloakrooms, the selection of chairmen to key committees was based on seniority, not performance. Little has changed since. Many of today's chairpersons, with a few exceptions, had mentors who served in Congress in the 1930s and 1940s. Some of those mentors were good, decent congressmen. Some were narrow-minded dinosaurs. And others were outright thieves.

For a newly elected congressman in 2012, his or her primary priority—on day one in office—was to fundraise approximately $2 million for their political party within the next six months. Six months was an important juncture for each party because if the freshman congressman couldn't accomplish that goal, within that timeframe, their value to their party was suspect. What a wonderful and time-honored way to introduce fresh minds, with fresh ideas, to Congress.

Over the next thirty minutes, Adams reviewed his reasons for appointing Ted David to the vice presidency. Firstly, he'd heard from multiple intelligence sources that David had a secret, offshore savings account that had rapidly grown in the past couple of years. It appeared that he was using the power and influence of his office at State to make money on the side. If they could uncover evidence of his wrongdoings, he might be controllable.

Secondly, there was no questioning David's ability to dazzle and mesmerize voters of all shapes, sizes, and intellects. At fifty-seven years of age and six feet in height, he was physically fit with an athletic build and a swarthy complexion. A full mien of slightly wavy and graying brown hair, coupled with inviting, smoke brown eyes, and a big smile suggested to many that he had future in Hollywood, should he ever leave politics.

With his stamp of approval on moderately conservative legislation, he could likely sell it to far left legislators who didn't want to unnecessarily cross swords with the leader of their party. Therefore, if Adams and McCracken could somehow shoehorn Lena Jones into David's 2012 presidential ticket, as the vice presidential nominee, she could hopefully carry the torch of the American Party.

Lena Jones was the Justice Department's first Afro-American and first female to fill the position of associate attorney general, the third-highest post in the department. She was also a registered Democrat who shared Adams's vision of the American Party.

In light of McCracken's surprise resignation, and his fast-fading health, Adams realized that his hopes for a David-Jones presidential ticket were now subject to a tight timeline. Several agreements needed to be settled before McCracken officially resigned, in the next week or so. Their first hurdle was to sell David on taking the post of vice president. The *carrot* would be his visibility and his ability to run for president while holding the prestigious position of vice president. Per the Hatch Act, only sitting presidents and vice presidents could campaign for a position in a partisan election, while other executive branch employees could not. In David's current position as secretary of state, he'd have to resign from State before he could commence his presidential campaign.

There was also the matter of an ironclad understanding attached to David's appointment to the vice presidency. In the unlikely *event* that anything *unforeseen* befell President Adams, like dying—during his remaining ten months in office—David would ascend to the presidency, which would again leave the post of vice president vacant. David would have to agree, prior to his appointment as vice president, to nominate Lena to his vacated vice presidential post. Adams and McCracken would naturally understate, or neglect, any discussion of *unforeseen events* when they pitched their idea to David.

David's ascendency to the presidency, and Lena's to vice president, would occur under the provisions detailed in the 25th Amendment of the U.S. Constitution. In the aftermath of President John F. Kennedy's assassination, this amendment was enacted by Congress to cover procedures covering the replacement of the president or vice president in the case of death, removal, resignation, or incapacitation. It had only happened once before during the Nixon administration. Gerald Ford assumed the office of vice president of the U.S. on December 6, 1973. The following year, on August 9, 1974, he ascended to the presidency when Richard Nixon resigned from office.

While all these health and political matters were unfolding, Adams would quickly and quietly dig into David's illegal activities. In his previous life as a wildcat oil driller in Texas, he'd experienced his share of disappointing dealings with unethical individuals, namely crooks. He'd learned two hard, expensive lessons from those dealings. Firstly, crooks surrounded themselves with other crooks. And, secondly, crooks were driven by greed. They would double-cross or reveal incriminating evidence on their ringleader, at the drop of a hat, if it meant a little extra booty for themselves. If caught in the act of a crime, they also wouldn't hesitate to spill the beans on their ringleader, if it resulted in a little less time for themself behind bars. Therefore, he needed hard evidence on David's illegal activities, and he knew just the person to call for such an assignment. His longtime friend, Mike Hall—from Martin High School in Laredo, Texas—was now the CIA's station chief in Kabul. Nearly all of David's deposits in his secret savings account originated from Afghanistan.

Incontrovertible proof of David's criminal activities would ensure that David kept his promise to appoint Lena to the vice presidency, *and* that she became his Democratic vice presidential running mate. It would also provide her with the *stick* she could use to secretly direct David's presidency be it for months or four more years. All of these occurrences were, in Adams's view, manageable and achievable, save for one. This was an election year. Come November 6, 2012, voters would decide the future fate of the David-Jones presidential ticket.

CHAPTER 10

LENA JONES

Robert F. Kennedy

Department of Justice Building, 5ᵗʰ floor

Office of the Associate Attorney General

April 2, 2012 | Monday 11:28 a.m.

LENA JONES CALMLY sat in her leather office chair as she impassively listened to the overwrought individual who sat before her. Had this meeting been video recorded and the sound muted, it would have appeared that she was being reprimanded for committing a violent crime.

Her visitor, Charles T. Hightower, Jr., was a deputy assistant attorney general who managed one of the most high profile sections in the Justice Department's Criminal Division. His section—one of six in the Criminal Division—handled matters related to organized crime, gang crimes, capital cases, and special prosecutions.

"FBI wiretap applications are none of your goddamn business. Keep your nose out of that," said Hightower as he became more agitated and repeatedly stabbed a pointed finger at her.

Lena was undeterred. With an arched eyebrow and a hint of a smile, she continued to prod and probe. "What about your email correspondence with the FBI regarding sketchy wiretaps?"

"Same thing. Stay away!"

"I see! Is there anything else I can do to make your job easier?" she asked, with a smirk.

Hightower didn't recognize her sarcasm. "No, except that I'm going to have a word with your boss, Smithson, about your meddling in criminal matters."

Ah-ha, a threat at last! She wasn't surprised, but she was intrigued with his reply. Austin Knight, the assistant attorney general for the Criminal Division, was Hightower's immediate superior, not Smithson. Usually, one didn't bypass one's immediate superior at Justice and speak directly with his boss's boss unless the two enjoyed a special relationship or were chummy. In this case, she suspected it was a little of both.

This seemingly informal and casual rapport Hightower maintained with Knight and Smithson fueled her suspicion that they were the parties at Justice who were encouraging others to stray from the letter of the law. This trio enforced laws and administered justice as they "saw fit." *Saw fit* meant their enlightened interpretation of federal statutes and laws, irrespective of the intent of those who created them… Congress and the president. Their *saw fit* doctrine also ignored the history of how laws were conceived, modified, and improved. They denigrated the entire law-making process. Why? Because these self-styled movers and shakers couldn't imagine, nor accept, that their holier-than-thou interpretation of laws was anything but appropriate and long overdue.

Lena's dad was a retired sergeant from the Emeryville, California, Police Department. He'd put in thirty hard years on the job in a city, adjacent to Oakland, that often had the highest per capita crime rates in the entire San Francisco Bay area. After listening to his accounts of the nonsensical application of some laws, and the even more preposterous conduct of some defense attorneys—all while she shared the same household with him for twenty-six years—she had no sympathy whatsoever for those who committed serious crimes. And even less sympathy for bleeding-heart hypocrites who opposed laws and police behavior that they, in their sanctified opinion, viewed as oppressive. As her dad said to her a thousand times, *Guess who will scream the loudest when they're mugged on a dark street?* In the blink of an eye, the cop hater who spat on cops at a rally the week before now expects immediate and preferential treatment.

This trio, or *conspiratorial troika* in her opinion, fell into that same knee-jerk category as the hypocrites, with one major exception. They significantly influenced how laws were applied. When one read about double standards or two-sets of laws, that wasn't fiction. That was a reality, especially in Washington.

"How do you feel about our former Attorney General, Garret Cutler, being held in a Mexican jail?" probed Lena.

"That's a fucking national disgrace," howled Hightower. "Allowing Mexico to incarcerate our sitting attorney general is unconscionable!"

"Former, not sitting," corrected Lena. "And, per our treaties with Mexico, they have every right to incarcerate a foreigner who they believe has violated their laws."

Hightower's angry eyes narrowed at the woman who initially reminded him of the Hollywood beauty, Halle Berry, and now reminded him of that judge bitch who had him spend a night in jail for a contempt of court sanction.

Lena elected to test the sincerity of Hightower's theatrics. "I'm surprised that his imprisonment has upset you so. I thought you'd be pleased. I heard that you and he hated one another in law school and that that carried over into this department. Didn't that have something to do with him nosing you out for the presidency of your school's *Law Review* publication?"

"Fuck you!" he barked.

Lena stood and calmly strode to her office door. She opened it, returned to her desk, and coolly leaned back in her office chair, with her interlocked hands resting on her chest. The broad-shouldered former All-PAC-10 gymnast with bright almond eyes knew that Hightower had a short fuse. *Perhaps the silent treatment will push him over the edge. If he loses his temper, everyone on the floor will have a better understanding of this prick's real character.*

Hightower was blessed with energetic patrician facial features that were framed with a full head of black wavy hair. Luminous hazel eyes added to his overall allure, especially for women. He'd played football for one year at the University of Virginia, as a fullback, and was a foot taller than Lena's height of five-foot-three.

Lena fully understood most women's initial attraction to the stately looking forty-five-year-old. However, after interacting with him at Justice during the last year or so, she'd become well aware of his shortcomings. Chief among those flaws was his absence of common sense, his lust for power, and his propensity to exploit his good looks in his relationships with women.

He'd recently knocked up an attractive twenty-five-year-old, junior attorney at Justice. If they were to marry, she'd be his third wife and would bear his fourth child. But, he balked at marriage and support for the child, contending vehemently that he wasn't the father. Paternity tests proved otherwise, according to intra-office gossip.

Hightower next pressed his ex-girlfriend to get an abortion. She declined, and he became even more vehement. So much so that the young mother-to-be successfully filed a restraining order against the father-to-be. In light of the restraining order, and the genuine threat of harm to the pregnant woman, it would have usually ended his career at Justice. But these were not normal times. He had the support of several heavyweight attorneys at Justice. And, he was the only child of a very wealthy Virginia family who enjoyed close ties with several very senior legislators in Washington.

Hightower's parents lived in Poquoson, Virginia, not far from the Newport News shipyard. The family's wealth was derived from its ownership of VA Trucking, which was one of the largest privately owned trucking companies in the U.S.

During the silence, Lena's mind drifted back to December 2010, sixteen months earlier. Her approval to her post of associate general attorney—the third-highest post at Justice—passed by the slimmest of margins in the Senate. Despite her hybrid political beliefs, in the socially conservative American Party, she was ruthlessly quizzed about unsubstantiated and planted rumors that she felt were flat out insulting. To an outsider, it would have appeared that the Senate was interrogating the embezzler of a widows and orphans trust fund or a child molester.

Particularly galling to her was the Senate's final vote on her confirmation. Every senator dutifully and mindlessly cast their vote exactly along their party lines. *What then was the purpose of all the vitriol that was slung at her during her hearings?* Her critics, she bitterly learned, had no interest in learning the truth or looking out for the country's best interests. All of their words and actions were solely crafted for two purposes alone, to smear her and make them look good!

The confirmation of a new attorney general, to replace Garret Cutler, was proving to be an even more contentious process than hers. After twenty months of Senate dickering and dithering, the post still remained vacant. Some of the dickering was likely related to the circumstances surrounding Cutler's incarceration in Mexico and President Adams's seeming disinterest in attempting to extradite him back to the U.S. In light of this impasse, the president turned to his vice president, Tim McCracken, to manage Justice on an interim basis. McCracken had preceded Cutler as the attorney general.

In the case of former Attorney General Garret Cutler—a brilliant and unassuming moderate Democrat, according to the mainstream media—he was arrested by Mexican President Carlos Ortega in August of 2010 while visiting Mexico City on a supposedly mundane Department of Justice legal matter. In rapid succession, Cutler was charged with and convicted of masterminding a bizarre U.S. gunwalking scheme based on evidence that mysteriously fell into the hands of Ortega. The indisputable evidence included damning video and audiotapes of Cutler, and unidentified U.S. accomplices, planning and implementing the scheme. According to Mexican court records, Cutler's scheme was in some incomprehensible way going to result in the downfall of all of Mexico's drug cartel kingpins, and the significant reduction of drugs into the U.S. All this harebrained scheme accomplished, according to President Ortega, was to further arm the drug cartels in his country with thousands of U.S. semi-automatic rifles. Rifles that were used to continue killing tens of thousands of innocent Mexicans.

Media coverage of the case filled the airwaves, in both countries, for weeks. The big unanswered question to those viewers, and especially Democrats on the Hill, was… how was this damning evidence gathered without their knowledge. Highly classified and sensitive investigations were just labels. They held little meaning to both major parties. Perhaps the better question was, who delivered the damning evidence to him? Lena smiled inwardly with that knowledge while she watched Hightower squirm in his chair.

After a time, she decided her silent treatment had runs it course. It was time to move on. She set her elbows on her desk and leaned toward Hightower. Slowly, and very deliberately, she began to explain to him one of her principal goals in life. "Let's talk further about Cutler and his incarceration in a Mexican jail, which you feel is a national disgrace," began Lena with the penetrating and angry look of an eagle. "There were only two people in all of Washington who knew what Cutler was up to. The FBI stashed those two individuals in a Georgetown *safe house* while they examined the hard evidence of his gunwalking scheme. Someone from the FBI leaked the location of that safe house to an unknown person at Justice. That bastard, Hightower, then passed the safe house location on to a Mexican drug cartel kingpin. That kingpin was the one who provided the mega-funds to persuade Cutler, and others, to execute their crazy gunwalking scheme," said Lena with eyes that bored into Hightower.

Beads of sweat began form on his forehead, and he was shifting nervously in his chair.

"Do you follow what I'm saying?"

"Uh-huh," he mumbled.

"Once this kingpin was apprised of the safe house location, he ordered a team of assassins to kill its two occupants. As you well know, Kelly Mills and I were the two occupants. This was the second attempt on our lives," she again paused.

Hightower was now nervously and unconsciously chewing his fingernails.

"The day before we moved into the safe house, an assassin's gunshot wounded Kelly, and my next-door neighbor was killed by a car bomb that was meant for me. I survived the assassins' second attempt, Kelly didn't. You knew Kelly. She was Attorney General Garret Cutler's executive assistant. Their office suite was only a couple of doors down the hall from here."

Without breaking eye contact with Hightower, Lena stood, moved to the front of her desk, and folded her arms. She rested her hips against her desk and leaned toward him until she was inches from his face.

"If it takes until my dying days, I will find out who in Justice passed the safe house location on to that Mexican drug kingpin. Kelly and I were best friends!" With that declaration, she saw Hightower's eyes widen for an instant and betray a secret. In poker circles, it was known as a *tell*. She knew then that if he was not the perpetrator, he was somehow involved.

Uncontrollably, she then smashed the folded knuckles of her right hand into his chest. His eyes popped, and she heard the air escape from his lungs. He momentarily lost his breath. "Lastly, don't ever point your finger at me again, like you did earlier, or you'll regret it! Now, get out of my sight. You disgust me!"

After taking a moment to catch his breath, Hightower rose and moved to the door.

Dr. Mary Phillips stood in his path, blocking the doorway. She'd taken up a position there not long after Lena had opened the door and was impressed with her boss's interface with the pompous Casanova from the floor below. She obviously had no difficulty communicating with those who were twice her size and half as smart.

After a brief stare-down of Hightower, Mary cheekily inched to the side to let him pass. Turning back to Lena, she said, "You'd scheduled an 11:00 a.m. meeting with me. Are we still on?"

Lena stared at her new colleague and smiled. She'd transferred in from the State Department forty-five days earlier. In no time, the two had forged a friendly and trusting relationship. They were approximately the same age, both single and each possessed advanced educational degrees.

Lena held both her undergraduate degree and her Juris Doctor degree in law from the University of California, Berkeley. Mary held a doctor of philosophy degree in Central Asian Culture and Religion from the Harriman Institute, Columbia University, New York City.

"Let's get together after lunch, say 1:30 p.m. if that's OK with you? I've fallen behind on a report that I have to get out," Lena said.

"That works for me."

"Good. I'd like to go over with you some of the Afghanistan election law reforms that I've been thinking about. And, I'd like to get your latest take on what's happening in Afghanistan, particularly from a State and embassy point of view."

"Can do! I know the good and the bad. See you at 1:30 p.m."

"Great," said Lena tentatively. "On second thought, how about we do a walking-talking meeting. It's a beautiful day, and the cherry trees are in full bloom. We'll walk-talk down to the Tidal Basin near the Jefferson Memorial. Do you have walking shoes?"

"Yup."

"Let's meet in the Great Hall entry foyer then at 1:30 p.m."

Mary nodded and left.

... one hour and forty-five minutes later

Lena and Mary headed casually towards the exit of Justice's Great Hall, which was framed with a pair of twenty-foot doors. When they were feet from the doors, two large men, walking side-by-side, entered the building and immediately made a beeline for them. The two approaching men looked like a wall of professional football blockers. In this case, it was an overweight fullback coupled with a wide-bodied guard. The fullback was Hightower and the wide-bodied guard—with no neck—was the deputy attorney general, Max Smithson. They were returning from lunch, and, from the smell of their breath, they had partaken in more drink than food.

"Lena, Lena, Lena!" slurred Smithson disparagingly.

Lena smiled demurely but didn't respond.

Turning his eyes to the blonde who stood beside Lena, Smithson asked, "Who is this comely lass?"

"Max, this Dr. Mary Phillips. She recently transferred from State to Justice. She's going to assist my legal team in Kabul. As you know, Justice is helping the Afghans reform their election laws. She's served in Kabul on several prior occasions and speaks fluent Dari and Pashto."

Smithson rolled back and forth on his heels while he thought. His meaty face and beady black eyes studied Phillips. He recognized that name, but couldn't quite place the context. Finally, his mind cleared, and he said, "Ah, yes! I was in San Francisco several weeks ago for a fundraiser for Ted David, your former boss at State. He mentioned to me that one of his senior Foreign Service officers, a real looker he said, balked at returning to Kabul for an assignment. She couldn't handle the stress in a war zone, poor baby, and was going to transfer to a *cush job* at Justice. That's you," said Smithson as he jerked his thumb in Mary's direction.

When Lena saw Mary stiffen, she gently and imperceptibly placed a restraining hand on her forearm. She was all too familiar with Smithson's off-the-wall remarks that were solely intended to unnerve an adversary.

Switching subjects, Lena asked innocently, "A fundraiser for David? Were you the premier speaker?"

"Not at all! Some high-tech nerd spoke about the future of the Internet. I was there asking for money. I raised millions," he said boastfully. "As the secretary of state, David can't officially campaign for election to a partisan political office. He'll probably resign from State in the next couple of months and fully concentrate on the primaries and his run for the presidency. In the meantime, 'Ole' Max has seen to it that his campaign war chest is well funded. I've raised over twenty million dollars for his primary campaign. David is going to be the next president of the United States, and guess who'll be his attorney general?"

Lena caught the eye of a nearby, friendly reporter who was standing in the lobby. She raised a questioning eyebrow in the reporter's direction.

The reporter smiled, raised her cell phone, and wagged her index finger in a circular motion, which indicated that she was filming and recording the conversation. Political appointees of the president, particularly those whose appointments were subject to Senate approval— like Max's post as deputy attorney general— were subject to federal fundraising restrictions, per the Hatch Act. In short, they couldn't use the influence of their office to solicit political contributions at any time from anyone.

Lena discreetly flashed the reporter an approving wink.

"Ole Max" was many things, but he was not an idiot. He knew he wasn't allowed to fundraise, but, in his "heart of hearts," he didn't care. He was *a big deal* in Washington who liked to flaunt his power.

"I have no idea who'll be the next attorney general," replied Lena innocently.

"Ole Max! I've already lined up, for David, the support of every high-tech, bigwig in Silicon Valley. If I were you, I'd start sprucing up your resume. Same for you, doc!"

A crowd of attorneys and reporters was now beginning to gather around the four. "Oh, my gosh. What should I do?" replied Lena in an exaggerated tone.

"For starters, you should keep your nose out of matters that aren't any of your damn business!"

"What kind of matters?"

"Wiretaps are none of your goddamn business!" interjected Hightower in garbled speech.

Lena flashed them both an ingratiating smile, which added fuel to their escalating contempt. Their red faces became redder.

"He's right. That's not your department. You oversee civil stuff, non-violent matters. Me and him take care of the bad guys, criminal matters," crowed Smithson.

"And how is that going?"

"Perfect! Smooth sailing," he said.

"And, what about the gunwalking into Mexico in 2009 and 2010 that your criminal division accommodated. And your U.S. Attorney in Phoenix conveniently overlooked. And your buddy in the FBI mishandled. And your overly ambitious ATF manager implemented. That's what you call smooth sailing!"

"Go fuck yourself!" whispered Smithson, none to quietly.

The reporter and two nearby bystanders recorded his expletive on their cell phones.

A moment later, he added, "You report to me! I want to see you in my office in thirty minutes!"

"Since when do I report to you?" asked Lena, with another composed and demure smile that pushed Smithson over the edge.

"Since for goddamn forever!" he barked.

The number of listeners surrounding the four was now six to seven deep. All of them heard and recorded Smithson's last comment.

"You have obviously forgotten the acting attorney general's instruction to both of us less than a month ago."

"'Wuz' that?"

"Until a new attorney general is confirmed by the Senate, we both directly report to Vice President Tim McCracken, the acting attorney general. Under normal circumstances, you're #2, and I'm #3 in Justice's hierarchy. But, under McCracken, we're equals! Now, if you'll excuse me, Dr. Phillips and I are going to enjoy an outdoor meeting. We're headed to a quiet bench, near the Jefferson Memorial. We'll be discussing election reforms in Afghanistan, which, as you know, falls under my Office of Justice Programs."

The color of Smithson's and Hightower's faces were now verging on purple, and perspiration wrung the collars of their shirts. Smithson opened his mouth and was about to make another inappropriate comment when a third man, Austin Knight, vaulted into the group. Assistant Attorney General Knight for the Criminal Division was Hightower's immediate boss and the third member of this Justice troika. He grabbed Smithson and Hightower and did his best to physically drag the two toward a private Justice elevator. The image, Lena thought, was like watching a VW beetle tow two Humvees.

The private elevator was reserved for those senior Justice officials located on the fourth and fifth floors. As the elevator doors began to close, with the troika inside the cab, two other men raced toward the elevator. They arrived a second too late. Mary recognized the smaller of the two. She didn't know his name but remembered seeing him—with his distinctive red birthmark on the right side of his jaw— at State's headquarters in the Harry S. Truman Federal Building. He came and went from the building at odd hours of the day, and he always used the secretary of state's private elevator, which serviced Ted David's palatial, 7th-floor office.

She'd never seen in person nor met the second man, but she had an idea of who he was. Beena Waleed had sent her a short note and out-of-focus photograph of a clan leader and his granddaughter, Emma, after she'd set the young girl's leg in a cast at the Red Crescent Clinic in Jalalabad. The man in the photo was a good six-feet tall with broad shoulders. The individual before her possessed those features plus he had the countenance of a leader—high cheekbones, thoughtful eyes, and a well-trimmed brown mustache and beard. Beena's note had also mentioned that this clan leader had dealings with State and the CIA.

The man's attire added a further clue to his identity. He was dressed in a formal, knee-length, dark green silk jacket (kurta style), which featured intricate grey embroidery. On his head, he proudly wore an ornamental and well-preserved green-gray Afghan lungee turban. Only clan leaders wore that type of turban. This was Jan Zahir, the leader of the Zahir clan in the Khyber Agency of Pakistan's FATA. The photograph Beena sent her didn't do him justice. He was a much more regal and powerful in person.

Mary left Lena's side and hurried up to Zahir. She knew Lena would want to distance herself from the lobby and the reporters. And Zahir's escort likely didn't want anyone to speak with his Pakistani visitor.

In Pashto, she said, "I'm Beena Waleed's friend. We operate the New Hope Girls Schools together. If you're Jan Zahir, I would like to speak with you in private. Where are you staying?"

He leaned forward and cocked an ear in her direction as if he was hard of hearing. He then whispered rapidly in Pashto. "The Washington Marriott, 22nd Street, Northwest. My hosts—Smithson and Hightower at Justice and David at State—don't want me to speak with any outsiders. I'm glad you recognized me. I also want to speak to you. I trust Beena, and she trust's you. Now leave, I'm going to pretend to insult you." He suddenly straightened and brushed the palms of his hands back and forth in a cleansing, dismissive manner, as he said in understandable English, "Go! Leave me alone! I'm here to speak with men, not women."

... *minutes later*

Once Lena and Mary were several blocks from Justice, headed toward the Tidal Basin, Lena turned toward her friend and asked, "Who was the man you spoke to with the turban?"

"He's Jan Zahir, a clan leader from Pakistan's FATA. I've never met him before, but I recognized from a photo Beena Waleed sent me. As you know, Beena and I are the founders of two all-girls schools in Afghanistan. In terms of preferred terrorist targets in Afghanistan, all-girls schools don't rank far behind Western military targets. Having a clan leader like him on our side is invaluable. I've also heard that he's a valued ally of our CIA. He allegedly provides them with lots of intel on Taliban and al-Qaeda activities."

"I see. If he's tight with the CIA, why then was he headed to the private elevator that serves the senior officials at Justice?" asked Lena. After a moment of reflection, she added, "The shorter guy with your friend seemed to know Smithson and Hightower."

"I picked up on that as well. I don't know who he is, but I do know that he uses the private elevator at State when he visits Ted David. As for his and Zahir's business at Justice, I haven't a clue."

"Interesting!"

"Zahir whispered to me where he's staying in Washington. I'm going to contact him. I'll let you know what I learn."

Lena again turned toward Mary, this time with a new level of respect. "That was one helluva act you and he pulled off in the lobby. I got the impression he didn't want anything to do with you."

"That was the point. If you spend enough time in foreign countries, being sneaky becomes second nature."

"Hmm," grunted Lena. Switching subjects, she added, "Thanks for your help getting rid of those junior reporters who suddenly appeared and were following us to the Tidal Basin."

"Being bitchy with reporters is another trait I've developed overseas. Being nice is a sign of weakness."

"Other than that one senior reporter that I recognized in the Justice lobby, the rest were all strangers. A couple of years ago, I oversaw the reporters in the White House press room. They were, for the most part, very senior reporters," said Lena.

"I was in Afghanistan then. I remember hearing something about a media ombudsman in the White House. Was that you?" asked Mary.

"Yup! I was the first one. It was a 'transparency experiment' of President Adams's. He hoped it would improve the public's view of his administration and the major news media."

"Did it work?"

"It did…at first. Before my appointment, I was an NBS reporter covering the White House. So, I personally knew most of them. The majority of them were hard-working, trustworthy individuals. But, like everything else, there is always that 10% that screws things up for the other 90%. *Screw-ups* are everywhere in Washington. They're in Congress, the executive branch, and even the judicial branch."

"How would you describe screw-ups?" probed Mary.

"Are you setting me up? You've worked in Washington, on and off, for over twenty years. You know how things work here."

Mary smiled and said, "Yes, I do know how things work in this *Power Capital of the World*. And, I am well acquainted with screw-ups, though I refer to them as *assholes*. I'd like to hear your thoughts on them."

Lena thought for a moment before responding. "Screw-ups come in all shapes, sizes, and disguises. So, it's impossible to generalize about them. Screw-up clues, however, include their work habits, their personal history, and their ego. With those qualifications in mind, I'm not particularly trustful of those who abuse booze or drugs. Those who have a history of physically or verbally abusing their spouse, kids, or coworkers. Those congressmen and senators who are too lazy to carefully examine, or even read, the pros and cons of an important legislative matter and instead mindlessly frog-march to the beat of their party leaders. That goes for the news media and voters as well who are too close-minded to research voting issues. They all have brains! They should use them!"

"You left out ego!"

"Self-serving egotists, in my view, fall into two categories. Loudmouth wannabes and blatant bullshitters. A wannabe boasts about his or her *visions*. They typically have no record of accomplishment in either the public and private sector, and their visions are just that… dreams! They're easy to identify.

"Blatant bullshitters, on the other hand, are more insidious and difficult to identify. There is often a sliver of truth in what they profess. For example, America is a country of immigrants. We all came from another country. Does that mean we should have open borders and welcome everyone and anyone who comes to our shores? No! This is 2012. Our country has changed since the first English settlers arrived in Jamestown in 1607. But, to listen to some of our holier-than-thou politicians talk, or scream, you'd think nothing has changed. An updated and more pragmatic immigration policy is a worthy goal. Open borders is a pipedream," said Lena as she temporarily digressed. Returning to her original point, she added, "There are a lot of bullshitting politicos in Washington, and they're not confined to any one party."

Mary nodded. "I feel the same way about screw-ups. Tell me about the White House press corps? How did you get along with them?"

"I was like a judge who daily presided over a courtroom. My daily mantra was that news is based on facts, not suppositions or opinions. I had to constantly remind the reporters that if they were going to broadcast or publish suppositions or opinions, they had a duty to their viewers or readers to apprise them of that. Most of my challenges involved TV reporters. Whereas newspapers have an editorial section devoted to opinions, the major TV networks—perhaps because of the time constraints on their broadcasts—don't usually make a distinction between facts and opinions. They don't see anything wrong with coloring a news report with an opinion."

"Make any enemies?"

"I alienated a lot of hardline reporters along the way. The hardliners, those that are biased toward the Republicans or the Democrats, have a weird view of life."

"How so?"

"They feel that their party leaders can do no wrong. They're do-gooders, all the time! And, if any of those leaders do stumble in some obvious way, they have a difficult time accepting that. It's as if they were personally attacked. It's unusual behavior if you ask me," said Lena.

"I know what you mean. They have a sense of guilt or shame as if they were partially to blame for their leader's offense."

"Yes. It's like a victim's guilt or survivor's guilt. There is often an inexplicable level of self-blame. Victims of an assault often reason that if they had gone to the library before the grocery store, then they wouldn't have been mugged. I understand their thinking, but they shouldn't feel any self-blame. Shit happens!" said Lena.

"Shit does happen, and none of our leaders are perfect!"

A few minutes later, they found a quiet bench on a secondary walkway in East Potomac Park, a couple of hundred feet northeast of the Jefferson Memorial. It was a sunny afternoon, with the temperature in the mid-70s°F and light winds of 5-6 MPH. Cumulus clouds dotted the cobalt blue sky, and the cherry trees, with their pink petals, softened the earth. The waters of the 100-acre Tidal Basin undulated peacefully. Hundreds of visitors idly strolled along the wide sidewalk that bordered the basin, transfixed with the beauty and meaning of the place. Others sat quietly on the marble stairs of the memorial that overlooked the Tidal Basin. When the wind stirred a bit, it looked as if the heavens were blowing a blizzard of pink snowflakes across the park.

Mary thought aloud. "How can we discuss depressing world realities in such a magical setting as this?"

Lena nodded in agreement.

The two sat quietly together as they savored their idyllic setting.

After a time, Mary spoke. "Back in the Justice lobby, you didn't seem the least bit intimidated with Smithson. Can he make life difficult for you?"

"We've had professional run-ins before. He doesn't scare me. Anyways, he'll be out of Justice within the week."

"Because of his language or behavior?"

"Nope! Smithson's influence with the major news media will cover up that crap. He'll get nailed for his fundraising comment. Under the Hatch Act, executive branch employees, especially bigwigs like Smithson, are prohibited from using the power and influence of their office to solicit campaign donations."

"Do you think he'll eventually return?"

"Possibly. It's a presidential election year. Adams can't run again because he's already served two terms. McCracken will be carrying the American Party torch next fall during the presidential elections, but unfortunately, his party...err, my party too... doesn't have the resources to advance their moderate message across the country. I see Secretary of State Ted David getting the nod as the Democrats' presidential nominee and General McMillan as the Republicans' nominee." Lena paused for a moment to organize her views of both prospective candidates.

She continued, "General McMillan is a popular, plain-talking individual. A pragmatist! I like him. He reminds me of General Colin Powell. And, he reflects a socially conservative message, which is similar to the American Party. Ted David is a political animal to the core. I had several dealings with him in the 1990s when he was the U.S. Senator from California, and I was a senior attorney with the American Civil Liberties Union (ACLU) in San Francisco. This was years before I became a reporter for NBS.

"At one time or another, he held opposing positions on just about every major issue in the state. Whenever he delivered a speech in person, no one knew what he'd say or which side he'd take. That is unless you polled the crowd beforehand, which is what he always did."

"He concerns me in two ways," began Mary. "Firstly, he's been consumed with urging regime changes across the Middle East. Islamic leaders—primarily those associated with the Muslim Brotherhood—have convinced him that if they ran their various states, the civil and human rights of their citizenry would improve dramatically because they know what's best for them. Them being the Muslim majority. David's bought into their hype *…hook, line, and sinker!*

"In the short time that these fundamentalist Islamic leaders have been in power, particularly in Libya and Egypt, it's become evident to the citizenry that what's best for their leaders doesn't translate to what's best for them. Living conditions, job opportunities, better housing, healthcare, clean water, and fundamental human rights have taken a backseat to strict Sharia Law. And, life for non-Muslim believers in those countries, like the Coptic Christians in Egypt, has gone from bad to worse.

"Secondly, and this jibes with your comment about David's obsession with popularity polls, he and his close pals—the secretary of homeland security, the new deputy director of the FBI, and Smithson at Justice—are all sucking up to the far left by redefining the meaning of terrorists and terrorism. *And its improbable association with Islam.*"

Lena's head snapped towards Mary. Her comment about terrorists' association with Islam touched on a sensitive subject. She was a staunch supporter of all Americans' freedoms, be they related to religion, lifestyle, or whatever. "Improbable association with Islam! Explain!" said Lena with a clear edge in her voice.

Mary understood Lena's response. It wasn't the first time, nor would it be the last time, that a highly educated individual—unfamiliar with daily life in an Islamic country—questioned her view of Islam.

"OK, this may take some time."

"I have all the time in the world for this, Mary," replied Lena stiffly.

"How would you compare our King James Bible, the Hebrew Bible, and the Koran?"

"All three books lay out the basic tenets for Christianity, Judaism, and Islam."

"Wrong on Islam!"

After a time, Lena added, "I think the Koran has supporting tenets in the Summa."

"Warm. I think you mean the Sunna."

"Yeah, the Sunna."

"*The Koran* is God's, or Allah's, message to Mohammed revealed to him through the angel Gabriel, over twenty-three years. If you believe that

Mohammed was a prophet of Allah, you're a believer. The Sunna prescribes the way of Muslim life. There are two collections of texts or books that make up the Sunna. One is *the Sira,* which is basically the biography of Mohammed. The second is *the Hadith,* which is the recorded sayings or actions of Mohammed.

"The Hadith describes the traditions that should guide Muslim life. These three books—the Koran, Sira, and Hadith—make up what is referred to as the Islamic Trilogy. Approximately 50% of the text in this trilogy addresses non-believers. Under Sharia Law, non-believers have no rights or freedoms. And a fact that surprises most uninformed advocates of Islam is that the Koran comprises only 15% of the overall trilogy text. Are you with me so far?"

Lena nodded.

"Good! For me, the Hadith is the most significant part of the trilogy because it clearly describes the *dos and don'ts* of Muslim life. The don'ts under Sharia Law include no dancing, no alcohol, no freedom of expression, no cartoons that belittle Mohammed, no freedom of worship, no friendships with non-believers, etc. Sharia Law defines a Muslim's rights and freedoms like our Bill of Rights. Ergo, Sharia Law fundamentally crosses the line between church and state. We separate the two. They combine the two.

"Many of the Muslim practices that we read or hear about today are found in the Hadith, not the Koran. Muslims turn toward Mecca and pray five times every day. The Koran specifies three daily prayers, the Hadith five. And, when Mohammed lived in Mecca, he instructed his followers to pray toward Jerusalem. In Medina, he instructed them to turn toward Mecca.

"What I'm getting at is this. If you elect to research Islam further, you'll find there are two distinct interpretations of Islam. The Meccan Koran is a benign, *earlier* version of Islam. The Medinan Koran is a violent, *later* version. Thus, you have a colossal Koranic contradiction until you get to the rule of *abrogation,* which is found in both Korans. Simply stated, abrogation means that the *latter version of the Koran is better!*

"In Mohammed's early years in Mecca, I view him as a start-up preacher pitching a new religion. In those early days, his words fell on deaf ears. After he was forced to leave Mecca for Medina, he changed from a peaceful preacher to a violent preacher-dictator who ruled with a very heavy hand.

For example, stealing from local Medina merchants and their caravans was an accepted practice of his followers. And, when a rift developed between his followers and a local tribe of Jews, he had 500-800 Jewish males beheaded.

"During my early years in college, I held a naïve view of Islam. After spending most of my last twenty years posted in the capitals of all the major Middle Eastern countries, I've seen who 'rules those roosts' in those countries, and they aren't disciples of the benign Meccan Koran. Seeing and experiencing first hand the application of strict Sharia Law is not a pretty sight. I detest it! I'll loan you my copy of *Sharia Law for Non-Muslims*. Form your own opinions," closed Mary with a relaxed, but confident smile.

Lena didn't respond to Mary's closing. Privately, however, she liked the way Mary described Islam. There was no forced-feeding involved. Firebrand disciples of a cause or movement who tried to sell their singular view of a subject with pedantic and overbearing arguments never impressed her. She would take Mary up on her offer and read *Sharia Law for Non-Muslims*. And, she would form her own opinions.

She looked at her watch and grimaced. "I've got to get back to the office. I was hoping to learn more about Afghanistan and our State activities there. Say, I've been asked to organize at informal Easter dinner at the White House this Sunday. If you're available, why don't you join us? We can continue our discussions then."

"The White House! Are you sure I'd be welcome? Won't there be cabinet secretaries and other bigwigs there?"

"Not a one! There will be, of course, President Adams and Vice President McCracken …each with their wife…plus a handful of friends. Most of these *friends* were involved in the shutdown of 'Operation Fast and Furious.' Hook DeLuca, the ATF whistleblower of that fiasco…now, an FBI agent and a good friend of mine. Annie Youngblood and her husband, Bobby Ridger. Annie will be your special aide …think kick-ass protector… when you return to Kabul next September. And lastly, Brice Miller, he graduates from Annapolis in a couple of months. President Adams and his wife, Becky, are like Miller's second set of adopted parents. It'll be a small, intimate group."

"I'll be there. Thanks for thinking of me. In the meantime, I'll also see if I can dig up my copies of Khaled Hosseini's books, *The Kite Runner* and

A Thousand Splendid Suns. You'd enjoy reading those books. They present an excellent picture of both the goodness and cruelty of Afghans."

"I've already read them. Those stories are heartbreaking. Why would you suggest I read them if you oppose Islam?"

"I don't oppose goodness. I do oppose a religion that doesn't tolerate other religions. And I do oppose religious zealots, like Islamic fundamentalists who discriminate against women, tout jihad, and support corporeal laws—like beheading— for non-believers. In the Hadith, you can substitute the word *slave* for woman. Islam is more than a religion," said Mary with a level of vehemence and emotion that was clearly evident.

It was apparent to Lena that Islam's view of women upset her friend. "Let's sit for a moment, relax and enjoy the setting before we head back to the office," said Lena as she patted Mary's hand in a calming manner.

A minute later, the screeching stop of a vehicle—a couple of hundred feet behind them—interrupted their reverie.

Lena said, "I think the sounds of the real world are calling us. Perhaps it's time to leave."

As they both turned away from one another to collect their bags that rested beside them, an earsplitting rifle shot pierced the tranquility of their paradise. A millisecond later, the back of their wooden bench exploded. Both women were knocked to the ground with the impact of the blast. Wooden splinters peppered their arms and backs. They lay stunned on the gentle downward slope before them. A hail of gunfire followed, disintegrating the bench and chewing up the ground around them.

Mary turned to Lena, with eyes wide but focused and determined. She saw her boss lying in a prone position facing the shooter. Gripped in both her hands was a lightweight Sig Sauer P238 handgun. It was the same model her dad carried when he went on his backcountry hikes. She knew it held a seven-round magazine of .380 ACP ammo. She personally preferred and owned a 9 mm Ruger LC9 handgun, which was idly sitting in her gun safe at home.

"This son-of-a-bitch won't stop until he's on top of us. We need some cover. I'm going to fire a couple of shots at him to slow him down. When I do, let's get behind those trees on our left."

Long seconds later, the two were huddled tandem behind the trunk of a large tree. Rifle shots thumped into the tree's trunk, and chunks of turf erupted around them. The shooter was utilizing suppressing fire to protect his steady advance.

"I think the bastard is carrying an M4 with a thirty round ammo clip. I got a decent look at him when we moved," said Mary.

"We're dead meat if he's got more ammo than that," said Lena with a note of resignation. She knew their options for escape were limited. After ducking another round of gunfire, she said, "If you move behind that tree, twenty feet further to our left, it may distract him and give me a better shot at him."

"Got it! It's now or never. Nice knowing you!" shouted Mary over the sound of rifle shots as she sprinted to the tree. After a wild headfirst dive behind the tree, she realized that the cacophony of gunfire had ceased. All she heard was the pounding of her heart.

Behind her, she saw smoke drifting from the barrel of Lena's handgun. Taking a careful peek, from behind the tree, she saw that Lena had hit their attacker. He was rolling in the grass, away from his rifle. What she saw next froze her beating heart. "Shit, a second shooter," yelled Mary.

Without a second thought, she jumped to her feet and raced to the first shooter's discarded M4. Seconds later, she grabbed the M4 and dropped into a prone shooter's position. Looking up, she saw that the second shooter—150 feet away– had discarded his rifle and was fiddling with a very visible suicide vest, filled with explosives.

The man stopped and stared at Mary. He then turned toward the Jefferson Memorial. His eyes settled on a group of panicked school children—another 150 feet away—who were huddled around their teachers, crying and screaming. An evil smile curled his lips as he began to sprint toward them.

Mary yelled at what she guessed was a sixth-grade teacher. "Run! He's a suicide bomber." Her warning did little to disperse the kids and teacher. Terror froze them all in place. She took several calming breaths and aimed at the bomber's bouncing back. *Shit, this was the second time that she'd be in this same do-or-die position. Please God, don't fail me!* One shot, a second shot, then an empty click.

CHAPTER 11

HOOK DELUCA

Medstar Georgetown University Hospital Washington, D.C.

April 3, 2012 | Tuesday, 9:12 a.m.

ANTHONY "HOOK" DELUCA stepped out of the elevator onto the fourth floor of the hospital and was greeted by a wall of men. Four men were attired in business suits, two others were dressed in full tactical gear with M4 rifles slung across their chests.

"Secret Service. State your business and raise your arms to the side," said the humorless man closest to him.

"I'm FBI Special Agent Anthony DeLuca to see Lena Jones. She said I'd be on her approved visitors' list. She's expecting me," said Hook as a second man patted him down and removed his sidearm.

"Keep your arms to the side. Where are your FBI credentials?" asked the second man.

"Inside pocket of my windbreaker, left side. Is Lena OK? Has something happened?" he asked, worried by the high level of security. He was thirty-six-years-old and casually dressed in gray slacks, a light blue polo shirt, and a tan windbreaker.

While the second man was reviewing his credentials, a seventh man emerged from a hospital room, fifty feet further down the corridor. He wore an FBI windbreaker similar to DeLuca's. "Stand aside men. DeLuca is on her list. Lena Jones will make a visual confirmation."

A moment later, Lena's head peered around the door jam, and she smiled. "Hook, I'm just finishing up a discussion with a friend. It'll only be a few more minutes. Relax and have a coffee."

After Lena's visual confirmation, the humorless agent said, "You're cleared to visit her, but we have to retain your sidearm until you leave the hospital."

"Got it! Vigilance is good. I like that. Is the extra security related to yesterday's bombing?" asked Hook.

The humorless agent didn't reply.

After a long moment of silence, Hook moved to a nearby makeshift coffee station. After removing his windbreaker and tossing it over his shoulder, he poured himself a half-cup of coffee, sat in a folding plastic chair, rested his head against the wall, and closed his eyes. A week earlier, he'd been assigned to the FBI's Terrorist Screening Center. The center was shorthanded, really shorthanded, which meant he'd gotten about twelve hours of sleep in the past four days. He was awakened from his instant slumber by a gentle shake of his shoulder. It was Lena. She was wearing casual weekend attire, rather than a hospital gown.

After yesterday's shootout near the Jefferson Memorial, Lena and Mary expected a brief exam at the hospital before they were discharged. That didn't happen. Once the doctors removed large wooden splinters from each of their backsides—their attacker's first shot shattered the bench's wooden backrest—the hospital staff ushered them into an FBI secured, two-patient suite for "overnight observation." Their overnight stay in the hospital had more to do with their safety than the monitoring of their health.

"Come with me. I'd like to introduce you to my friend."

"Is this the blond bible-thumper that everyone in Justice is talking about, Mary Phillips?"

She admonished his wisecrack with an angry glare. "Hardly. She's in an empty hospital office somewhere, making phone calls. And she's not a bible-thumper! She has a doctoral degree in culture and religion."

"Same, same," he replied saucily. "By the way, what's the deal with the Secret Service agents. Is it related to yesterday's bombing? Are you a VIP now?"

Lena flashed him another look of censure as she waved him into her room. An instant later, his lethargy and wiseacre demeanor dissolved. Lena's friend was Vice President Tim McCracken.

"Tim and I have been discussing the vice presidency," smiled Lena with an unreadable expression.

McCracken had just filled her in on her role in President Adams's goals for the Ted David-Lena Jones presidential ticket. He'd also apprised her of Mike Hall's part in the plan.

Hook's eyes narrowed, curious about that subject. *Discussing the vice presidency? What was there to discuss about that. It was what it was!*

McCracken interrupted his thoughts when he extended his hand and said, "I was looking forward to meeting you at our White House get-together eighteen months ago. We were celebrating the disclosures you made that shutdown the ATF's gunwalking scam. If I remember correctly, you couldn't make it because you were reorganizing the Phoenix ATF office."

"Yes sir, Mr. Vice President," replied Hook officiously as he studied the solidly built man who gave him a firm handshake. At a tad under six feet in height, he possessed short sandy blond hair, a chiseled face, and clear blue eyes. His face and overall bearing reminded him of his long-ago company commander in the Force RECON Marines. Tough, no-nonsense, and trustworthy. His face was also free of the alcohol-induced red spider veins that were commonplace amongst men in their mid-fifties in Washington.

"Please call me Tim in informal settings like this, especially when we're amongst friends."

"OK, Tim! I go by Hook," he smiled as he traced his facial scar, which was the source of his nickname. It began near his left ear and curled along his jawline to within an inch of his Adam's apple. "This was the result of a knife fight I had with two hajjis in a dark alley in Fallujah, Iraq, in 2004. I was a lucky, young Marine!"

McCracken next traced his visible Air Force mark, a half-inch scar above his left eye. "A show-off, newbie F-16 pilot inexplicably turned into my F-15 and shattered my canopy. So much for our pretty faces!"

The two veterans, and Purple Heart recipients, felt an instant bond.

Hook continued with an explanation of his ATF management effort in Phoenix. "The ATF office in Phoenix was a mess. I eventually turned things around and turned over the management of the office to my former partner, Dan Weathers. He's got the office running like it should have been. I transferred out of the ATF into the FBI with the help of Lena, and I think you. Thank you for what you did for me," said Hook with a heartfelt note of sincerity.

McCracken wagged his head knowingly. When the head of a large department, in the public or private sector, fell from grace because of the disclosures of a whistleblower, the well-intentioned informant found himself dealing with a new set of problems. Fellow colleagues, who had tied their professional futures to their former leader, were often out for revenge. Hook's gunwalking disclosures ruined the careers of senior officials in not only the ATF but also the FBI and the U.S. Attorney's office.

"Change is good for all of us. I have a few more minutes and am going to refresh my coffee. I'd like to hear what you're doing now," said McCracken lightly.

After McCracken stepped out of the room to refresh his coffee, Hook looked at Lena. "Are you all right? Christ, I can't believe what happened yesterday to you, Phillips, and those school kids at the Tidal Basin."

"I'm physically OK. The docs removed several large splinters from my back, then sewed me up with just a couple of stitches. Mary required a couple of stitches as well. The shooter didn't hit either of us, and the bomb explosion was too far away."

"And psychologically?"

Lena turned away from Hook and moved slowly to the side table beside her bed. She grabbed a Kleenex from its box and slumped onto the side of the bed. With her back to Hook, she wiped the tears from her eyes and blew her nose. "I don't like getting goddamn shot at! And those poor kids…" she sniffled.

Just then, McCracken stepped back into the room. He'd been standing outside of the room, by the open door, and had overheard much of their conversation. His face was flushed with anger. "I don't like you getting shot at either. This is the third time you've been attacked while on my watch. Two dickhead terrorists waltz up to the Jefferson Memorial, in our goddamn capital. They try to shoot you and Mary Phillips, and they succeed in killing three innocent 6th graders with a fucking bomb. That is goddamn disgraceful and intolerable!"

Lena nodded dolefully. "Let's sit and talk about other things." After rearranging three chairs in a half-circle, they settled themselves, and Lena looked at Hook. "I would like to hear how things are going for you at the FBI. Personally, I thought you'd be at Fort Bragg in North Carolina undergoing some sort of paramilitary training."

"You want the long or short version?"

"I vote for the long version. I need to calm down before I say or do something I'm going to regret. I can't tell you how angry I am about yesterday's tragedy," grumbled McCracken.

"The news coverage has also bothered me," added Lena. "Lots of finger-pointing by congressmen and senators about our administration's lax national security."

Hook sat stiffly in place, unsure how he should proceed.

He wasn't a particularly big man at five-foot-eight, but he exuded a forceful presence. A presence that was accentuated by his wide shoulders, muscular forearms, black hair combed straight back, and classical Roman facial features that included a slightly downturned nose. And of course, there was the matter of his facial scar. It projected a sort of swashbuckling pirate persona, which appealed to him.

In light of McCracken's and Lena's present state of mind, he decided to ease into a description of his two assignments of the last month. His first assignment involved cross-training at the Department of Homeland Security (DHS). His second assignment, as of a week earlier, involved a promotion of sorts and stand-in responsibilities at a special desk in the FBI's Terrorist Screening Center. The terrorist screening, or absence of screening, in both of those departments could have contributed to yesterday's tragedy. He decided to tread carefully.

"My HRT training schedule included a month of military cross-training…"

"HRT?" asked Lena.

"My FBI Hostage Rescue Team…HRT!"

"Right."

Hook continued, "Nearly all of the FBI candidates in my HRT class have no understanding whatsoever of the military. All of their initial FBI training involved the civilian world and domestic investigations. They're not familiar with the military's chain of command, message traffic, hand signals, military combat gear—weapons, protective gear, night vision goggles, explosives, etc.— or how the military even travels in a combat zone."

"Uh-huh, so why the need for military training? I thought that the Hostage Rescue Teams were exclusively involved in the rescue of hostages on U.S. soil."

"Yes and no! HRT was initially set up after the murder of eleven Israeli athletes, by Palestinian terrorists, at the Munich Olympics in 1972. The live telecasts of that tragedy gave law enforcement agencies a glimpse of the future. Hence, the FBI's creation of HRT.

"But, after the events of 9/11, the FBI decided to take a more proactive approach toward the possibility of terrorism on U.S. soil. That decision led to the expanded mission of HRT, which involved terrorist interdictions beyond our borders. HRT agents have now been embedded with many of our JSOC…Joint Special Operations Command… teams for years. Those teams include SEAL Team 6, U.S. Army's Delta Force, and the 75th Ranger Regiment.

"We help these JSOC teams locate, identify, and interrogate both suspected and known terrorists. Zeroing in on them often involves many of the same tools and tactics… wiretaps, examining Internet communications, and checking financial records, etc. …that we use against organized crime syndicates in the U.S. We also help them identify and gather evidence at a terrorist's site, which could become important in the event of a subsequent trial. Our different skill sets complement one another. Whoever thought of this collaboration deserves a medal."

McCracken remained silent throughout Hook's HRT explanation. He was well aware of the FBI's expanded international role. He did, however, appreciatively purse his lips at Hook's compliment regarding the FBI-JSOC collaboration.

Lena next asked, "So, how did you avoid the training at Fort Bragg?"

"My team leader didn't think I needed a month or so of military cross-training. He knew that I served in the Marine Corps for seven years. He thought my time would be better spent furthering my cyber skills."

"So, you're now receiving additional cyber training at FBI headquarters. You're just across the street from my building," said Lena.

"Yes and no, again. At the outset of HRT training, we received a broad-brush overview of FBI cyber intelligence gathering. I apparently impressed my cyber instructors. When my team leader inquired about further cyber training for me, it set the wheels-a-turning inside the FBI. The Bureau was aware of my prior border experiences in Arizona with the ATF, so they decided that a couple of weeks of cross- training at the Department of Homeland Security (DHS) would make me all the more valuable."

"That makes sense. I'm pleased to hear that the FBI realized that. Large bureaucracies sometimes overlook past experiences," interjected McCracken.

Hook agreed and continued, "At DHS, I was teamed with a senior analyst who was working on the Customs and Border Protection (CBP) database. On my second or third day with this guy, his manager strolls by our cubicle and drops a list of seventy names on his desk and tells him… us… to delete their TECS records. No explanation, no nothing. Typical, tight assed bureaucrat."

McCracken grinned.

"Uh, this manager was from another planet, if you know what I mean," said Hook, in an attempt to moderate his comment about bureaucrats.

McCracken's grin broadened. He liked Hook.

"I think I know what TECS files are, but refresh my memory," asked Lena.

"TECS is short for Treasury Enforcement Communication System. TECS records contain the background history of all persons—U.S. residents and foreign visitors—who have entered or attempted to enter the U.S. These records are kept in an open archive database for primarily officers and agents who work at CBP, though other government agencies and their agents also have access to it. Its purpose is to record data on persons entering the U.S. It's a key screening aid for CBP agents.

"Agents post details in the database about suspicious or unusual persons who are attempting to enter the U.S. For example, if an agent at say a Maine-Canada border crossing decides to take a closer look at the background of an individual who is acting strangely at his checkpoint, he can… with a couple of keystrokes… search the database. He might find a useful note about the individual when he crossed into the U.S. a year earlier at say the New Hampshire-Canada border crossing."

"Are these notes opinions or hard intelligence?"

"A little of both. During my training with this DHS senior analyst, he used the actual case that I just described as a teaching example. The first part of the TECS record read, 'Subject interviewed. Bloodshot eyes and smells like a brewery. Lost his passport and wallet, probably not the first time.' That's a subjective observation. However, the investigating agent phoned the subject's employer, a nearby New Hampshire car dealer, and verified the following: 'Employer confirmed subject's U.S. citizenship and identified a prominent, but faded tattoo on the subject's left forearm.' Thus, the telling notes became part of the TECS record as a memoranda of information received (MOIR). It explained the weird behavior of the boozer, and it *absolved* him from any further CBP investigation or time delay at the border. He wasn't, in any way, a threat to our national security."

"In the case of this boozer," probed Lena, "was that the type of TECS record you and the analyst were instructed to delete?"

"Not even close! All seventy records covered suspicious foreign persons who threatened to file a lawsuit against the U.S. for improper visa screening and questioning. They felt it was a violation of their civil rights!"

"Excuse me!" said McCracken sternly. "They're not U.S. citizens! They don't possess the same civil rights as U.S. citizens. We can question them as we please."

"That's what I said. Management then fed me, and the whole office, a pile of pure BS. According to the old-timers' gripes in the breakroom, our candy-assed middle managers were getting pressure from management to avoid the unnecessary hassle and cost of legal defenses that could result in courtroom defeats and public embarrassments, especially if it involved questioning Muslims who were linked to various Islamic groups. They represented a majority of the names on the deletion list. All questions involving religion are a 'no, no' these days."

McCracken assumed control of the conversation while he thought aloud. "The lawsuit threat likely came from one of the many Islamic foundations that are popping up all around the country."

"Correct!" said Hook.

"Some, but not all, have benevolent, well-meaning goals."

"Right again!"

"Others are nothing more than fronts for terrorist groups," continued McCracken matter-of-factly.

Hook tipped his head in agreement and added, "A couple of weeks ago, a formal complaint was circulated around my DHS office. The complaint was from a not-so-well-meaning Islamic foundation. The complaint, I later learned, was also sent to the CBP, the FBI, and Justice."

"I didn't see any formal complaint!" said Lena.

With a knowing smile pasted on his face, Hook said, "You wouldn't have. My guess is that the complaint was delivered to only certain individuals at Justice. And those certain individuals will only disclose it when the timing most benefits their personal agenda."

"I haven't seen or heard of the damn complaint either!" growled McCracken.

"Same, same applies to you, Tim. The two lowlights of the complaint are," began Hook, as he recited the details from memory. "One, all U.S. agencies that are involved in the security checks of foreign persons who are requesting entry into the U.S. have, and still are, routinely violating the 1st Amendment rights of those said individuals—"

"Hold it! Our 1st Amendment rights apply to U.S. citizens, not foreign persons. Now, once a foreign person enters the U.S., either legally or illegally, their rights expand. But that's a separate matter from visa screening," interrupted McCracken, red-faced and clearly agitated.

Hook flashed a stoic look while inwardly agreeing with McCracken's assessment. "Two, our nationally accepted security phrase of 'See Something, Say Something' is racist. It's a form of profiling and a violation of Muslims' civil rights. Muslims, the complaint stated, includes every Muslim on the planet."

With that last comment, Lena could see that her close friend and long-time mentor, McCracken, was about to explode. She attempted to defuse the moment with a benign observation. "I can see that the questioning of a Muslim by a Border Patrol agent may get a little dicey if the agent finds a note in the individual's TECS file related to say Hezbollah, Hamas, or al-Qaeda. But our agents are entitled, rather required, to probe further into those relationships or associations. That's their job, border security. For example, over the years, we've questioned thousands of Northern Ireland

Catholics about their association with the IRA before they've entered the U.S. Terrorism, in any form, is an issue that the U.S. takes very seriously."

"Absolutely!" snapped McCracken. "Why should we exclude every Muslim on the planet from security screening into the U.S. That's ridiculous! Christ, Osama bin Laden was a Sunni. What makes Muslims so special?"

Hook withdrew a folded Xerox paper from his windbreaker pocket. "Lena, I have another bombshell! I was going to forward you this FBI notice last week, but I became sidetracked. DHS kept me busy."

"Is this a notice you received because you're an FBI agent?" asked Lena.

"No, it's broader in scope. The FBI circulated this notice to CBP, DHS, and Justice."

"I would have been copied on this notice then. What does it say?"

"This letter modifies the FBI's screening policies for foreign persons entering the U.S. It's dated March 22, 2012, twelve days ago." He paused as he searched the document for the phrase that made his blood boil. "Ah, here it is. 'The *mere association* of an individual with an illicit …violent extremist group… should not automatically determine that the individual is acting in furtherance of that organization's illicit activities.' The modification goes on to reassert that investigations can't be based *solely* on race, ethnicity, national origin, or religious affiliation."

Lena made an offhand comment as she thought, "That last part about race, ethnicity, etc. That's standard stuff. There is no questioning that."

"I understand," said Hook, before adding, "though I don't entirely agree with it. But that's a subject for another discussion. Concerning 'mere association with an extremist group' and 'automatic determination,' I understand what the author is trying to accomplish. He or she doesn't want background investigators to make automatic, superficial risk assessments.

"But I don't like the wording…'mere association.' Consider a visa applicant—be they Muslim or not—who we've learned has attended one or more bomb-making classes that has been taught by a known terrorist. Do they qualify for a visa if they simply attended the classes, but didn't assemble a bomb? Under our current standards, yes, they get a 'free pass' because they weren't *actively involved* in making a bomb. They were *merely associated with an extremist group!*

"Next, background checks. Is it reasonable for a foreign person to presume that they can simply waltz into any country they desire without undergoing some form of a background check? No, it' not! That person should realize that their present and former activities—including their circle of known associates—are taken into consideration before they get a pat on the back and a *welcome aboard greeting.*

"Furthermore, a U.S. visa applicant should also realize, or be reminded of the fact, that ranting, raving, and/or delivering tidal waves of complaints isn't a substitute for an impartial screening," closed Hook with a harrumph.

"Feeling better?" smiled Lena.

"Sort of, if it weren't for the fact that we've lost our way. Our weak-kneed DHS screening managers have been intimidated. They are so petrified that senior management will fire them or label them a racist if they deny any Muslim an entry visa that they're virtually issuing all them visas.

"A recent case in point, I attempted to disapprove a visa application of a Muslim who readily admitted that he was a member and active supporter of Hamas. My boss reversed my denial on two counts. One, Hamas is an Islamic religious organization that is comprised of Sunnis. I couldn't deny his application because he was a Sunni. Two—"

"Hold it again! Hamas is also a universally recognized terrorist organization. Their members don't get a free pass into the U.S.," asserted McCracken.

Both Hook and Lena unconsciously nodded in agreement.

Hook continued, "Two, I didn't have proof that he was making bombs or furthering terrorism. But," he paused for emphasis, "I did have proof. I explained that the public homepage of the applicant's Facebook account had posted instructions on how to make and detonate and an IED (improvised explosive device). Additionally, his homepage had a picture of him throwing a Molotov cocktail (a firebomb) at Israeli policemen in Tel Aviv.

"My asshole boss, first said, what's wrong with that! When I got in his face, he apologized for his anti-Semitic remark. He then robotically and thoughtlessly stated that we couldn't review an applicant's Facebook account because it was a violation of their privacy. I countered that it was an open-to-the-public account. Doesn't matter, he said, and he overrode my denial. We're giving suspicious persons a free pass and compromising the safety of the country."

"Goddamn it!" burst McCracken. "Hook's absolutely right. DHS is being played. Did you voice those concerns to management?"

"Yeah! My boss, who I'm certain is a little unstable, screamed at me. He said I was a racist and an Islamophobe. He told me in one-syllable words to do what I was told. He and his boss were the ones who earlier ordered me, and my colleague, to delete the seventy records because those individuals were, I later learned, on a 'hands-off list,'" said Hook.

"Hands-off list?" asked McCracken incredulously. "DHS doesn't, or shouldn't, have such a list. After 9/11, the attorney general tasked the FBI with maintaining The Terrorist Watchlist, which is often referred to as the 'Watchlist.' The FBI also oversees an even more discriminating list known as the 'No Fly List.' The individuals on the No Fly List have undergone a higher level of scrutiny than those on the Watchlist," paused McCracken as he stood and began pacing. "Did any of the names or records on this *hands-off list* jump out at you?"

"Yes, twenty-two of them made me want to puke. Both DHS and the FBI investigated those cases. I next, inconspicuously, contacted the lead investigator on each case. All of them were involved in either the field intelligence report (FIR) or the suspicious activity report (SAR). I learned from my phone conversations with them, and their supporting documentation in the files, that all twenty-two of these individuals are hardcore jihadists who want to kill as many Americans as they possibly can.

"None of these investigations were superficial. Each investigation involved deep international background checks, hundreds of hours of domestic surveillance, and countless interviews with their known associates. The mountain of evidence on each one of these guys was incontrovertible. The investigators went bonkers when I told them that I was ordered to delete their files."

McCracken massaged his forehead with one hand as his head shook resignedly from side to side. "Son of a bitch! Son of a bitch!"

While McCracken was weighing his course of action, Lena intervened in a backhanded, but beguiling fashion. "Because I know that your are a compliant and obedient type of individual, with a nonexistent bullshit meter, are you still working at DHS?"

Hook laughed.

"Yes, just what I thought! They sent you back to the FBI posthaste," replied Lena sarcastically. "In addition to that paper, you withdrew from your windbreaker pocket; is there anything else in that pocket that you'd like to share with us, like a thumb drive with all the stored data on those seventy records that you so diligently deleted."

Hook laughed again as he dug into the pocket of his windbreaker. He withdrew a thumb drive, handed it to Lena, and said, "All seventy files are on that drive. The worst of the lot is in the folder entitled '22.' The files include a photo of each person."

Lena unconsciously tapped the thumb drive against her cheek as she thought.

McCracken's pacing increased.

Hook continued, "The news media hasn't got their hands on a photo of the terrorist that you shot and killed yesterday. But if I were you, I wouldn't wait too long before you ask someone you trust to perform a facial comparison of your victim with the individuals in my '22' folder. Politically sensitive bodies have a tendency of getting mysteriously cremated or pictures and fingerprints transferred to others or faces being blown off with a shotgun blast."

"Shit, shit, shit! Lena, give me that thumb drive," said McCracken excitedly. "I'm going to look into this right now. I'm heading to the FBI. I trust the director, Tom Milton, but not his recently promoted deputy, Byron Weeks."

Lena agreed with McCracken's assessment of Weeks. She had worked with Weeks on several cases and didn't like him. Though he seemingly got results, she believed his successes were the result of others' tireless efforts. Sadly, no one would ever know how he advanced to the upper echelon of the FBI because he so intimidated his staff that none of them would ever question or challenge his tactics or views on a case. Nor was he one to let facts interfere with his predisposed narrative, especially when it involved a high profile case. His history of heartless and immediate transfers from Washington, to Podunk offices, or forced early retirements were legendary within the Bureau.

Just before McCracken raced out of the room, he looked at Hook and said with a sincere expression, "Good work Hook! We need more men like you In Washington. I'll see you Sunday for Easter dinner in the White House."

Lena turned toward Hook and asked, "Can you stay longer? I'd like to introduce you to Mary Phillips. She should be back at any moment."

"No problem. I told my training supervisor at the FBI that I'd be visiting you this morning."

"Great! How about a short break? I'd like to freshen up and make a quick call to my office."

"Will do. I could also use a strong cup of coffee, like a double espresso. I passed a coffee shop in the lobby when I arrived. Can I get you anything?"

"A latte, please."

"Got it. And I want to hear about your Easter party. I haven't received my invitation. Are we going to have a grown-up Easter egg roll on the South Lawn of the White House after the kids' fun and games?"

"I'll fill you in on the Easter dinner when you return with the coffee," smiled Lena.

Once Hook left, it was her turn to start pacing. She was replaying in her mind a comment Mary had made yesterday at the Tidal Basin. *The secretary of Homeland Security, the new deputy director of the FBI, and Smithson at Justice are all pandering to the far left by redefining the meaning of terrorists and terrorism. And its improbable association with Islam.*

She moved to the side of her bed and grabbed her cell phone off the side table. She dialed Mary, who answered on the third ring. "Where are you? I've got an FBI friend visiting me. I think you'd be interested in hearing what he has to say regarding the FBI and their redefinition of terrorism."

"I'm on the second floor in a vacant admin office. I've been busy making phone calls. I'll be back to the room in a couple of minutes. You won't believe what I've learned!"

"Nor, what I've learned!" said Lena as she ended the call, and took a deep, weary sigh. She was tired. *I'll just stretch out on the bed, close my eyes and take a little snooze until Hook returns,* she thought.

When Hook returned, Lena was lightly snoring atop her made bed. He eased onto the bed beside her and placed an arm around her shoulders. A minute later, she jerked to the side and moaned. He suspected that the post-bombing screams of sixth graders were ripping through her mind. He gave her a gentle shake that woke with a start. Fear and panic filled her eyes.

"What? Where am I?" she cried.

"You're in the hospital. You've been here since yesterday afternoon. I'm here with you. You're safe. You had a bad nightmare, likely a flashback of yesterday's bombing," said Hook as he grabbed a nearby box of Kleenex, set it on his lap, and handed her a tissue.

"Yes, yes, of course. I just dozed off. Nothing more," she said, wiping her eyes.

Hook was familiar with the distant and terrified look he'd seen on Lena's face. He'd seen that look on the faces of tough-as-nails Marines. He'd also heard those same Marines moan or scream in the middle of the night. When she began to vigorously rub her arms, he saw the goosebumps. Getting shot at or attacked by an adversary was one thing. Seeing a terrorist, a couple of hundred feet away, blow up children was in a separate, depraved category all its own. He sadly realized that Lena was now a member, along with himself, of the *I Hope to God that I Never See that Again Club.*

Moments earlier, Mary stopped short of the open doorway of her hospital room. She scrutinized the dark, handsome man with the scar on the left side of his jaw, who was calmly sitting on the bed beside her boss. They were talking in whispers and sipping coffee. A box of Kleenex rested on his lap, and he had an arm draped around her boss's shoulders as if he was comforting a child. This was Lena's FBI friend that she said she'd be interested in meeting. This also happened to be, she guessed, the same FBI agent with the unusual nickname of Hook. Lena had spoken about him several times before. His scar was a dead giveaway for the nickname.

If she remembered correctly, his background involved stints as a Force RECON Marine, a policeman in Philadelphia—while he earned his college degree at Temple University's night school—and an ATF special agent. He was now an FBI special agent who, according to Lena, was undergoing further training in the FBI's elite Hostage Rescue Team (HRT) program.

She announced her presence with a knock on the door and a clearing of her throat. Lena and Hook instantly looked up and smiled. Character traits like insensitive, boorish, and overbearing shaped her former conceptions of Hook. Those notions now seemed the exact opposite of what she was seeing and feeling. He also possessed the most sympathetic and alluring brown eyes she'd ever seen.

Hook slipped off the bed and awkwardly stepped toward her. He, too, was expecting something entirely different than the blonde beauty who filled the doorway. From what Lena had told him, he was expecting a spare, straight-laced religious scholar, with wire-rimmed glasses and a bible tucked under her arm. Instead, he found himself staring at the well-proportioned figure of a woman, with her hands on her hips, who was dressed in a black, form-fitting spandex outfit. With luxuriant blond hair, peaches and cream complexion, and deep blue eyes, he guessed she was in her early thirties. His estimate was low by a good ten years or so.

Hook extended his hand and mumbled, "Anthony DeLuca. Nice to make your acquaintance."

"Acquaintance!" snickered Mary as she seductively arched an eyebrow. She took his hand. It was warm and soft. Taking a step closer to him, she placed her other hand on their grip and shamelessly caressed his hand. An electric charge raced between them. "Mary Phillips, Hook!"

Lena inwardly chuckled at their initial attraction. After a time, she said, "Why don't you two pull up chairs beside my bed. If you don't mind, I'm going to stay put. I'm comfortable. I'm anxious to hear what you've learned, Mary."

After the chairs were rearranged, Mary began. "I made three calls. The first was to my co-founder of our two girls schools in Afghanistan, Beena Waleed. I reached her at our Jalalabad school, just before she left for dinner. I questioned her further about Jan Zahir. He's the man with the turban who I spoke to briefly yesterday in the lobby of Justice."

Lena now remembered the man.

"Beena explained that he's gone out of his way to renew a past relationship with her family. He's a pro-American, Pashtun tribal leader who was best friends with her deceased uncle, Ahmad Shah Massoud. Massoud was the leader of the Northern Alliance in Afghanistan until al-Qaeda assassins killed him two days before 9/11. He and Zahir were allies of our CIA. Zahir has apparently continued, and strengthened, his relationship with the CIA. His longtime handler, Mike Hall, is now the CIA station chief in Kabul. I've met Hall a few times at the embassy. He seems like a decent guy, but he's definitely all business."

Lena nodded. She replayed, in her mind, Mary's discussion about Zahir during yesterday's walk to the Tidal Basin. "Are you going to meet Zahir?"

"He was my second call. I reached him in his room at the Marriott this morning. We spoke in Pashto, and I asked him to call me back from a payphone in the lobby of the Marriott, which he did. I knew his calls would be monitored. The CIA had previously made arrangements to meet with him— despite a barrage of very determined objections from State and Justice— before he arrived in Washington. The CIA meeting with him is set for 7:00 p.m. tonight at their headquarters. Zahir requested my presence at this meeting. The CIA agreed, and they're picking me up at my house at 6:00 p.m."

"The plot thickens," mused Lena.

"More than you think. I only had a minute with Zahir on the lobby phone before he caught sight of his babysitter from Justice, who was looking for him. He'd heard about the shooting and bombing yesterday afternoon. He thought I was the primary target. He feels that the president of Afghanistan, Hakim Qazi, and his police chief, Safi Khan, are worried that I know too much about their crooked insider wheeling and dealing."

Lena took a long moment to consider that presumption. She'd thought that yesterday's attack was yet another Mexican drug cartel hit directed at her. *Apparently not*, according to this clan leader. Continuing with this line of thought, it became clear to her that significant political and financial issues—related to the war in Afghanistan—were obviously at play here, in Washington. And none of the key players involved in that subterfuge were beyond engaging terrorists to kill a senior U.S. official on U.S. soil, and to prospectively mask that shooting with a suicide bombing.

Mary continued, "Zahir told me that Smithson and Hightower, Jr., have offered him *big money*, even a piece of their stolen truck racket in Afghanistan—"

"Stolen truck racket! What's that about?" interrupted Lena incredulously.

"I'm not sure. I've only heard rumors," began Mary. "Insiders at our embassy in Kabul *may be* tipping the Taliban on the schedules and routes of ISAF and U.S. truck convoys in Afghanistan. I also don't know if the thieves are real Taliban or crooks posing as the Taliban. That's the extent of my knowledge."

"Jesus Christ! That's disgraceful! Is Justice in Kabul investigating any of this?"

"Not that I know of, but I'm just getting to know your staff in Kabul. If Smithson and Hightower are involved in this racket, I'd guess there is no way an investigation could get underway. By the way, a majority of the fuel trucks that operate in Afghanistan were either sold by or brokered by… VA Trucking!"

"Are you goddamn kidding," screeched Lena as she vaulted off the bed. "That's Casanova's father's company."

"Exactly! I was in the doorway of your office yesterday morning when you took Hightower, Jr., to task for some of his sketchy dealings in the Criminal Division. I'd say sketchy dealings run in the Hightower family."

Lena paced the room, her mind racing, trying to form a solution. Unfortunately, there were no simple answers. Frustrated, she plopped back into her chair and groaned, "What a mess!"

Mary nodded in agreement and continued, "So Smithson and Hightower have offered Zahir big money and a piece of their stolen truck racket in Afghanistan for half or more for his Khyber Pass toll collection treaty. Zahir also believes that Safi Khan, the police chief in Kabul, is involved in these Smithson-Hightower, Jr., negotiations. If he doesn't accept Smithson and Hightower's demands, they've threatened to terminate U.S. intelligence services with his clan and even help a nearby Pashtun tribe take over his village."

"Big money? Any idea on how many dollars that might be?" sighed Lena plaintively.

"It's got to be in the millions. The Khyber Pass is the key logistics route into Afghanistan. Whoever controls that pass controls Afghanistan."

Hook chimed in. "You both need increased protection. These dickheads are killing people. They're not screwing around."

Lena and Mary barely acknowledged Hook's recommendation.

Mary charged ahead with a description of her third phone call. It was to the president of VA Trucking, Mr. Charles T. Hightower, Sr. When she was connected to Hightower's executive assistant, a very officious woman who sounded like she ran the company, she was initially disappointed. Hightower was in an important board meeting, explained the assistant, and couldn't be disturbed.

Unfazed, she convincingly intimated that she was part of the FBI team that was investigating the numerous thefts of VA Trucking's fuel trucks in Afghanistan. She next asked the assistant, in an obsequious manner, if she could possibly help her with her inquiry. Mary's kindly request sealed the deal. Miss Know-it-all couldn't restrain herself.

"She gave me a treasure trove of inside information," began Mary, "all of which she believed was public knowledge. Max Smithson and Hightower, Sr., were regular golfing partners. All of VA Trucking's orders—for the sale or lease of fuel trucks in Afghanistan— cross Smithson's desk at Justice, in one misbegotten form or another. Smithson's office specifically instructed VA Trucking to install ultra-secure, GPS wireless tracking devices on all of the fuel trucks that were headed to ISAF or U.S. fuel delivery contractors in Afghanistan. And…you'll never guess who possesses the sole receiver for those tracking devices?" queried Mary, with the bearing of Sherlock Holmes.

Lena shrugged her shoulders and spread her hands. She had no clue.

"Kabul police chief, Safi Khan. Furthermore, the delivery of this one-off receiver was handled through…none other than… our own Diplomatic Security (DS) staff at the U.S. Embassy in Kabul."

Lena and Hook unconsciously shook their heads in disbelief and disgust.

"Know-it-all closed our conversation by sweetly informing me, since I was such a good listener, that Hightower's son—Charles T. Hightower, Jr.—would likely become the president of the United States after Ted David's eight years in the White House."

Minutes later, after a break for more coffee, the three of them resumed their discussions.

Mary looked from Hook to Lena and asked calmly, "So what have you learned about the FBI's redefinition of terrorism?"

"Hook explained to Vice President Tim McCracken and me that—"

"McCracken was here?" she interrupted.

"Yes, we're friends. I thought you knew that."

"I had no idea."

"I was one of his assistants before I was nominated by President Adams to become the associate attorney general."

"I guess I missed all that during my last tour in Kabul."

"Anyways, Hook described to us the flaws in Homeland Security's (DHS) screening of suspicions foreign persons. He also confirmed your belief that DHS, and possibly even the FBI, are unilaterally redefining the meaning of terrorists and terrorism. McCracken left for the director of the FBI's office thirty minutes ago."

Mary leaned into Hook and gave him an unexpected kiss on the cheek. "I knew I had you pegged right! You're one of the good guys!"

"Ah… ah!" Hook stopped and stammered with a flushed face.

Lena laughed. "'Cat got your tongue?' I didn't think I'd ever see the day! Now that you're back at the FBI, what have they got you doing?"

Hook composed himself and smiled at Mary. "Thank you for the kiss." Turning to Lena, he said, "When I returned to the FBI, they promoted me. Go figure! They've temporarily assigned me to the Terrorist Screening Center, which they manage. The assignment is for ninety days. It will mean a roll-back in my HRT training class. When you helped me get into HRT, I know that some of your motivation was based on having me stationed in Afghanistan when Mary," he paused, as he pointed a finger at his new admirer, "returned to Kabul, next September. It's now looking like I might not arrive until November or December. Is that OK?" he tentatively asked.

Lena turned toward Mary with a questioning look.

Mary thought for a moment before responding, "Two terrorists tried to kill us yesterday. I think we should table this matter for the time being."

"Yes, your right. Let's not get ahead of ourselves. We'll see how things unfold over the next month or so. But, as far as I'm concerned, you can rest assured that you won't get administratively dismissed from HRT because of this ninety-day FBI assignment."

"Thanks! I appreciate that. During my first couple of days at the center, I was helping a couple of admin types update the Terrorist Screening Database. Input into the database comes from a variety of sources… DHS, Justice, State, Defense, the FBI, and a large, select pool of U.S. and international intelligence agencies, border patrols and law enforcement departments. That changed last Wednesday when someone in human resources took a closer look at my military and law enforcement background. I was switched to the *No Fly List* desk on Thursday. 'No Fly' is a list of persons who pose *the most credible threat* of committing an act of terrorism against the U.S.… usually related in some way with aircraft. It's a shorter list than the center's

Watchlist. The twenty-two persons that I described to you and McCracken earlier should have been at the top of the No Fly List."

Lena was silent for several long seconds as she thought. "Let's return to your recent stint at the DHS for a moment. Do you have any idea of who, outside of Homeland Security, may have provided the names on their unauthorized hands-off list?"

Her stomach churned when Hook smirked, and he again dug into the pocket of his windbreaker for yet another note. With a scrunched facial expression, she emitted a torrent of semi-decipherable profanities under her breath.

Hook handed her a 3"x5" card with the names of individuals listed on both sides.

Mary saw her friend's face turn gray.

"Son-of-a-bitch! Cabinet members, a couple of members of the House Select Committee on Intelligence, and several senior senators!"

"Why didn't you mention this when McCracken was here?"

"Because I didn't think the time was right to apprise him of another security lapse. He looked like he was 'loaded for bear' when he left here for the FBI."

"Uh-huh! Uh-huh!" muttered Lena distractedly. Her thoughts were focused on the implications of Hook's latest disclosure. Very high-powered individuals in Washington didn't want the names of these seventy suspicious persons to catch the attention of the FBI. That was why these bastards intercepted those records and had them deleted in a less discriminating setting, Homeland Security. Rather than being a *gatekeeper*, Homeland Security had secretly become the *graveyard* for the records of very dangerous persons.

"What would prompt these individuals to compromise our national security?" asked Mary.

"You mean aside from money and increased power?" asked Hook.

Mary delivered an affirmative, but despondent grunt.

"I'll give you a two part answer," he began. "Firstly, all the names on that list are either appointed elitists or elected officials who live in a deluded bubble and/or have never seen the face of evil. None of them have ever closed the terrified, dead eyes of a teenage girl who was raped, beaten, and discarded beside her tortured-to-death parents. Never seen the scattered flesh and body parts of a farmer's market blown to smithereens by a suicide bomber. And, never smelled the unforgettable stench of fifty dead adults and children baked to death in a locked truck trailer in the middle of a hot desert.

"As for their delusions, they would rather see ten avowed jihadists enter the U.S. than risk the prospect of denying one of them the wondrous opportunity to rescind their fundamentalist Islamic beliefs and accept American ideals...democracy, human rights, liberty, opportunity, and equality."

Mary interrupted Hook with a condensed hadith quote from *The Reliance of the Traveler*. "'A Muslim believer may not be killed except for three reasons: as punishment for murder, for adultery, or for apostasy.'"

Lena immediately interrupted Mary. "What's *The Reliance of the Traveler?* You make it sound like you're quoting from a law book."

"It is a law book. It's the definitive text for Islamic law and the most widely accepted manual for Shafi'I (Sunni) jurisprudence," paused Mary. She'd explained to her friend yesterday that Islam was *more than a religion*. But with Lena, and other friends and colleagues, they had difficulty fully grasping that concept after one explanation.

"I think I know what *apostasy* means, but help me?" asked Hook.

"Apostasy is the act of leaving Islam, and it's a capital crime...*punishable by death!*" said Mary.

He massaged his jaw as he considered that definition. "So, in the unlikely event that one of these jihadists—who received an underserved *free pass* into the U.S.— rejected Islam and embraced another religion and accepted our American ideals, he would become a target of the other nine jihadists."

"Yes and no," said Mary, with a seductive smile that stirred his loins.

God, she was beautiful! He was having difficulty concentrating on her commentary.

"A Muslim doesn't necessarily have to totally reject Islam or even embrace another religion to become a target. If he or she simply moderates their Islamic beliefs that warrants a killing in the eyes of fundamentalists," said Mary, momentarily pausing. She angled her chair toward him and placed a hand on his forearm.

Her touch sent a high-voltage surge through his body.

"I interrupted you. You were talking about elitists and elected government officials," she purred.

Deep breaths, he thought to himself. "Ah yeees... my second point!" he said slowly, while mightily attempting to focus his thoughts on visa screening, rather than having sex with Mary. "Their views... their views would change in a millisecond should anyone of their endorsed jihadists blow up a school and kill children. Only then would their fervor, for unqualified entry into the U.S., perform an immediate about-face, and they'd blame others for the tragedy. We're seeing that now, after yesterday's bombing. The FBI and DHS didn't do their jobs. Those who enabled the bastards to enter the country are blameless.

"I'd also add that the rank and file of the FBI, CBP, and other law enforcement agencies that protect our national security aren't idiots. They all have two to four years of a college education. Many of them interface with dozens of individuals every day. Do they make mistakes? Sure they do. We all make mistakes. But, for the most part, their errors are corrected ... either by management or themselves.

"Take me, for example. I was first a Marine in Iraq, then a cop in the Badlands of North Philly, and...most recently...an ATF agent covering the Arizona-Mexico border. Over the course of a month, I interfaced with thousands of honest people and hundreds of lying SOBs. I, and others like me, develop an unscientific sixth sense for trouble based on our actual experiences, not on hearsay or a one-off occurrence. Is this sixth sense 100% reliable? No, but I'd say it's 90% reliable. It's saved my life on more than one occasion. Plus, evil is not modest. It has a penchant for announcing its presence.

"Thus, when I, and others like me, are ordered to ignore the suspicious activity of a foreign visitor and not ask them straight forward questions regarding the purpose of their visit... we're not doing our job. When we're ordered to neglect a visitor's association with known violent terrorist groups and not scrutinize an asshole who's trying to intimidate me and create a distraction because he's hiding something...we're not doing our job. When these workplace mandates exist, like now, our national security plays directly into the evil hands of terrorists, and our entire screening process becomes a farce."

Lena was silently impressed. She agreed with Hook's analysis as she pondered, and began to revise, her own view of politicians and idealists. *They didn't grasp the concept of cause and effect. They could not and would not ever admit that there were consequences for their actions. Politicians were especially expert in avoiding or deflecting blame when a policy or plan they advocated turned into a disaster.* She'd learned from her father, a retired police sergeant, that when one makes a mistake, they own up to their error and try to make matters right.

"Like I said before, 'He's one of the good guys!'" said Mary as she placed another kiss on Hook's cheek.

Lust, more than embarrassment, caused his face to turn beet red.

Just then, Lena's cell phone rang. She saw the caller was the vice president. "Hello, Tim. This is Lena. Any luck at the FBI?"

"I'm in the director of the FBI's office," he began with an obvious note of agitation in his voice. "Hold on a minute while I put you on his speakerphone."

After overhearing that comment, Mary jumped to her feet and whispered to Lena. "Put this call on your cell phone's speaker. If it's OK with you, I'm going to record this conversation on my cell phone." Lena silently agreed. Mary activated her recorder and carefully placed her cell phone beside Mary's.

Moments later, McCracken began speaking. "Director Tom Milton is present and sitting beside me is his deputy, Byron Weeks. We have Hook's thumb drive in the director's computer. The photos of Hook's most suspicious persons in his '22' folder are clear and legible. The problem we have is that the face of the shooter that Lena shot yesterday has been blown off. It's unrecognizable."

Another voice then aggressively chimed in. "This is Deputy Director Weeks. I personally handled yesterday's shooting and bombing investigating from the very first minutes. I can't tell you how royally pissed off I am at this new FBI agent, Anthony DeLuca, who was forced upon us by higher-ups. He has inappropriately inserted himself into an extremely important and sensitive investigation.

"Furthermore, he stole files from the Department of Homeland Security (DHS), and he's intimated that they have been maintaining a hands-off list, which is absolutely false. Lastly, he has apparently alleged that everyone in this '22' folder of his should have been on our No Fly List. I'm personally going to see that he's kicked out of the FBI and charged with a number of crimes."

Lena and Hook sat frozen in place.

Mary moved to the phone and said, "This is Dr. Mary Phillips, Weeks. I was the individual who shot the bomber yesterday."

"I know who you are. If you were a better shot, three sixth graders wouldn't have lost their lives yesterday," replied Weeks coldly.

Angered with that mean-spirited and distorted remark, Lena interjected, "If she hadn't acted quickly and grabbed the first shooter's rifle, all thirty-five students and three teachers would have been killed. The rifle, as you know, only had two remaining rounds left in its magazine when she took aim at the running and bobbing second shooter with the suicide bomb. He was also a good seventy yards away."

"That's a load of crap! She had nearly a full magazine in the rifle when she grabbed it. The rifle still had half a clip remaining when we retrieved it," said Weeks defiantly.

Mary placed a restraining hand on Lena's shoulder and gave her a mysterious wink as she leaned toward the speaker of Lena's cell phone. "What about the first shooter's face? I'm pretty sure Lena's shots didn't hit his head."

"My goddamn office is only a few blocks from the scene. I was the first FBI agent on the scene. The first shooter's face was blown off, and there was half a clip of ammo still in your rifle. And, just so I'm absolutely clear, if I read or hear any news media reports that contradict these findings, I'll know damn well who the source was. And, you can damn well bet you'll regret it!"

"Well then, Weeks," continued Mary evenly, "one of us is a liar! You see, the first thing I did after the bomb exploded was to take a picture of the first shooter's face with my cell phone. It wasn't blown off. My next picture was of the rifle's magazine. After firing only two shots with the rifle, I heard the empty click sound when I pulled the trigger. I immediately pulled the magazine out of its rifle seat to see if there was a jam that I could hopefully clear, but it was empty."

Mary paused for effect before continuing, "I'm from Maine, and I often hunted with my dad. I'm a good shot. I wished yesterday, as I still do now, that I'd taken down that bomber further from the children. After my picture taking, which lasted only a few seconds, I administered first aid to the wounded children. I've seen your mug on TV. I know that there were at least two other FBI agents on site before you arrived. Three teachers can also confirm that detail."

Long silence.

"Director Milton, what's your cell phone number?" asked Mary. "I'll send you my pictures of the first shooter's face and the rifle magazine. We'll hold on this end until you receive the photos. My guess is that the shooter's face will match up with one of the individuals in Agent DeLuca's '22' folder."

Less than sixty seconds later, Mary, Lena, and Hook heard chairs toppling, the sound of punches being landed and a muffled growl, "…you lying son-of-a-bitch!" An instant later, their phone connection was terminated.

CHAPTER 12

CIA HEADQUARTERS

Langley, VA

April 3, 2012 | Tuesday, 6:18 p.m.

LENA JONES HAD never visited the CIA's headquarters before. She now stood before a large plate glass window, in the director's plush office on the 7th floor, gazing at the forest that surrounded the building. Mike Hall was sitting at a small conference table, behind her, catching up on his day's emails. She and Hall were in the office to discuss a few matters before he met with Jan Zahir and Mary Phillips at 7:00 p.m., in a nearby conference room. She planned on privately viewing Hall's meeting from the director's office, on a closed-circuit TV.

The director was off-site as were most of the other CIA senior officials who raced about the 7th floor during regular business hours. It was quiet, and the lights in the office were dimmed. She pensively studied the forest that surrounded the building. In the darkening sky, the long, naked arms of the trees announced just a hint of springtime growth. Then, as if a symphony conductor had tapped his baton against his music stand, their arms seemingly came to life. They swayed in harmony with a freshening breeze. Their tempo mysteriously grew as if they were on center stage. Adjacent trees, in the wings, hardly quivered. Twirling arms dipped and darted in a dance she found mesmerizing. Suddenly, a bolt of lightning lit the sky, its thunder like that of crashing cymbals, startled her.

Were the forces of nature trying to send her a message? Was that the cre-

scendo? Forgotten memories from a long-ago literature class at U.C. Berkeley began to flood her mind. *You're alone in a shadowy, dark forest! Are you lost, or not? If lost, how did you lose your way? Should you stop and rest? Push ahead? Or, quit and try to escape from the forest!* "Christ!" she said softly to herself. Dante Alighieri's *Inferno,* the first part of *The Divine Comedy (1320).* "Those were his themes and dilemmas!"

"Did you say something?" Hall asked.

"No, just talking to myself. We don't have much time before your meeting with Zahir and the others. I think there are a couple of matters we should discuss beforehand," she said purposefully as she stepped toward Hall.

They each knew of the other's involvement in the Adams-McCracken American Party succession plan. President Jed Adams had personally explained the plan to Mike Hall—his longtime friend from Laredo, Texas—that morning in the White House. And Vice President Tim McCracken had outlined it to Lena at the hospital.

Once they were settled around the table. Lena began, "I spoke briefly with FBI Director Milton just before I arrived here. He's got his deputy director, Byron Weeks, dead to rights on his involvement with the Jefferson Memorial bombers. Weeks had their names taken off his No-Fly List, and it looks like he conspired with Agnew at Homeland Security to have their TECS files deleted. I also think he was the one at the FBI who leaked my safe house location to the Mexican cartel kingpin a couple of years ago. Whether or not he collaborated with someone else in Justice, regarding that leak, is still not clear."

"If I remember correctly, your friend Kelly Mills was killed, and an FBI agent was seriously wounded during that cartel hit."

"Yes, she was. Her last shots saved my life. One of my life's goals is to bring to justice the bastard, or bastards, who leaked that location."

Hall had met Lena briefly a couple of times before. His recollections of her were that she was friendly, but very focused when it involved her work. He elected not to tell to her that he, too, had spoken with Milton. With the president's prior approval, he had filled Milton in on Adams's succession plan, and their need for incontrovertible proof of Ted David's crimes. Milton and Hall had worked together on several high-profile investigations in the past twenty years. In the process, the two had become trusting friends. Thus, unbeknownst to Lena, there was another very powerful man in Washington who liked the idea of guiding and controlling David's prospective presidency.

Hall asked, "Do you think the general public...rather the major news media...will buy your eventual leap in political status from associate attorney general to the vice presidency?"

"No, I don't. There is, however, an interim step that you may not be aware of."

Hall's thick of eyebrows rose a fraction, and his angular, six-foot-two body shifted slightly. Her intimation surprised him. *Had Adams forgotten to apprise him of a critical step in his succession plan?*

"Deputy Attorney General Max Smithson ran his mouth yesterday afternoon in the lobby of Justice, an hour before the bombing. In slurred, drunken speech, he publicly announced, in front of a lobby full of reporters, that he'd been raising campaign funds for Ted David's run for the presidency."

Hall laughed. "Booze will do it every time! It turns smart people into idiots. So, he'll be forced to resign his post as deputy attorney general because of his Hatch Act fundraising violation, and you'll assume his position."

"You're warm. The end result is even better. Next Monday, President Adams will make several announcements. He'll disclose the reasons for McCracken's resignation from the vice presidency and announce his replacement, Ted David. Next, he'll ever so sadly explain Max Smithson's Hatch Act oversights and his honorable decision to resign from Justice. Lastly, he'll note that in light of the few months remaining in his final term in office that he's appointing me to the *acting post* of attorney general. He wants to avoid the possibility of any lengthy partisan debate over my *permanent nomination*. David's appointment, however, should easily sail through both houses of Congress."

"David and his Democratic Party will love the idea," added Hall. "He's thrown into the limelight of the White House, and he can actively campaign for the presidency, which is something he couldn't do—per existing ethic rules— in his lesser role as secretary of state."

"Exactly!" she smiled. "David's nomination is, of course, contingent upon his side agreement to appoint me as his vice president should our dear friend, President Jed Adams, die in the next nine months."

"I like the idea of your appointment to the vice presidency, but not the reason for your ascendency. Adams's death! He and I are close friends."

Lena grimly nodded in understanding.

"Adams is one of our great presidents," he continued. "He's been a quiet supporter of me the last few years. He's helped my career."

"He may have opened a door or two for you, but your rise through your ranks is the result of your accomplishments. I've read your CIA file. Not everyone takes advantage of an opportunity. Take Ted David for example, he elected to profit from his opportunity at State, rather than advance State's international goals."

After a time of reflection, Lena said, "There is one additional condition to David's side agreement with President Adams. I run as David's vice president on his party's presidential ticket."

Hall rubbed a couple of fingers across his pursed lips as he thought. "That may be easier said than done!"

"We …Adams, McCracken, and I …understand. There will be moans and groans from a few *wannabe vice presidents* in his party, but I think those voices will soon die out. The current polls have the Democrats and Republicans running neck and neck. Democratic leadership will realize that my addition to David's presidential ticket, as a black female, may very well tip the scales in their favor come election day, November 6, 2012. Plus, I'm still a registered Democrat!"

Like Lena moments earlier, he too now thought of a long-ago college course. Rather than literature, however, his memory was of a political science class. Adams's succession plan reminded him of the renowned, or reviled, depending on whose side you were on, the Italian politician and philosopher, Niccolo Machiavelli, who believed that "the ends justifies the means."

After a time, he said resolutely, "Clever and cunning! We're now a team. Our job in the next nine months is to gather enough hard evidence on David's illegal activities so that, if the Ted David-Lena Jones ticket is elected, you're the behind-the-scenes person who's calling the shots in the White House."

"That's it! Now, please fill me in on your CIA career. I've read your CIA file," she began as she withdrew a file from her briefcase and laid it in the table. "It seems to me that, in your early years, your superiors did their level best to either drive you out of the agency and/or sabotage your family life. Have you got enemies that I should know about?"

Hall's penetrating gray eyes widened, acknowledging her insight. He liked her direct questions and her understanding of the Company's indifference towards the lives of their case officers.

"I have no specific enemies, nor any specific backers…other than say, President Adams. In the private sector, you may get a pat on the back from your boss for a job well done. In the Company, you learn early on that management is stingy with praise and generous with reprimands. That's enough said about that.

"I'll give you a big-picture overview of my career. I grew up in Laredo, Texas, not far from President Jed Adams's ranch. He and I went to the same high school, though he was several years ahead of me. He went to Texas Tech after high school and then into the oil industry. We were reunited in 2002 at a high school reunion. He was then the junior U.S. Senator from Texas, and I was a CIA case officer, just returned to Washington from Kabul. I worked closely with our military and the Brits in kicking the Taliban out of Afghanistan," said Hall, pausing to further summarize his well-traveled background.

In the meantime, Lena studied him. His longish, curly brown hair and honest face gave the impression of a kindhearted person. His posture—with his head tilted backward, legs crossed, and his arms folded across his chest—projected a slightly divergent trait, that of say a discriminating rancher appraising cattle at an auction. Then, there was his penchant for wearing Western attire. He was currently wearing a stylish Western cut blazer and a formal Western dress shirt, matched with a decorative, turquoise bolo tie. She doubted that he owned a single traditional suit, a button-down white dress shirt, or a club tie. His clothes, like the person, said that he was a proud Texan who didn't care what others thought of him.

Turning her attention to his CIA file, while he explained his transition from the Army to the CIA, she read that he was divorced in 1999. *Not surprising*, she thought when she considered his overseas CIA postings—Aden,

Mogadishu, Bagdad, Riyadh, Bahrain, and Doha. His fluency in just about every major language spoken in the Middle East likely contributed to his run of nearly non-stop overseas assignments. That factor alone undermined the strongest of families.

"My dad was a sergeant in the Army's Green Berets. He was killed in Vietnam in 1967 when I was ten-years-old. Twenty years later, my family learned that he was killed in Laos, not Vietnam, during a covert CIA mission. He was a larger than life type of guy. I loved him and wanted to be just like him when I grew up. After high school, I went to Texas A&M and majored in International Studies, with a minor in a language... Arabic! At A&M, I enrolled in the Corps, U.S. Army ROTC. Upon my graduation, I was commissioned as a 2nd lieutenant. My goal was to become—"

With an understanding smile, Lena guessed, "A Green Beret!"

"Yes, that all went up in smoke in 1983 in Beirut, Lebanon. I was in the infantry and had been accepted into the first phase of training that could lead to becoming a Green Beret. But, before I started that training, twenty other U.S. Army soldiers and I were sent to Beirut, Lebanon. My unit, along with 1,800 U.S. Marines, plus other soldiers from France, Italy, and the U.K., were on a peacekeeping mission in Lebanon and stationed in Beirut. In 1983, Lebanon was in the midst of a complex civil war (1975-1990). Bad actors from all over the Middle East wanted a piece of the country, particularly Beirut. Beirut was generally referred to, at that time, as the 'Paris of the Middle East.' Though once the civil war ended, parts of it weren't very charming. They were more reminiscent of the bombed devastation of Dresden, Germany—post World War II—than Paris.

"Terrorist groups like the PLO, the Muslim Brotherhood, and Hezbollah were present. State governments—like Iran, Iraq, Syria, Jordan, and Israel—were also involved. Their interests covered a range of issues, from political objectives to territorial considerations.

"After a few months in Beirut, I was able to speak passable Farsi. So, early on Sunday morning, October 23, 1983, I had just finished questioning a suspicious Iranian at the police office on the Beirut Airport and was walking back to my quarters. My quarters were located in the Marine Corps barracks building. I was approximately 1,000 feet from the building when the terrorists' suicide bomb went off. I remember a bright light then nothing.

"I woke up in a makeshift first aid tent five hours later. I was severely concussed. Flying debris from the explosion tore up my left leg. A second terrorist car bomb hit the French barracks, two miles away. Deaths from those two bombings totaled 220 U.S. Marines, 58 French paratroopers, 17 CIA agents, and several of my close Army buddies. It was awful!

"Hezbollah—a group of extremist Shias, formed in Lebanon and backed by Iran—was primarily responsible for the bombing. Syria and the Assad regime played a lesser role in the attack."

"Thanks to modern medicine, my left leg is now stronger and better than my other leg. Too bad today's medical capabilities weren't available in 1983, or I would have become a Green Beret. After being medically discharged, I joined the CIA."

Lena thought about what Hall had just said. On the one hand, it was a reflection of who he was. *His dad had been killed in Laos during a covert CIA mission. He'd lost friends in the terrorist Marine Corps barracks bombing in Beirut. He, too, had been seriously injured in that attack. Nevertheless, he still wanted to become a Green Beret. Service and sacrifice for his country were in his blood.*

On the other hand, his comments prompted her to reflect on those she worked with in her executive branch of the government. She estimated that less than 5% of senior management in her executive branch were veterans. And that percentage likely shrank even further when it involved a change of leadership in the White House. Newly elected presidents were obliged to promote their party's functionaries and reward campaign staffers and donors. Prestige, power, and fanciful idealism motivated these appointed newcomers to the White House.

After working in Washington for the past five years, it was evident to her that middle-aged veterans, with family obligations, had no interest in pursuing a career in politics. Fanciful idealism wouldn't feed or clothe their families. They couldn't afford to screw around with the vagaries of politics and elections. A sad consequence of this reality was that it further distanced White House newcomers from the real meaning of service and sacrifice to one's country. Scheduling a press conference or ensuring that a limousine arrived at its appointed place on time hardly qualified as service to the country. And it certainly didn't have any relation to sacrifice.

She looked at her watch and suggested, "Let's break and continue this discussion after your meeting with Zahir."

"Good idea," he said, as he stood and flicked on a wall switch. A wall-mounted TV, near their table, began to illuminate. "You can see and hear everything that occurs in my meeting. With this clicker, you can adjust the volume, switch to captions… if we speak in Urdu… and replay portions of our meeting."

"Should we apprise them that I'm watching and listening?" she asked.

"That's your call!"

"Don't tell them. I trust Mary, but I don't know much about Zahir."

Just then, Hall's CIA cell phone vibrated. He read the message and turned to Lena. "FBI Special Agent Anthony DeLuca has apparently accompanied Dr. Mary Phillips to this meeting. Is that OK with you, or would you rather he cool his heels in our coffee shop?"

"He can attend the meeting. He'll be in Kabul within the next year, working with the FBI's HRT. I think it will be good for him to meet Zahir. I also implicitly trust him, in more ways than you can imagine," she said.

"Got it," he replied in an unusual and unquestioning manner. FBI Director Tom Milton's hours-earlier comments to him regarding Hook's discovery of visa screening lapses had already sold him on the man. "By the way, if you want me to ask a special question, type your question on this secure tablet. It will pop up on my tablet in the conference room," he said, as he slid a book size computer tablet toward her.

Minutes later, the meeting began with Jan Zahir at one end of the small conference table and Hall at the opposite end. On Hall's left sat Mary Phillips and Hook DeLuca. To his right sat, two males in their mid-twenties. From their uniforms, Lena could tell that they were 1st class midshipmen from the United States Naval Academy, located in nearby Annapolis, Maryland. One of them was Brice Miller.

She'd first met Miller in August of 2010 in the Yellow Oval Room at the White House during a reception President Adams had organized. The reception and dinner honored those individuals who were involved in the discovery and shutdown of a government condoned activity known as "Operation Fast and Furious."

Miller was injured in a gunfight during the final hours of that fiasco while temporarily attached to a Marine Corps Force RECON unit. His unit, which was in the midst of a joint U.S. Air Force-Marine Corps desert exercise in Arizona, was ordered to the dry, barren hills north of Nogales, Arizona, to capture and arrest a large group of semi-automatic rifle buyers and sellers. His attachment to this Force RECON unit was a consequence of the Naval Academy's summer indoctrination program that exposed midshipmen to various naval and Marine Corps career paths. Prior to his admission to the Naval Academy, he'd been a highly decorated gunnery sergeant in the Marine Corps.

Lena typed out a question on her tablet. "Who is the man with Miller, and why are they present? Do they hold proper security clearances?"

Hall saw the note and chided himself, with an absentminded rap of his knuckles on the table. "Folks, please excuse me. I'll be just a minute." Moments later in the corridor, he unmuted the audible control of his tablet and said, "Lena, do you copy?"

"Yes, I copy. I've met Miller before. Why are the two of them in your meeting? Shouldn't they be in class?"

"They both graduate and get commissioned next month. The young man with Miller is Yossi Levy. He's an Israeli and Miller's roommate at the academy. His dad holds the third-highest post in Mossad. I'll fill you in on their roles in a plan I'm working on after the meeting. I should have explained this to you beforehand."

Lena acknowledged her understanding, and Hall returned to the conference room. When he returned, Hook was casually chatting with Miller. He quickly learned from their conversation that Hook was the former ATF special agent and whistleblower who had initially contacted a U.S. senator about "Operation Fast and Furious."

The two then explained that they had both fought together against the rip-crew in the Fast and Furious, Bellota Canyon, shoot-out in 2010. Furthermore, they had each served, at one time, in the Marine Corps' "3/5" battalion known as Darkhorse. Hall knew nothing about their shared background experiences, but he liked it. It added an extra degree of cohesion to the plan he was formulating.

His attention next turned to Yossi and Mary, who were conversing in intimate, rapid-fire Arabic. *They seemed as if they were related!*

Mary suddenly stopped in mid-sentence and flashed Hall her heart-stopping smile. In Arabic, she said, "I first met this Adonis twelve years ago in Tel Aviv!"

Yossi imperceptibly blushed, and Hall smiled.

Hall replied to her in Arabic, "Why don't you tell us about this... in English!"

"In late 2000, State temporarily reassigned me to Tel Aviv from Cairo. President Clinton, at the time, was doing his best to broker a peace agreement between the Palestinians and the Israelis. Prime Minister Ehud Barak, an Israeli dove if there ever was one, dealt with Palestinian Chairman Yasser Arafat, an inflexible terrorist to the core. Yossi's dad, a rising mid-level Mossad agent at the time, was working eighteen-hour days trying to keep the peace in the West Bank. Arafat's short-term objectives for that hot spot were just the opposite.

"Arafat hoped that world opinion would turn in his favor if the world viewed, on TV, Israeli police brutally suppress peaceful Palestinian protests in the West Bank. What did unfold, broadcast on TV news channels around the world, was just the opposite. Israeli police exercised unimaginable levels of restraint, while Arafat directed and personally orchestrated ever-increasing levels of violent Palestinian protests. When his hateful plan ran out of steam, and world opinion turned against him, he simply reneged on all of his promised peace compromises. The peace agreements went up in smoke, and $30 billion in reparations to displaced Palestinians evaporated." The recollection of that wasted opportunity caused Mary's eyes to tear-up and her speech to break, then stop entirely.

Yossi finished her thoughts. "During those negotiations, Mary often came to our house for dinner. That's when I first met her. My dad spent hours with her discussing cultural, behavioral, and historical details that influenced Palestinian thinking. He was trying everything in his power to bring peace to the region. Sadly, he, like President Clinton, was just grasping at straws. Peace was a repudiation of Arafat's being. He had no interest in peace. Mary's description of him was accurate ... Arafat was a terrorist to the core!

"I was a twelve-year-old kid, who was awestruck ...and lovesick...

with this blonde Westerner. She hasn't change… but I have. I'm more into brunettes these days!" smiled Yossi.

Brice gave his roommate a friendly jab in the ribs. "Hey! We're here for serious business."

"What's more serious than beautiful women," smiled the lean, five-foot-seven, olive-skinned Israeli.

Hall bowed his head thoughtfully. "Do you speak any other languages?"

"When I served in the IDF (Israeli Defense Forces), I was sent to an intensive language school where I learned Farsi."

Hall queried him in Farsi, "Are you fluent in it or just passable?"

"Fluent. How about you?"

"Fluent as well."

"I'm passable," interjected Mary.

Hall unconsciously tapped a forefinger on the tabletop. The success ratio of his soon to be disclosed plan was improving.

Turning to Zahir, he said in English, "I'll conduct this meeting in English. There are two matters that I'm going to cover tonight. If you don't understand what I'm saying, please don't hesitate to stop me. I'll convey my meaning to you in either Pashto or Urdu."

"I prefer Pashto. Just like you do with me in Jalalabad!" said Zahir.

Hall nodded and continued, "Last December, two individuals from Justice sent a lame-brained messenger, named Bill, to Afghanistan. Bill, with the backing of our ambassador in Kabul—and personal written instructions from Secretary of State Ted David—insisted that I meet with him immediately in Jalalabad. The messenger's purpose was to inform me of an imminent threat against our embassy in Kabul."

Mary saw Hall stiffen. A message from Lena had popped up on his computer tablet. "Who were the two from Justice?"

"Excuse me for a moment. I have a time-sensitive query that I have to respond to." He quickly typed a short reply that said he'd divulge that in the next few minutes.

He continued, "A colleague of mine, from Britain's SIS, and I met with Bill at FOB Fenty. FOB Fenty is one of our military bases that encompasses the Nangarhar Province airport in Jalalabad. Jan Zahir was also present at that meeting. His clan is my most valued source of intelligence throughout the Pakistan FATA and parts of eastern Afghanistan. The CIA and I have benefitted from their solid intelligence since we kicked the Taliban out of Afghanistan in December 2001."

"Mike," interjected Zahir, "please describe to them our earlier business."

"Yes, of course," began Hall. "In 1999, I was officially assigned to the CIA's office in Frankfurt, Germany. I spent three-quarters my time in Germany supporting—as best as I could, with limited CIA funding—Ahmad Shah Massoud's Northern Alliance. They were battling not only the Taliban then, but also Pakistan. The rest of the time, I was in Dushanbe, Tajikistan, aiding our supply lines to Massoud. I occasionally flew into Afghanistan in one of Massoud's helicopters. My last trip into Afghanistan was aboard an old Russian helo that they left behind because it was unsafe to fly. Ten years later, it was in worse condition.

"In mid-September 1999, I met Jan Zahir on my last trip to Massoud's home base in the Panjshir Valley. He was delivering supplies to his close friend, Massoud. He offered to provide me with intelligence on Taliban and al-Qaeda activities in the FATA. All free of charge then," said Hall with a wink.

Zahir smiled, "That is what you call a 'pleaser!'"

"I think you're referring to the sales term 'teaser,' though free intelligence does *please* me!"

"Yes, yes. Since then, we've become friends and allies."

"Very good friends and allies," added Hall. "Back to Bill in Jalalabad. He didn't really have a lot to say. He didn't know the date of the attack, other than it was *imminent*. Nor did he have any idea of the magnitude of the attack. Was it a single suicide bomber or a well-orchestrated assault like last September's Haqqani Network attack in Kabul?

"He did, however, provide us with the coordinates of the Pashtun village that was harboring the terrorists. He expressly told me that the CIA should immediately destroy the village with a drone attack. The target coordinates were of Zahir's village.

"Zahir later learned from Bill, after a little prodding, the details of his assignment. Smithson and Hightower retained him for $25,000. Secretary of State Ted David subsequently gave him written instructions, which included the target coordinates, and paid him half of his fee. After meeting with us at FOB Fenty, he met with the police chief of Kabul, Safi Khan, and others, in a Jalalabad warehouse. Safi gave him the second half of his fee." Turning back to Zahir, he asked, "Regarding your current meetings with Smithson and Hightower, I gather they aren't aware of Bill's post-warehouse conversation with you."

Zahir shook his and said, "No, they don't have a clue. Bill isn't particularly smart, but he is smart enough to know when to keep his mouth shut. Smithson and Hightower are anxious to buy half, or all, of my Khyber Pass toll rights."

"Interesting, very interesting! Hold those thoughts for a moment," said Hall as he looked at Yossi. "The second matter involves your father. He called me three days ago. He told me about a shipment of thirty MANPADS that Libyan al-Qaeda agents are planning to send to a terrorist group in Pakistan. That group, Tehrik-i-Taliban Pakistan (TTP), is located in the Kurram Agency of Pakistan's FATA."

Zahir abruptly intervened, "TTP headquarters in Kurram is little more than a day's horseback ride from my village. They are very bad, very cruel Islamic fundamentalists. One of their favorite targets is schools. They have killed many students," said Zahir.

A moment later, Mary asked, "What are MANPADS?"

Hall absently chewed the inside of his cheek as he thought how best to respond. "A quick overview of MANPADS, or Stingers, and their relationship to the mess that is now unfolding in Libya. MANPADS is short for man-portable-shoulder-launched-air-defense-system. These weapons are deadly to any type of low flying aircraft. Low flying meaning up to an elevation of 10,000 feet. We, the CIA, delivered thousands of these weapons to the Afghanistan mujahideen in the 1980s when they battled the Russians. MANPADS decimated their helicopter force. A fact that contributed greatly to their withdrawal from Afghanistan after ten years," paused Hall. He next added astutely, "Shortly after that, Russia went broke. Wars aren't cheap!

"As for Libya, Libyan rebels killed their country's de facto leader, Colonel Muammar Gaddafi, on October 20, 2011... a little less than six months ago. During Gaddafi's forty-two-year rein, Libya acquired approximately 20,000 MANPADS. A MANPADS stockpile that was the largest of any non-MANPADS producing country in the world. When Secretary of State

Ted David initially persuaded President Adams in 2009 that Gaddafi and his oppressive regime had to be replaced, he claimed that there were only two Libyans who were capable of leading a pro-democratic regime change. They were General Younis and Mustapha Abdul Jalil, Libya's Minister of Justice. The problem that each of these prospective rebel leaders faced, however, was that they had no weapons and no money to buy weapons. Gaddafi controlled Libya's purse strings, and his military was well-armed. Speeches and chest-thumping could only carry a rebel force so far.

"So, David got together with a couple of his like-minded visionaries, including my former boss in the CIA. They developed and executed, with presidential and congressional approval, a modest $60 billion weapons sale to Saudi Arabia in 2010. Unsaid, in this widely publicized deal, was that at least 90% of these weapons were to be covertly transferred from Saudi Arabia to there neighbor Qatar. From Qatar, the weapons would then be delivered to David's chosen Libyan rebel leaders in Tripoli— General Younis and/or Abdul Jalil. The 'fly in the ointment,' which David apparently over-looked while he aggressively twisted arms and greased palms to consummate this arrangement was that the Qataris and Saudis hated one another.

"Also neglected by David, and his clique of not-so-knowledgeable visionaries, was the Qataris' view of General Younis and Abdul Jalil. The Qataris didn't feel either man was the right man to lead a new Libya. Younis was a moderate Muslim, who routinely opposed many of Qatar's friends in eastern Libya, al-Qaeda jihadists. As for the soft-spoken Abdul Jalil, they didn't view him as a hard-charging, pro-Qatari rebel leader, though he did become the nominal chairman of the Libyan rebels' Transitional National Council (TNC) in Tripoli.

"The Qataris preferred leader was Abdelhakim Belhaj* in Benghazi. He was the leader of the al-Qaeda terrorist group—the Libyan Islamic Fight-ing Group (LIFG)—in eastern Libya. The Qataris kept their promise and delivered all of the U.S. sourced weapons to a Libyan rebel leader, Belhaj. David's chosen leaders remained empty-handed.

---

* General Younis, Mustapha Abdul Jali, and Abdelhakim Belhaj are mentioned here for background purposes only. Mustapha Abdul Jali, a onetime judge who became the Minister of Justice, often ruled against Gaddafi's regime. He was also widely respected in Libya as a strong proponent of human rights.

"Abdul Jalil immediately complained to the U.S. that his TNC wasn't receiving any weapons. This concerned Belhaj because he figured he needed at least twelve more months before he could defeat Gaddafi and consolidate his political influence in western Libya. He decided he could 'kill two birds with one stone.' Belhaj had General Younis murdered, which put Abdul Jalil in a difficult position. Either hope for an end of the civil war in Libya and select Belhaj as the TNC's commander of the Tripoli Military Council or experience the same fate his friend Younis met. He appointed Belhaj to the post. When that happened, David realized that the winds of political reform had fully shifted a 180°. He and his pals were now facing the headwind of a hurricane and dealing with a longtime al-Qaeda supporter."

"I know Belhaj," interjected Zahir. "He fought with the mujahideen in 1988-1989."

"Was he pro-Afghanistan?" asked Brice.

"No, he was *anti-Soviet Union*, pro-Pakistan," replied Zahir. "He returned to Libya in 1992. That's when he formed the Libyan Islamic Fighting Group (LIFG). His group tried to assassinate Gaddafi three times. After his last failed assassination attempt, Gaddafi chased him out of the country, and he fled to London, along with some of his LIFG commanders.

"In 1998, he began to spend much of his time in Jalalabad with Mullah Omar. Mullah Omar was the founder and leader of the Afghanistan Taliban. The two were virtually stationed in my backyard. I provided my friends in the CIA and SIS intelligence on Belhaj's travel plans in 2004."

"You were the *one*!" exclaimed Mary.

"Possibly!" said Zahir with a grin like a Cheshire cat.

"*One what?* Fill me in," asked Hook, now curious.

"SIS, and I think the CIA, grabbed Belhaj at the Kuala Lumpur International Airport in 2004 and returned him to Libya for questioning and imprisonment. The Qataris eventually got him released from prison last year. He's now up to his same old tricks," said Yossi.

"Yossi, dear, he renounced his ties to al-Qaeda in prison," baited Mary with an innocent smirk.

"Oh, yes! You're referring to his 'revisions dispatch' from his prison cell," began Yossi. "He forsook his long-held Islamic fundamentalist beliefs. It was such a tender and heartfelt message. I don't think England's leaders bought one word of it. He now claims that SIS (MI6) overzealously questioned him…as in torture… about his links to al-Qaeda before they returned him to Gaddafi and a Libyan prison. At first, I thought he was after hush money from England, but now I'm not so sure.

"There are close to one million Muslims living in and around London. Belhaj is a charismatic figure. If he told his followers that 'the moon was made of green cheese,' they'd believe him. He can steer popular opinion," said Yossi pausing. As an afterthought, he added, "If Belhaj becomes the president of Libya, Sharia Law will become the law of that land within minutes, and Ted David's vision of a regime change in Libya will have succeeded, though not quite the way he'd hoped."

"Yossi, you seem to be quite well informed and well-read," observed Hall.

"I'm no better informed or read than 99% of my fellow Israeli citizens, which is a little over eight million at last count. As an international intelligence expert, you know full well that nearly every Muslim in the Middle East would like nothing more than to see Israel wiped off the face of the earth. Be it a clan, like the Zahirs, or a country, like Israel, we understand what it's like to have a target on your back. When one finds himself in that position, political correctness takes a back seat to survival," closed Yossi.

Heads nodded somberly in the conference room. Even Lena, who was remotely watching and listening to the meeting in the director's office, found herself subconsciously nodding in agreement.

Hall resumed control of the meeting. "One other, not so minor, detail. Once Gaddafi was killed, it wasn't long before the surviving elements of his loyal army crumbled. Belhaj quickly and efficiently added Gaddafi's arsenal of weapons to his already well-stocked inventory of Qatari weapons. MANPADS began to appear in black market weapons bazaars throughout the Middle East. A few weeks ago, a U.S. Army H-47 Chinook helicopter was shot down in Afghanistan with a MANPAD that came from the batch of weapons the Qataris delivered to Belhaj. As we speak, there are several other shootdowns of Western aircraft that our government, and other countries, are quietly investigating.

"David wisely announced recently that State has set aside $40 million for a buyback program of Libyan MANPADS. In the meantime, he and his circle of fast-fading friends were praying that no further friendly aircraft would be shot down with a U.S. MANPAD. A shootdown of a defenseless commercial airliner would terribly impact their political careers," closed Hall with a grim expression. He stood, stretched, and moved to the coffee bar for a coffee refill.

Bill had apprised Hall of David's secret MANPADS buyback program, four months earlier during their meeting in Jalalabad. He elected to keep that detail, and the dismal results of the program, private for the time being.

While Hall was pouring coffee, Yossi said, "A month ago, I visited with my dad here in Washington. He was meeting with U.S. intelligence agencies. He told me Israel was investigating Belhaj's possible sale to Iran of 480 MANPADS."

Hall walked thoughtfully back to his seat at the table. Once he settled himself, he stared hard at Yossi and said, "This information goes no further than these walls."

Yossi nodded in understanding.

"Mossad and we have confirmed that sale. Furthermore, Iran directed an indeterminate number of those MANPADS to Hamas in Gaza. Fortunately, your country's AH-64 Apache helicopters are armed with anti-MAN-PADS defenses."

"Thank you, Mr. Hall. I shall keep that information secret," said Yossi with a tight but irritated expression. He knew his dad would apprise his two cousins—a male and female—of that fact. They were both AH-64 Apache pilots. His next question was even more vexing for Hall. "Why did you allow all these goddamn MANPADS into Libya in the first place? A year ago, the United Nations passed a resolution for full-scale NATO intervention in Libya as well as a No Fly Zone there. Gaddafi's air force was effectively grounded one year ago."

Hook and Miller shared a subtle and knowing glance. Yossi's question went right to the heart of the matter. They were both curious to see how Hall would respond. Would he feed them a typical line of Washington BS or tell the truth? His answer would give them better insight into the character of the man who likely had plans to send them into harm's way—in the very near future.

Hall cocked his head to the side as he thought. "That's a damn good question. There is no simple answer. Firstly, once 'big government' sets its wheels in motion, there is very little that can stop it. Secondly, in the beginning, the Libyan rebels *did need weapons*. I'd say we… State, Defense, and the CIA… went overboard in that area. My former boss was involved in that decision. When Abdul Jalil complained that his TNC wasn't being armed, my current boss opposed the delivery of more MANPADS to Libya. His opposition was based on a fact and a hunch. The U.N. had passed a No Fly Zone resolution. MANPADS weren't needed in Libya. His strong hunch, or main concern, was that if we sent more MANPADS to the TNC that they would eventually fall into the wrong hands, which they have!"

Yossi wasn't through. "Is Belhaj delivering MANPADS to his al-Qaeda friends in Syria? The U.S. news media speculates that is happening."

The worsening political and human nightmare that was unfolding in Syria had every Western country, with an ounce of compassion, searching for a solution. Sadly, there were no simple answers.

Hall scratched the back of his neck as he composed his response. "It's my *belief* that… sometime within the past year… a plan was concocted, here in Washington, to deliver *MANPADS and other heavy weapons* to moderate Syrian rebels. This plan was to be implemented by pro-West Libyan rebels. I further believe that the architects of that plan were David, my current CIA boss, plus the head of the National Security Staff, Bud Lowe. That decision, however, was based on General Younis becoming the chairman of the Transitional National Council (TNC) or, at the very least, the commander of the Tripoli Military Council. When Belhaj had Younis assassinated, and he became the head of the military council, everything rapidly turned to *shit!* 'Pigs will fly' before Belhaj ever sends a single MANPAD to a moderate, pro-democracy Syrian rebel.

"Belhaj is the problem, and the U.S., particularly David at State, has no way now to stop, or even slow, his arming of deadly al-Qaeda groups throughout the Middle East." Hall stopped to collect his thoughts on a particularly touchy issue, which was now receiving worldwide attention. "Turkey is now screaming at David because Belhaj, with support from the Qataris, has begun to ship ever-increasing caches of weapons to ports in their country. All of these weapons are destined—via secret and circuitous routes—for Islamic fundamentalist rebel groups in Syria. Groups that we know are aligned with al-Qaeda and are not moderate, nor pro-democracy.

"The Turks don't want those weapons to fall into unfriendly hands. I understand that. David understands that. Turkey is currently pro-U.S. and anti-al-Qaeda, but that equation could change in the blink of the eye. Adding to our fragile relationship with Turkey is our pro-Iraqi Kurd support, which flies in the face of their view of the Kurds.

"One final point about Belhaj. A reliable intel friend of my mine in Niger told me that Belhaj sent 800 older MANPADS to repair shops in Agadez, Niger, for refurbishing. From there, my friend tells me, they're likely headed to al-Qaeda groups in North Africa—Mali, Algeria, Chad, Somalia, and Kenya. Belhaj has also sent an unknown number of MANPADS to his friends in Egypt and Yemen.

"David, my current CIA boss, and Bud Lowe are scrambling big-time to *keep the lid* on this MANPADS proliferation problem," continued Hall, "but, I don't think they'll succeed. France, Great Britain, and Israel are intercepting and reporting the sightings of these MANPADS all over the Middle East."

With a clenched jaw and a forced smile, Hall turned his attention to Zahir in an attempt to steer their discussions away from the growing MANPADS problem. "Tell us more about Smithsons and Hightower's interest in acquiring your rights to Khyber Pass toll collections. And, why their seemingly *big hurry* now? I apologize for my drawn-out discussion of MANPADS."

Zahir nodded while he slowly swept his cold, stern eyes over the other visitors. "MANPADS is a serious matter, Mike. Without the MANPADS that your CIA gave Ahmad Shah Massoud and me, we couldn't have beaten the Russians. MANPADS in the wrong hands is very bad. Imagine the problems you'd have if a U.S. MANPAD shot down an airliner on approach to the Srinagar Airport in Jammu and Kashmir, India?"

Hall despondently shook his head agreement.

"Or, an airliner at the Imam Khomeini International Airport in Tehran, Iran? That would be very bad for the U.S.!" added Yossi.

"My current boss is quite aware of the idiotic risks he's inherited from his predecessor. Defense has still got their heads buried in the sand, and Ted David at State is curiously indifferent—or, he believes in miracles!" said Hall.

"Or, he enjoys a seven-figure balance in an offshore savings account that he controls under some fabricated corporate name," said Hook, who'd been quiet thus far.

Hall's head nodded sullenly. Hook touched on a valid point. He said what everyone was thinking.

"My Khyber Pass toll collections," began Zahir authoritatively. "I think the reason for their urgency is because the Khyber Pass has been closed since the Salala Incident last November. Smithson, Hightower, and their greedy partner, Safi Khan, probably believe that my clan is hurting because there are no tolls. They also probably believe that they could make a fortune in black market fuel sales to the ISAF if they could persuade a few Pakistanis to overlook nighttime fuel deliveries. Furthermore, when the pass does reopen, they likely think that they can double or triple the tolls."

"Doesn't your toll collection treaty prohibit that?" asked Hall.

"Yes, it does. But Paki officials are driven by greed, dislike of the West, and dislike of those who—like my clan—support the West. Their dislike is stoked by Islamic fundamentalists and their belief that the West, primarily the U.S., does whatever India desires. Some Paki officials believe that it was my clan who tipped the U.S. on the location of Osama bin Laden's home in Abbottabad, Pakistan, last May."

"That's ridiculous. We gathered our intelligence for that mission exclusive of you and our other spies. You didn't contribute anything," Hall said vehemently.

"Tell that to your friends at the Pakistan ISI."

Hall stared at Zahir for a long moment before he said, in exasperation, "Those assholes! They're their own worst enemy."

Zahir simply nodded.

"Please explain to the others the details of your Khyber Pass concession. It may better help them better understand the motives of your prospective buyers."

Zahir scratched his neatly trimmed beard as he ordered his thoughts. "I will first explain the standing of my clan's Khyber Pass agreement with Pakistan. By the way, it's not a concession. It's a binding government treaty with my clan."

Hall nodded for Zahir to continue. Over the next few minutes, he presented a detailed history of his clan and how their Khyber Pass toll rights came into being. He began his narration in 1770, then touched on notable events and battles in 1842, 1893,* and 1924.

"Shortly after the British left India in 1947, and India and Pakistan became separate independent countries, war broke out between those two countries over control of Kashmir. We fought on the side of the Pakistanis in that battle but lost. Battles still rage over control of the Jammu and Kashmir area, but we are no longer involved there. Because we supported Pakistan in that war, they rewarded my clan with permanent property rights. These rights are in writing in a treaty between the Pakistan government and the Zahir clan. When Pakistan signed our treaty, it was no different than a hundred other treaties they had signed with other clans. It was, and still is, the only way Pakistan could maintain roads or other public facilities in remote areas of the country.

"Our duties in this treaty require us to patrol, protect, and maintain the Khyber Pass. In return, we can collect tolls for the maintenance of the pass and borrow money, secured by our treaty, for road improvements. Our toll prices must be reasonable and allow for only a modest profit. If Safi Khan were involved with this treaty, he'd triple the tolls. I have known him for forty years. He is a greedy man with no heart.

"There is one unusual fact that affects our treaty. Those who live in the FATA, like the Zahirs, are predominantly ethnic Pashtuns. We are a minority in Pakistan, but a majority in Afghanistan. The Pakistan Constitution gives Pashtuns the right to self-govern the FATA. Thus, we have what you call 'standing' because we are Pashtuns, and our Khyber Pass treaty involves property rights that are within Pakistan's borders. It is what you call, I think, a 'binding agreement,'" said Zahir pausing.

Mary replied to Zahir in Pashto, "Your understanding of *standing* and a *binding agreement* is correct. The U.S. has many binding agreements, like treaties, with other countries. Your English is very good Malik Jan Zahir. I am impressed."

"Thank you, Mary, for those kind words," said Zahir, in English. "I have Mike Hall, and now Beena, to thank for my English speech. I have more

---

* In 1893, Great Britain established a new border between "British India" and Afghanistan known as the Durand Line. The Zahir clan found itself twenty miles inside British India even though the British had never defeated them in a battle.

to say about self-governing. Each clan or tribe determines their own laws and penalties for breaking laws. In my clan, I am in charge of all that. I'm guided by my moderate Islamic beliefs and fairness. That makes the Zahirs a target for Islamic fundamentalists... or extremists... who live near us in the FATA. Those tribes wander, plunder, and don't believe in clan borders. Some of them would like to take away our Khyber Pass treaty and even take over our homes."

Over the next few minutes, Zahir presented additional details on his clan. He carefully avoided any comment on the modest financial impact his clan was experiencing because of the absence of Khyber Pass toll collections. Though Hall was aware of his ISAF approved fuel storage enterprise, he wasn't inclined to share those details with anyone who didn't have a need to know.

After Zahir concluded, Brice asked, "Does the U.S. have any idea how long the Khyber Pass will be closed?"

Hall replied, "It could be days, or it could be years. No one knows. I've heard it's adding at least $100 million more per month to the ISAF's fuel bill."

"My recollection is that the ISAF consumes, between jet fuel and diesel, approximately forty-five million gallons of fuel per month. I also seem to remember that 75% of all fuel deliveries into Afghanistan come through the Khyber Pass. Is that right?" asked Brice.

Before his induction to the Naval Academy, July 2, 2008, Brice Miller had served multiple combat tours in Iraq as a Marine. During his last combat tour, as the Corps's youngest gunnery sergeant, he was charged with a number of responsibilities. One of his most important responsibilities—in his mind—was to ensure that his platoon (43 Marines), or company (180 Marines), didn't run out of ammunition, fuel for its vehicles, food, and water. In a widespread military mission, like Afghanistan, logistic support could mean the difference between life or death.

"A little high for fuel. Low for other supplies," replied Hall.

"What routes are being used now to get fuel into Afghanistan?" Brice asked casually.

"Fuel is coming in from ports on the Baltic and Black Seas," said Hall.

Yossi nearly came out of his seat, "Jesus, if the ISAF has to depend on fuel deliveries from the Baltic and Black Seas, they're screwed! It can be done, but it's got to be costly and clumsy. It'd be like transporting produce today from Florida to Washington with draft horses and wagons.

"By my math," continued Yossi, rapidly tapping the tabletop as if it were a calculator, "a $100 million monthly border closure headache, divided by forty-five million gallons equals a $2.22 per gallon monthly fuel surcharge."

Hall replied, "It's probably closer to $3.00 per gallon surcharge because a little over 20% of ISAF's monthly fuel deliveries come into Bagram— on a fixed price basis—via Red Star, Mina, and Gazprom in Manas, Kyrgyzstan."

"Let's say, on a pre-border closure basis, twenty-five million gallons of fuel came through the Khyber Pass monthly," estimated Yossi.

All heads shook in agreement.

"The ISAF is currently paying, say, a $3.00 per gallon shipping premium and not liking it. If Pakistan proclaims tomorrow that they intend to keep their border crossings closed for the next five years, does the ISAF close shop and walk away from Afghanistan?"

All heads shook their heads. No, they wouldn't!

"A bean counter in the Pakistan government has already apprised his boss that, with respect to *just the Khyber Pass*, they could increase ISAF fuel fees and tariffs upwards to $75 million per month... and still keep the ISAF on the *proverbial hook*. That's just for fuel. *It doesn't include other supplies.* Nor does it include fuel passing into Afghanistan via Quetta in southern Pakistan. With Quetta in the mix, that's the $100 million monthly fuel headache the ISAF is facing."

Heads again shook in agreement.

Yossi was shocked. He couldn't believe the financial enormity of ISAF's fuel problem. After a time, he began to think aloud, "In a perfect world, all of that $100 million would go into the Pakistani government coffers. But, this is Central Asia. At best, half would ever get that far. Pakistanis leaders would first line their pockets with cash." He suddenly paused, and his finger tapping ceased.

After several long moments, he continued, "The reason I'm taking so long to analyze this problem is that my thoughts are divided. One side of my brain reflects my Israeli experiences and thinking; the other half reflects my U.S., or Naval Academy, thinking. In the case of the U.S., and the ISAF, this fuel issue is a *headache,* but it's *not a deal-breaker!* They're not going to walk away from Afghanistan at this stage of the game.

"Let's say that since September 11, 2001, the U.S., Brits and the rest of ISAF have expended over $500 billion in chasing down Osama bin Laden, restoring some form of democratic government to Afghanistan, and rebuilding the country. That estimate is likely on the low side. My U.S. thinking tells me two things. One, the Pakis will take full advantage of this border closure opportunity, ISAF and U.S. relations be damned. Two, once the Paki officials have set up their new offshore savings accounts, my guess is that the ISAF and U.S. will have no choice but to agree upon at least a $50 million per month uptick in Pakistani fuel tariffs before the border is reopened," closed Yossi.

"We'll just reduce annual foreign aid to Pakistan by an equal amount," said Hall plaintively.

Mary chimed in, "That's easier said than done, Mike. I'm familiar with how those dollars flow through State to USAID and eventually to each foreign country. We'd be lucky to recoup 50% of increased costs."

Everyone's view of Pakistan dimmed another notch.

Brice interjected, "Yossi, tells us about your Israeli thoughts."

"My Israeli solution!"

Brice folded his arms across his broad chest, leaned back in his chair, and nodded. The seams of his white U.S. Navy short-sleeved summer shirt strained with the effort. The rock hard five-foot-ten, steely-eyed, blonde midshipman looked very much like a no-nonsense 2nd lieutenant in the Marine Corps, a rank he would ascend to in the next couple of months.

"Your relations...ISAF's and the U.S.'s...with the Afghan Taliban remind me of Israel's relationship with the Palestinian extremists, specifically Hamas. Hamas has no interest in compromise, nor any interest in what's best for a majority of Palestinians. As you say in the U.S., 'it's their way or the highway.' Many of your naïve and/or historically ignorant politicians who have never felt, tasted or seen the hand of evil believe that throwing money... usually *big bucks*... at a problem can cure all ills. All that does is *postpone a final outcome.* Nothing has been resolved. Israelis don't favor that option, nor can they afford it. It's a waste of money."

"Is that your answer?" Brice asked.

Yossi clasped his hands together, rested them on the tabletop, and bobbed his head affirmatively. Without providing any details of a prospective Israeli solution, Yossi's answer revealed his thoughts on the Taliban's and Hamas's intransigence and Pakistan's greed.

Zahir returned the discussions back to the Khyber Pass. "If Safi and his friends controlled the Khyber Pass, he would figure out some way to smuggle fully-loaded 20,000-gallon fuel trucks through the pass, under the cover of darkness. Per Yossi's fuel equation, he'd make at least an extra $60,000 per fuel truck delivery.

"My Khyber Pass treaty has value to black marketeers, like Safi. I don't think that way. I'm a Pakistani Pashtun who has close ties with Afghanistan. My clan wouldn't attempt to illegally profit from this problem," paused Zahir, before adding. "This border closure also hurts Pakistan. There is trade between Afghanistan and Pakistan, plus many jobs at stake in Pakistan. The Pakistan government must understand this. The pass can't stay closed for five more years, or there will be another war inside Pakistan."

Hall looked at his watch with weary eyes. This meeting had run longer than he'd expected. "I'm going to wrap this meeting up. I think we all have a better understanding of this MANPADS problem and this Pakistani border issue. My boss and I are developing a plan that will involve all of you. The execution of this plan will occur in early June, after the graduation and commissioning of 1st Class Midshipmen Miller and Yossi on May 29, 2012, at Annapolis.

"With the help of Mossad, we've learned how the thirty MANPADS will be delivered to Hakimullah Mehsud's terrorist group, Tehrik-i-Taliban Pakistan (TTP). From Benghazi, they will first cross the desert to Cairo. In Cairo, they will be flown to the Incirlik Air Base in Turkey and then on to Jalalabad. This appears to be a trial shipment. If all goes well, I'm certain that Belhaj will send more MANPADS to TTP.

"At Incirlik, I've made arrangements with the Turkish government to switch out the brand new Libyan MANPADS with CIA modified MANPADS. The CIA has agreed to let the Turks keep the new ones in exchange for their cooperation with this matter.

"The CIA MANPADS have a tracker planted deep inside each of the missile's engine. We'll learn where each missile is sent. Furthermore, the guidance system of each missile has been reprogrammed to return the missile to its original firing position, shortly after launching, and explode."

Yossi smiled as he elbowed Miller in the side and whispered, none too quietly, "That's a good example of an Israeli solution!"

Hall didn't appreciate the interruption and flashed Yossi a scowl. "Miller and Yossi will oversee this switch in Incirlik and accompany our MANPADS on its final flight to the Jalalabad Airport. With the help of Zahir in Jalalabad, they will continue to track the movement of the MANPADS. They're going to be trucked from the airport to the New Hope Girls School in Jalalabad."

Turning to Mary, who had visibly stiffened with his mention of her school, he continued, "Hakimullah Mehsud has planned to take delivery of these missiles at your school, in early June. Your school will be in summer recess, and no pupils will be present." He paused to interject, "He complained to his Libyan confederates that he preferred an earlier MANPADS delivery date, but they couldn't logistically accommodate him. Besides destroying the school, Mehsud was hoping he could kill all the students. The actual delivery date is a day or two after your school recesses for the summer.

"He's worse than Safi Khan, an evil bastard to his core!" said Mary pausing. "I suspect this *MANPADS interdiction* is primarily an attempt by the U.S. to mend relations with Pakistan, and the Pakistan ISI, in light of the Salala Incident."

Hall agreeably rocked back and forth in his chair. "There are two reasons. One, is yes, it will hopefully help our relations with Pakistan. TTP is dedicated to overthrowing the Pakistani government. And two, we want to prevent al-Qaeda and Belhaj from introducing MANPADS into the Afghanistan military theatre. We also don't want TTP killing school kids anywhere, be they in Afghanistan or Pakistan.

"If Mehsud personally shows up at your school, we would ideally like to arrest him and allow, if possible, the tinkered MANPADS to getaway. Mary, I will speak with your boss Lena Jones about having you back in Afghanistan during this time. That's it for now. I'll be getting together with you individually as my plans develop. Your drivers are waiting for you outside to take you all home," closed Hall.

He stood and was about to leave the room when Zahir rose from his chair and leaned into him. "A couple of final points. You should hear this. As we all know, the Haqqani Network was behind the attack on your embassy last September. What you likely don't know is that they engaged Safi, for a fee of $50,000, to have someone open the security gates of that twelve-story, unfinished office building that overlooks your embassy. That *someone* works at your embassy, and his nickname is Cannon. I don't know his real name. The Haqqanis commenced their attack from that building."

Though neither Hall nor Mary was aware of Safi's involvement in the attack, they nodded knowingly about the origin of the attack.

Staring at Mary, Zahir continued, "A week before the attack, Safi..." He paused, searching for the correct English words.

Mary stoically interjected, "He tried to rape me, but I fought him off,"

"Yes," said Zahir sympathetically. "But, you offended his manhood. Do you know the meaning of *Ghairat* in Pashtun culture?"

Mary slowly nodded as her body slowly collapsed into Hook.

Hook put an arm around her shoulders and whispered, "Do you want to leave now? You've had a rough couple of days."

"In a moment," she murmured. Turning to Zahir, she said, "I offended his social standing. In his case, revenge was required."

"Revenge for Safi meant your death!" began Zahir. "He told the Haqqani's that he'd cut his $50,000 fee in half if they killed you during the attack. When they failed, he demanded the full $50,000 payment. The Haqqani's balked, explaining that they'd lost three good men in their failed assassination attempt of you. Rather than negotiate a compromise with them, Safi disrespected the founder of the network, Jalaluddin Haqqani, and his son, Sirajuddin. The Haqqanis didn't pay him a cent, and they've since ended their relationship with him. I believe that Safi, and to a lesser degree Qazi, was behind the attempt on your life yesterday. Greed motivates Safi. For Qazi, greed and holding on to his power guides his actions.

"Concerning my meetings with Smithson and Hightower the last few days, they have insulted me. They're like Safi. All they care about is money. They've made me extravagant offers for my toll collection, but I've refused. I'd dishonor my clan and my forebears if I did such a thing.

"The three of them are bad men with no principles. They're involved with stealing fuel trucks that transport fuel from Pakistan to your ISAF. Trucks that my men protect when they cross the Khyber Pass into Afghanistan. They also shakedown ISAF supply vehicles and military convoys with phony toll collections on secure roads in the interior of Afghanistan."

"Shit!" spat Hall. Though the CIA wasn't responsible for investigating or policing criminal activities in Afghanistan— they utilized political and military methods to prevent or thwart terrorism—he should have been made aware of these crimes.

"Firstly, these three bad men, and Ted David, want to bomb my village. Secondly, they want to take over my toll collections. Lastly, they will want to displace my clan from its home. I see Safi Khan behind all these actions. And, after hearing more about his relations with the TTP—their acquisition of MANPADS and destroying a girls school in Jalalabad—I think he's changed sides. He's left the Haqqanis and is helping the TTP.

"He knows that they target girls schools and that they need a new home. The Pakistani military has forced most of them out of the Swat Valley, north of Islamabad, and they've been kicked out of eastern Afghanistan. They are also being forcibly removed from their current base in the Kurram Agency of the FATA, a strong Shiite area. Safi has told the TTP leaders that he can deliver my village and valley to them."

In the silence that followed, those present—including Lena—agreed with Zahir's theory.

Hook finally broke the silence. "Hall, I'd like to help you out in any way I can with this MANPADS operation. Even if it means pleading with my FBI sponsor."

"I don't think that will be necessary Hook, but I appreciate it. I think your boss will be more than willing to accommodate your request, especially in light of your disclosure of those *suspicious persons files*."

"Suspicious persons files? My boss? I don't get it? Are you referring to my FBI sponsor, Lena Jones?"

"No, your real boss...FBI Director Tom Milton. He's now your *secret admirer!*"

CHAPTER 13

HELP AND COMFORT

CIA Headquarters | Langley, VA
April 3, 2012 | Tuesday, 9:07 p.m.

WITH HIS RIGHT hand tucked securely inside Mary Phillips's left arm, Hook DeLuca steadied Mary as they exited CIA headquarters and headed toward his car in the parking lot. "You've had a couple of long days. I'll take you home and get you settled."

She murmured something indecipherable as her head slumped against his shoulder.

"OK, just a few more steps and your chauffeur will have you buckled into his chariot."

"Ah, Prince Charming, I like that."

Thirty minutes later, they reached her townhome. Hook again steadied her as he guided her into her home.

"The bedroom," she whispered as she pointed weakly to the rear of her home.

"OK, honey. Easy does it." Moments later, he laid her gently on her bed and removed her shoes. "Would you like anything to drink? Tea, water …whiskey!" he said with a smirk.

She smiled weakly. "Ice water and a couple of aspirin. The aspirin is next to the kitchen sink."

He moved slowly into and around the kitchen, giving Mary time to undress and slip into bed. On the refrigerator door, he studied a couple photos held in place with magnets. Mary and Lena smiling and relaxing in a coffee shop. She and an unknown older man…probably her dad…with his arm around her shoulders on a hilltop, surrounded by a multi-colored sea of late September trees. Red maples, fire cherries, large aspens, and alders. Lastly, there was a photo of her with an attractive, petite woman who was wearing an Islamic cover. From what she had told him, he guessed the smaller woman was her friend and co-founder of the two New Hope Girls Schools in Afghanistan, Beena Waleed. The two were standing together, with arms interlinked, in front of a large group of young girls. The girls were also covered, and none looked older than fifteen. Behind the group of girls was an aged single-story building, doubtless one of their two schools.

From the bedroom, he heard Mary call out provocatively, "Prince Charming, Cinderella awaits you!"

With a water glass in one hand and a couple of aspirin in the other, he stepped into her bedroom. The lights were dimmed, and she was sitting upright in bed, cushioned with a couple of pillows. She had changed, but not into a matronly, flannel nightgown. She was dressed, though barely, in a frilly and revealing black teddy. The type that he'd seen displayed in the storefront window of a Victoria's Secret.

He sat awkwardly, on the edge of her bed, and timidly handed her the water and aspirin. *God, she is gorgeous!*

After washing down the aspirin with several sips of water, she returned the glass to him and patted the bed beside her. "I'm sore, achy and mentally exhausted. I would love to have you hold me and comfort me through the night," she said with a suggestive and enticing grin. "That is…if you're interested?"

Tongue-tied again, like earlier in the day at the hospital, he nodded wide-eyed and muttered a throaty, "Uh-huh!"

"Come the morning, I expect I'll be seriously interested in more stimu-lating…and sweaty… activities. By the way, I'm on the *pill,* so not to worry!" She said with a glint in her eye and an ever-widening, lascivious smile.

Now marginally composed, but fully aroused, Hook croaked, "I can do that. Help and comfort for my fair lady."

… 5:30 a.m.

A whimper and cry woke Hook from his deep sleep. The room was dark but partially lit by the first rays of the morning sun against the curtains. His eyes studied his strange surroundings. He wondered for just an instant where he was, and then he remembered. He felt Mary's warm body beside him. Her head rested on his shoulder, and an arm lay across his chest. A louder, muffled cry...deep from within Mary's throat...prompted him to give her a gentle, wakening jostle.

Her eyes slowly opened, then smiled.

"Bad dream?"

"Yeah, the bombing!" She gripped him harder and implored, "You're here. Hold me!"

"You're safe. Don't worry. I'm not leaving."

She gave him another firm hug as her eyes dreamily closed, and she fell back asleep.

An hour later, he was jostled awake with a loving prod from her. He rolled toward her and found her gleaming and inviting bright eyes studying him. They both searched one another's faces for a very long time. She then slowly moved to a sitting position and pulled off her teddy. She wore no panties. His eyes widened.

When she pushed the bed sheets back, his manhood was large and hard. She tenderly rolled over him until she straddled him. Her blonde, silky hair spilled across his face as she leaned into him. Her lips, then her tongue, found one of his ears. She huskily whispered, "The stitches in my back are a little tender. Are you OK with this position?"

Just before their lips met, he broadly smiled and crooned, "I'll make do!"

He ran his hands over her perfectly formed breasts as she moaned and swayed gently back and forth. They unconsciously began to fuse. Kisses washed over faces, ears, and necks. She leaned forward and slid her hands behind his head. As she pulled his mouth to her breasts and hardening nipples, his hands moved down her smooth, strong legs. First feeling their firmness, then kneading them.

As the rhythm of their undulating increased, her head lolled from side to side, and she gasped, "I'm close."

"Me too!"

In his last moments of lucid thought, he felt Mary slather his prick with a lubricant and gently guide him into her. In unison, they rocked together… words of affection flowed with their tempo… until time stopped, and their universes exploded. Their bodies merged, as if they were one, in a loving, but fierce embrace. Neither one was wanted the moment to end.

After a time, their embrace softened, and he felt warm tears fall upon his cheek. "You OK?" he asked gently.

"More than OK!"

He took several moments to form his reply. "I've never felt like this before."

"Nor I," she sniffled.

They held their embrace, disconnected from time and the call of responsibilities.

After a very long time, she gave him a loving poke. "You awake?"

"Uh-huh."

"How about a repeat?"

"That can't be repeated!"

"Maybe not, but let's try!"

CHAPTER 14

THE FIRST REAL DATE

Chiara's Ristorante Georgetown area | Washington, DC
April 11, 2012 | Wednesday, 5:36 p.m.

HOURS BEFORE HOOK picked up Mary, for their first real date, she was in an absolute tizzy. No matter how she tried to calm herself, nothing worked. She felt like an adolescent schoolgirl before her first date with a high school heartthrob. Her anxiety was such that she began to chew her fingernails, a nervous habit she'd broken twenty years earlier.

Hook had made the difficult-to-get dinner reservation for them at Chiara's Ristorante in Georgetown. In "Washington Today's" yearly review of local restaurants, Chiara's Ristorante was a perennial favorite in the category of Best Italian Restaurants. She'd never dined there before but knew—from her reading of their reviews— that it was a cozy restaurant, with limited seating for up to eighty diners. Its specialties were Sicilian dishes that were influenced by Greek, Spanish, and Arab cultures. Hook's choice of this restaurant, and his apparent familiarity with it, sparked her curiosity and added to her anxiety. She viewed him as more of a "meat and potatoes" man. And she, sure as hell, didn't want to embarrass herself, or her best-ever lover, in front of a packed house of highbrow socialites.

When they entered the restaurant, she was immediately impressed with its layout. A stone archway led into a light-beamed, high-ceiling dining area that was encircled with canary yellow plaster walls and accented with ornate white crown molding. Dinner tables—neatly covered with white, linen tablecloths—were discreetly arranged upon a floor of aged, red tiles and separated with tall potted plants or miniature palms.

A short slender woman with gray hair, fashionably pulled into a bun, suddenly appeared by Hook's side. She silently clutched one of his hands and began to lead him to a private window table in the rear of the restaurant. As she followed the two, she studied the Italian oil paintings and white marble statues that filled the walls and alcoves of the restaurant. The setting reminded her of an elegant Italian villa that one might find overlooking a vineyard.

It was early for dinner—a good thirty minutes before their regular opening, she noted when they entered the restaurant—and only a few other tables were occupied. The nearest diners were a good forty feet away. Their table was separated from them by a half-wall wreathed with flowing plants, and it overlooked a well-tended garden in the rear of the building. A natural stonewall, absent any mortar and approximately twenty-feet high, bordered the back of the garden. The wall was awash with creeping wisteria, their dazzling lavender color dissolving gently with the sinking sun.

Once they were seated, the short woman wordlessly shoved menus at them and placed her hands on her narrow hips. She studied Hook. It was an intense, unreadable look.

"Come stai Mio Bambino? Sembri stanco! Vorresti un espresso per stimolarti? Non puoi deludere questa bella donna!" said the woman, as her eyes moved from Hook to Mary. How are you My Child? You look tired! Would you like an espresso to stimulate you? You can't disappoint this beautiful woman!

Hook blushed slightly and replied, *"Questa è la nostra prima vera data, Chiara."*

The absence of other diners and the hostess's observations in Italian seemed to have a calming effect on Mary. She took one of Hook's hands in hers, then met Chiara's steady gaze and said easily, "Chiara, he is correct. This is our first real date. And if our relationship is to survive, your child better not disappoint me tonight. He is a keeper! *Mi capisci?"* Do you understand me?

"Capisco e questo è fantastico!" I understand and this is great! Chiara next moved behind Hook—whose face was flushed with embarrassment—and

gave him a motherly hug. Switching to English, she said, "Hook's mother, God bless her soul, and I were best friends. Our two families emigrated from Sicily to the U.S. in 1962. We settled in Philadelphia. Our family went into the restaurant business, and Hook's family sold Italian delicacies—cheeses, olives, and meats. How long have you known this handsome man?"

"We met a few days ago!" smiled Mary.

He placed one of his hands atop of one hers and sputtered, "You speak Italian?"

"Passable, plus four others."

"Questa donna è un angelo non rovinare tutto!" crowed Chiara, as she gave Hook a loving slap on the back of his head. This woman is an angel don't screw this up! "We've got your favorite on the menu tonight, *pasta alla Norma.*"

"I'll have that, and we'll share a bottle of your Novella," said Hook.

Mary turned to Chiara. "Please tell me about your pasta alla Norma and Novella."

"Pasta alla Norma is one of our house specialties and a favorite of many of our regulars. It's sautéed eggplant over penne rigate. We don't use macaroni style shells in our dish. We add our homemade tomato sauce plus lightly salted ricotta and basil. As for the wine, the Novella is quite popular. It has a robust, fruity flavor. You'll like it!" replied Chiara knowledgeably.

Mary nodded, "I'll go with that then. Robust is good for tonight," she said as she winked at Hook, her earlier anxiety now a distant memory. He blushed, and Chiara grinned as she left for the kitchen.

Hook had dated a fair number of women in the past, a few he had even lived with. One relationship lasted nearly a year. He generally viewed himself as experienced and worldly when it came to women. He wasn't intimidated by them or reticent in their presence. Mary, however, was in a league of her own. There was nothing ordinary about her, despite her surprising spat of jitters when he arrived at doorstep, an hour earlier. Her intelligence, beauty, and seductive smile had a way of both clouding his thinking and guiding his emotions. Realizing that he'd fallen "head over heels" for her, he'd decided a few days earlier—in a rare moment of clarity— that a modest background check on his lover might be appropriate.

He called several friends at Justice and State. Several of them had worked with her. Others, who only knew of her by name, checked with close friends who did know her. Their feedback amused him, mainly because those he queried assumed he'd be reporting to her. While he smiled distractedly, he reflected on his findings, none of which were ambiguous. *Don't ever lie to her! If you carry out one of her assignments indifferently, you'll regret it. But, if you've done your best and failed, she won't crucify you. And, lastly, forget about asking her out on a date. She's either gay or pretty damn picky!*

While he was ruminating, Chiara arrived with their wine. She expertly opened the bottle and poured a tasting portion into Hook's wineglass.

"Good! It's fine," he said absently as he sipped it.

After filling both of their glasses, Chiara said, "The wine is not good, it's excellent! Furthermore, I've been watching you. I doubt Mary is a mind reader. Communication and compromise builds relationships. Don't ever forget that *Mio Bambino!*" she said as she gave him another loving whack on the back of his head and returned to the kitchen.

They touched glasses and concurrently said, "To us!"

Moments later, Mary arched an eyebrow and smiled. "I hear you've been checking up on me."

Red-faced, he said, "Just confirming my feelings!"

"Any surprises, *Mio Bambino?*"

"Just one, and I've ruled that one out."

"What's that?"

"That you're gay," he said with smiling eyes.

She began to laugh, then he followed. Within seconds, they were each convulsed with laughter.

After a time, they collected themselves and chatted idly, until a waiter arrived at their table. With a flourish, he formally placed a warm plate between them, which held two medium-sized pan-friend crab cakes seasoned with a cilantro-lime sauce. "Compliments of the house!" he proudly pronounced.

Between mouthfuls, she said, "These are the best I've ever had. They're not dry or overcooked, and I love the sauce. The Italian chef obviously knows something about Chesapeake Bay cuisine."

"The chef...rather chefs...are Chiara's niece and nephew. They both sharpened their craft at a restaurant in Catania, Sicily, that's owned by one of Chiara's longtime friends. They also gained some local experience when they helped out another friend of Chiara's. That friend owns a restaurant on the harbor in St. Michaels, Maryland."

"Very impressive!" she murmured. "Tell me what you know about Annie Youngblood. I sat next to her at Easter dinner, last Sunday, in the White House. I learned that she's a sixth-grade teacher who loves her class in Dennis, Montana. She apparently is going to leave teaching and get involved with law enforcement, quite possibly with the FBI. She said Lena is going to help her with her FBI application."

"Lena's mentioned the same thing to me. It's a good idea, and it's justified. The FBI is always on the lookout for qualified Native Americans to help them with Indian affairs in the Western states. She may even get an eventual posting—as a single agent— at an FBI satellite office in Dennis, Montana, her hometown.

"But she won't receive any FBI training before Hall's MANPADS operation in June."

"In the month before the operation, Lena has enrolled her in an accelerated, one-on-one training program with a private security contractor. She'll miss the last couple of weeks of her school year."

"She looks fit, but she's small. I'd guess five-foot-six, and she couldn't weigh more than 120 pounds. To be honest with you, I'm a little concerned about her lack of experience and ability to protect me in Afghanistan. She's a schoolteacher! Does she even know how to load a gun?" asked Mary.

"Firstly, my FBI training schedule has again been modified. During Hall's operation, I'll be shadowing you in Kabul and Jalalabad. Secondly, I hope Annie has time to guard me. She isn't your typical schoolteacher," said Hook pausing to recollect the details of her prior accomplishments. "She has a black belt in jiu-jitsu and was the NRA female World Shooting Champ in 2010. I wouldn't be surprised if her security coach learns more from her than she from him."

"Really!"

"Yeah, really! And that's not the half of it. From what my Marine Corps buddy, Brice Miller, told me she's got ice water running in her veins, and I've personally seen her *gift.* "

"Gift? I trust you're not referring to mystic powers!"

He smiled and said, "This is what happened. Twenty months ago, when I was an ATF agent, I helped the Marines take down a Mexican rip-crew in an area just north of Nogales, Arizona, known as Bellota Canyon. I was helping four Marines tie-up twenty rip-crew captives that had just surrendered. Annie was collecting their weapons. All of a sudden, she straightens, and her head tilts toward the sky. She grabs an M4 carbine and trots off to a nearby hilltop that the rip-crew once held. A good minute later, we hear the distant sound of vehicles approaching. She somehow sensed that vehicles were arriving."

"She has good hearing," countered Mary.

"I have good hearing. I walked point with my Marine squad in Iraq. I could hear a grasshopper hop from fifty-feet away. Annie has special senses."

"Hmm!"

"Her uncle, Tom Youngblood, is the last Youngblood in a long line of Arapaho shamen."

Mary wagged her head, unconvinced.

"So, the vehicles rumble up a steep dirt road to our plateau. We don't know if it's good guys or bad guys. We grab our weapons and hunker down. Fortunately, it turns out to be good guys, the FBI, and local law enforcement. The head FBI guy—Special Agent-in-Charge Herbert Tabb, Phoenix office— turns out, however, to be a bad guy. He was one of a handful of bent guys in the FBI, ATF, and Justice, who enabled thousands of semi-automatic rifles to be delivered into the hands of the Mexican drug cartels.

"Tabb immediately marches up to the rip-crew leader and unties him. He then begins to reprimand us, he's screaming. With wild eyes, he tells us this guy is one of his prized informants and untouchable. It turned out later that he was a registered FBI informant, but the only informing he did was to his cartel boss. Tabb hadn't gotten a lick of intelligence from him. It was a one-way street that solely benefitted the cartel.

"So, we're standing there, face to face. Tabb looks like a Western gunslinger, with matched, six-shooter pistols sitting in open holsters. The rip-crew leader grabs one of his pistols and takes aim at a Phoenix TV news reporter, Maria Perez. She'd just arrived with the local law enforcement. None of us, except for a Phoenix cop, knew of her relationship with the rip-crew's cartel boss. She'd relentlessly criticized him on Phoenix TV. Plus, three months earlier, she'd shot and killed the boss's uncle on her doorstep with a Sig Sauer P-238. The uncle had been sent to assassinate her."

Mary flashed Hook an unusual look as she delicately placed her fork on the table and reached for her handbag. "My dad carries a P-238 when we go hiking in Maine. Lena also carries one. It saved our lives last week. I prefer this," she said as she discreetly lifted a pistol a fraction above the tabletop. "This is my 9 mm Ruger LC9. It was in my gun safe at home last week. I'll now never leave home without it."

He nodded and casually pulled away the left side of his blue blazer, which revealed his pistol that was tucked into a shoulder holster.

"That looks like a Glock 23."

"That's a good guess. I'm impressed. You know you're handguns. It's a Glock 22, a standard FBI sidearm."

"Ah! A little bigger pistol with a magazine that can take fifteen rounds instead of thirteen. I like more firepower," she smiled.

He replied with a grin. "The couple that loves together, packs together. I suggest you return your artillery to your handbag before Chiara returns and has a heart attack."

Moments later, their waiter arrived with their dinners, and further conversation all but ended.

Minutes later, Mary was the first to speak. "Geez, this Pasta alla Norma is delicious."

"Yup!" Hook looked up from his meal and flashed Mary a crooked smile. "I love this dish. It's second only to sex."

"A distant second, I hope! By the way, from the size of that plate, I think you received a double portion."

"Chiara spoils me!"

Mary remained silent as she sipped her wine and studied her lover. He was a man of many passions. Sex obviously, excellent food now, and the conviction to do what was right... regardless of the professional consequences. He was the ATF agent who blew the whistle on the government's gunwalking scam, and he exposed—only days earlier—the visa and No Fly List corruption that had taken hold in Homeland Security and the FBI. *Definitely a keeper, but also one with a growing list of enemies,* she thought. "Back to Bellota Canyon, what happened to Perez?"

"An instant before the rip-crew leader shoots Perez—the Phoenix cop, a childhood friend—steps in front of her and takes a bullet in the head. The two tumble to the ground. He's dead before he reaches the ground. She's uninjured. The leader then turns the pistol on Annie's husband, Bobby. A moment before he pulls the trigger, his head explodes. It's a perfect headshot from Annie's hilltop, a good 150 yards away.

"Tabb, then, goes berserk. His prized informant is dead. He draws his other pistol and aims it at Captain Jim Grimes, USMC. He was in charge of the Marine unit that subdued the rip-crew. No one thinks he'll really pull the trigger, except for Brice Miller. He dives in front of Grimes at the last instant and takes a shot in the chest. His Kevlar vest saves him. Both men tumble to the ground. But Tabb isn't through. He steps toward them and raises his pistol for a second shot. Annie shoots the pistol out of his hand, another 150-yard perfect shot!

"According to Brice, that's the second time she's saved his life. In 2008, she nailed a terrorist, in the Yellowstone shootout, who leveled his pistol at him from a distance of ten feet. That 250-yard shot, with a Marine Corps sniper rifle, was uphill and delivered through a forest of trees."

"Sounds like she does know how to load a gun!" she smiled, before adding, "You also said that she has ice water in her veins. What did you mean by that?"

"In that same Yellowstone attack, the terrorists got the upper hand. At the peak of the shootout, Annie scrambled toward the lead terrorist who was issuing orders to his men. He was positioned on a roadbed fifteen feet above her hillside location. The bad guys were setting up a machine gun to fire at five busloads of school kids who were running for their lives. Her bravery, nerve, or whatever it was surprised the leader. Before he could collect himself and draw his sidearm, she shot him with a .45 caliber pistol. That act apparently swung the tide of the battle in favor of the good guys."

"That was ballsy! You've convinced me. She's just the opposite of what I thought."

"I also think that because of her size and dark complexion that she could easily blend in with the older girls in your Jalalabad school. She could be an inside, undercover agent when Hall executes his MANPADS operation."

"School will be in recess. There shouldn't be any schoolgirls present during the operation. But you're right about her blending in with the girls."

Changing to a different subject, she asked, "What do you think of President Adams's succession plan? That was quite an Easter dinner revelation."

Hook turned his head, checking to see if anyone could overhear them. The nearest party was leaving. No one could hear them. "At first, I was shocked that they would divulge those details to us. But after thinking about it, it makes sense, especially in your case. You know more about the dirty Afghan dealings of President Hakim Qazi and Police Chief Safi Khan than anyone else. Plus, from what Hall and Zahir told us last week at the CIA, they're all connected to David, Smithson, and Hightower in one way or another."

She nodded and reached for her wineglass. After taking a sip, she said plainly, "FBI Director Tom Milton trusts you. You'll be his eyes in Afghanistan. You'll also be a hidden asset of Hall's."

He massaged his jaw while he considered her comment. After a time, he elected to change the subject. "I didn't know Jed Adams was in such bad shape. He looked awful last Sunday."

"He did. I was surprised that he made it through dinner. His wife, Becky, all but fed him."

"McCracken's wife wasn't much better. You could tell he really loves her. Resigning was a good idea. He'll be with her till her last breath. The same goes for Becky with Jed."

"Both good men and great Americans." Moving on, she said, "I doubt there will be any delays with Congress's approval of Ted David as vice president."

"None that I can see. Having Lena in the wings...to take over the vice presidency if Adams passes...is forward-thinking. I like that idea."

"Me too," she said. "What do you think of Hall's MANPADS plan?"

"I like it. It's a first step toward mending relations with Pakistan, and it seems to be a good way to crack down on Tehrik-i-Taliban (TTP). I've also been checking up on Safi Khan. He seems to have a stranglehold on police matters, not only in Kabul but throughout the country. I don't think changing alliances—from the Haqqani Network to the TTP—will compromise his influence in Afghanistan."

"Safi Khan and TTP!" groused Mary with a tight-lipped grimace. "That's a bad combination... a senior Afghan insider and heartless killers that target school children. I like the fact that Hall's got TTP in his crosshairs. From what Zahir was saying about Hall's support of the Afghan mujahideen in the 1980s, I got the impression that he rather enjoys killing bad guys."

"Absolutely! By the way, do you have any idea who Safi's informant is in the embassy?" he asked.

"The guy nicknamed Cannon?"

He nodded.

"I think it's Lane Peters. He's a senior DS security specialist at the embassy. He used to escort me around Kabul during my last tour. He's not friendly, and he's a stickler about security. During my unforgettable drive from the embassy to Bagram last September, one of Peters's DS colleagues, Joe Michaels, was a fellow passenger in our armored Toyota SUV. Michaels said that he thought Peters was into 'sketchy stuff.' Selling intelligence and/or weapons to the bad guys. A couple of Michaels's Army buddies told him that Peters was kicked out of the Army for doing that in Iraq. He received an *Other than Honorable Discharge (OTH)* from the Army, according to Michaels."

Hook remained silent for several long moments while he considered Mary's comments. *If* Peters did the things she said, he would have been court-martialed and sent to Leavenworth Prison for years. After serving his sentence, he would have then received a *Dishonorable Discharge (DD)*, *not* an *Other than Honorable Discharge (OTH)*. But, if Peters somehow had his charges reduced, and he did receive an *OTH,* that alone would have precluded him from applying to Diplomatic Security (DS) for a security position. Michael's story didn't make sense. He decided to research the matter.

"Earth to Hook, come in Hook! What do you think of Brice and Yossi's involvement with Hall's MANPADS plan?" said Mary with a questioning look.

"Sorry, just thinking. I think it's a good idea. Brice knows his way around a battlefield. I've checked up on him. Before being admitted to the Naval Academy, with an age waiver, he was the youngest gunnery sergeant in the Corps. He received a Silver Star for pulling several of his buddies from a burning HUMVEE in Fallujah. He then returned to the HUMVEE's .50-caliber gun-turret and drove away a boatload of al-Qaeda insurgents who were on the verge of overrunning his unit. That incident occurred during the second battle of Fallujah, Iraq, in November 2004."

Smiling, he placed an index finger on his face and traced his faded knife scar from his ear, along his jawline, to an inch from his Adam's apple. "That's where I got my nick!"

"It's hardly a nick, *Mio Amante!*"

"Ah!" he smiled broadly. "I've graduated from your *baby* to your *lover.* I like the sound of that, especially when you say it in Italian. It adds an element of zest to our relationship!"

She flashed him a seductive smile and coolly sipped more of her wine.

That look of hers could arouse him in a heartbeat, which it was currently doing. He subtly rearranged the linen napkin in his lap to avoid any embarrassment, should Chiara suddenly arrive. "In addition to Brice's Silver Star…" he began with garbled speech.

"Cat got your tongue…again?" purred Mary.

He politely smiled and took a sip of water. "Once a Marine, always a Marine! Marines can control their emotions!"

She leaned toward him, while one of her hands deftly moved along the inside of one of his legs. "Ah, what have we got here? Did you secretly slip a cucumber into your pants when I wasn't looking?" she said with a lewd smirk.

He shifted his chair to the side, out of range of her hand, and crossed his legs. With a goofy smile creasing his lips, he said playfully, "Let's conserve our energy for your bedroom and act like mature adults."

She laughed a loud, exuberant laugh and fell back into her chair, giggling. "*Conserve our energy!* I'm not into eco-friendly lovemaking."

Blushing, he turned slightly to see if anyone had noticed their exchange. "You know what I mean. Now, back to Brice…"

Fifty-feet away, partially hidden by a large potted plant, was Chiara. With glowing eyes and a satisfied smile, she silently sent her best wishes their way.

"…in addition to his Silver Star, Brice has three Purple Hearts, the Defense Superior Service Medal, the Navy and Marine Corps Medal, plus several lesser medals. This is a timely 'tweener' assignment for him."

"*Tweener?* What does that mean? And how did Brice Miller get involved in Hall's MANPADS operation?"

"His involvement?" he thought. "First, he's Yossi's roommate at Annapolis. Yossi's dad and Mossad provided the initial MANPADS intelligence. That got the ball rolling. Then, Hall, who is a close friend of President Adams, may have mentioned Annapolis during his MANPADS briefing of Adams. Adams and his wife, Becky, have no children. From what I've heard, they've become quite close to Brice during his four years at Annapolis. He's stayed with them in the White House multiple times, especially during holidays. They first met Brice after he, Annie, and others thwarted that terrorist attack in Yellowstone National Park in 2008. The principals were invited to the White House for a celebratory dinner. Adams repeated the dinner invitation after the Bellota Canyon debacle in 2010.

"Hall, Adams, and Brice are all from West Texas. Brice was from a broken home. His high school football coach's family informally adopted him. I think, so too, have the Adams. That's my best guess on how Brice may have initially come to Hall's attention.

"As for the *tweener assignment,* Hall and the CIA have got their hands on a very experienced Marine *between* his graduation from the Naval Academy and his reporting to the Corps's The Basic School (TBS) in Quantico, Virginia. Once Brice reports to Quantico, his life and career are strictly controlled and jealously guarded by the iron fists of the Marine Corps. And, from my experiences in the Corps, that means everything is done by the book. No secret assignments, like this. No bending the rules. No missions, without the full support and oversight of the Corps."

"I see. That's good to know. In a way, I'm like that! I watch over my New Hope Schools and Beena Waleed like a mother hen. Beena is as close to a daughter as I'll ever have."

He understood the intent of her simile while inwardly chuckling at her comparison. Comparing a hen to Marines was a stretch. Bit by bit, however, he was learning what was important to his lover.

Continuing with his discussion of Brice, he added, "Brice's roommate... and your onetime admirer... Yossi Levy is no slouch, either. He served in the Israel Defense Force (IDF) for three years before receiving his acceptance, as well as an age waiver, to Annapolis. The IDF awarded him the Medal of

Distinguished Service in 2006 for his courage and extreme bravery during a Gaza tunnel battle. It's their third-highest medal and one that is not lightly awarded. He also speaks Farsi, and he looks like he's from Libya. He's a good fit."

After a comfortable period of silence, he took one of her hands in his. "Did you miss me last night?"

"Yes, I cried my self to sleep, but not over you."

He saw the glimmer of tears begin to well in the corner of her eyes. Looking her hard in the eye, he asked, "Flashbacks on the bombing?"

"Uh-huh!" she whispered as she wiped a tear off her cheek with her free hand.

"Sad about not nailing the bomber further from the kids?"

She hiccupped and nodded.

He massaged her hand for several moments before responding. "I've read the FBI's revised incident report on the bombing. Director Milton called me into his office today after lunch and showed me the report. He'd received it only an hour earlier from his internal review board. He'd ordered a new investigation after learning of Byron Weeks's misrepresentations of the incident. Do you want to hear the gist of it?"

She removed her one hand from his and studied him. His face was impassive, with no indication or clue about the report's findings. "No! I did my best. That's all that matters!"

He liked her answer but disregarded it. "Your two seventy-yard shots that brought down the bomber were rated as 'high expert.' The report also stated that the shooter, you," he paused briefly to accurately recall the report's conclusion. "You exhibited a high degree of initiative and competency in retrieving an unfamiliar rifle and accurately firing two stopping shots that prevented the suicide bomber from advancing further toward a group of school children. The investigator's closing comment stated that without your quick reaction and expert shots, during an incident where your life was also at risk, there would have certainly been a greater loss of life and more serious injuries."

"Thanks for telling me that. It helps! But, but..." she cried as her chest heaved, and a stream of tears rolled down her cheeks.

Hook moved his chair beside her and wrapped an arm around her shoulders.

Her head turned into his chest, and she cried like a baby. Her cathartic release was unseen by all in the restaurant, save for Chiara. She'd read last week's newspaper accounts of the incident and the description of the unnamed, tall blonde woman from Justice who'd shot the suicide bomber. From what Hook told her when he made his dinner reservation, she correctly guessed who Mary was and why she was crying.

Hook held her tightly against his chest and patted her shoulder as he whispered into her ear. "People like us are different from most others. When life's fair-weather turns into a thunderstorm, we don't compromise our principles and take shortcuts. We stay the course and afterward lick our wounds. Wounds that are often psychological and unseen. That price comes with being who we are. We have to focus on the positives. You saved the lives of thirty-two sixth graders and three teachers last week. Sadly, three students didn't make it. In time, you'll get better, and this experience will make you stronger."

After finishing their dinner and declining coffee and desert, Chiara stepped inconspicuously to their side. She silently bobbed her head toward the entry lobby. Hook and Mary followed her gaze. The lobby was packed with diners anxiously waiting to be seated at their reserved tables.

"Notice anything unusual?" Chiara asked.

"Lots of customers want to be seated," said Hook.

"Take a closer look!"

"They're looking at you," said Mary.

"No, they're looking at you! My waiters have loose lips. I, unfortunately, mentioned to one of them that I thought you were the woman who shot the suicide bomber last week. They pulled up your picture on social media and confirmed my suspicion. I'm so sorry!"

"That's life. Mary is now famous. She'll get used to it," said Hook, a little too insensitively to Chiara's liking.

He received another whack on the back of his head. "Grow up, *Mio Bambino!* Ladies deserve better treatment, especially this one. *Trattala come una divinità!*" Treat her like a goddess!

Mary stood and hugged Chiara. She then whispered into her ear.

Chiara returned her whisper, but just loud enough for Hook to hear her salacious and sexy advice. She refused Hook's offer to pay for their dinner with an unexpected and leading reply. *"Pasti gratis qui fino a quando non sei sposato!"* Free meals here until you're married! Arm in arm, she then guided them to a rear exit.

The race to Mary's townhome, in Hook's Dodge Charger, was made all the more exciting by their passionate kissing and caressing across two bucket-seats, and Hook's need to somehow keep an eye on the road.

Once they arrived at Mary's front door, she feverishly searched through her handbag for her keys. After a few expletives, she found them and then unsteadily dropped them in a potted plant that rested beside the door. Hook retrieved them and coolly unlocked the front door. What happened next was far from cool. It was frenzied, passionate, and downright sizzling. Partially dressed sex standing, in the front hallway, against a closet door. Naked sex in Mary's shower. And finally, one last hurrah in Mary's king-size bed before they fell asleep in each other's arms, satiated and exhausted.

CHAPTER 15

VICE PRESIDENT TED DAVID

Harry S. Truman Building, Washington, D.C.
Office of the Secretary of State
April 27, 2012 | Friday, 11:28 a.m.

VICE PRESIDENT TED David weaved his way around packed boxes, destined for his new office in the West Wing, and settled into his well-worn, leather desk chair. He leaned back in his chair and rested his crossed feet on his desktop.

Max Smithson, David's recently appointed presidential campaign manager and chief fundraiser, sat opposite him. Smithson showed no signs whatsoever of his tearful and seemingly heartfelt resignation of several weeks earlier. He'd been forced from his post as deputy attorney general at Justice for Hatch Act fundraising violations. His well-orchestrated resignation—beside the Spirit of Justice statue in the Great Hall of the Robert F. Kennedy Department of Justice Building—received national news media attention. More importantly, it achieved its intended political result. Biased news media outlets and fellow party members, from coast-to-coast, screamed at the injustice of it. The Hatch Act of 1939, in their opinion, was antiquated and was never intended to punish such an upstanding public servant as Smithson.

"So, how did your first campaign speech as vice president go yesterday in Albany?" asked Smithson.

"All of our New York state politicians showed up. Plus, most of the

Madison & Lee College (M&L) student body was present. The weather was a little cool, but it was sunny. I made the speech from the steps of the student union building. All told, there were probably 3,000 people in attendance."

David's approval to the post of vice presidency sailed through both Houses of Congress in record time. The Democrats loved the idea that he could campaign for the presidency while still holding office. The Republicans liked the idea because they thought it might minimize his coast-to-coast presidential campaign stumping. He had to stay close to home, in Washington, to attend to his new responsibilities. They reasoned that the less he flashed his dazzling smile and beat his campaign drum around the country, during state primaries, the better it was for them.

The major news media wondered briefly how this unusual event came to pass—the appointment of Ted David, a non-American Party supporter, to the vice presidency—but no one really knew. Excepting that is President Adams; his former vice president, Tim McCraken; his new vice president, Ted David; FBI Director Tom Milton; Acting Attorney General Lena Jones and a handful of other tight-lipped insiders. Those insiders included Mike Hall, Mary Phillips, and Hook DeLuca. Little could the news media imagine how stranger events would soon become.

Before David's appointment to the vice presidency, he was generally viewed as the presumptive presidential nominee for the Democratic Party. Now, as the sitting vice president, he believed that his presidential nomination prospects were a virtual lock. He couldn't imagine that any Democrat would vote against him in a state primary, especially since he'd been appointed, and endorsed, to his new post by a president from an opposing political party, the American Party. State primaries would automatically fall in his favor, like tumbling dominoes. He was his party's man for the top spot! Thus, the only issue to be decided before the Democratic National Convention in September was who would be his vice-presidential running mate.

And even that debate was, in his mind, a no-brainer. President Adams's backroom requirements—to appoint Lena Jones to the vice presidency, in the event of his death, and to have her run as his vice president on his party's presidential ticket—were hardly concessions. Having a black female, and the current acting attorney general, no less, as his running mate was a "win, win" proposition. Furthermore, she was admired and respected by his party's loyalists, as well as those who supported the American Party. Come next November, she would tip his tight election prospects—whether she was still at Justice or his vice president—into a guaranteed win.

Once David was sworn into office, and the hoopla surrounding his inauguration had died down, Lena would learn—at the pinnacle of her political career—the meaning of being totally irrelevant. He'd send her packing to the adjacent Eisenhower Executive Office Building, where she and her staff could count paperclips for the next four years. Her token office in the White House would go to someone on his staff, like Hightower, Jr. She'd have no say in any of his decisions.

"I don't care who was there. What did you cover in your campaign speech, and were there any hardball questions?" pressed Smithson, in his typically blunt manner.

"I spoke about immigration and the benefits of open borders. The kids and reporters ate up my 'We're all immigrants' line."

"I heard that there was a question about the relaxation of visa standards for…unfriendly foreign visitors."

"Unfriendly as in a jihadist," cracked David with a foolish smile.

"Goddamn it, David! Watch what you say. If you ever let slip with a comment like that in public, your shot at the presidency will disappear in a flash."

"Chill out, Smithson. I was just kidding. Now that I'm the vice president, Islamic fundamentalists will never screw with us on U.S. soil. They love me!"

"I wouldn't count on that!"

"Anyways, concerning visas, I passed the buck. I told the crowd that my buddy…Jim Agnew, the Secretary of Homeland Security (DHS)… was in charge of that stuff. They bought it!"

"Watch what you say about your connections at DHS and the FBI. The news media knows that it's only a matter of days before Agnew resigns. Deputy Director, Byron Weeks of the FBI has already resigned and our buddy …Hightower, Jr., …is in the midst of filing charges against him. The news media is already intimating that Agnew and Weeks accepted bribes in exchange for visas to suspicious persons and/or the removal of their names from the No-Fly List. The two Taliban jihadists who were behind the recent Washington bombing…" Smithson suddenly stopped.

David's face was blank. He'd forgotten about the attack.

Smithson unconsciously chewed on the inside of his lip as he attempted to check his irritation. He continued, with barely controlled speech, "… the bombing of a couple of weeks ago, near the Jefferson Memorial. The two bombers bought their way into the country."

"Right!" said David, still clueless.

"Three 6th grade school kids were killed in their attack and ten others injured!"

"Yes, of course! Very tragic! It slipped my mind. A lot has happened in the last couple of weeks. Can I be tied to that bombing? I suspect our partner in Kabul, Safi Khan, was behind that attack. I thought he was only going after Mary Phillips."

Smithson's face turned red. He silently marched to the office's Audio-Visual (AV) receiver and turned up the volume. He didn't want listening devices to record this private, and quite incriminating, chat with David.

Audio recording devices were often installed in senior government offices for a variety of purposes. The occupants of those offices were usually apprised of their presence, but not always. Even with that prior knowledge, it wasn't uncommon for an occupant to let slip an embarrassing comment that could easily be passed on anonymously, by a disgruntled or jealous colleague, to a member of the press.

At this point in time—the move of David's files and furniture from State to the West Wing—neither David nor Smithson were aware of FBI Director Tom Milton's high level of contempt toward each of them. Nor were they fully aware of the allegations that Byron Weeks made, in front of then Vice President Tim McCracken, in Milton's office on April 3, 2012.

Bloodied and sniveling, after being pummeled by his older and out-of-shape boss, Milton, Weeks spilled his heart out during that April 3rd meeting. He knew that Safi Khan was behind the Jefferson Memorial bombing attack. He also knew that David, Smithson, and Hightower were partners with Khan, and president Hakim Qazi, in various fuel truck and toll collection scams in Afghanistan. Between juvenile whimpers, he then bawled that he didn't possess any hard evidence to support his allegations. His uncorroborated claims—to an old school, just-the-facts type of investigator—further angered Milton. When Weeks blabbered apologetically—possibly in the hope of receiving some form of absolution from his boss—that Dr. Mary Phillips was the intended target at the Jefferson Memorial, not the 6th-grade class, Milton had to be pulled off Weeks a second time.

Moments after Weeks was dragged out of his office, Milton was on the phone. In no particular order, he wanted the straight dope on the bombing, and he wanted to know more about David, Smithson, and Hightower's nefarious dealings in Afghanistan. It wasn't long before he found himself speaking securely with the CIA's station chief in Kabul, Mike Hall, who just happened to be back in Washington for meetings.

Hall shared, with his longtime friend, his intelligence and suspicions about David. He also disclosed to him, with the prior approval of Adams, the president's ingenious plan for the survival of his American Party. Milton repaid his confidences by filling him in on Weeks's minutes-earlier, tell-all confession.

Within twenty-four hours, Milton had multiple, state-of-the-art recording devices planted throughout David's State office. He additionally made plans to have another set of devices planted in the vice president's office in the West Wing, once McCracken moved out. These new recording devices, unbeknownst to David and Smithson, had little difficulty eliminating background music.

Smithson slid his chair closer to David's desk and lowered his voice. "Our errand boy, Bill, was our go-between in all of our dealings with Agnew and Weeks. They both probably suspect that we were involved in some way, but they have no direct proof. I think Bill's usefulness to us has run its course. I see an accidental death in his future. What do you think?"

David nodded his head in agreement and said, "Very accidental and very untraceable. Even with my personal instructions, the jerk couldn't persuade the CIA to bomb an insignificant Pashtun village in the FATA, which no one in the U.S. has ever heard of, including me. The Jefferson Memorial bombing was yet another example of crappy execution. If I'm elected president next November, Smithson, I can't afford any more fuckups!"

It's your job to make sure that my instructions get followed. That is if you want to be the next attorney general."

Smithson kept his short-fuse temper in check as he faked a compliant nod of his head. David's threat and his singular focus on *his career* was testing his patience.

"Knowing Hightower, Jr.," continued David, "the charges against Agnew and Weeks will likely be written-up in such an abstruse and difficult-to-prove fashion that nothing will ever come of it. He'll protect his friends. By the way, I'm having lunch with both Hightowers in the Eisenhower Executive Office Building at noon. Pakistan's border closure is hurting his father's business, VA Trucking. He's not selling any more fuel trucks to carriers in Pakistan, and he's likely got a long list of truck lessees who are in arrears on their lease payments. I suspect they want to see if there is anything I can do to prod Pakistan into reopening their borders into Afghanistan."

"I doubt there is anything you can do to unclog that mess. There are already major players, like the ISAF, who are pressuring Pakistan. That border closure is costing the ISAF an extra $100 million per month in higher fuel costs. The Hightowers will probably also piss and moan about our reduced revenue stream from Safi's truck shakedown enterprises. That too has been hurt by the border closure."

David absently smiled in agreement. He turned his head in the direction of the music receiver. A hard metal tune was playing. "This is crap. Are we through with discussing sensitive stuff?"

Smithson nodded and turned off the music.

Though David didn't particularly enjoy hard metal music, his main purpose in turning off the music was to divert their conversation from the Hightowers. Were he to be elected president, he'd also promised Hightower, Jr. the post of attorney general "Back to your campaign speech," began Smithson, "I heard from a reporter that there was a group of protesters at your speech yesterday who were making a stink about Islam's view of non-believers."

"Yeah, there were about fifteen of them, and they were handing out leaflets that contained quotes from the Hadith. As you know, Islam's view of non-believers isn't very tolerant or sympathetic, especially among Islamic fundamentalists."

Smithson interjected, "That's an understatement. They believe they should all be killed."

"Anyways," parried David, "I handled the situation. I had my starry-eyed, student campaign staff grab all their leaflets. They then screamed at the protesters, called them Islamophobes, and chased them off. I even shouted at the smart-alecks. 'My dad was an Iranian Muslim!' It was a beautiful sight!" boasted David.

Smithson cringed while he delivered another warning, "Be careful of what you say. The press knows that your natural father was not an Iranian, nor a Muslim."

"Chill out, Smithson! Do you think for one second that those kids will make a distinction between my natural father and stepfather? Shit, seventy-five percent of them won't even bother to register and vote," mocked David.

"I'd also keep those stats to yourself!" grumbled Smithson. With his speedy congressional approval to the vice presidency, David's arrogance had been supercharged. His current level of sanctimonious behavior was already beginning to wear on him.

"OK, I'll stick to banging my Islam drum. Islam is the religion of love! Their cultured and urbane 'profs' love that. God forbid they ever have to travel to Mogadishu, Bagdad, Beirut, Damascus, or Benghazi."

Each of those cities was a center of violent intra-Muslim conflicts or noted for their intolerance of everything Western. Everything Western included clean drinking water, sewage systems, public schools that allowed girls to attend, electricity to homes, and modern medicine. It also included all Western tourists.

Also included on that list of cities, thought Smithson, *were parts of London, Paris, Brussels, Amsterdam, Berlin, Munich, and Barcelona.* Several years earlier, he'd promised his first-year college daughter an all-expenses-paid European trip if she maintained her Dean's List academic standing through graduation. She had kept her end of the deal, but he was now backpedaling. He was throwing in a used car in exchange for a destination change to Australia, New Zealand, or anywhere in South America, except Venezuela. His daughter wouldn't hear of it. A deal was a deal!

"You're a lock to be the next Democratic candidate for president. Don't give *the right* any chance to critique your speeches," urged Smithson.

"Yeah, yeah, yeah! Take it easy! Listen, I've got to leave for my lunch." He stood, unconsciously brushed his wavy brown hair to the side, and without a goodbye or thanks to Smithson strutted out of his office.

CHAPTER 16

MANPADS IN JALALABAD

FOB Fenty | Jalalabad Airport
June 5, 2012 | Tuesday, 1:42 p.m.

ONCE THE PROPELLERS of the U.S. Air Force C-130 Hercules came to a stop, the pilot lowered the rear cargo ramp, and one of his crewmembers released the combined exit door-external stairs. Before Brice Miller and Yossi Levy stepped out of the aircraft, they turned upwards, toward the cockpit, and thanked the pilot and his crew for a safe flight.

The pilot looked down at them and smiled. "Did you like our reclining seats and in-flight meals?"

Brice smiled and gave the pilot a thumbs-up gesture. "Loved the horse-cock sandwiches, and the web seating was the best ever!"

The pilot laughed and said, "Stay safe, boys!"

After exiting the aircraft, they moved toward the aircraft's rear cargo ramp. Moments later, two nearby panel trucks and a forklift arrived. It was a windy, clear day with the air temperature hovering around 95°F. The concrete taxiway was, at least, thirty degrees warmer. While Brice reviewed the off-loading instructions with the aircraft's loadmaster, Yossi spoke to the two Afghan truck drivers in Farsi. Minutes later, Brice and Yossi trooped into the tired and partially air-conditioned passenger terminal of the Jalalabad Airport. FOB Fenty encompassed the airport.

Standing behind a second-story bay window, they scrutinized the movement of their valuable cargo. Thirty 36"(H) X60"(L) X 30"(W) crates that were secured to custom-built pallets, two crates per pallet, were loaded into the panel trucks. Each 250-pound crate was stamped and sealed in accordance with U.S. Department of Defense cargo regulations. The cargo manifest description read, "Agricultural Equipment," which was partially accurate. Except for a specially modified roll of plastic netting—to protect crops from birds—which was placed in the bottom of each crate, the crates contained a various assortment of tools. Shovels, hoes, rakes, and other miscellaneous farm tools. Inside each heavily shrink-wrapped roll of netting was an undetectable MANPAD. Undetectable, that is, except for its weight, which was five times the weight of a standard roll of netting.

Both men were tired. Their day had started ten hours earlier when they observed the loading of their cargo at the Incirlik Air Base in Turkey. Because their cargo would be the first to be off-loaded at Jalalabad, they patiently watched the loadmasters secure all types of first-on cargo that totaled approximately 28,000 pounds. Once the aircraft was loaded and airborne, they expected a seven-hour flight. With headwinds and mid-air refueling by a KC-135 Stratotanker, their 2,400-mile flight took a little over eight hours. Eight hours in the cargo bay of a noisy as hell C-130.

The ring of the burner cell phone, which Yossi had taken from the Egyptian, Mostafa, at Incirlik, startled him. He answered the call in Farsi, "Hello!"

"Mostafa?"

He recognized an American accent. He continued in Farsi, "Yes! Who is calling?"

"You don't recognize my voice?" replied the speaker in Farsi.

"No, but I know it's not Safi Khan. I've had a long day. Who is this?" he growled.

"Very good! This is Mike Hall," he replied in English. "There has been a change in plans."

The first phase of Hall's MANPADS operation had unfolded without incident. Yossi, Brice, and a couple of others had smoothly arrested Mostafa and a turncoat American USAID volunteer when their Cairo to Incirlik flight landed in Turkey. In the course of the arrest, the USAID volunteer let slip that Safi was supposed to pay him and Mostafa, $5,000 each, for accompanying the MANPADS. The contents of each crate were next rearranged to accommodate a special roll of netting that contained a re-engineered MANPAD.

Before the arrest of the two al-Qaeda agents at Incirlik, Hall's counterintelligence team in Kabul had been monitoring Mostafa's cell phone conversations with Kabul's police chief, Safi Khan. In the New Hope Girls School, Jalalabad, his team had also planted numerous listening devices and pre-positioned weapons in hidden locations. The weapons included several M4 carbines and handguns, flashbang grenades, tear gas canisters, and a half dozen syringes filled with an incapacitating agent. The pre-positioned weapons were concealed in inconspicuous locations just in case something went astray.

The scheduled delivery date of the MANPADS to Tehrik-i-Taliban (TTP) was set for the next day, June 6, 2012. The day after the girls had been dismissed for summer recess. Mary, Beena, Hook, Annie, and a contingent of four Navy SEALS would be the only ones present at the school when the MANPADS transaction occurred. Annie would be disguised as a student volunteer and Hook as an old and feeble janitor.

The four SEALs would be hidden in a storage shed at the rear of the schoolhouse. They would also be connected to Hall's communications links, which included listening devices inside the school. The door to the shed was secured with a rusted, un-pickable lock to prevent the bad guys from investigating it. The SEALs form of ingress and egress would be via an undetectable sliding panel on the side opposite the shed's door. They'd be called upon in the event the exchange went bad, or the TTP clansmen attempted to harm the women or damage the empty school.

Hall's operation was intended to accomplish three goals. His first goal was to record incriminating discussions between Safi Khan and the Tehrik-i-Taliban (TTP) clansmen at the school. The second goal was to peacefully turn over the keys to the two panel trucks—loaded with the tinkered MANPADS—to the TTP clansmen and let them go on their merry way. Lastly, he hoped to apprehend Safi and extract from him—by threatening to disclose to his current terrorist partners, his new relationship with TTP—the details of his many scams involving David, Smithson, Hightower, and Qazi.

His carefully planned operation began to unravel two hours earlier when a member of his CIA team listened in on three of Safi Khan's phone calls. The first incoming call was from a man named Cannon. Cannon said he'd gotten into Mary Phillips's room at the U.S. Embassy, Kabul, with his security key, and found revealing notes on her desk calendar. The notes read: "June 5- MANPADS arrive, last day of classes" and "June 6- MANPADS delivery."

Safi thanked Cannon, and then made a call to someone Hall's team was quite familiar with, Hakimullah Mehsud. Mehsud and Mullah Fazlullah were the co-leaders of Tehrik-i-Taliban (TTP). Mehsud instructed Safi to pick-up the MANPADS that afternoon, *a day earlier than planned.* He also reminded Safi that he expected him, and his partner, Cannon, to be present at the school for the transfer of the MANPADS to several of his men. Safi was holding the second half of Mehsud's payment, $75,000, for the thirty MANPADS, and an additional $5,000 for each of Belhaj's men who were accompanying the weapons Safi then called Cannon back and explained to him the change in plans. Cannon said he'd immediately leave the embassy and estimated that his hundred-mile drive, from Kabul to Jalalabad, would take three hours. He'd meet Safi and their new TTP partners at the originally scheduled meeting place, Phillips's all-girls school.

Unfortunately, Hall hadn't received this intelligence until a few minutes earlier.

"Thus, you may expect a call, at any moment, from Safi ordering you to take the MANPADS directly to the school."

"What about the SEALs? Will they be on station?"

"No, they're out of town. They fly into Jalalabad tonight. I'm rounding up some of my men and sending them to the school as we speak. But I can't guarantee that they'll be in place when you arrive."

"What about getting the students out of the school?"

"There's a problem with that too. No one is answering the school phone, and our four insiders—Mary, Beena, Annie, and Hook—are at the school, conducting a dress rehearsal for tomorrow's supposed exchange. I can't reach any of them either. TTP must be using a cell phone jammer."

"Shit!"

"Yes, so you've got to improvise and—"

"I have an incoming call. The screen says it's Safi. I'll call you back afterwards.

Hall realized that his prospects for completing a successful operation were rapidly disintegrating. He wasn't at the starting blocks of an attack where a simple "abort" command would suffice. He was in the middle of a complex, multi-pronged undertaking that now involved the lives of at least one hundred students and an unknown number of teachers and staff. He needed help. After a moment of reflection, he hit the name of a familiar name on his cell phone call list, Jan Zahir.

"How are you, my friend? Ready for tomorrow's operation?" answered Zahir. "My people are in place to follow Mehsud's TTP men to their hide-out."

"Change of plans," replied Hall, with an unmistakable note of urgency. "The MANPADS delivery is going down this afternoon. Mehsud moved the delivery date up. Someone from our embassy tipped Safi, and Safi tipped Mehsud. I think Mehsud's men... I don't know how many... are already at the school. I haven't been able to reach anyone there. And Mary, Beena, Annie Youngblood, and Hook's cell phones aren't working. The bastards have either collected them, or they're jamming them. They went to the school today to rehearse tomorrow's plan. There are also at least six teachers...maybe more, including staff... and over a hundred girls at the school. All likely hostages!" grumbled Hall.

Zahir remained silent for several long moments as he thought. "I have two women in their early twenties who are trained assassins. They each look like they're fifteen-years-old. They'll easily pass as students. They use knives and syringes for their assignments. I can have them at the front door of your school in one hour. They'll carry books with them and explain they are cousins who live in the same house. They'll dream up some excuse for their tardiness."

"Today is the last day of school before the summer recess if that's of any help."

"Maybe, OK. I'll pass that on to them. They'll be with my assistant, Farid. You've met him before. They'll walk by the main entrance of the cricket stadium on their way to the school. If you have any last-minute instructions for them, that's where you can deliver them. Is there any way they can recognize this Annie Youngblood? And, Hook is probably the only male in the building."

"That's right...I forgot...you haven't met Annie Youngblood. She's Mary's personal guard...an expert shot and she has a black belt in Ju-Jitsu. She's short, five-foot-six, but all the girls at the school are probably around that height," he said, more to himself, trying to remember other identifying highlights. "She'll likely have the broadest shoulders of anyone of the schoolgirls. I think...I think her covering veil is off-white with light blue and pink stripes. Hook will be disguised as an old janitor. Hopefully, they're wearing their disguises. They should be!"

"Yes, hopefully! Farid will be with the two women at the cricket stadium. Bye."

Hall either forgot or wasn't aware of Zahir's relationship with Beena. Thus, when he asked him for help, he had no idea of the type of response he was initiating.

Zahir immediately called Farid into his office and gave him instructions. He next phoned his one and only spy in the Kabul police force, Din Pirooz. Pirooz had been investigating a robbery in Kabul, which led him to Jalalabad. He'd had lunch with him just the day before. Though Pirooz wasn't a member of his clan, the two shared an intense hatred of Safi Khan.

"Hello, who's this?" answered Pirooz warily.

"Your luncheon friend from yesterday?"

He recognized the voice but thought a moment before answering. He knew that Safi had a staff of loyal crooked cops who routinely eavesdropped on the personal cell phone calls of their honest duty-bound brethren. "Ah yes, the merchant who heard things about the robbery in Kabul. Has your memory improved?" he said with contrived sarcasm.

"It has! Are you still in Jalalabad?"

"It so happens that I am. I'm at a sporting goods store, near the cricket stadium, buying a jersey for my nephew in Kabul. Would you like to meet?"

"Are you at the store with the large picture of a cricket bowler above it?"

"I am."

"I'll meet you there in fifteen minutes," closed Zahir. He next waved to Ali and Farid, who just finished his call with one of the girl assassins.

"Bring your pistols and get the rifles, plus extra ammunition. Hurry, we're headed to the cricket stadium. Ali, you'll drive."

Three minutes later, Ali was behind the wheel of Zahir's rusted and dented Toyota Corolla, racing toward the cricket stadium.

Approximately twenty-five minutes later, there was a curious collection of cohorts in an empty alley between the entrance of the cricket stadium and the adjacent sporting goods store. Hall's team was comprised of two CIA operatives, stationed in Kabul, and the two new panel truck drivers, Brice Miller and Yossi Levy. Absent from the meeting was his communications crew, who were in the midst of rapidly setting up their comms van, a half block from the school. Jan Zahir's rapidly assembled team included his two bodyguards, Farid and Ali; two early-twenties female assassins; and a friend and spy on the Kabul Police force, Din Pirooz.

In the feverish minutes before they all met, Hall learned from Yossi that Safi had never met either of the two al-Qaeda agents—Mostafa and the turncoat USAID worker—which he and Miller were posing as. From Zahir, he also learned that he'd enlisted the help of Kabul policeman, who might well help them gain access to the schoolhouse.

In the alley Hall and Zahir explained to the others—with the aid of a small grease board, complete with the property's details —the general layout of the school and its grounds. They had both visited the schoolhouse several times in the last few weeks. On the grease board, Hall had sketched the rectangular shape of the approximately 30,000 square foot lot and the 15,000 square foot, one-story building (See Figure 1). The single-story, concrete-block building once served as the primary telephone switch facility for all of Jalalabad. Ten-foot chain-link, security fences surrounded the sides and rear of the property for security purposes.

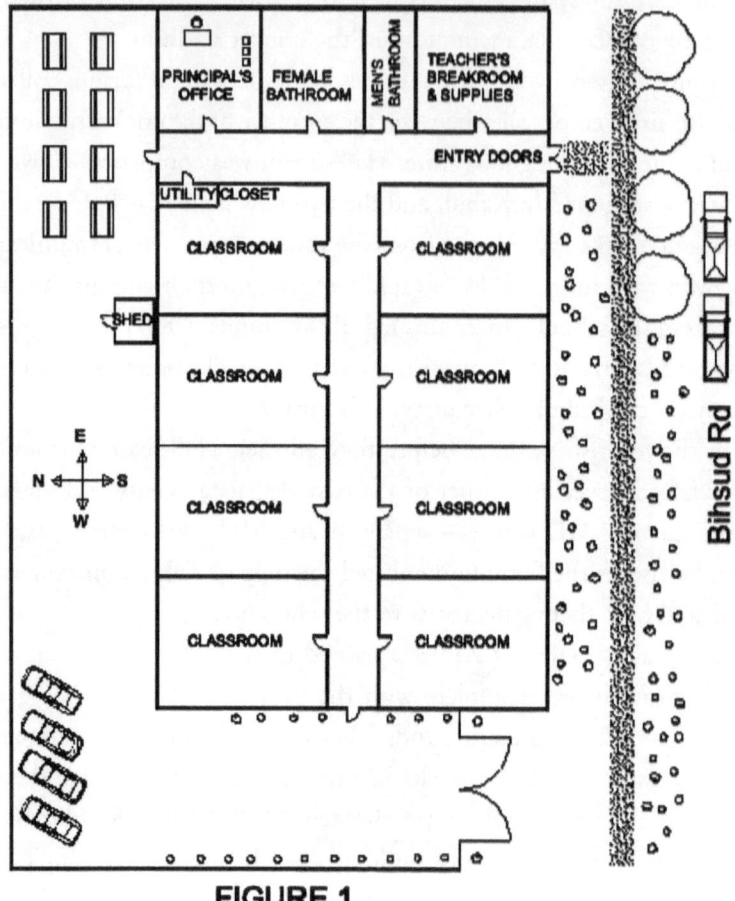

New Hope Girls School, Jalalabad, Afghanistan.

FIGURE 1

He next focused on the layout of the rectangular school. The longest side of the building, 150 feet, was oriented on the property in an east to west fashion, parallel to Bihsud Road. The east side of the school abutted the ten-foot wall, and the school's main, double-door entrance—on the south side of the building—was separated from the street by approximately twenty feet. On the west side of the property was a thirty-five-foot wide driveway that provided access to the rear yard of the school. A small storage shed was located on the north side of the building, near the building's rear exit. A third exit door, on the western side of the building, opened onto the driveway. Four parking stalls and eight picnic tables with benches, covered with a shade canopy, filled the majority of the school's rear yard.

Upon entering the school, there was a multi-use breakroom-supply room on one's right and a twelve-foot wide hallway on the left, which led to the west side-building exit. Classrooms, on each side of the hallway, ran the length of the building. Classrooms on only the south side (the street side) of the building each had three large, barred-windows. On the north side of the building, there were no windows. All these details were noted on his sketch, along with the locations and descriptions of the hidden weapons.

"I'm not a military man," said Hall, as he looked first to Zahir, then Brice and Yossi. "My prime concern is the safety of the children. What would you recommend?"

Yossi immediately responded. "This isn't my first hostage situation at a schoolhouse. Israeli policy firstly advises negotiation."

Zahir spat and rocked on his heels. "That's not possible. Tehrik-i-Taliban (TTP) is in control here. Safi may think he is, but he's not. TTP clansmen are animals. The more outrageous their crime, the more publicity they get. Killing students is what they specialize in."

After a moment, Yossi continued, "Failing a negotiation, your only option is surprise…coupled with shock and awe. They're going to start shooting students the instant they feel threatened."

With a mixture of anger and resignation, Hall imperceptibly wagged his head in understanding.

"I agree with Yossi," began Brice, "but before we do anything, we need to get some idea of what we're facing. Are there four terrorists in the building or ten? Are the students locked in classrooms or being guarded in the hallway? Are the terrorists going to blow up the school or burn it down? Then, we figure out some way to get as many of our people inside the building as we can before we do anything."

While pausing to consider other options, Brice's eyes fell on Zahir's friend Pirooz, who was formally attired in a neatly starched police uniform. Beside Pirooz were two petite women. Each of them held an armful of books, and they both looked as if they were fifteen-years-old.

"How about this," he continued. "Yossi enters the building first *without the keys* to the panel trucks. Safi will want the keys before he hands over any cash. Yossi explains that he wants to see the money first before he gets the keys to the trucks. In the meantime, he surveys the situation. How many gunmen? How they're armed and where they're located. Safi, hopefully, shows him the cash. When he's escorted outside by one of the gunmen, he'll run into Pirooz and the two female assassins who will be carrying their schoolbooks. Inside their books will be fragmentation and flashbang grenades, which we'll provide. They'll have to tear apart a couple of books to hide them.

"While Pirooz distracts the gunman, Yossi will lean into the cab of his truck and grab his keys. While in the cab, he'll quietly brief one of Hall's operatives on the situation inside the building. The operative will be hidden on the opposite side of the truck."

Turning to Yossi, he added, "Leave the windows of your truck open." Turning his attention next to Hall, he asked, "What's the vehicular and pedestrian traffic like in that area? You're operative can't be too conspicuous."

"It's a busy place, lots of traffic of all types. I like your thinking," said Hall.

Brice next turned toward Zahir and said, "Once we have Yossi's intel, you and your men will take up a position near the building's rear exit. You may have a fence to deal with, or you might be able to waltz down the driveway. You'll be connected to Hall's communication net. Once you hear a flashbang go off… detonated by one of your assassins… your team will breach the school through that rear exit.

"Yossi will have a pistol in his boot. I'll be armed with an M4 carbine and take-up a position near the front entry door. Introducing me to the jihadists, inside the school, will screw things up. Just the sight of a Westerner will increase their craving for bloodlust. We don't want that."

Brice next asked Zahir to translate his instructions to the two women. "One of them will set off a single flashbang grenade when either one, or Annie, feels the time is right. This will be a judgment call for them. The instant that flashbang goes off, we attack. They should close their eyes and hold their ears once they activate the flashbang. It's bright and loud as all get-out. They'll only have a couple of seconds before it goes off."

Hall addressed Yossi, "Once you return to Safi's location in the school, give the truck keys to whoever you think is the TTP leader." Turning to

Brice, he added, "If it's possible, let at least two TTP men exit the building and escape in the trucks."

"That's a lot of 'possibles and hopefullys.' We'll do our best," said Zahir with a hard look. "Describe again, for me and the others, who else is in the building and how they are disguised...or not!"

Twenty minutes later, Yossi and Brice parked in front of the aged girls school. Beige stucco had been poorly applied to the wall facing the street. Much of the façade was peeling and sun-bleached, with plaster wire netting visible along much of its base. A decorative rock garden filled the narrow front yard and hid some of the netting. Large terracotta planters, containing red and yellow roses, sat on each side of the wide double-door entrance. The wooden doors were a faded light blue, with highly polished brass doorknobs. Despite the age of the building, someone had clearly made an effort to make the school as welcoming and inviting as possible.

Before Yossi hopped out of his truck, he ensured that all the windows of his truck were open. He was dressed in a long-sleeve, light green shirt that hung loosely over his hips and tan baggy pants. He marched up to the front doors and tried the doorknob, but it was locked. He pounded the side of his fist against the door and barked, in Farsi, the secret passwords, "Delivery of thirty desks!" Just as he raised his fist to pound the door again, the door suddenly opened, and a tall, bearded man roughly pulled him inside.

Three additional men, with semi-automatic rifles aimed at his chest, motioned him toward the rear of the building. On his right was the empty breakroom and a couple of bathrooms. On his left, he passed the school's wide hallway that ran the length of the building. The interior of the building was well lit. Young girls—none no more than fifteen or sixteen-years-old—were sitting on the floor, lining both sides of the hallway. Some were whimpering. Most had interlocked their arms with adjacent friends and were silent. And Petrified! All of their faces were downturned in a submissive manner, no doubt in response to their captors' threats.

Sitting in the wide hallway, a few feet from the entryway, was a wide-shouldered girl with an off-white veil that was highlighted with blue and pink stripes. He subtly winked at her. She slightly nodded as one of her hands calmly rubbed her chin, in the shape of a handgun, while her other hand patted her hip. Annie was armed. (See Figure 2 below left).

Just before he was pushed into a larger room, the principal's office he surmised, he saw "Janitor" Hook standing by the rear exit door, leaning against the open doorway of a utility closet. Fortunately, he was wearing his disguise. He looked like a seventy-years-old version of Quasimodo, the fictional hunchback of Notre Dame.

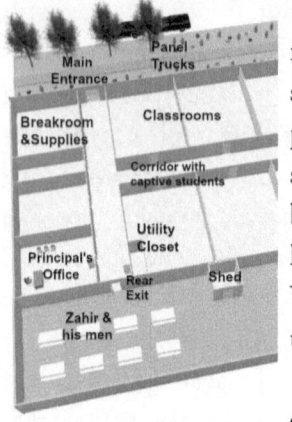

Hidden inside the closet were an M4 carbine, flashbang grenades, tear gas canisters, and four syringes filled with an incapacitating agent. Hook placed his free hand near the bicep of his opposite arm and signaled— by pressing his thumb between his index finger and middle finger, emulating an injection—that he possessed a syringe. When he next flashed Yossi four fingers, it meant that he was carrying four syringes.

Sitting behind a desk in the principal's large office was a bald-headed man of medium height with bulging shoulders and a massive chest. An unkempt mustache partially cloaked his cruel lips, and heavy eyebrows bordered his narrow, dark eyes. He guessed that this was Safi Khan. His father was no doubt a Russian— likely from one of the "stans" countries in the old Soviet Union— and junior was likely a world-class weightlifter. *Shit, it will take a .50 caliber round to take down this bear of a man,* he thought.

The numerous ribbons festooned across the breast of his uniform shirt, coupled with the stars on his shoulder boards, confirmed his belief that this was indeed the Kabul police chief. Standing to his side were two of his henchmen, also dressed in Afghanistan National Police uniforms. They were guarding two adjacent female prisoners, Mary Phillips and Beena Waleed. Both women were slumped in chairs, hands bound, and each held in place by a henchman. Their faces were bruised and battered. Phillips had a badly cut lip, with blood running over her chin and spilling onto her white blouse.

"Give me the keys to the two trucks," commanded Safi in Farsi.

Yossi straightened. He'd learned long ago, from his days in the Israeli Defense Forces, that acquiescence was a sign of weakness. He stepped toward Safi, placed his hands on the front edge of the desk, and leaned toward him. In measured and assertive Farsi, he said, "Belhaj in Libya explained the deal to my leader in Cairo. You and your TTP partners pay $150,000 for these thirty MANPADS. The second half of that payment, $75,000, is due now, upon my delivery of the weapons to you. Furthermore, you owe my partner and me $5,000 each for accompanying these missiles," smiled Yossi.

Safi's dark eyes closed a fraction as he studied Yossi. After a time, he grabbed a satchel that sat on the floor. He placed it on the desktop and counted banded-stacks of U.S. hundred dollar bills. He disdainfully pushed the stacks toward Yossi and ordered, "Count it!"

A hint of a smile crossed Yossi's face as he nodded slightly and began to expertly count the stack of bills. "This is just $10,000. Where's the rest of the money?"

In the next instant, Safi thrust the satchel toward him. A blizzard of banded-stacks of cash flew into his chest.

Shit, the bastard was quick for a guy his size. Once he confirmed the amounts, he slipped the delivery fees into a side pocket. He then refilled the satchel that Safi had thrown at him with the $75,000. Just as he began to lift the satchel, one of Safi's meaty hands darted out and slapped the bag from his hand.

Safi addressed the tall man who'd earlier pulled Yossi into the schoolhouse. He was obviously the leader of the four-man TTP team. "Go with him. Count the crates, check for the MANPADS, and get the keys to the trucks." Turning his attention back to Yossi, with lifeless eyes and a hostile sneer, he said, "First an inventory! The final payment is due upon our receipt of exactly thirty crates, which better carry thirty MANPADS."

The bastard sounds like an accountant, thought Yossi, as he followed Tall Man out of the office.

The two had just reached the sidewalk—near the closest panel truck—when Pirooz and the two women, posing as students, intercepted them. Brice Miller was hiding behind a car, a safe distance behind the second truck. Pirooz came to attention and stepped in front of Tall Man, stopping him in his tracks. In an overbearing manner, he said, "I'm here to see Safi Khan. Official business! He's expecting me. These two students gave me directions to the school. They're returning books."

In the meantime, Yossi opened the door to the nearest truck, leaned in, and reached for the keys. In a soft whisper, he asked, "Can you hear me?"

"Yes," came an equally quiet CIA agent.

In the next few seconds, he gave the agent a rapid-fire report on the situation inside the schoolhouse. He closed by saying that the tall terrorist, the one who was speaking with Pirooz, was the leader of the four-man TTP team. He'd give him the keys to the getaway trucks.

The terrorist who was half-listening to Pirooz, moved to the open driver's door of the panel truck and barked at Yossi, "Hurry up!"

After retrieving the keys from the first truck and closing the driver's door, he turned towards Tall Man, "Follow me. I'll show you the crates."

After unlocking the rear sliding door of the panel truck, Tall Man counted the crates. He also randomly opened two crates to confirm the presence of a MANPAD. He repeated the procedure on the second truck.

"Good?" asked Yossi.

Tall Man grunted an approval and grabbed the keys from Yossi's hand. He then roughly pushed Yossi, along with Pirooz, and the two female students into the schoolhouse. The two women were immediately ordered to sit in the hallway, beside the other girls. Yossi and Pirooz followed Tall Man into Safi's office.

Tall Man's three associates lit cigarettes and sat in chairs that were situated against the wall, opposite the breakroom, near the front doors.

Hook, standing by the utility closet and the rear exit, asked, "Cigarette?"

One of the three turned toward him and flipped him the bird. None of them could see what was happening in the wide hallway, behind them, where the schoolgirls were sequestered. The two late-arriving students were quietly briefing Annie, in broken English, on the rescue plan.

Meanwhile, in the office, Pirooz didn't attempt to cover up his unexpected presence with the pretext of police business. Years of pent-up emotions spewed from him. He roared at Safi as he detailed his involvement in payoffs, murders, and the attack on the U.S. Embassy last September.

Safi ignored his expected tirade.

At the mention of the September attack, Mary lifted her head and said weakly, "You tried to have me killed that day, but you failed. You're an animal!"

Safi turned and rolled his chair toward her. "I won't fail a second time.

After I'm finished with you, you'll wish that I succeeded the first time," he said with a merciless smile.

Mustering her last ounces of energy, Mary imperceptibly raised her battered face toward Safi and shrilly stated, "You and Qazi are crooks of the lowest order. You steal from your allies…the U.S., Great Britain, Germany, France, Italy, Canada, and others. Hijacking fuel trucks, shaking down truck drivers, skimming foreign aid funds for all types of Afghan services and facilities… schools, hospitals, freshwater plants, sewage systems, roads. You don't give a shit about your own people!"

"Ah, stealing! I've learned a lot from my U.S. partners…David, Smithson, and Hightower. We only steal millions. Your U.S. politicians steal billions," said Safi with a grisly and repulsive grin. "Bridges and roads that never get built, innovative 'green businesses' that never make a dime, a fleet of Afghan Air Force cargo airplanes that can't fly, and the granddaddy of them all… home loans to individuals who couldn't qualify to buy a car. Your Fannie Mae and Freddie Mac bailout was what …$125 billion!"*

Despite her beaten and battered condition, Mary was surprised by Safi's comment. *Somewhere in the reprobate's depraved mind, there was an awareness of the U.S.'s financial mismanagement.* "They don't steal, they misappropriate!" she countered.

"Ah, more Western doubletalk," he jeered. "Then, my partners and I are only guilty of misappropriation. If it's not a crime in Washington, it's not a crime here." Pausing and temporarily ignoring the setting, he leaned back in his chair and clasped his hands behind his head as he began to proudly prognosticate. "Come November, I think my valued friend and business partner, Ted David, will be elected the next president of the United States. My businesses should thrive with him in office. But all this talk has nothing to do with my task at hand." Just then, his cell phone rang.

With a quick glance at the caller identification, he answered the call

---

* Safi's reference was to sixteen Italian made, twin-engine cargo planes (C-27As) that the U.S. requisitioned for the Afghan Air Force. The total price, from an Italian aircraft manufacturer, was $600 million. Unfortunately, the purchase price neglected to include a reasonable and ready supply of spare parts for the aircraft. After a handful of missions and several failed attempts to qualify the airlift-capability of the fleet, the entire fleet was grounded in 2011. In 2012, the aircraft lay rusting at one end of the Kabul International Airport.

and flashed Mary a malicious grin. "Ah, my insider at the U.S. Embassy. Cannon, where are you?"

"I'm forty-five minutes away. There was a bad accident on the road," said Cannon.

Mary heard the reply and said, "Tell DS Specialist Lane Peters, he can go to hell! I know he's your mole at the embassy."

Safi Khan's black eyes smiled, and a crude smirk crossed his lips. "Bad guess, Phillips! I couldn't buy Peters's cooperation. Specialist Joe Michaels is my mole. He's made me millions."

"Goddamn it, Safi! What are you doing? Nobody at the embassy knows that I'm your mole," screeched Cannon over the phone.

"Calm down, Cannon. Phillips's days …rather minutes… are numbered. Your identity will die with her," he chuckled.

"Michaels couldn't be all that valuable to you," began Mary, loudly enough for Michaels to hear. "We were both passengers in the embassy shuttle vehicle that was taking us to the Bagram Airfield, last September. The one you engaged the Haqqani's to blow up with an RPG."

With a forced note of sincerity, he said, "I didn't know he was in that vehicle!"

Mary mimicked his insincerity, "Oh, really! Weren't you the one who insisted that he change our driver that day? Jamal Waleed was supposed to drive us to the airport."

"Enough, you arrogant, Western bitch! It's time I permanently wiped that smile off your face," he said as he terminated Cannon's call.

Turning away from Mary, he reached for his pistol that he'd slipped into a desk drawer. Halfway through his turn, his eyes widened in shock, and he froze. Tall Man had neglected to disarm Pirooz.

With his pistol drawn and aimed at Safi, Pirooz's speech brimmed with venom. "My brother and four other fellow police officers were killed during that twenty-hour Haqqani attack last September in Kabul. No memorial service for those good men. Not even a kind press release. You played a key role in that tragedy."

One of Safi's men reached for his sidearm. Pirooz shot him in the forehead. An instant later, he shot and killed the second police officer.

At that moment, Yossi sensed that Tall Man, standing behind him, was drawing one of his weapons. He flung an elbow at his throat while he violently kicked the heel of a foot into his knee. Tall Man dropped his pistol and began to fall, but not before he wrapped an arm over Yossi's shoulders and pulled him to the floor with him. Yossi's head slammed against the cold concrete floor, momentarily stunning him.

He remembered broken scenes that followed. *The office door flew open. One of the terrorists stepped into the office. He clumsily raised his AK-47 semi-automatic rifle and fired a three-round burst. A single round caught Pirooz in the shoulder and spun him to the floor. Safi stood with a pistol in his hand. He began to move around his desk to finish off Pirooz.*

Yossi, now more cognizant, then heard the familiar sound of a cylindrical object roll along the floor of the outer hallway and come to a stop by the principal's open office door. Despite bending his body into a tucked position—like a diver—closing his eyes and pressing his hands against his ears, the proximity of the flashbang grenade's detonation disoriented not only him but everyone else in the principal's office.

Hook leaped over him and raced toward Safi, who was staggering around the front of his desk. Tall Man and the terrorist, who'd shot Pirooz, were on their knees, also slowly recovering. Before Hook could disarm Safi, he fired two unsteady shots at Mary. Hook jumped onto his back. With a syringe in each hand, he simultaneously jabbed them into each side of Safi's neck. After a brief violent struggle—like being on the bucking back of a Brahma bull at a Western rodeo—Safi collapsed, unconscious. Hook rushed to Mary's sprawling body, which was inert in a growing pool of blood. He undid her bound hands, then Beena's.

Raising himself to one knee, Yossi was conscious of a hail of gunfire in the outside hallway. He next heard Zahir bark, from the rear of the building, "Grenade, get out of the building!" Several moments later, the building-jarring explosion of a fragmentation grenade knocked him back to the floor.

He vaguely remembered more gunfire as he again struggled back to his knees. *Hook and Mary were lying together on the floor, covered in blood, and partially obscured by the large desk. Beena lay seemingly unconscious beside Mary, with blood staining her blouse.* As he attempted to stand, he recalled the fleeting image of a pistol barrel sailing toward his head.

Twenty minutes later, while sitting on a chair in one of the school's empty classrooms—with a cold compress held against his head—Yossi learned from Brice what had happened after he'd been knocked unconscious.

"The tall terrorist or one of his men knocked you out. Those two then escaped in the trucks," said Brice, leaning against a student desk.

"Lucky for them. If I ever see Tall Man and his buddy again, they're 'dead meat!' My head is killing me."

"I'll take you to the infirmary at FOB Fenty in a couple of minutes. The ambulances from the base just left here with Mary Phillips, Annie Youngblood, Pirooz, and one of Zahir's men, Farid. Beena Waleed didn't make it. She's dead. Hall had Safi whisked away somewhere else."

"How about the schoolgirls?"

"They're all shook up, but none of them were hurt. A damn miracle!" said Brice.

"Targeting school kids. Evil bastards! Tell me what happened to Beena. My last memory of her was while I was facedown on the floor. She was lying next to Mary and looked unconscious," said Yossi.

After several deep breaths, Brice calmed himself and described what he'd learned from Pirooz. "According to Pirooz, who was also lying on the floor of the office with a shoulder wound, Safi fired two shots at Mary before Hook jumped on his back and incapacitated him with two injections. One shot hit Mary in the chest, and the other just grazed Beena's head. That probably knocked her out. You, then, were apparently trying to stand when Tall Man pistol-whipped you and knocked you back to the floor."

"Uggh," groaned Yossi. "The compress helps, but my head is pounding. What happened at your end?"

"One of the terrorists chucked a frag grenade at Zahir and his men. It blew open the front and rear doors of the school. Farid caught a piece of shrapnel in the leg. Nothing major, he'll recover." Brice paused, closed his eyes, and massaged his forehead.

Yossi could tell he was replaying the events in his mind.

"Moments later, the two terrorists, who were stationed near the school's main entrance doors, emerged through the smoke and dust of the grenade explosion. Tall Man and another terrorist followed seconds later. Tall Man tossed a set of truck keys to the guy who was with him and ordered the other two back into the schoolhouse. He instructed them to shoot all the girls," paused Brice, now standing with his hands on his hips.

"That's what Hall told me," he continued. "I didn't understand a word Tall Man said, but I understood his facial expression and body language. The son of a bitch wanted the girls massacred. Seconds later, Tall Man and the other guy sped away in the panel trucks."

"Was Tall Man going to come back and pick-up his buddies?" asked Yossi.

"No. One of the CIA operatives spotted the vehicle they arrived in. It was parked down the block and had two AK-47s laying on the backseat, in plain sight."

"Uh-huh," murmured Yossi.

"I'd taken up a position, behind a parked car, that was directly across the street from the school's front doors. I took dead aim at the first terrorist, who staggered out of the building through the smoke and dust. When all of a sudden, he and the other three terrorists were swallowed up in a sea of screaming girls, who were wildly running out of the school. I couldn't take a shot at any of them for fear of hitting one of the girls." Brice again stopped and took a few more deep breaths.

Continuing, he said, "A CIA operative used a crowbar to pry open the exit door at the far western end of the hallway. That exit led to the building's driveway and safety. The operative tried to usher the girls out of the school, through that exit, but they were all in a panic. They ran every which way. I presumed that they'd take advantage of that escape route—"

"But they didn't!" said Yossi, completing Brice's critique. "They didn't know what was happening. With all the explosions and gunfire, they ran for their lives! And some of the frightened girls compromised your line of fire."

Brice nodded with a dejected grunt. "When the two shooters re-entered the school, they nearly tripped over Annie. She was kneeling, arms extended, with both hands gripping her pistol. I heard her order the terrorists to drop their weapons. They either didn't understand her or didn't care. I watched them raise their rifles toward her when all hell broke loose. One AK-47 fired on full automatic, the other rifle jammed. Annie shot and killed the active shooter, but in the process, he clipped her leg with a round. It knocked her down, and her pistol skittered away.

"By then, the second shooter had cleared the jam on his AK-47. He was taking aim at the schoolgirls, while Annie tried crawling to her pistol. The bastard stepped on the ankle of her good leg. She couldn't move. He then yelled something at the girls. I didn't understand what he said. Hall told me later that he said, 'Eat dirt, you filthy pigs!'

"I couldn't take a shot because girls were still racing through the front doors." Brice dropped his head and massaged his forehead with both hands. "I screwed up!"

"What happened next?" pressed Yossi.

"Beena flew into the second shooter who was taking aim at a group of girls. They tumbled to the floor. She had a tactical knife. I don't know where the knife came from?"

Yossi instinctively reached behind his back for his thin-handled knife with a five-inch blade, which was held in place in the middle of his back, beneath his untucked green shirt. His fingers touched an empty sheath. Unbeknownst to Brice, he'd strapped the sheathed knife to his belt before they'd arrived at the school. "She must have grabbed my knife while I was out on the floor! When I came to, my shirt was halfway up my chest."

"She stabbed the guy three or four times, screaming something at him all the while. He only got one shot off during her attack, but that's all it took. It entered below her chin and came out the top of her head." With that image embedded in his mind, Brice's chest heaved as he let out a grieving gasp. "An instant later, Zahir finished the bastard off. He then started crying and repeating a phrase I didn't understand."

After a time, he continued while blankly staring at the street through the classroom's windows. "I made a rookie mistake that could have cost Annie her life and did cost Beena hers. My firing position was all wrong. I set up for a head-on shot, directly in line with the front doors of the school. I didn't consider the possibility that panicky schoolgirls might use that exit to escape. They prevented me from shooting the terrorists. At the very least, I should have set obliquely to the front doors so that I didn't have *background and foreground* civilians compromising my shot."

"Things could have turned out a whole lot worse!"

"But not on account of anything I did!" pined Brice, clearly upset with his actions.

"Wrong! You were the one who conceived the rescue plan. 'Get more good guys and gals inside the school!' That was your idea."

But not at the price of Beena's life. According to Mary and Zahir, she was one of the best, young female doctors in the whole damn country. Her death is a national tragedy!"

"It was a tragedy, but given the circumstances, I'd bet she'd do it again!" said Yossi pausing. "Do you have any idea what her final words were?"

"Yeah! Zahir told me. 'These are my girls…my girls!'" he said before silent tears began to streak his face.

"And Zahir's words?" pressed Yossi, with one final question.

"He spoke in Pashto, as if he was saying a prayer. The only phrase I recognized was 'the Lioness of Panjshir!' I don't know what that means."

After a time, Brice moved to Yossi's side and slipped a hand inside one of his arms. Helping him to his feet, he said, "Let's get you checked out at FOB Fenty. I'd hate to see you start your next *cush assignment* resting beside a swimming pool, restricted to limited duty."

Yossi flashed his former Annapolis roommate a crooked smirk. "Shayetet 13! They make your Navy SEALs look like pussycats. I report next Monday to the Atlit Naval Base. When do you report to Quantico?"

"Same as you, next Monday. Formal training for The Basic School starts the following day."

… *fifteen minutes after Brice and Yossi left for the infirmary at FOB Fenty.*

Cannon parked his government sedan a half-block away from the still smoking schoolhouse. Several newly-arrived U.S. Army investigators were taking photos and securing the site. He flashed his DS badge at an investigator and asked, "What happened? I had a meeting scheduled here with Dr. Mary Phillips."

"A terrorist shootout of some kind. None of us know the details. We arrived just as the ambulances and the morgue van were leaving. Four wounded were taken to the infirmary at FOB Fenty. Five KIAs (killed in action) were loaded into a van and likely taken to a local morgue. The KIAs looked like they were all local nationals. Two Afghan cops in uniform, two

Taliban in mufti, and one small Afghan woman, who could have been a teacher."

"Did you get a look at the survivors?" asked Cannon.

"A quick look. Two women. One was an attractive blonde woman, looked like an American. She took a shot in the chest and was in bad shape. I don't think she'll make it. The second, smaller woman was dressed like the locals, except I heard her talk. Her accent sounded like she was from Wyoming or Montana. She had a minor leg wound. Then, there were two men. A male, mid-twenties, dressed in mufti. He looked like a local. Minor leg wound. Lastly, a tall Afghan cop with black hair. He took a shot in the shoulder."

Cannon nodded appreciatively. The Army investigator, a sergeant he saw, was experienced. He took note of not only the woundeds' injuries, but also their hair color, speech, dress, and age. "What about the deceased? Could you describe them?"

"They were loaded into the van when I arrived, but I got a pretty good look at them. There were two Afghan cops, one medium-sized Afghan woman...she could have been a teacher... and two young, scraggily Afghan males who smelled like they hadn't showered in a year. My guess is that they were terrorists."

"The two dead cops. Were either of them bald and muscular?" asked Cannon.

The investigator thought for a moment. "Yes, one was bald and very muscular. I think I've seen his face in the newspapers. He might be a senior cop in the Jalalabad police force."

Cannon inwardly smiled. He didn't feel compelled to correct the investigator's observation. The bald cop was Safi Khan. He knew that Safi always traveled with two henchmen cops. Therefore, all three Kabul cops were accounted for. Two were dead, one of which was Safi, and the third had been wounded.

He realized that this might be an opportune time to hasten Mary's demise. A visit to the FOB Fenty infirmary and her sudden, though probable, death would preserve his unknown identity. Had he known that the CIA was listening in all of Safi's phone calls and that their audio bugs, in the principal's office, had also recorded his identity, he might have skipped his next stop.

"Thanks for the update. It sounds like the person I was scheduled to meet is it at the infirmary," he said as he shook hands with the investigator and turned back toward his car.

Ten minutes later, Michaels was waved through the security gate at FOB Fenty. After passing a row of plywood structures, painted olive-drab, and a couple of larger light metal buildings, Michaels arrived at the infirmary. Near the entrance of the infirmary, he eased into an empty parking stall that was sandwiched between two other identical government vehicles. Just before he exited his car, he noticed Mike Hall. Hall was standing outside of the infirmary entrance, checking his emails on his secure Blackberry.

Michaels was unaware of the two cell phone calls that Hall had recently received. The first call was from his CIA plant at the schoolhouse, the well-disguised Army sergeant-investigator. The last call was from the Army sergeant-in-charge of the main security gate at FOB Fenty. His target, Michaels, had entered the base and was headed toward the infirmary.

Out of the corner of his eye, Hall saw Michaels park. He concluded his fake email review, opened the front door of the infirmary, and signaled someone to join him outside. Seconds later, a stocky, six-foot Army security guard arrived at his side. Feigning the need for a private conversation, he softly repeated his devious plan into the guard's ear as he guided him to a stop near the front of Michaels's car.

Meanwhile, Michaels was busily sliding down in his driver's seat until he was hidden from sight.

Hall's next conversation with the guard was far less discreet. His loud and authoritative instructions were spoken in a way that guaranteed Michaels heard his every word. "His name is Joe Michaels, and he's a DS security specialist at our embassy. You and your men have to protect Mary Phillips. She may have learned more about his crimes… tipping sketchy toll collectors on the times and routes of our military convoys… before she was shot at the school."

"Sketchy? What does that mean?"

"Sometimes the collectors just demand tolls. Other times they sell their information to the Taliban. No matter how you look at it, disclosing that kind of information to third parties is bad. Trucks get blown up, and men are killed."

While the guard somberly shook his head in agreement, he asked, "How's Phillips doing?"

"It looked bad at first, but it was just a flesh wound," began Hall with a wink, though he knew she was in critical condition. "She's sedated now. I'll probably be able to speak with her in an hour or so. I'll know more then. In the meantime, keep a close eye on her. Here are copies of Michaels's picture. Give them to your men. If they see him, have them detain him. I've got a lot of questions for that guy. The guards at the base's entrance gate are also going to keep an eye out for him."

"If Michaels is guilty of compromising our convoys, can I shoot him? I've had friends killed on convoys that were tipped to the Taliban."

"You'll be second in line, behind me," said Hall with an unmistakable note of sincerity. "Let's go inside and brief your men."

After a time, Michaels inched behind the wheel of his car. He started his car, carefully backed out of his parking stall, and slowly turned his vehicle toward the base's exit. He wasn't a religious man, but he now prayed that the guards manning the base's *exit gate* hadn't been told to watch out for him. A minute later, he uneventfully passed through the exit and turned *east* toward the Torkham Border Crossing, and Pakistan.

Once he traversed the Khyber Pass and arrived safely in Peshawar, Pakistan, his escape would be complete. In his briefcase—or his "go case"—he had his fuel ledger, two sets of phony identification papers, and $100,000 in U.S. cash. His ledger also contained the Deutsch Bank account numbers and passwords for all of his partners and accomplices. The way things were now unfolding, his net worth could easily increase a hundredfold within the next twenty-four hours.

Hall's cell phone rang. "Hall here, sergeant. Did our man turn east?"

"He did Chief. How did you know?"

"Just a hunch sergeant. Your boys did good. There'll be a $100 credit at the base's watering hole for you and your men tonight."

Hall then turned to Jan Zahir, who was standing beside him. "He's on his way. All I need is his ledger. You can keep whatever else he has."

Jan raised an eyebrow, as he countered, "My toll collectors won't have any problem stopping him. He may have a pile of cash with him?""

"It's all yours. I just want the ledger."

"One of my men was killed during a convoy holdup that he and Safi engineered. I'd like to turn him over to the dead man's widow. Do you want his remains back?"

Hall held Jan's eyes as he said evenly, "I'm not going to, in any way, interfere with the widow's observance of *Pashtunwali.*"

CHAPTER 17

CLOSURES AND NEW BEGINNINGS

CIA Annex Kabul

June 8, 2012 | Friday, 9:30 a.m.
(and the following days)

MIKE HALL LEANED forward over his desk, with folded arms, while he studied the demure young lady—in her late twenties or early thirties—who sat ramrod straight in the chair before him. Her hands were primly clasped together in her lap, her face was impassive, and her clear, gray eyes were focused on him. Her posture and presence reminded him of his long-ago sixth-grade teacher in Laredo, Texas, a strict schoolmarm if there ever was one.

Though he'd spoken with Amy Blake, over the phone, several times in the past few days, this was his first face-to-face meeting with her. She worked for Treasury's Financial Crimes Enforcement Network (FinCEN) in Washington as an investigator. Her current, full-time assignment required her to travel to Kabul every few months. Her present ten-day visit was coming to a close, and she was scheduled to fly back to Washington on Monday, June 11.

Except for her serious bearing, she was an extremely attractive woman with auburn hair, swept to the right side of her head in a trendy, pixie style. Full lips, with just a touch of red lipstick, complemented her evenly-toned complexion. Her attire—high-waisted, fashionable blue pants, simple black flats, and a sleek, light gray lab coat, which she wore over a beige, V-neck top—added to her professional, but no-nonsense, image. She could have easily passed as a financial executive at a major corporation.

After Hall introduced her to Hook, he got right to the point. "I wanted Hook to hear what you previously explained to me over the phone. It may have some bearing on his on-going assignment," he said, pausing to accurately summarize her activities. "Our U.S. Treasury has secretly bought up promissory notes held by multiple Dubai real estate developers as well as bad loans from the Kabul Bank."

"None of that was secret. The Dubai developers knew I was representing the U.S. Treasury. The notes, with personal guarantees, that Treasury acquired were for condominiums Qazi and his insiders bought there," replied Amy in a confidant and composed manner.

"I thought the Kabul Bank was dead and buried," said Hall.

"Dead, but not buried. We bought the Kabul Bank loans last year during an assumption period, fully approved and authorized by the World Bank. Those bad loans totaled approximately $1 billion."

"OK, I got it. So, you bought up these loan obligations, then you, Lena Jones and someone from State—"

"Her name is Susanna Thomas. You know her, she's our acting Secretary of State. She took over State when David became vice president. She also happens to be a close friend of Mary Phillips, as am I."

"Uh-huh, you and Thomas then spoke with the banking officials in both England and Germany."

"Yes! We asked them to freeze all the banking accounts of the borrowers while we legally proceeded against them for the full satisfaction of their loan obligations. With a few minor exceptions, all of their accounts were maintained in banks in London and Frankfurt."

"Were these the borrowers' personal accounts?"

"A few were, but a majority of their funds is held in *phony, baloney* shell corporations."

"Can you pierce the legal protections of these off-shore shell corporations? And, has this ever been done before?"

"I've spoken at length with my counterparts in London and Frankfurt... and our own legal experts at Treasury and Justice about piercing shell corporations. If the beneficial owners of those shell corporations have committed crimes directly against the U.S…. or interests of the U.S….then, yes, we can freeze the assets of shell corporations. We do, however, require the support of our friends in London and Frankfurt to accomplish this.

"Because they also happened to be allied militarily with us in Afghanistan, and they share our view of President Qazi and his cronies, they've been quite cooperative. The debt obligations that we're seeking to recover total approximately $1.5 billion. We're also going after an additional $500 million in direct U.S. aid that we believe these scoundrels illegally skimmed. Our friends in London and Frankfurt will get a well-deserved, generous commission on whatever monies we recover.

"As for your second question… no, this has never been done before. We, the U.S., has never pursued a civil case—for say theft, default on a loan, or a negligent financial loss—against the sitting president of a country. Further, we've never moved against the president of a country that we're occupying and trying to defend. It's somewhat counterproductive, unless, that is, the U.S. government concludes that they're fed up with dealing with a mentally unstable and thieving president who views us as worse than the Russians."

"Won't this screw up our mission in Afghanistan?"

"I don't think so, though I'm just a lowly investigator at FinCEN."

Yeah, right! A lowly investigator with a very ingenious mind! thought Hall with a suspicious smirk. Blake's understanding of the complexities of international banking laws, coupled with her high level of creativity, didn't jibe with her alleged position at Treasury. Someone with juice at FinCEN must have started their career at the CIA. Vague and non-descript job classifications were standard operating procedure in the Company.

Both men felt that her plan was not only brilliant but perfectly timed. All the participating countries in the ISAF were fed up with Qazi and his insiders' duplicity. But, considering the magnitude of the dollars involved and the boldness of the scheme, they also concluded that Blake must have had someone at the highest level of the U.S. government pre-approve it and gather consensus approval from other significant ISAF stakeholders. The question was, who? Hook guessed it was Lena Jones, in her new role as acting Attorney General. Hall thought it had to be his longtime friend from Laredo, Texas—President Jed Adams. Even though he was on his deathbed, Adams was a tough old coot who couldn't stand to see anyone or any country take advantage of the U.S.'s democratic and humanitarian goals. As far as Hall was concerned, Afghanistan's 2014 presidential election—to hopefully displace Qazi—couldn't come soon enough.

"By the way," continued Amy, "I heard that you interrogated Safi Khan. Did he tell you that Vice President Ted David is one of his principal partners in his multi-pronged scams? I would be surprised if those weren't the first words out of his mouth."

Hall rocked back in his chair, pressed his palms together and rested his chin on his fingertips as he thought. Blake's unexpected and perplexing remark had caught him off guard. *How much did Blake know about Safi Khan's network of partners? It likely had to be significant if she was going to freeze their bank accounts in Europe.*

Amy sensed Hall's reluctance to openly divulge his level of intelligence. Spooks were often like that. Affable and inquisitive one moment and subdued and silent the next. Rather than pester him, she elected to move on. "I'm freezing the accounts of approximately fifty shell corporations. I know the names and addresses of all the managing partners and members. Furthermore, I'm attaching the personal bank accounts of fifteen individuals."

Hall interrupted, "I thought you said you were primarily going after the principals in the shell corporations."

"The fifteen individuals are also members of the shell corporations. The gross value of shell corporation assets is approximately $3 billion. The asset value of the personal bank accounts is only $18 million."

Hook whistled, and Hall shook his head in disgust as he growled, "Goddamn Greed!"

Blake sighed. "Yes! It's disgusting. David's, Qazi's, and Safi's personal bank account balances are each $3.1 million; Hightower, Jr.'s, and Smithson's balances are each $2.0 million; Michaels's balance is $1.2 million; Hightower, Sr.'s, balance is $1.0 million; and the remainder, $2.5 million, is in various smaller accounts, under the names of local Afghans who supported and executed Safi and Michaels's scams. I can also tell you that the current balances in these personal accounts reflect only 60-70% of their gross deposits. Each individual moved money out of their accounts. Furthermore, these balances are 'a drop in the bucket' when compared to the large multi-million dollar deposits that went into the shell accounts of these major league embezzlers…Qazi, Safi, and their insiders."

The magnitude of this public trust betrayal, by the most powerful leaders in Afghanistan and a decadent few in the U.S., left Hall and Hook speechless.

"Qazi, Safi, and other high ranking Afghanistan ministers will scream and shout when I take over their accounts. Do you have any thoughts on how I, or *we*, can get ahead of them and minimize their public outrage?"

Her question again caught him off guard, especially the *we* part. Gradually, however, his disposition improved, and a sly grin began to emerge. "If the Afghan people were to learn of their leaders' thieving from say a monetarily unrelated, third parties like Pakistan or even the Taliban—"

"They'd never reach the city limits of Kabul," said Hook, with a grisly and satisfying grin. "Half the country would want to hang them!"

"They'll keep their mouths shut." The certainty in Hall's voice indicated that he agreed with Hook. "I'm turning over Safi Khan to Din Pirooz this afternoon. I'm through questioning him. Pirooz is going to be charging him with the attempted murder of Mary Phillips and being an accomplice in the killing of Beena Waleed. Reporters, from all the ISAF countries, are keeping close tabs on the progress of this case. Qazi, if he's still as calculating as I know he is, will likely keep his nose out of the case…at least at this stage." Hall paused as another thought crossed his mind.

Continuing, he said, "I think this may be an opportune time for our ambassador to encourage Qazi to replace his disgraced police chief with Din Pirooz. Safi, after all, attempted to kill one of our senior Foreign Service officers." Hall didn't feel it necessary to inform Blake that this was the third Safi-Qazi sanctioned attempt on Phillips's life.

Hook cocked his eyebrows and grinned. "Excellent idea. I like it!"

Turning to Blake, Hall asked, "When do you execute your recovery plan?"

"We first arrest and take into custody all the perpetrators. That action occurs during a sixty-minute global window. We don't want the parties to communicate with one another. Concurrently, we deliver and record all the documentation related to the freezing and attaching of bank accounts. That may take a couple of hours longer. All of this will take place sometime in the next ten to fourteen days. I'll let you know the exact date when it's agreed upon with our British and German partners."

Just then, Hook's cell phone vibrated with a text message from Lena Jones. It read: *I'm at Mary's bedside at Walter Reed Medical Center. The trauma docs wanted to check her out before they transfer her tomorrow to MedStar Georgetown University Hospital. Her evacuation from the Landstuhl Medical Center in Germany went smoothly. She's in good condition, and the docs expect that she'll fully recover. She sends her love and misses you!"*

His head drooped, and he began weeping, then bawling like a child.

"Good news, I hope?" inquired Hall, with sympathetic eyes that were rapidly filling with tears.

"Lena is with Mary at Walter Reed. The docs expect her to make a full recovery."

With that news, Blake began to sniffle, then cry. A couple of days earlier, she'd heard from a nurse friend at FOB Fenty infirmary that Mary had been shot in the chest during a classified mission in Jalalabad. Her condition, upon her arrival at the infirmary, was listed as critical.

Hall looked at his watch and stood, indicating that their meeting was over. Moving around his desk, he extended his hand to Hook. "I spoke with your FBI boss, Director Tom Milton, this morning. Your services here, for the time being, are over. Why don't you pack your bags and catch the next flight out of Bagram to the States. I'm sure Mary misses you, and she'll need help dealing with the loss of her friend, Beena Waleed."

Hook rose from his chair, neglected his hand, and hugged him. "One last question," he began while taking a step back, "is there any news on the whereabouts of Joe Michaels, a.k.a. Cannon? "

"No news on his whereabouts. I have confirmed that he drove through the Torkham Border Crossing several hours after the Jalalabad school shooting last Tuesday. But there is no information from Pakistan on whether he made it to Peshawar. I did, however, recover his fuel ledger. It's quite incriminating. It has the names and bank account details of all his partners."

Hook believed that Hall's answer was truthful, but not particularly thorough. If he didn't make it to Peshawar, Pakistan, it meant that he was waylaid somewhere along the Khyber Pass. And since the pass ran through the Khyber Agency of the FATA, Jan Zahir's home turf, it wasn't a stretch to presume that Zahir had something to do with Michaels's disappearance. He wisely decided to let the matter rest.

"Did you have any luck finding out how he got the nickname Cannon?" asked Hook. "I searched lots of military databases. I thought maybe he served an artillery unit. I came up empty."

"Safi told me that he gave him the nickname. He has a tattoo on his shoulder that depicts two crossed cigars with a grape centered below the cigars. The crossed cigars looked like cannon barrels. That was the basis then for his nickname, Cannon."

"Cigars and a grape! What's the significance of that?" asked Hook.

"I had the same question. It apparently reflects his main goal in life… *living the good life.* Smoking Cuban cigars, drinking fine wines, owning expensive cars…those kinds of things."

"And attaining those luxuries, as quickly as possible, by whatever means necessary. In his case, that meant crime. *Good riddance to bad rubbish!*" grumbled Hook.

Hall nodded and turned toward Amy. "If you'd like to stay on for a few minutes, I can share with you the bank account details from Cannon's fuel ledger. It's just names, account numbers, deposits, and passwords. No current balances."

Blake stood and stepped toward the two men. "I've extended my temporary assignment here for a few more days. I've spoken with and met Beena's brother Jamal. He's taking over management of the New Hope Girls schools with none other than Din Pirooz's wife, Aziza. She graduated from Heidelberg University a few years ago, with a degree in sociology. Currently, she's an interpreter at the German Embassy here in Kabul. Two of her nieces attend the New Hope Schools, and she's fluent in English as well as German and Dari. Tell Mary that I'll keep an eye on the schools' finances for as long as she likes. You can also assure her that Qazi's minister of finance, Jamee Nabi, won't be making any more attempts to appropriate the New Hope Girls Schools' operating capital at CityTrust, Kabul. The schools' current account balance of $872,000 is safe and secure!"

"Appropriate!" repeated Hook, with a questioning squint of his eyes.

"Yes, as in stealing. Nabi has repeatedly tried to transfer those funds to a mysterious state school account that he and Qazi control. CityTrust and

I have told him that the New Hope Girls Schools are funded by a non-governmental organization (NGO) and are totally independent of Afghanistan's state school system." With an angry flushed face, Blake paused to collect herself. "During the development of my recovery plan, I paid special attention to Nabi's personal bank accounts. When I'm through with that prick, he won't have a nickel to his name!"

It only took Hall and Hook a second to digest her comment before they both shared the same thought, *Don't mess with Blake!*

"Regarding the New Hope School, there is one final matter that you should both be aware of. Yesterday, I received $100,000, in cash, from Jan Zahir's clan to start a Beena Waleed College Scholarship Fund." Turning to Hook, he added, "That may, in some small way, help Mary recover. Please send her my best wishes."

"Same for me," offered Amy.

With tears running down his cheeks, Hook extended an arm toward Blake and drew her into a three-person hug.

June 9, 2012, Saturday, 12:31 p.m., MedStar Georgetown University Hospital

Lena Jones sat comfortably— in a cushioned chair, in the corner of Mary Phillips's hospital room—quietly admiring the loving behavior of recently arrived, Hook DeLuca. When he arrived, a few minutes earlier, he gave her a heartfelt hug, stowed his bags in the opposite corner of the room, and settled himself on a spot near the head of Mary's bed. She was soundly sleeping. Bottles of medicines and fluids hung from an IV stand on the opposite side of her bed. A spider web of sensors, connected to diagnostic monitors, tracked her vital signs. He lightly placed a hand over one hers while he gently stroked her hair and whispered to her.

Though he'd gotten five hours of sleep during his seventeen-hour flight from Kabul to Washington, it was a tortured and restless sleep that was hardly refreshing. Lena thought he looked like hell. Bloodshot eyes, hair a tangled and greasy mess, and a days-old quarter-inch beard.

During his long flight, thoughts of DS Security Specialist Joe Michaels, and his *good life* aspirations, kept popping into his mind. Easy money, expensive cars, Cuban cigars, and drinking fine wines. When Michaels was caught—that is, if he was still alive—he was going to jail for a very long time. He might even face the death penalty if he was found guilty of one or more capital crimes. Murder, treason, terrorism.

The same sordid ambitions also applied to David, Smithson, and Hightower. They were partners with, Safi Khan. The ringleader involved in the near massacre of hundred schoolgirls in Jalalabad, and the actual bombing at the Jefferson Memorial that did kill three school children. *All of this for what?* he continued to ask himself. A few extra dollars and more political power! Greed and deceit!

Suddenly, Mary's eyes began to flutter and then open. Turning her head toward Hook, it took her a moment to focus and realize who was sitting beside her. "I've missed you. I knew you would come back to me," she said weakly before her eyes again closed, and she drifted off to sleep.

Hook stood and moved a chair beside Lena.

"She's been like that for the last few hours, in and out of sleep. The docs and nurses say that's a good thing. She's resting and healing. All of her vital signs are good."

He grunted.

"You look awful. You should go home and get some sleep."

"Any news on Annie Youngblood's condition?"

Lena filled him on her rapidly improving condition and closed by mentioning that she'd start her FBI training at the FBI Academy, in Quantico, in two weeks.

He then began to explain to her Amy Blake's financial recovery plan, when Lena stopped him in mid-sentence. "I know all about it. The Treasury secretary, State's acting secretary, Susanna Thomas, and I have had multiple meetings together with Amy at President Jed Adams's bedside."

He thought for a moment before framing his next question. Leaning toward her, he whispered, "How about incriminating intel on David?"

She smiled broadly and whispered, for a full minute, into his ear. The gist of her update was that Hall possessed multiple audio and videotapes of his interrogations of Safi Khan, plus he had a recording of Safi's conversation with Mary before he shot her at the schoolhouse.

Continuing with her update, she summarized FBI Director Tom Milton's findings regarding the "Visas for Sale" program; the combined Mary Phillips assassination attempt and Jefferson Memorial bombing; and the proposed drone bombing of the Zahir clan village. An intermediary, known as Bill, delivered the drone attack coordinates to Hall last December, per David's handwritten instructions on State stationery. Milton was now in possession of that document, courtesy of Mike Hall and Malik Jan Zahir. Lastly, she explained that Milton also possessed several highly incriminating audio recordings, between David and Smithson, which took place in David's State office.

After delivering her update, she leaned back in her chair and said aloud, "Milton has Bill in custody. He's personally handling his interrogation. Bill, not surprisingly, worked for Hightower, Sr., at VA Trucking." Pausing, she shifted uncomfortably in her chair and flashed Hook a despondent look. "That's the long and the short of this sorry mess," she said with an obvious note of anger and not a trace of accomplishment.

"I'd say that's enough crime to put David, Smithson, and Hightower *...the rotten three...* away for a thousand years."

Overwhelming emotions limited her pained reply. "Put away two of the three. David may well become our next president!"

June 11, 2012, Monday morning, 6:42 a.m. ...

U.S. Press Release, Washington, D.C.-*Flash*: Former FBI Deputy Director Byron Weeks was found shot to death this morning on a local running trail, near the Potomac River. Pinned on his chest, according to the person who discovered the body, was a note. The note read: "The security of our citizenry isn't a game. Agnew could be next! A friend of Julie, Kathy, and Brian." These names refer to the three eleven-year-old victims of the terrorist bombing near the Jefferson Memorial that occurred on April 2, 2012. Weeks resigned from his FBI post one day after the bombing and, according to an anonymous source, had been cooperating with the Justice Department, and a recently convened federal grand jury. Rumors have been swirling on Capitol Hill that he and other highly placed government officials were involved in a scheme, currently known as "Visas for Sale." The scheme apparently involved issuing U.S. visas to "highly suspicious persons" for a fee. All of these applicants' previous visa applications had been denied.

June 15, 2012, Friday morning, 9:31 a.m. ...

U.S. Press Release, Washington, D.C.-*Flash*: President Jed Adams died quietly this morning in the presidential bedroom of the White House. At his side, during his final moments, were his wife, Becky; former vice president, Tim McCracken; Acting Attorney General Lena Jones; 2nd Lieutenant Brice Miller, USMC; and the White House physician. Complications related to his advanced level of Parkinson's disease are believed to be the cause of his death.

June 18, 2012, Monday, 10:09 a.m. ...

U.S. Press Release, Washington, D.C.-*Flash*: Former Vice President Ted David was sworn into the office of President of the United States. He becomes the 45th President of the United States. Rumors from numerous high-ranking senators and congressmen have been circulating in Washington that President Ted David will nominate Acting Attorney General Lena Jones as his vice president, rather than his longtime friend Max Smithson. This unexpected turn of events has surprised and angered many of President David's longtime friends, as well as several vocal far-left Democrats who view Lena Jones as a moderate Democrat, with centrist views. With only seven months remaining in this presidential term, Jones's confirmation to the post of vice president is expected to be swiftly approved by Congress.

June 19, 2012, Tuesday, 11:07 a.m. ...

U.S. Press Release, Washington, D.C.-*Flash*: This morning, in the conference center of the Robert F. Kennedy Department of Justice Building, Acting Attorney General and Vice President Nominee Lena Jones personally delivered seventeen indictments to senior government officials.

Details to follow- A single television network, CBC Washington, was invited to film and record this live and extremely unusual event. According to CBC Washington, the sole condition of their exclusive news recording required them to provide all competing major TV networks with copies of their recording, absent their network logo and commentary, prior to 4:00 p.m. EST so that those networks could broadcast the details of this event on their evening news reports. It's believed that Jones, formerly a media ombudsman on President Adams's staff, organized this breaking news event to avoid reporter histrionics that have, of late, interrupted and obfuscated announcements in the White House press room.

... 4:17 p.m.

U.S. Press Release, Washington, D.C.-*Flash Update:* Earlier today, a federal grand jury in Washington handed down seventeen indictments to high profile senior government officials, legislators, and one judge. The charges outlined in the indictment are related to the "22 File" that was leaked from the Department of Homeland Security (DHS) last April. The twenty-two "highly suspicious persons" specified in that file were granted U.S. visas in exchange for large bribes paid to government officials. Two of the named individuals in the "22 File" were killed in the terrorist bombing of April 2, 2012, which occurred near the Jefferson Memorial in Washington, D.C. The remaining twenty "suspicious" persons have been returned to their countries of origin.

The charges outlined in the indictments cover public corruption, specifically bribery and terrorism. The unusual terrorism charge, according to the White House press secretary, is based on evidence gathered from the public FACEBOOK postings of each individual named in the "22 File." Those who have been indicted aided and abetted the entry into the U.S. of generally known and widely recognized terrorists. The charges also detail DHS's willful neglect of a number of federal security statues and the contravention of their own, longstanding visa standards and guidelines.

Of particular note was the fact that legislators from both the Democratic and Republican Parties received indictments. An appeals court judge in California was also among those indicted.

The closing moments of the indictment announcement promise to provide interesting TV viewing tonight. Congressman Jim Badda (D), from a district in Michigan, took offense to the fact that everyone named in the "22 File" was a Muslim. Lena Jones confirmed that was true, but that they were all Islamic terrorists with publicly pronounced goals to harm the U.S. An abbreviated transcript of their exchange follows:

Jones- They don't get a free pass...or even a paid pass...just because they're Muslims.

Badda- That's religious discrimination. Our 1st Amendment doesn't allow that.

Jones- It doesn't allow discrimination based solely on one's religion. You and your pals' success in muddying that distinction is over.

Badda- (Long pause) The shooting death of Byron Weeks yesterday in our country's capital was disgraceful. It's another reason why we should get rid of guns.

Jones- If I wasn't armed last April, I wouldn't be standing before you now, and thirty-two more sixth-graders and three teachers would be dead. Yesterday's shooting, which I view as inexcusable, was born by the failing of U.S. security protocols. Protocols that you undermined. The murder of Weeks isn't a gun issue.

Badda- That'll change! Congress makes the laws!

Jones- Yes, you do. You make laws that the president has the right to approve or veto. In the case of a presidential veto, the Congress can override a veto based on a two-thirds vote in each house. But, all our laws have to comply with the intent of our Constitution. If they don't, our Supreme Court will settle the matter. (Long pause).

Since I'm privy to the crimes that you've committed and the bribes that you've accepted, if I were you, I'd be more concerned about the blowback you might receive from your customers [those who paid you bribes] in Yemen, Libya, and Egypt. They might not feel that they've gotten what they paid for.

June 21, 2012, Thursday, 2:16 p.m. ...

U.S. Press Release, Washington, D.C.-*Flash*: A housekeeper found Former Deputy Attorney General Max Smithson dead this afternoon in his home. Unconfirmed rumors suggest that the cause of death was a self-inflicted gunshot to the head. Smithson unexpectedly resigned from his post of deputy attorney general at the Justice Department in mid-April. It's believed that President Adams pressured him to resign amidst allegations that he violated several Hatch Act provisions while actively fundraising for then Secretary of State Ted David's presidential campaign. After his resignation, he was promptly retained by David as his presidential campaign manager.

Additionally, rumors began to swirl at the Diplomatic Security (DS) headquarters in Arlington, Virginia, last week that an unnamed DS security specialist stationed in Kabul was involved with Smithson and one of Smithson's longtime friends, Charles T. Hightower, Sr.—owner and the president of VA Trucking in Newport News, Virginia—in some type of multi-million dollar

fuel truck scam in Afghanistan. Also mentioned in this unconfirmed scam was Kabul's chief of police, Safi Khan. Though Khan
is currently under investigation for his role in the recent shooting
death of a prominent Afghan female, Dr. Beena Waleed, he is
widely known as one of President Hakim Qazi's closest advisers
and friends.

VA Trucking is one of the largest privately owned trucking
companies in the U.S. Hightower's son at the Justice Department—
Deputy Assistant Attorney General, Criminal Division, Charles T.
Hightower, Jr.—has not been available for comment.

June 25, 2012, Monday, 9:23 a.m. ...

U.S. Press Release, Washington, D.C.-*Routine:* FBI sources have
confirmed rumors that Deputy Assistant Attorney General, Criminal Division, Charles T. Hightower, Jr., has fled the United States.
According to the FBI's law enforcement contacts in Mexico, officers
with the Policia Federal spotted Hightower in the company of a
Sinaloa drug cartel lieutenant, last Saturday night, in a club in
Nogales, Sonora, Mexico.

June 27, 2012, Wednesday, 5:32 p.m. ...

U.S. Press Release, Washington, D.C.-*Routine:* The divorced
wife of former Secretary of Homeland Security Jim Agnew found
her ex-husband marginally responsive this afternoon. Agnew was
renting a small two-story townhome in the Georgetown area of
Washington, D.C. Emergency Medical Services (EMS) personnel,
on the scene, reported that they found the patient nearly comatose
at the bottom of the second story stairway. He had no feeling in
his lower extremities and could not speak coherently.

Arriving police detectives found no evidence of foul play. The condition of the townhome and the odor of alcohol on the patient's clothing prompted an unnamed detective to speculate that excessive alcohol consumption may have caused Agnew to fall down the steps.

Agnew was relieved of his cabinet-level position at Homeland Security last April, days after the Jefferson Memorial bombing, by then President Jed Adams. According to an anonymous source, Agnew had been cooperating with the FBI in their investigation of highly placed government officials who were involved in a scheme, currently known as "Visas for Sale." It's believed that the Justice Department offered him some form of prosecutorial leniency in exchange for his cooperation.

July 3, 2012, Tuesday, 7:32 p.m. EST (10:32 a.m. Islamabad, Pakistan) ...

U.S. Press Release, Washington, D.C. (Central Asia desk)-*Flash:* Acting Secretary of State Susanna Thomas announced this evening that a deal had been reached with leaders of the Pakistan government to immediately re-open the Khyber Pass and other border routes from Pakistan into Afghanistan. The exact terms of the deal are still unclear at this time, but the main stumbling blocks between the two parties have been resolved. Thomas offered a direct apology to the Pakistan government for the friendly-fire accident—known as the Salala Incident—that occurred last November when U.S. forces, under the command of the ISAF, accidentally killed twenty-four Pakistan soldiers and wounded thirteen others. A payment by the U.S., on behalf of the ISAF, to the Pakistan government of $1 billion was also a condition of the deal. Pakistan's demand for an additional cross-border transit fee of $5,000 per truck was not accepted by either the U.S. or ISAF.

In an unrelated matter, President Qazi has promoted Din Pirooz to the post of chief of police, Kabul. He succeeds Safi Khan, who was not available for comment. The U.S. and ISAF commands commented favorably on Pirooz's promotion.

July 4, 2012, Wednesday Tuesday, 5:45 p.m. EST (8:15 a.m. Kabul, Afghanistan) ...

U.S. Press Release, Washington, D.C. (Central Asia desk)-*Flash:* A spokesperson for the U.S. Embassy, Kabul, reported this morning that one of the first fuel trucks to transit the just opened Khyber Pass, from Pakistan into Afghanistan, observed the body of a male hanging over the roadway, approximately five miles east of the Torkham Border Crossing checkpoint in Afghanistan. The body, impaled on what appeared to be a flagpole, was initially reported as that of former Kabul police chief, Safi Khan.

Chief of Police Din Pirooz's comment on the sighting was brief. He explained that Safi Khan had inexplicably escaped police custody several days earlier and that without crime scene photos, he couldn't confirm or deny the identity of the body. He further added that the location of the alleged crime was not only outside of his jurisdiction (Kabul) but also outside the jurisdiction of the Islamic Republic of Afghanistan. The sighting was located in the Khyber Agency of the FATA, which is part of Pakistan.

Closing Historical Notes on Tehrik-i-Taliban Pakistan (TTP)

2012- When Malala Yousafzai was fifteen-years-old, she was shot in the head by an assassin while returning home in a school bus in the Swat Valley of Pakistan. The assassin, a member of Tehrik-i-Taliban Pakistan (TTP), targeted Malala because she was an outspoken advocate of the right of all children to an education. Though gravely wounded, she eventually recovered from her injury, as did two of her classmates who received lesser injuries.

Two years later, at the age of seventeen, she and Kailish Satyarthi were jointly awarded the Nobel Peace Prize "for their struggle against the suppression of children and young people, and for the right of all children to an education." Malala became the youngest person ever to win the prize.

"I didn't want my future to be imprisoned in my four walls and just cooking and giving birth." Malala Yousafzai

November 1, 2013- A U.S. drone strike killed the leader of TTP, Hakimullah Mehsud, in the North Waziristan Agency (FATA), Pakistan. Mullah Fazlullah assumed the leadership of TTP.

December 16, 2014- World leaders universally condemned TTP's attack on an army public school in Peshawar, Pakistan. The massacre that was planned and directed by Mullah Fazlullah, the leader of TTP, killed 133 school children and 13 civilians.

Pakistan's '9/11'—"This horrible act of terrorism has changed me completely. I don't have even a bit of mercy for any kind of terrorist in any part of the world," says Khan (a female Muslim and resident of Peshawar) from Peshawar in north-west Pakistan, where the Taliban attacked an army –run school on Tuesday, killing 141 people including 132 children.

"I had always despised the Taliban but I had a soft corner for the religious parties who take part in politics and those so-called Islamic schools," said Khan. "But after this unbelievable day they lost all kind of sympathy that I had for them."

As the *Guardian's* South Asian correspondent Jason Burke explained:

The school in Peshawar is a blunt reminder that the Middle East does not have a monopoly on Islamic militant violence. For many years, it

was Afghanistan and Pakistan – the latter dubbed "the world's most dangerous place" by a U.S. magazine in 2007 – that were the primary concern of security and law-enforcement agencies around the world. *

An earlier, December 14, 2014, Jason Burke quote- Islamist militants, from one faction or another in the province of Khyber Pakhtunkhwa, have destroyed more than a thousand schools in the past five years. These institutions symbolise government authority and are seen as un-Islamic. This school [the Peshawar army-run school] is at the edge of a military "cantonment" in Peshawar, the capital of the province.

June 14, 2018- A U.S. drone strike killed the leader of TTP,† Mullah Fazlullah, in the Kunar Province, Afghanistan.

---

* Fishwick, Carmen and Burke, Jason. "Peshawar school massacre: 'This is Pakistan's 9/11 – now is the time to act'" *The Guardian.* December 19, 2014

† Tehrik-i-Taliban Pakistan (TTP) is an alliance of militant networks formed in 2007 to unify opposition against the Pakistani military. TTP's stated objectives are the expulsion of Islamabad's influence in the Federally Administered Trade Areas (FATA) and neighboring Pakhtunkhwa Province in Pakistan; the implementation of strict Sharia Law throughout Pakistan; and the expulsion of Coalition (ISAF) troops in Afghanistan. TTP leaders also publicly say that the group seeks to establish an Islamic caliphate in Pakistan that would require the overthrow of the Pakistani Government. TTP has historically maintained close ties to senior al-Qaeda leaders, including al-Qaeda's former head of operations for Pakistan.

Office of the U.S. Director of National Intelligence, "Counter Terrorism Guide," https://www.dni.gov/nctc/groups/ttp.html

A summary of the "9/11" tragedy

(Includes America's response during the following 103 days)

September 11, 2001, 8:46 a.m. EST-Flight 11 from Boston's Logan International Airport crashes in the North Tower of the World Trade Center. Within the next seventy-seven minutes, the flights of three additional hijacked aircraft come to an end. Two of the planes fly into their targets, the Pentagon and the South Tower of the World Trade Center. Courageous passengers overwhelmed the hijackers of the third aircraft, and it crashed into an empty field near Shanksville, Pennsylvania.

September 13, 2001- The U.S. government releases a videotape, absent the audio portion, that they believe connects Osama bin Laden to the "9/11" attacks. Within weeks, the FBI verifies the connection of the airline hijackers to al-Qaeda.

September 16, 2001- Pakistan's president, General Pervez Musharraf, pledges to assist U.S. in the arrest of Osama bin Laden. On the heels of this offer, widespread protests and demonstrations opposing his pledge occur throughout his country.

September 20, 2001- U.S. President George Bush announces "War on Terror." To those responsible for the 9/11 attacks, he states that all current evidence points to al-Qaeda and its leader, Osama bin Laden. He also orders the leader of the Taliban, Mullah Omar, to hand over all al-Qaeda leaders to the U.S. and allow international peacekeepers to inspect terrorist training camps.

September 21, 2001- In response to President Bush's requests, Mullah Omar is interviewed by the publicly-funded radio channel, *Voice of America*. During the interview, Mullah Omar focuses his talk on three topics. The U.S. is responsible for the despair of good Muslims in all Islamic countries. He's not afraid of an attack by the U.S. on his Taliban… "the infidels will never succeed!" And, lastly, he will not turn over Osama bin Laden to the U.S. "No good

Muslim would ever do anything like that," he avows. "If they did, it would mean the end of Islam."

September 24, 2001- Mullah Omar announces that if the U.S. attacks his Taliban, his believers are free to start planting poppy seeds again for the production of opium. In 2000, he had issued an edict against the cultivation of poppies, and Afghanistan's opium crop was nearly eradicated. At the time of this prohibition, his Taliban had been criticized the world over for his human rights violations. There were two obvious reasons behind his edict and possibly a third. His first goal was to garner international respectability and financial aid for his Taliban. The U.S. gave him $43 million for his onetime poppy eradication effort. The second reason, which disappeared within one year, was that "growing opium was un-Islamic." A possible third reason was to increase the value of his accumulated stockpile of opium. Southern Afghanistan accounted for 90% or more of the world's illicit opium production.

In his 2001 backpedaling on opium production, he also added that his believers could only grow the crop, not consume any of it.

September 25, 2001- Mullah Omar was again in the news. During an interview with a Pakistani journalist, he gave another reason for *not* turning over Osama bin Laden to the U.S. "I don't want to go down in history as someone who betrayed his guest. I am willing to give my life, my regime. Since we have given him refuge, I cannot throw him out now." Under the code of ethics of *Pashtunwali,* a Pashtun cannot betray a guest. Unsaid by Mullah Omar was the fact that Osama bin Laden was not just *any guest.* He had been the primary benefactor of Mullah Omar's Taliban since his arrival in Afghanistan in 1996. Also unmentioned, at this time—and overshadowed by the events of 9/11—was the matter of Ahmad Shah Massoud's assassination by two of Osama bin Laden's hitmen. With Massoud's passing, the Taliban had little fear of the Northern Alliance. Mullah Omar believed that he would soon rule the country, and he doubted that any foreign country, even the U.S., would ever dare to repeat the same mistake the Russians made in 1979 when they invaded Afghanistan.

October 7, 2001- "Operation Enduring Freedom" commences. The U.S. and British begin the bombing of Taliban forces. Approximately 1,000 U.S. special forces— comprised of Green Berets, Delta Force operators, and SEAL Team 6—are gathered in Afghanistan to fight alongside Marshal Fahim's Northern Alliance. On this day, Osama bin Laden also issues a warning, broadcast over *Al Jazeera TV* stations, "May Allah mete them [the U.S.] the punishment they deserve!" In the next sixty days, the exact opposite occurs.

November 9-13, 2001- The Taliban retreats from major cities in northern Afghanistan. On November 13, the Taliban flee Kabul.

December 5, 2001- The U.N. Security Council passes a resolution establishing an interim peacekeeping force in Kabul. Two weeks later, another resolution is passed that establishes a NATO-led security force, the International Security Assistance Force (ISAF). ISAF's mission is to assist Afghanistan in setting up an Afghan National Security Force—a force comprised of their army, air force, national police, local police and an intelligence department—and to help the country rebuild its government institutions.

December 6-17, 2001- The U.S. confirms the location of Osama bin Laden in the Tora Bora cave complex of the White Mountains. Round the clock bombing of a six by six mile area commences. The CIA asks President Bush for more U.S. special forces to surround the area and prevent the escape of key al-Qaeda and Taliban leaders.

A debate ensues within the White House. Is the U.S.'s mission to remove the terrorists from Afghanistan or kill them? Is Osama bin Laden the commander of an army or simply their spiritual leader? In the first two months of U.S. troop involvement in Afghanistan, a light U.S. military footprint has appealed to the Afghans. They've willingly aided and fought beside U.S. forces. Now, at Tora Bora's final hour, should the U.S. supplement their forces with thousands more of in-country troops to seal off the area—and possibly alienate the Pashtun mountain tribes—or should a light U.S. footprint again carry the day? The U.S. opts for the light footprint approach. On December 15, Osama bin Laden is spotted by Jan Zahir's men riding out of the mountains, on horseback, into the safe and welcome haven of Pakistan. Hundreds of other al-Qaeda and Taliban fighters follow him.

December 9, 2001- Kandahar, the former base of operations for the Taliban in southern Afghanistan, falls and Mullah Omar flees the country. A few days later, ISAF and the U.S. announced that the Taliban and al-Qaeda no longer hold any major cities in the country and most, if not all, of them have left the country.

December 13, 2001- A videotape is recovered in a home in Jalalabad. On the tape, Osama bin Laden is seen laughing and boasting about the hijackers that he sent to the U.S. U.S. intelligence confirms the authenticity of the tape and estimate that it was recorded one month earlier. Analysts surmise that the purpose of the tape was to impress his Wahhabi benefactors in Saudi Arabia.

December 22, 2001- A new Afghan government formally assumes control of the country.

Casualties

September 9 to December 22, 2001

Panjshir Valley (9/9/2001)- 4 killed- Ahmad Shah Massoud and an aide plus 2 al-Qaeda assassins.

United States "9/11" Attack (number killed, per *Wikipedia*)

2,135 U.S. citizens

372 Non-U.S. citizens

344 Firefighters

71 Law enforcement officers

55 Military personnel

19 al-Qaeda hijackers

Total killed- 2,996

Total killed + related deaths+ wounded= Approximate total 6,000: 11 pregnancies lost; 1,400 first responder, subsequent deaths; and 1,140 civilians who lived, worked, or studied in the general vicinity of "Ground Zero" and its toxins have contracted cancer. As of September 2018, over 20,000 individuals—approximately 80% were "first responders"—have filed for compensation under the 9/11 Victims Compensation Fund. Compensation eligibility requires proof of an illness that one incurred as a result of the attack.

Operation Enduring Freedom-Afghanistan and the Tora Bora area of FATA (number killed, October 7- December 22, 2001)

12 U.S. military

1 CIA agent

10,000 (low estimate) Taliban and al-Qaeda fighters

1,500-2,000 Afghan civilians (estimate) killed by retreating Taliban and al-Qaeda fighters, or accidental fire from Operation Enduring Freedom fighters.

Unknown- Northern Alliance and supporting Afghan provincial fighters